THE SHADE OF
WISDOM

BY
CLIFF KYLE

SPIRIT REIGN
PUBLISHING
A Division of Spirit Reign Communications

Copyright © 2013 Cliff Kyle.

All rights reserved. No part of this book may be used or reproduced by any means, graphic, electronic, or mechanical, including photocopying, recording, taping or by any information storage retrieval system without the written permission of the publisher except in the case of brief quotations embodied in critical articles and reviews.

Cover: Daryl Anderson, Sr.

Interior Page design & layout: Ornan Anthony of OA.Blueprints, LLC

Author Photo by: J Adams Photography of Beaumont, Texas

Published by: Spirit Reign Communications

Printed in the United States of America

ISBN: 978-1-940002-12-5 (PB)
ISBN: 978-1-940002-13-2(ePUB)
ISBN: 978-1-940002-14-9 (ePDF)

SPIRIT REIGN
PUBLISHING
A Division of Spirit Reign Communications

Contents

Acknowledgments 5

Foreword 7

Introduction 8

Chapter 1 'Family Prayer' 13

Chapter 2 'Do Not Forsake Assembly' 25

Chapter 3 'The Bull or the Prophet' 39

Chapter 4 'Walking With The One Who Has Power' 51

Chapter 5 'Marriages' 65

Chapter 6 'What Is Your Character?' 91

Chapter 7 'Gold in the Hill' 109

Chapter 8 'Be a True Godly Friend' 131

Chapter 9 'God Hears You' 145

Chapter 10 'Enter The Most Holy Place' 161

Chapter 11 'Are You Receiving Your Preparation?' 177

Chapter 12 'On What Does Your Faith Rest?' 195

Chapter 13 'Who Made You The Judge?' 207

Chapter 14 'Can God Find You?' 223

Chapter 15 'Solid Foundation' 239

Chapter 16 'Restoration For Your Soul' 259

Chapter 17 'Why Pray?' 269

Chapter 18 'Jesus Christ Is Real And He Is Coming' 285

About The Author 303

References 304

DEDICATION

To Shirley Kyle, my wife. Thank you very much for loving me especially through the process of writing this book. I shall always love you.

To Willie Mae (Gilford) Kyle, my mother. In her memory.

ACKNOWLEDGEMENTS

There have been many friends and family members who have both encouraged and inspired the content of this book. My wife, Shirley has been a reader and one who journals for years. I have watched her devour books including God's Word then write what God has spoken to her. It instilled in me to one day write something that she would not only enjoy reading but also gain encouragement. She read the first manuscript and provided both edits and inspiration. My daughter, Shon Peebles, is also an avid reader. In addition, as a skilled editor, she assisted with dialogue and story content. Her husband, Eric Peebles, encouraged me to pull the book off the shelf after it sat for more that ten years after I wrote the initial manuscript. My son, Clifton Kyle, Jr. and his wife, Karen, supported and encouraged me to finally get it done. My sister, Darlyne Dorsey, and her granddaughter, Nyaiah Harris, read chapters and provided valuable feedback. My brother, Clinon Kyle, will find many similarities in this book to our lives as siblings growing up in the South. Our relationships with family and friends are key in God's kingdom. My relationships have both ignited and fueled the underpinning messages throughout this book. One such relationship is with my daughter, Rhonda Ramsour. In addition, Mother Bernice Parham constantly encouraged me to write the many messages that I received as I read the bible. When I chaired the Prayer Ministry, it was her encouragement that caused me to write daily devotions to the prayer warriors. Many of those devotions found their way into this book. In addition, she read and provided insightful feedback. My accountability partners (Gerald Mundy, Steve Coffey, Greg Smith, Ken Stephens, Hersey Jenkins, Paul Peoples, Greg Pearson, and Al Reynolds) demonstrated life styles that inspired many stories in the book. They also poured over early versions of the manuscript. They were and continue to be a great help to me. Ms. Connie Taylor read the manuscript and provided valuable insight to restructuring chapters and content within chapters. Andrew Jackson read the manuscript, corrected the use of words, validated references to characters, and assisted with the flow from chapter to chapter. My pastor, Rev. Robert l. Stevenson, kept me aligned with God's word. While this is a novel whose characters are fictional, their stories and the scriptural messages of their stories are very helpful to many individuals to say the least. Therefore, his reading of the manuscript was of utmost importance. Many more friends and family members were the inspiration behind many of the stories in this book. To all of you, I am grateful for your love of Christ and obedience to His Word.

I am deeply indebted to Rev. Eric Thomas who graciously agreed to write the Forward. His life story is the foundation to his book, Secrets To Success. The publishing of his story in book form was a great encouragement to publish this book, The Shade Of Wisdom.

Finally, my brother, Elder Louis Kyle, is the reason I can call Jesus Christ my Lord and Savior. He led me to Christ and became one of my first mentors. Had that not happened, whose knows where I would be today?

A SPECIAL MESSAGE TO MY GRANDCHILDREN

To: Keisha Igbazua, D.J. Ramsour, Kyle Peebles, Meghan Ramsour, Justin Peebles, Grant Peebles, Trevor Peebles, Payton Peebles, Kennedy Kyle, Kendall Kyle, Karsyn Kyle, Kourtlyn Kyle, and Terva Igbazua (my first great-grandson) - Live a life of integrity grounded in the Word of God. Accept Jesus Christ as your Lord and Savior then live the abundant life. Remember to Stay Focused!!! Have Fun!!! Keep Your Sense of Humor!!! Continue To Pray!!!

FOREWORD

Wisdom is an invaluable gift. In this book, The Shade of Wisdom, Cliff Kyle takes you on a journey driven by the helm of wisdom. Wisdom reveals to the reader a simple truth, life is full of personal choices. Contrary to what society is led to believe; people are the victim of their circumstance, nothing more nothing less! Cliff Kyle not only shatters that belief but provides his readers with the skills needed to make wise choices. What makes Wisdom unique and sets it apart from books in its genre, is the source in which the wisdom is provided. Cliff Kyle reveals that wisdom can come from the most unexpected places and can be delivered by the most unexpected people. The method that Cliff used to intertwine the life of Willie Johnson into biblical principals is remarkable. It's easy to relate to the characters in the book. The life long experiences in this story is one that will keep you searching through the book for more and more principles.

Yet we all know that while it is easier for some people to grab life changing principles with enthusiasm, such is not the case for every individual. A number of individuals find it very difficult to make the type of choice that will set them up for success. If this is the case for someone you love and desperately long to help overcome some of their negative habits, The Shade of Wisdom is a great gift.

The stories of Willie Johnson will come with the lack of or refusal of sound counsel. I am confident that these stories will and more importantly, the principles found in Wisdom, will bring you a much fuller, peaceful and productive life.

No matter where you are in your life or someone you love, this book can help you make the most out of the rest of your life by:

Challenging you to make the most of every life decision
Challenging your negative perceptions about life
Discovering the power of choices and decisions
Letting go of your past and embracing your future
Find the true meaning of life and
Give you renewed strength to live your Maximum life!
This is a novel for the ages.

Foreword written by Eric Thomas

INTRODUCTION

'The Shade Of Wisdom' is a novel with a message. It teaches and counsels in very illustrative and imaginative ways using the life stories of a fictional character named Willie. It is a guide on how and when to pray. However, rather than being a list of topics with sample prayers, it instructs in the context of situational stories. Witnessing can be a challenge for some of us. Yet, the book demonstrates how God will place opportunities to spread the gospel right before our eyes if we would just be observant.

Our character is developed in early childhood, teenage, and young adult experiences. The stories in Willie's life attempt to raise an awareness of building character. The astute reader will learn that we have an opportunity to reshape our character if we yield to God's plan.

The foundation of God's love is relationships. Willie's relationships with his father, mother, siblings, friends, children, and wife are highlighted throughout the book. Pay particular attention to other relationships as well. In each relationship, there is fundamental teaching for all of us. We learn how to deal with difficult relationships and the impact they have on our lives. We embrace nurturing relationships like the accountability group Willie joins later in his life and the mentoring relationship he has with his great-aunt. Some relationships are shameful to us. The truth is that shame is a cover up for pride. We somehow believe that the negativity in the life of another reflects on us. Thus, this is nothing more than pride deeply rooted in our character.

So, Willie tells his story. The milestones in his life from an early age not only shaped his character but also helped identify God's call upon his life. Many of these events while seemingly routine life experiences are actually signature stories relating to God's divine purpose for Willie.

Early in his childhood, his mother, Doris, introduced him to God. She was a kind, gentle, and frail woman who nurtured her six children with the love of

Christ. However, her husband left her when the youngest was three and the oldest was thirteen. Her limited marketplace skills allowed her to provide for her family as a seamstress in the neighborhood cleaners. She worked six days a week. As a result, the oldest of the children, Christine, pitched in on a daily basis as surrogate father, nanny, maid, tutor, and big brother. She, after all, was the eldest and the remaining children were all boys. There was Ralph, Tommie and Jesse (twins), William, then James, the youngest.

The housing projects where the family lived were initially stable. However, it quickly deteriorated. It was a rough neighborhood filled with gangs, violence, drugs, poverty, alcohol, and broken homes. Yet, as was the case in many neighborhoods of the 1940's, 1950's, and 1960's, all the parents of the neighborhood cared for those who lived there. So, when any of the boys got out of hand, Christine and Doris could rest assured that some other parent would administer proper discipline, like a whippin when necessary.

Willie was an intelligent child. And, he was smart, too. He knew when to display his academic prowess and when to let it lay low. It was this awareness that enabled him to survive the gangs, drugs, and prostitution all around him. Or, so he thought. He would later realize that it was Christ who dispatched His angels from before the creation of the world to surround and protect Willie until such a time as this.

Willie would eventually leave this neighborhood and city. He would enter college, find Jesus Christ, and then begin a journey, a quest that had no end. Willie would accept Christ, travel the globe, and spend many years getting cleansed by the washing with water through the word as God prepared him for the prophetic mantle. Yet, pride would enter. He would reach a point where he thought that he could master much of life with what God had placed in him and his wife. Through a great deal of pain, he would find that only by complete surrender to Christ is life lived in abundance.

After breaking him, God would send him on a mission. Through this experience, Willie realizes the prophetic call upon his life. It would be the most incredible twelve days he had ever lived.

If you are breathing, this book has something for you. As you journey with Willie through his successes and failures, the discerning reader will notice God's teachings on repentance, fasting, healing, and faith. Every event and episode of Willie's life is a representation of God's work in the lives of His children. Don't miss the teachings on salvation, grief, persistent obedience, the book of Ephesians, God's eternal story, and much, much more.

Allow the Holy Spirit to fill you as you read. Then like Willie, you will be able witness God's promise made through the prophet Joel.

"And afterward, I will pour out my Spirit on all people. Your sons and daughters will prophesy, your old men will dream dreams, your young men will see visions." (Joel 2:28 NIV)

1

FAMILY PRAYER

"SNAAAAKE!! SNAAAAKE!!"

I took off, flying down the dirt road toward Pappa Johnson's house. I ran as fast as my 10-year-old legs could take me, kicking up sandy red dirt and dust everywhere. I was huffing and puffing. Two of my brothers and I had been playing in Pappa's back yard near the chicken coop when all of a sudden this 30 foot long snake appeared out of nowhere. The snake was midnight black, long and slender, like a fat water hose. It fixed its eyes on me and slithered slowly as if it was approaching easy prey. The ground was hot enough to fry an egg on it. The rising heat and piercing sunrays almost kept me from seeing the snake at all. The reflection of a black, shiny, moving object was the only thing that saved me.

"Willie, slow down. The snake went the other way. Slow down," my brother Tommie yelled.

My sprint became a trot, and then I slowly came to a walk. After stopping, I grabbed my knees and asked, 'How do ya, know?"

Tommie's twin, Jesse responded, "Cause I saw him. I picked up a stick, and then ran him in the other direction. I watched him crawl away."

"Man, you sure are scared of snakes," snickered Tommie. "I don't know why you like to come up here to the country so much. Snakes are everywhere around here."

"I know. Did you see the size of that thing? He was thirty feet long."

"No he wasn't. That's just your imagination."

"Uh huh. Yes, he was too. I saw him first."

"Yeah, but you didn't stick around long enough to really see him."

"I'm not going to stick around either. Snakes are bad business."

We had been coming to Raeford every summer since before Daddy left Mamma. Christine, our sister, usually came too. However, now eighteen years old, she found better things to do back in Fayetteville. Besides, it was a welcomed break for her. Our dad TJ, left Mamma when Christine was thirteen. Chrissie, as we called her, was up at the break of dawn every morning helping Mamma to get us boys ready for school. She would make breakfast and march us into the bathroom one by one. All five of us. She would check faces, teeth, hands, and arm pits. After making sure that we ate all of our breakfast, she would march us out the front door. James, my youngest brother and I, still walked to the neighborhood elementary school about a quarter of a mile away. Tommie and Jesse took the Jr. High School bus and Ralph, my oldest brother, usually took the High School bus with Christine. Mamma would be busy mending socks and underwear then ironing shirts and pants. She was out the door on her way to work usually before all of the boys were out of the bathroom. She would give us each a hug, a kiss, a word of encouragement, and a nickel.

That summer Jesse, Tommie, James, and I stayed with Pappa, our great grandfather. Ralph stayed with Uncle Eddie, my grandfather's brother, for a couple of weeks. He liked staying there so that he and Eddie Jr. could hang out at the Cave, go swimming, and go hunting whenever they wanted to. Chrissie and Mamma stayed back in Fayetteville and enjoyed as much of a restful summer as they could before the Fall of the year came. Mamma was beginning to feel a little stress though because it was Chrissie's last summer at home before heading off to college. She had been a big help around the house. Now it was time for her to get on with the rest of her life.

"Chrissie, do you think Ralph is ready to step up and take charge of the boys after you leave? I get a little concerned about them, you know, between the times I leave for work and when I get home in the evening."

"They'll be alright. Ralph is slowing down a little. Tommie and Jesse are getting up there in age. Willie isn't much trouble. A little sneaky but not much trouble! James is the only concern. He has four brothers to look after him. So they'll be alright."

"They are all just getting so big. And, this neighborhood is getting rougher and rougher especially for boys."

"Mamma we've been through this before. Everyone knows you and respects you. They know me and they know the boys. You don't have anything to worry about."

"I know…. I know…"

****

It was Ralph's last night in Raeford for the summer. And he was going to make the most of it. Earlier that day, he, Eddie Jr., and some other cousins went swimming in the creek. They all gathered at Uncle Eddie's house, helped Eddie Jr. with his chores, and then took a short cut through the back pasture to the creek. It was a lazy hot day which made it a good day for a swim. So from late morning to early afternoon, they jumped in, dove, and dunked each other in the cool running spring water. Swimming in that creek was common for most of the children and teenagers of that community. They were barely there an hour before several others joined them.

Since the crowd was mostly youth and early teens, Ralph and the other boys did not stay as long as usual. Instead, they wandered in the woods staking out good hunting spots and looking forward to a teenage dance that was being held that evening at its usual place, the Cave. It was the local teenage juke joint located next door to Aunt Alice's store. Aunt Alice, Uncle Eddie, my grandfather and eleven others were siblings. Since Uncle Eddie's house was on the opposite side of the Cave, Ralph was spending the night in the ideal place for what he had in mind. The boys made their way back home, rested for a while, and then got ready for the dance. Uncle Eddie gave his usual warning to Ralph and Eddie Jr.

"Don't stay out too late, boys. I want you back by midnight."

"No problem Dad," Eddie Jr. answered.

The party got going early. Most of the usual crowd was there by 9:00pm. Earl, Andrea, Phyllis, Candace, Nancy, Aaron and just about everyone else that Ralph expected to be there, showed up. The dance hall was dark. The only light came from red and blue bulbs appropriately placed around the room. A person could hardly see whoever was dancing right in front of them. That was a good thing for those who danced off beat or wore out of style clothes. Neither one of those was the case for Ralph, though. He was one of the best dancers in the area and dressed sharp. Such was the case that night as he stayed on the dance floor doing the shake, the twist, the jerk, the wautoosie, and all the latest dances. The sounds of Diana Ross and the Supremes, Marvin Gaye, the Impressions, and The Temptations bounced off the walls. He danced with every girl at the place. Most of them were his cousins but two of them were new girls who came over from Sparta, a neighboring town about ten miles away.

Raeford is in a dry county. That means there was no alcohol at either the Cave or Aunt Alice's store. Besides, this was a teenage hangout. But Ralph wanted to impress the new girls from Sparta, so, he coaxed Eddie Jr. into stealing his dad's car. The plan was to drive with the girls to Greensboro, pick up some beer, then be back well before midnight.

"Come on Eddie Jr. You know that Uncle Eddie and Aunt Hattie (his wife) fall asleep early. All we have to do is sneak up to his night stand, pick up the keys easy, and we are on our way."

"He'll hear us crank up the car."

"No he won't. We'll put it in neutral, push it down the street, and then crank it up a half mile away."

"Boy, you are wild. It'll never work."

"Yes it will too. I do it all the time at home. I usually get my little brother Willie, to crawl into Mamma's room to get the keys though. He's the quietest."

"Willie is all the way up at Pappa's. And, he will never let us take him out of the house at this time of night."

"We won't need Willie this time. I know how to do it. I saw where Uncle Eddie laid the keys. They are on top of his Bible. It'll be easy."

Ralph and Eddie Jr. then told the girls from Sparta that they were going to get Eddie Jr.'s car. They lied that he lived a mile away. It would take them a couple of minutes before they would be back.

"Shhhh! They are going to wake up if you don't shut up." Ralph lay perfectly still on his belly on the floor and contemplated his first move. He began to inch forward slower than a turtle, taking just half an inch at a time. He didn't dare make a sudden move. Slow, easy movements were best. He had to be patient. He got closer and closer to the bed. The floor creaked. He had to wait. Uncle Eddie turned over in the bed. Ralph motioned Eddie Jr. with his finger on his lips to be still and be quiet. He then continued to move toward the bed. When he got into position, he reached up toward the nightstand. His hand stretched out one finger at a time. Ralph walked each finger one by one until he finally reached the keys. Now, lifting the keys was the real tricky part. It was important to lift them in such a way that prevented them from clanging together thus making a noise.

Ralph got a firm grip on one of the keys on the ring. Then slowly, ever so slowly, he lifted the key ring. Each key moved toward the center of the ring as he lifted. He was careful to make sure that each key remained touching the Bible while he lifted. If any key swung free, it could clang against another and make a noise. He had to pay special attention to the shorter keys. They would come off the Bible first. Slowly, Ralph lifted. One by one, they came up. No noise. So far, so good. As the final key was lifted, he squeezed the entire bunch of them in his palm. With a closed fist clenched tightly around the keys, Ralph smoothly lowered his hand and buried it in his armpit. He then curled his arm under his body and slowly made his way back to the doorway.

"You got them?" asked Eddie Jr.

"Yeah. Now be quiet. Put the car in neutral. Then let's push it down the hill."

"OK," Eddie Jr. responded.

Ralph said, "I'll give it a shove. You jump in. Then at the bottom of the hill, crank it up."

Uncle Eddie was a local businessman. He owned a trucking company that cut timber then hauled it to the local paper mills. He had established himself over the last few years as reliable, cost effective, and efficient. Therefore, his business had grown substantially. As a result, he bought a new car every year. Since he owned two, no car was more than two years old. Ralph and Eddie Jr. stole the newer of the two, the red convertible mustang. The girls would be impressed. They drove up with Ralph riding shotgun. The girls were beaming. Ralph jumped in the back seat with his date. Off to Greensboro they went.

They stopped on a dark dirt road on the way back to drink the beer. They guzzled. The girls were a little "woozy".

"Hey Ralph, slow down, Man. You've already had four in the last twenty minutes. Are you trying to drink up the whole case before we get back?"

"I'm alright. You just handle your business."

"Look it's getting late. We had better get back before the Cave closes. I gotta take a leak. I'll be right back."

Eddie Jr. headed for a tree off the side of the rode while the girls giggled. Ralph had everyone switch while Eddie Jr. was gone. He wanted to drive Uncle Eddie's new car. He blew the horn.

"Eddie Jr.! Let's go. I'll have us back in plenty of time to party hearty some more."

"Oh no you don't. I had better drive."

As Eddie Jr. reached for the front door, Ralph pulled away just a little. He did it again and again and again each time Eddie Jr. caught up and reached. Finally, Eddie Jr. gave up and sat in the back with a warning that Ralph had better drive carefully.

Ralph eased them off the dirt road, out of the woods, and then screeched the tires onto the only paved road that led to the Cave. He pressed the pedal to the medal and zoomed around the curves. He tossed the girls and Eddie Jr. from side to side. They screamed. He laughed. All of a sudden, a deer flashed onto the highway. Ralph was going too fast. He slammed on the breaks and jerked the steering wheel to the right barely missing the now frightened deer. The car rolled down the ditch, passed within inches of two trees, and then came to a stop at the edge of Cow Creek.

"Are you crazy? You almost got us killed!!" said Eddie Jr.

Ralph was still shaking with fright. He could hardly move. But, thank God. No one was hurt. The car only got a little mud and some burned rubber on the tires for the wear. They had thrown the empty beer cans out at the last stop. The only thing shook up in the car was Ralph, the girls, Eddie Jr., and the unopened beer. Eddie Jr. then threw the beer in the woods.

"I'm driving the rest of the way," he said.

No one said a word when they got back to the Cave. It was nearly closing time. They went in, had a few dances, and said goodnight.

That night, the boys lay quietly in their beds. Their minds raced with the events of the evening. Softly, they began to whisper. They talked about the dance, the girls, the beer, and the car. Occasionally, one would laugh a little louder than expected. The other would warn that the laugh could awaken Uncle Eddie or Aunt Hattie.

"Don't worry," Ralph said on one occasion. "They can't hear us. We got away with the keys and the car. Didn't we?"

"Be quite!" Eddie Jr. said.

"Besides, that ceiling fan is making enough racket to drown out a live band if we had one in here," continued Ralph. "If you or Uncle Eddie don't tighten up that thing with a screw, one of these days it is going to come tumbling down."

"Shut up and go to sleep," said Eddie Jr.

It was not unusual to sleep with the windows open, screen on, and fan twirling. Such was the case this night. The crickets, the frogs, and the ceiling fan harmonized into a lullaby that put the two of them into a needed deep sleep.

"How was the dance last night, boys?" Uncle Eddie asked.

"Oh. It was OK. A couple of new girls came from Sparta to liven things up a bit. But, other than that, nothing exciting happened," lied Ralph.

"I'm glad you had a good time. Your granddaddy will be here in a few minutes. Yawl be going to Pappa's house to spend the day before the family prayer tonight. When you get back to Fayetteville tomorrow, say hello to your mamma and Christine for me."

****

There was a little coolness in the air that morning. The clouds were moving in. It looked like rain. Pappa had promised us that we could walk down to Aunt Alice's store. That was always an exciting event. But we had to hurry if we were going to beat the rain. The walk was about a mile and a half if you went around the curves. You could cut about a half mile off the walk if you went through the woods, though. Tommie and Jesse knew that they could not run off and leave James and me. But, they took the short cut through the woods while keeping an eye on the two of us.

"Yawl better keep up. You know it going to rain," Tommie called.

"Tommie, why don't you carry James? We might be able to get there a little sooner," said Jesse.

"You carry him. Or let him run. He's a big boy now. Plus, he's heavy."

I encouraged James, "Come on, man. Let's run."

We all made it to the store before the clouds burst. When the rain came, it was like a monsoon. This was not a drizzle. It did not build slowly then burst into a heavy rain. The raindrops came all at once. They were like pellets hitting the ground. They hit with so much force that they caused the tree branches to dance vibrantly. The tree trunks swayed back and forth in response to the heavy wind. The sky became dark bluish gray in color and lightning skipped about the skies. Thunder rumbled and roared. It was loud. That kind of rain would make you run for dear life if you were caught in the midst of it. It quickly soaked the ground and made puddles and pools everywhere. Since we were inside Aunt Alice's store, we felt safe and secure.

Aunt Alice was the best country storeowner in the world. She always allowed us to have as much candy as we wanted. This time was better than usual. We couldn't go outside in the rain. So we just sat and gorged ourselves on candy, cookies, cake, and potato chips. No customers were in the store today. Just us, but that was enough. Some days, the store was full of customers. The old lady from down the street, the scary looking man who only has one leg and lived alone behind the store, and a mean, very large lady were regulars. The mean lady hated children, or at least she seemed to. She would always come in all sweaty and complaining about how some bad kids had picked her flowers or ran on her grass. She complained about everything. She always held the screen door open too long as she entered the store and let it slam when she left. Aunt Alice never liked to see her coming because she never had enough money to pay.

"Put it on my tab," she'd say. Of course, it was a tab that never got paid. One egg here, two cups of milk there, never a whole container or package of anything. Why Aunt Alice let her keep up this routine was beyond me.

Then the rain stopped as suddenly as it started. There was a rundown schoolyard across the highway from the store. It was one of our favorite places to play. An old tire swing was there. There was a sand pit and a seesaw too. We scooted across the road.

"Yawl look out for the cars," she called. Our cousins, Aunt Alice's three daughters were always at the store. They went over to the schoolyard with us. Uncle Eddie's four daughters joined us. Other children in the neighborhood also joined us. We ran, played, and just had a good old time.

Soon, it was time to head back to Pappa's, and Tommie had a trick up his sleeve. Earlier he had put something in his pocket when we were in Aunt Alice's store. Aunt Alice had turned away to count the peppermints and gumballs when Tommie reached on the counter near the cold medicine. He moved ever so slowly so as not to alert Aunt Alice. Why had he needed cold medicine? He wasn't sick. But it wasn't the same package that cold medicine came in. It was a thin blue and white box. It looked almost like a candy or gum box. I hadn't paid much more attention to it than that at the time. On the way home, Tommie told James that he had chocolate candy and offered some of it to him. James gladly took a big chunk and ate it.

The rain had stopped and it was cool. We took the long way back to Pappa's. Tommie and Jesse were snickering all the way. We got about a quarter mile away when James got a funny look on his face.

"I got to doo doo. I got to doo doo!"

Tommie and Jesse roared. They were laughing their heads off. I asked James what was wrong. He could only scrunch up his face and say again, "I got to doo doo. I got to doo doo!" He put one hand under his butt and took off running. He ran all the way to Pappa's. By this time, Tommie and Jesse told me that it was stool softener that James ate. Now I was laughing too. You had to see this scene. James with one hand on his butt, running as fast as he could, yelling all the way, "I got to doo doo! I got to doo doo!"

Pappa only had an outhouse. James ran past the front porch along the side of the house, past the chicken coop, and to the outhouse about another 100 yards away. He made it. But he stayed in there a long time.

"James. You alright?"

"Shut up."

"Come on, man. You alright?"

"I told you to shut up. I'm all right. And, I'm telling Pappa too."

They should have known better and I should have known better than to join them in the laughter. Pappa was the wisest man in the country. He was the son of a Cherokee Indian woman and a half white man. He had light skin and curly hair. He was only average height and build but his stature in the community made him seem tall and big. Everyone looked up to him. He was a strong man of prayer and often spoke a prophetic word. Not everyone understood him. But he was kind and gentle. He never looked down his nose at anyone and never raised his voice. When James told on us, we knew that we had a teaching coming.

"Now boys, you know that it was wrong to treat your little brother that way. You could have seriously hurt him. I want all of you to apologize, give him a big hug, and a kiss. "

"Jesus teaches us to love one another. We are to be kind and compassionate to one another."

"And James, you are to forgive your brothers just as in Christ God forgave you."

"I want all of you to remember these words. Love must be sincere. Hate what is evil; cling to what is good. Be devoted to one another in brotherly love. Honor one another above yourselves. Never be lacking in zeal, but keep your spiritual fervor, serving the Lord. Be joyful in hope, patient in affliction, and faithful in prayer. Share with God's people who are in need. Practice hospitality."

"OK. Pappa."

"No, I want all of you to really memorize these words. They are found in Romans Chapter 12, verses 9 through 13. At the end of the summer, I want each of you to recite them to me word for word. Don't miss a single syllable."

"Now go get washed up. Supper will be ready soon. Then I want all of you on the front porch until we start the family prayer."

After supper and cleaning the kitchen, we all rushed to the front porch. About two months earlier, my great grandmother, Pappa's wife, died. She was buried in the family cemetery not far away. That cemetery is on the site of the annual Homecoming, a community wide event that occurred the second weekend of August. It honors the founders of Raeford. Pappa's house was a sharp shooter with one hallway right down the middle of the house. I sat on the front porch on the steps that were directly in front of the middle of the house. I could see down the hallway from the front door to the back door.

As we sat ready for Pappa to begin, I heard footsteps coming down the hallway. Thump. Thump. Thump. I wondered who it could be. Everyone was either on the front porch or in the front yard as usual. No one was in the house. But, the footsteps continued. Thump. Thump. Thump. They got closer and closer to me. It was now pretty dark outside and there were no lights on in the house. So when I looked back down the hallway and saw my great grandmother walking toward me, I nearly jumped out of my skin. I screamed and ran up the steps to Pappa. I told him what I heard and what I saw.

He told me to look around at the front door. Sure enough, it was a living person. But it was only our cousin who had walked from her house in the back through Pappa's house on her way to the prayer meeting.

What a relief………………………..

Pappa hosted the weekly family prayer in his front yard every Saturday night. Raeford is a small community of about 600 people. I used to swear that every one of them was related in some way. It sure seemed that way. Pappa was the eldest of seventeen children. My grandfather, Grampa Ellis, was the eldest of Pappa's fourteen children. And, most of them still lived in Raeford. Some had married and moved away but many stayed in this little community. Pappa called all of the family together for prayer every week.

Tonight Pappa taught first from Ephesians. He continued the message that he had given to the four of us earlier on love. His prayer focused on Ephesians Chapter 6. He prayed that the children would obey their parents. The parents would instruct the children. Everyone would work honestly and earnestly for a living. Then, he entered into spiritual warfare for the family based on Ephesians Chapter 6:10 –18. "Every family member is to be encouraged with renewed strength and anointing. God's strength is seen in many ways.

1) His power, vigor, might, energy, and fervency in our daily lives.
2) To influence, have authority, and have resources for the battles.
3) To withstand an attack.

Remember that Ephesians 6:10 - 18 begins with being strong in the Lord and the power of His might. The Greek word for strong here means to receive the empowerment of God's might. God is preparing us. Receive the preparation. Put on the full armor. Receive renewed strength and anointing. Then, stand. Unified in prayer, let us stand."

This kind of prayer always interested me a great deal. I was focused. Years later, I would remember these Saturday night family prayers and their impact on my life.

2

Do Not Forsake Assembly

"Boys! I got a letter from Daddy. He is coming home!" screamed Chrissie. She had been waiting for months to hear from him. Me, too.

Our Dad left Mamma and moved to California when I was five years old. Every summer, we would visit our grandparents, his parents, in Raeford. After they moved to Fayetteville, we continued our visits to Raeford and stayed with Uncle Eddie, Aunt Helen, or Pappa. When Grampa Ellis and Gramma, our dad's parents, moved to Fayetteville, we visited them on the weekends about once a month. Gramma would have each of us to write a letter to our Daddy every time we visited. He never wrote back. Sometimes, I would imagine that he was on a ship in a far off land. Maybe he was busy inventing something really important. Of course, deep down inside, I knew that he just didn't care. Gramma had been promising that he would write soon. Then she told us that he would be returning to Fayetteville. Boy was I excited!!

I had long wished that he and Mamma would get back together. I wanted a father in the house. Although none of my friends in Lincoln Grove Village had a father in the house, it seemed like all the smart kids in the Greenspoint neighborhood in Fayetteville had a father and I wanted to be like them. Plus, I had fantasized about my Daddy taking us fishing, going camping, and having fun in Raeford.

"Let me read it. Let me read it," pleaded Ralph.

"I want to read it, too," James said.

"Me too!"

"Me too!"

"Me too!"

Everybody wanted to read that letter. Daddy had finally written to us. Although the letter was addressed to Christine, we all claimed it was our letter, too. In the letter, Daddy told us exactly when he was coming. He would arrive at 3:00pm on Christmas Eve. He would be coming at Christmas time and not going back to California. Hot dog!! Daddy was coming home. I could hardly contain myself. When we told Mamma, it didn't seem to matter to her one way or another. She seemed really happy for us, though. Although she didn't seem to have any personal excitement, I just knew that would change as soon as he arrived.

That was the longest wait for Christmas in my life. Each day seemed like a month. Not much else seemed to matter. High School football in North Carolina is king. It was common for the weekly family focus to be on the next Friday or Saturday night game. Especially since Ralph was a super star on the team. He played halfback. Ralph was the fastest man on the team. Naturally, we were excited to watch him play. Now as a junior, he was the Captain of the team. He had played on varsity since his freshman year and started last year. Long touchdown runs of 30, 40, or sometimes 70 yards were common for Ralph. But this season, football took second place to the arrival of our Daddy at Christmas.

I dreamed of what it would be like when he returned. I had always dreamed a lot. Every night I would dream something usually pretty vivid. Some dreams were even in color. I remember this one weird dream I had of Daddy.

> My Daddy had come back from California to buy a house. He had a woman and other people with him. I went to where he was. I was glad to see him. I asked if he had heard about Ralph. He asked who was Ralph. I told him, his son Ralph. He told me Ralph had called the 'house'. But since Daddy was never home, he missed the call but got the message. I was thinking the 'house' was either the house where his parents lived or his house in California. He then asked me why I didn't ask about Johnny. I told him that I didn't know Johnny. He told me that Johnny was his son from California.

The next scene in the dream is of him in a barbershop surrounded by bodyguards. I was angry with him. I wanted to spend more time with him. But he was not interested. I kicked the legs of the barber chair from beneath him. He fell then looked up at me with a smirk on his face. I got on the floor next to him to tell him that at another date and time, I would fight him. His bodyguards stepped in. I said I would fight him man to man with no weapons or any help. One of his guards lifted me up, pointed a gun and a gasoline can at me and told me if I ever approached my Daddy again, he would light me up. Daddy just looked at me from the floor. I left.

That was a very weird dream to me. I didn't understand it and I didn't like it. Why had I wanted to fight my daddy? A couple of weeks later, I had another pretty weird dream. Ralph had told the four of us about the car incident with him and Eddie Jr. from the previous summer. It was an exciting story. But we knew that it was dangerous. We looked up to Ralph. He led an exciting life. He always seemed to go against the grain, push the limits, and live on the edge. He was handsome, popular, a good dancer, an outstanding athlete, and as intelligent as he wanted to be. But there was something else about him. He was different. I didn't know exactly what it was. He just knew things.

In this dream, Ralph had stolen Grampa Ellis's car. Uncle Eddie had purchased Eddie Jr. his first car. The two of them were racing to Morehead City beach along Highway 96. The boys had done this before. The first one to Morehead City beach would buy a month's worth of soda pop for the other. This time was a little different. It was foggy following a rainstorm and it was difficult to see. Eddie Jr. edged in front of Ralph. Ralph then leaped in front and sped faster and faster down the winding roads. The dream went silent and then flames were in my face as I watched Ralph's car explode on the side of a hill. He had made a wrong turn in his excitement over finally beating Eddie Jr. In this dream, Ralph died from the accident.

I didn't like this dream either. I told no one about either dream. I just kept them to myself. After football season, basketball began. Now this was the sport for the twins, Tommie and Jesse. Since Ralph was the football star, they focused on something else. They were pretty good athletes and could play just about any sport that they wanted. They just wanted to excel at something that Ralph chose not to play. So, basketball was it. They were now freshmen in High School but played on the Jr. Varsity team. They had grown pretty tall. They played the two forward positions opposite each other. It was fun to watch them.

However, as Christmas approached, basketball was just barely getting started. It was mostly practice and a couple of non-conference tournaments before the holiday season arrived. It was just as well because Tommie and Jesse could not concentrate as Christmas got nearer.

Finally, the Christmas season arrived. Daddy would arrive in Fayetteville soon. He would stay with Grampa Ellis until he got a house. We all were anxious to go see him. During the day on Christmas Eve, all of us got Daddy a present. Christine took us to Bridgeway Shopping Center, which is the strip mall in town. It had your basic clothing, jewelry, and shoe retailers with an assortment of specialty shops, ice cream parlors, and restaurants. She purchased a picture frame then wrapped a poem she had written along with a photo of herself in some bright red shiny paper with Christmas bulbs on it. Ralph got him some Ole Spice cologne. The twins each got him a box of handkerchiefs. I found a beautiful key chain at J.J. Blueberry's. It was gold plated with an eighteen-inch chain that connected to his belt buckle. And James got him a necktie that sang Jingle Bells when you pressed it in the middle. We were ready.

Gramma picked us up about mid-afternoon before Daddy was scheduled to get in. We would all be there waiting on him when he drove up.

"What kind of car do you think he'll be driving?" Ralph asked Christine.

"I don't know, boy. And it doesn't matter."

"I bet he has a really cool car."

"Yeah, it's probably red," Jesse joined in.

"What if it's a convertible?" Tommie asked.

I didn't care what kind of car he had. That was probably one of the last things on my mind. I just wanted to see him. I wanted him to hug me and pick me up.

"Look, a car is pulling into the driveway!" said Christine.

"It's a station wagon with a trailer on the back. And lots of people are in it," Ralph observed.

Gramma ran out of the door to greet them. It was Daddy all right. He got out of the driver side. A woman got out of the passenger side. And, three children got out of the back seats. What was this? I couldn't believe it. Who are these people getting out of the car with my Daddy? I didn't like the looks of this.

"Daddeee!! Daddeee!!" Christine shouted with excitement as she threw her arms around his neck. Tommie and Jesse ran out to greet him too, with

James close behind. Ralph and I stayed inside. I kept peeping out the window while Ralph stood in a daze. Grampa Ellis had not gone outside either.

    Daddy came in the front door with the crowd in tow behind him. First, there was Gramma, then Christine, the strange woman, the three kids, James, Jesse, and then Tommie. Daddy was a big man. He was 6'6 and 280lbs. His natural high yellow skin color had tanned some. But he was still pretty close to the color of Pappa. He had muscles everywhere. Even his eyebrows it seemed had muscles. And he smoked very large cigars. He was a man's man. He had more nicknames than anybody I ever heard of. His given name was Thomas Jesse Johnson. But they called him TJ, Bo, Chief, Daddy T, and Rooster.

    He rubbed my head and said, "Hey, sport. I want you to meet your new little brothers and sister."

    (What!! I thought. New brothers and sister!!! And, doesn't he even know my name?)

    "Grant and Jacob are twins. Valerie is their older sister. And this is my wife, Marilyn. She's your new step-mother."

    "Ralph. Look at you. You are all grown up. Come give me a hug."
With that, Ralph bolted for the front door. He was out the door in a flash and running as fast as he could down the street. Grampa Ellis ran to the door behind him.

    "Ralph!! Get back here!! What's the matter with you?"

    Instinctively, I knew what was wrong. I wanted to run out of the door too. But someone would soon catch me. They couldn't catch Ralph. He was too fast. My life was ruined. Daddy came home with a ready-made family. He had replaced us. What was I going to do? There was no way for him and Mamma to get back together, not now, not EVER!

****

    Grampa Ellis brought us home around 7:00pm. The rest of the afternoon was a bore. Christine, Tommie, Jesse, and James seemed to be having a good time telling Daddy all of the things they had been doing and listening to his tales from California. I just wanted to go home. I was glad when Gramma said that we had better not stay too long and make Mamma angry.

    Ralph had already run and walked the five miles back to the house. Of course, he had told Mamma everything that happened. While she might have been thinking all kinds of bad things about Daddy upsetting Ralph and me that way, she never said a word. She just opened her arms when we got in. She hugged each one of us. Her hugs were something special, too. It was like a bear was hugging me. It seemed like she squeezed so hard that I would melt into her skin. I would literally sink into her body. Her hugs felt good. This one was especially good. It confirmed her love for each one of us.

"Mamma, Daddy came home with three children and a wife. Can you believe that?" I blurted out

"I heard," she said. "You know, your Daddy can do whatever he likes. He's a grown man."

"But he could have told us. He could have written. It didn't have to be a surprise," I said.

"What difference does it make?" was Christine's response. "He's still our Daddy."

"Not mine," said Ralph.

"Mine neither," I agreed.

"Both of you should be ashamed of yourselves. He is your father. And there's nothing you can do about it. God's word says, "Children, obey your parents in everything, for this pleases the Lord."

"Parent?" Ralph questioned. I shook my head in agreement.

"Whether you like it or not, he is your parent. You don't have to agree with everything that he does. But, you do have to obey him. So before this gets too far out of hand, I want both of you to settle it in your hearts right now that T.J. Johnson is your father and there is no other."

It was still Christmas Eve, so we got into our routine of putting on red pajamas, finishing the decorations on the tree, baking cookies, drinking eggnog, playing Christmas carols on the record player, and wrapping the last presents. Christmas had always been fun. But he messed this one up.

****

The school year went by quickly. During the winter and spring, while Chrissie was back at college, we all ran track, and visited Daddy on the weekends. At least, most of us did. Ralph always had track or baseball or something that would keep him so busy that he couldn't or wouldn't visit. The rest of us were busy a lot, too. But we found time to make it to his house at least twice a month. Daddy started a cement construction company with the help of his brothers and Grampa Ellis. He gained the favor of many businessmen. As a result, his business grew faster than expected. His laborers were mostly relatives. Many of them, like Ben, were from Raeford. We called him 'Shot Gun'. Every Friday, Daddy would pay his men from his kitchen table piled high with cash. It was always a party at his house on Fridays. He had washtubs of beer on ice, domino tables, card games, gambling shack in the back, and the blues playing. He was making some money.

When the summer started, Ralph, Tommie, and Jesse went to work for him. Ralph wasn't too excited about it. But, it put money in his pocket. Before too long, he had saved up enough and convinced Daddy to give him the difference so that he could buy a used car. It was a purple Dodge 444 with big tires on it.

"Tommie, Jesse, and Willie, want to go for a ride?" Ralph didn't have to ask that question too many times. We were in that car lickety split.

"I wanna go too," James begged.

"You're too little. Go back in the house with Mamma."

We were gone before he got inside and told Mamma that Ralph was leaving again. He went speeding down University Avenue at about 60 miles an hour. When he got out of the city limits, he took that car up to 95 mph pretty easily. I was getting a little nervous. He could tell. He slowed down, cruised around by the swimming pool for people to see us, and then drove back home. That was fun.

"Ralph, if you leave like that one more time without telling me, I'm taking those keys," Mamma scolded when we returned. "I have a mind not to let you go with your Daddy to the beach tonight. How are you going to act?"

Ralph apologized then went into our bedroom to get ready for the beach. Daddy had promised to give him a beach party for his birthday in Morehead City, no less. Daddy loaned his trucks to many of Ralph's friends so that a lot of people could go. Ralph, of course, would drive his car. Everyone would meet at Daddy's house then leave in a caravan.

Ralph and three of his buddies piled in his car and took off.

"See yawl in Morehead City," he said as he sped off leaving the caravan in his wake.

It was about 9:30pm that night when the phone rang. To my surprise, when I answered, it was Daddy. He asked for Mamma. I held the phone until she came and stood nearby. She said nothing. Just listened. Then all of a sudden, she screamed.

"NO! NO! NO! NO!" It was a blood-curdling scream. Something was wrong. She dropped the phone and fell on her face still screaming.

"Please God. NO! NO, NO!" I didn't know what to do. I let the phone dangle. I joined Mamma on the floor. James came running in. Chrissie was at summer school. Tommie and Jesse were spending the night at friends. Mamma was crying and not making much sense. I couldn't understand a word she was saying. Something was terribly wrong. I heard Daddy on the phone.

"Doris! Doris!" I picked up the receiver and yelled at him.

"What did you tell her? What did you say to her? She doesn't want to talk to you!" I hung up. Mamma heard me and reached for James and me. She gave us one of her hugs. It was a strong hug like before but she wasn't letting go. She squeezed so hard this time that I thought I heard my bones pop. I asked her what was wrong. She told me to call Tommie and Jesse. They needed to come home. I asked her again with tears in my eyes,

"What's wrong, Mamma?"

She only repeated that I needed to get in touch with Tommie and Jesse, then call Christine, and tell her to come home. Now I was really nervous. I was crying when I dialed the phone numbers. Mamma couldn't stop crying. James was crying. I was crying but didn't know why.

Christine drove that hour and a half from college in about 45 minutes. Tommie and Jesse got there about the same time. Mamma was quieter but still crying. She just held James and me until everybody got there. Christine took control and tried to get her to talk. We all feared the worse. Ralph was not there and Daddy had called. I told them everything that happened. While I was talking, the phone rang again. It was Daddy again.

"Chrissie, there was nothing I could do. Ralph took off with his friends before we were ready to leave. You know how that boy is."

"What are you talking about Daddy?"

"He was gone before I could catch him. When we got to the ferry, police cars were everywhere. Ralph lost control of his car, ran through the gates, and plunged into Morehead City bay. He drowned. He's dead Chrissie. Ralph is dead!"

****

      The funeral was three weeks before the Raeford Community Homecoming. It was a big one. Our family is big. His classmates and teammates were there. A couple of college coaches even came. Ralph was well liked. It was a very sad day for Mamma and the rest of us. I didn't think that she would ever forgive Daddy for giving Ralph a party at Morehead City beach. By the time Homecoming rolled around, she was calming down. At least she could attend the event. Raeford was her hometown, too.

      Her father, Joshua Freeman (Big Daddy), came to Raeford from Virginia with her mother, brother, and sister about two years after she was born. Her mother, Big Mamma, used to tell stories of the feuds between the Freeman's and the Johnson's that resulted from Big Daddy moving next door to Grampa Ellis. Big Daddy was constantly running the Johnson boys away from his girls. But TJ was able to catch Doris and run off with her.

      This Homecoming was to be a special one for several reasons. I had promised Mamma that I would get baptized this time. Plus, with Ralph now dead, I was a little afraid not to get baptized. In addition, Grampa Ellis would be preaching the Sunday sermon. So I was sure that Ralph would get a second eulogy.

      We got to Pappa's just before supper on Saturday night. All of us were there, Christine, Tommie, Jesse, James, and me. As usual, we sat on the front porch immediately after supper and before most of the rest of the family arrived for prayer. The air was still. Everything was quiet and so were we. I sat in my spot on the steps. James sat next to me. The herd of cows across the highway started to lie down for the evening. Yet for some odd reason, the bull that was serenading one of the cows fascinated me. I had seen this before. It was an ordinary event in the country. However, this time I was fixated. There was something about the birth that would result from this union that captivated me. Maybe it was because Ralph had recently died that I thought of a NEW BIRTH. Maybe not!

      The family prayer was no less captivating. Pappa was his usual self. He taught from Hebrews 10:24 – 25. The message was Do Not Forsake Assembly. He told us that the central theme of this message was unity. Pappa continued,

      "When He gave me this subject a couple of days ago, I thought that I knew what God would talk about. Initially I thought that the message was about praying together. I thought it was about being unified in our prayer life and prayer times. And, it is extremely important to pray with each other and pray for each other. The word says so. Hear this. "And let us consider how we may spur one another on toward love and good deeds. Let us not give up meeting together, as some are in the habit of doing, but let us encourage one another—and all the more as you see the Day approaching."[1] In addition, "Confess your faults one to another, and pray one for another, that ye may be healed. The effectual fervent prayer of a righteous man availeth much."[2]

God is so good. God has given me experiences and used some of you to show me that this message goes far beyond praying for and with each other. I know that this unity message is about the highest command God has given us for each other. It is about loving each other. He has so much to say on this topic because it is so important to Him. Allow me to share just one or two things God has to say about this love that unifies. "You, my brothers, were called to be free. But do not use your freedom to indulge the sinful nature; rather, serve one another in love. The entire law is summed up in a single command: "Love your neighbor as yourself." If you keep on biting and devouring each other, watch out or you will be destroyed by each other.[3] May the Lord make your love increase and overflow for each other and for everyone else, just as ours does for you. May He strengthen your hearts so that you will be blameless and holy in the presence of our God and Father when our Lord Jesus comes with all His holy ones.[4] Bear with each other, and forgive whatever grievances you may have against one another. Forgive as the Lord forgave you. And over all these virtues put on love, which binds them all together in perfect unity.""[5]

What does this message mean to you today? There are relationships in your life that are in need of a 'love fix'. They need repair. The unity that must result from the repair can only be achieved through love. And our prayers must be rooted in love. You have a spouse, family member, co-worker, ministry fellow, or friend with whom you must be reunited. There is a stronger bond of love that is waiting to unify you. There is healing in Gilead because there is a balm in Gilead. Some of you know what I am talking about. As soon as I started speaking this and even now, I know that God is speaking directly to many of you. You have relationships that are in need of a 'love fix'. I want you to pray, find yourself some love and unity scriptures, meditate on them, then obey what God tells you to do. If you need a scripture or someone to pray with, just let me know. I am happy to be your servant."

****

Grampa Ellis's sermon the next day was a continuation of Pappa's message. Holy Spirit united the two of them. He taught from Genesis to Revelation. "The bible teaches about God's character and ways. We know that as God revealed Himself to the prophets of old, He quite often exacted punishment against evil. As He walked the earth as Jesus Christ, love and compassion became His dominant theme. Now, during this dispensation of the Holy Spirit, He is teaching, guiding, and counseling us on how to live Godly lives on a daily basis. So, in all that we get, we must get a full understanding of His word.[6]"

"God taught further, through Paul, that everyone who wants to live a Godly life in Christ Jesus will be persecuted.[7] We should be prepared to preach the word in season and out of season. We should correct, rebuke, and encourage with great patience and careful instruction.[8] How do we properly view this power of self in light of God's word? Here is something to think about.

- Be sure of the call upon your life.[9]
- When we suffer, suffer for Christ not another person.[10]
- We must walk in the light of God's word and pray that our loved ones also walk in that same light. Then, we will have fellowship with one another.[11]

As we take the whole of God's word on power, we must be careful to always leave room for the Holy Spirit to teach, guide, and counsel us.[12] If we read God's word only to get the letter of the law, we can get false messages, followed by sin, and thus become separated from God.[13]"

I listened intently to what God was saying through Grampa Ellis. But I did not fully understand all of it. I just knew that I wanted him to get to the end so that the baptisms could start. As soon as the sermon was done and following the call to accept Christ, this church baptized all candidates. There were only three of us that day, an uncle, a cousin, and me. Christine, Ralph, Tommie and Jesse had all been baptized previously. James was to be baptized in a year or so. I was the first of this group of three to wade into the water. Grampa Ellis and one of the Deacons got in the water with me. He prayed, and then they dunked me.

I wrapped the drying towel around me and sat on the bench to wait for the other two. Years later, I would realize that all that happened to me that day was that I got wet. I had not really yet accepted Jesus Christ as Lord and Savior. I just wanted to make Mamma happy. Something strange did come over me as I sat there though. All of a sudden, I was in a daze. I reflected back on several months before Daddy came back from California. I remembered my two dreams and got shivers. I dreamed Daddy came back with a son and I dreamed that Ralph was killed in a car accident. Both of those things proved true!!

3

The Bull or the Prophet

"Great is Thy faith-ful-ness, O God my Fa-ther, There is no shad-ow of turn-ing with Thee; Thou changest not, Thy com-pas-sions, they fail not, As Thou hast been Thou for-ev-er wilt be, "Great is Thy faith-ful-ness! Great is Thy faith-ful-ness! Morn-ing by morn-ing new mer-cies I see; All I have need-ed Thy hand hath pro-vid-ed, Great is Thy faith-ful-ness, Lord un-to me!"

This song by my cousin from California rocked the house. It was the Raeford Annual Homecoming Sunday and we were in the middle of the Family Tributes. The annual worship service always started in this way. Representatives from each family in Raeford would sing, read a poem, make a statement, or otherwise give tribute to the eldest person who had ever lived in the community from that family. It was always in alphabetical order.

Eddie Jr. Alberts	Thomas Henderson
Joseph Bennett	Harvey Johnson
'Bud' Brunson	Chad Lankey
Hal Chestnut	S.T. Leday
John Ervin	Herman Powell
Joshua Freeman	Samuel Reynolds
Daniel Hines	Agnes Simpson

Our family always sang because of the beautiful gift of singing bestowed on so many of the females in the Johnson family. Some of the men could sing exceptionally well too. But, the women by far excelled in singing from their hearts with music in their voices. I was not included in the group who could sing. So I made a point of getting to the church early enough to get a good seat for the Family Tributes but far enough in the back to sneak out when the worship service started. During my early years, me and the rest of my male cousins had much better things to do like walking in the woods and going swimming in the creek.

For that particular service, I got a good seat about three rows from the back. While listening to a different cousin from the Lankey side of the family recite the same poem that he reads every year, I drifted to thinking about the previous year's escapades. Tommie, Jesse, me and five or six other cousins slipped off from The Shade Tree when no one was looking and made our break to the woods. The trail was a familiar one. From the cemetery, we would cut behind Mr. Powell's house to the dirt road that curved past Aunt Helen's and stopped at the field where Henry Hines kept his cows. We were always careful cutting through that field because he had a bad bull in there.

"Better look out for that bull," Tommie said.

"You just don't mess with him if he shows up. I know you," said Cousin George.

"I ain't messin with that bull. He can outrun us in these bushes," Tommie responded.

We walked along the trail picking up and throwing sticks at rocks and trees. We just talked about much of nothing. We noticed that Cousin Austin wasn't with us this time. He was as big a prankster as Tommie. I wondered what he was up to.

"The bull's comiiiiiinng!!!!" It was Tommie. He had wondered off looking for the bull. He found him and picked at him until the bull was now charging. This bull was huge. He stood about five feet tall and weighted nearly a thousand pounds. He looked to be about as wide as he was tall. His horns were curled and came to an ice pick point. His dark brown coat was sprinkled with red spots. He had a frightful red face with splotches of white than ran between his eyes and stopped at the top of his lips. These very big lips were blood red.

"Look out!! Look out!!" everyone yelled as we split in nine different directions. Tommie was pretty fast. He quickly caught up with the rest of us and went past. The bull latched onto Cousin Marcus. Marcus was moving!!

"Run Marcus!! Run!!" We all yelled.

The bull was bearing down on Marcus. He was doomed.

"Go to the creek!" Marcus was zigging and zagging across the field. The bull was just a few feet from him now.

"Run Marcus!! Run!!"

The bull kept charging. We stopped running away long enough to look back and see Marcus disappear around the bend. We ran forward. We had to see what happened to Marcus. As we got close enough to see, we noticed that the bull had stopped. Snot was coming out of his nose. He had his head bent and moving it from side to side. No one dared get any closer. Marcus was nowhere to be found. He had run to the other side of the creek and jumped in.

"Snap". It was a twig beneath my feet as I walked backwards. In an instant, the bull turned and saw us about a hundred yards away.

"We better get out of here," Jessie said.

"That bull looks mad."

"Last one in the creek is a rotten egg," yelled Tommie. And off he went.

We all went skinny dipping in the creek. That's the only way to swim. Plus, most of us had on suits. We couldn't go swimming in them. As we ran toward the creek, we started shedding clothes. We had to hold them long enough to get to the creek then hang them on branches. But off they came none-the-less. Splash. Splash. Splash. Splash. Splash. One by one, we hit the water. The creek was a fast running creek with clear cool water. Marcus had already climbed out by the time we got there and was hanging his clothes on a tree to dry. Splash. Back in he came. We kicked up water. Dived in. Jumped in. Dunked each other. And played tag in the water. We knew to stay active so as to keep the water moccasins away. As long as we were frolicking in the water, the snakes would leave us alone.

"Hey, who is that messing with our clothes," Jesse noticed.

"Surprise!" It was cousin Austin. He was clicking pictures with his mother's new instamatic camera.

"Cut that out," we shouted.

Click. Click. Click. He snapped three or four pictures before anyone could get out of the water and chase him off. But he only went far enough away to keep anyone from taking the camera from him. While we got out of the creek, click. Click. Click. He kept backing up, clicking all the way. We hustled getting our clothes back on.

****

"Willie!! Willie!! Pay attention. You're daydreaming, again." It was Mamma. I was trapped. I had stayed in the church too long. The Family Tributes were finished and the worship service had begun. Mamma made me scoot to the middle and sat right next to me. I couldn't get out.

Just before the sermon started Pappa stood and spoke this prophetic word.

"My son, I bless you my son. I have given you eyes to see through the darkness. I have given you strength. I have given you courage to go where few men would go. But you have the courage and, you have the strength. You are one of my Mighty Men. I have given you the ability to go and to tread upon serpents. These are unholy spirits. You will be treading upon hard, hot coal and lava. It will be hot. But you will be protected because I am with you. You won't be injured because my spirit will be covering you and my angels will be shielding you. You are going to be able to handle all that I give you because I have given you all that you need. You are a maximum man. It is California or bust for you. You are an intense man. The job that I have for you takes a man with strength, courage and endurance. You are going to carry a heavy spiritual load for me. But you can do it because you have my Spirit. You have a full measure of my Spirit. And as you step forth, you are going to have everything you need. So step forth. Step out of the boat. You have everything that you need."

"Who is he talking to Mamma?" I asked. "Is he talking about Daddy? He said something about California."

"Shhh. I don't know who he's talking about. He's just directing the prophecy to the church. The person he's talking to knows though."

I wondered who he could be talking to. I looked around and everyone was fixed on him. When Pappa spoke, it was like E.F. Hutton speaking. Everyone listened.

"Son, I've made you a man of valor, a man of war. I have called you to this because you are mighty. I have given you much strength and much determination. You are the one that will not compromise. You are going in to possess the land. You will be going into my land. You will possess it. And, and fear not because I will always be with you. There will never be a time that I will leave you. You will always possess the land. I will send forth angels before you. I will be your rear guard. And you will always defeat the enemy."

Then he sat down without speaking another word. Wow! His words kept ringing in my ears. Was he talking about Daddy? He must have been.

He mentioned California. Daddy had been in California. Who was he talking about? I kept looking at him. He always sat on the benches on the left of the pulpit. He was not a Pastor or Preacher. So he couldn't sit in the pulpit. But it seemed that he could talk whenever he wanted to. The floor was always given to him whenever he stood up. I watched him for the rest of the service. He remained fairly absorbed. He praised with the music and said Amen to the Pastor's sermon. Yet, through it all, he maintained a serious look on his face. He never gave a hint to whom he was talking. He didn't look at anyone. He didn't wink. He didn't smile. He didn't wave. He did nothing like that. So, who was he talking to?

****

It was eating time at The Shade Tree. After Homecoming Sunday worship service, the family would gather at the Shade Tree to eat. The food was spread out on this long, long, long table. All the cars would have their trunks facing the table and form a huge circle around the Shade Tree, the table, and the church. This was a fun time. All of the families would get together. The eldest Johnson to ever live in Raeford was Harvey Johnson, Pappa's daddy. This is a portion of his family tree.

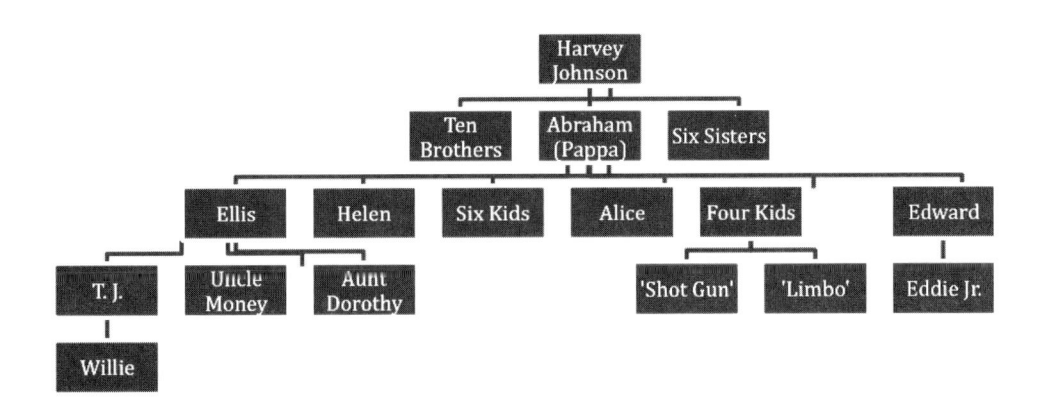

```
                         Harvey
                         Johnson
                            |
        ┌───────────────────┼───────────────────┐
      Ten              Abraham              Six Sisters
    Brothers           (Pappa)
                          |
   ┌────────┬────────┬────┴────┬────────┬────────┐
 Ellis    Helen   Six Kids   Alice   Four Kids  Edward
   |        |                          |          |
 ┌─┴─┐  ┌───┴───┐                  ┌───┴───┐      |
T.J. Uncle    Aunt                'Shot Gun' 'Limbo' Eddie Jr.
     Money   Dorothy
 |
Willie
```

43

The eldest Freeman (my mother's maiden name) was Joshua Freeman. His family tree is this.

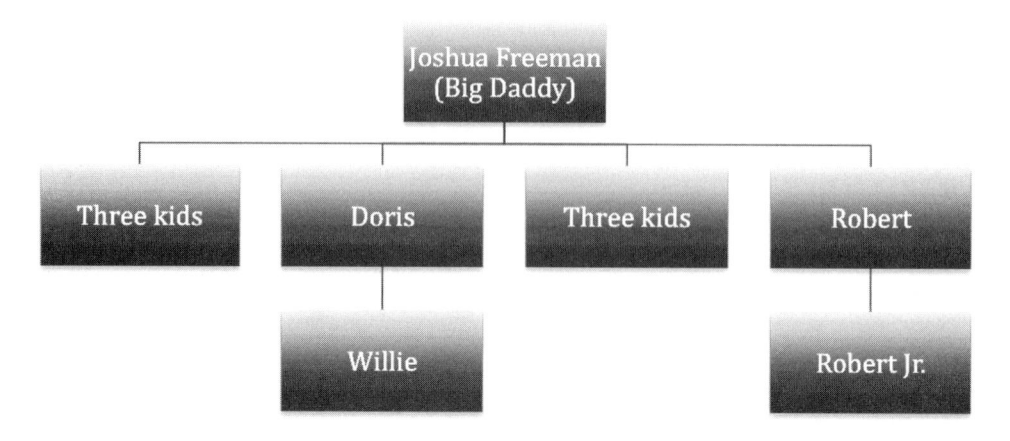

```
                    Joshua Freeman
                      (Big Daddy)
        ┌──────────┬──────┴──────┬──────────┐
    Three kids   Doris        Three kids   Robert
                   │                          │
                 Willie                    Robert Jr.
```

Abraham Johnson's wife, my great grandmother, was a Reynolds. We called her Mamma Liz but her real name was Elizabeth Reynolds. This is her family tree.

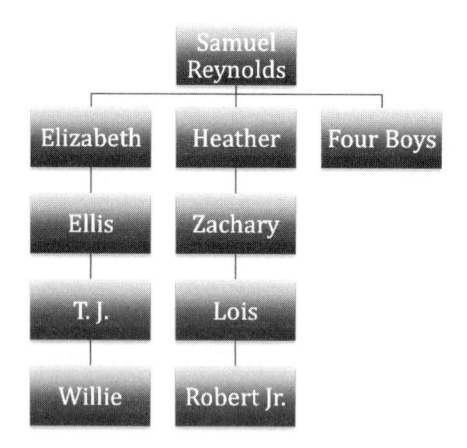

```
                Samuel
               Reynolds
        ┌─────────┼─────────┐
    Elizabeth  Heather   Four Boys
        │         │
      Ellis    Zachary
        │         │
       T.J.     Lois
        │         │
      Willie  Robert Jr.
```

Now, I want you to follow this. Doris married TJ. Robert Freeman married Lois. So, I am the first cousin of Robert Freeman, Jr. on the Freeman side but third cousins on the Reynolds side. It gets deeper than that. Zachary married a Hamilton. Her sister married Ellis. So, if you came down the Hamilton line, both Robert, Jr. and I would show up a third time as second cousins. Now, Lois' mother is a Traylor. Gramma, Grampa Ellis' wife, is a Traylor. Gramma's brother married Lois' Aunt, her mother's sister. So, if you follow the Traylor family tree, you will find me and Robert Jr. a fourth time. See what I mean. It seems like everybody in this community is related one way or another.

While it was fun meeting and greeting all the cousins, it had its challenges too. For example the Freeman family and the Johnson family did not get along. Why did that have to happen to me? We always drove to The Shade Tree with my Mamma, a Freeman. She parked her car next to her mother, Big Mamma. Her brothers and sisters parked their cars next to each other near Big Mamma. Directly across the way, on the other side of The Shade Tree, the Johnson family would park. Gramma, my Daddy's mamma, would make it a point to have her car in a straight line from Big Mamma's. Then the tug of war would begin with us in the middle.

Of course, we had to eat with Mamma first, then Big Mamma made sure we had plenty to eat from the back of her trunk. All the while Gramma would be beckoning us to come to her car.

"Willie, come see Gramma," I would hear her calling. I knew what she wanted. She wanted to stuff me with food, too. I had to eat some of her food or she would be upset. So back and forth we would go between both sets of Grandparents. Hugging one then, hugging the other. Kissing one then, kissing the other. Eating cake from one car then eating pie from the other. That's why we would sneak away most of the time. We needed to walk and swim just to get all of that food down our stomachs.

The Shade Tree was the center of all the action. The church was beneath its leaves and the family gravesites are all around it. After eating, it was tradition to walk the graveyard to 'visit with family.' I eventually came to know that this was the beginning of much of the spiritualism that sprung up in the family. People would actually talk to the dead people in the graves. Some would claim to hear voices talking back that very day. The activity of simply respecting those who had gone on to glory was being perverted into spiritualism.

It was always wise to be out of there before nightfall because of the 'spookiness' that surrounded the cemetery. We would usually be out by late afternoon, well before dark. It was common to go from house to house visiting relatives. Since all of the Freeman family had either moved from Raeford or died, the closest relative to visit was either the Johnsons or the Reynolds family. Of course, the favorite spot was Pappa's. Mamma took us there and asked that Daddy bring us home early. He agreed. So off we went. Grampa Ellis and Uncle Money, Daddy's brother, went there too.

James and I headed to the backyard. We always found something to get into. Daddy sent Jacob and Grant (his boys from California) with us.

"Yawl better leave them chickens alone," we heard Grampa Ellis say.

What does he know? We just went to the other side. It was fun to shoo them and watch them fly. A chicken couldn't fly very far. So, we would just shoo them all over the back yard. Jacob and Grant were having fun too. As we were shooing the chickens, they got a little too close to the mother goose that was walking her baby geese to the pond down the way. The two little boys were just waving their hands and running after the chickens. They didn't pay any attention to the mother goose. But when they got too close, she squawked and flew after Grant.

He started yelling.

"Help!! Help!! Help!!" That mother goose was all over his head. She was pecking and he was running. It was a funny sight. Me and James broke out laughing. The mother goose was not hurting him. But he sure was scared.

"What going on out here?" Daddy questioned. He could see the goose chasing Grant. He came to the rescue. He grabbed up Grant in his arms and ran the goose off. Jacob ran and grabbed one of his legs. James and I were still laughing but not too loud now. Daddy didn't look happy.

"We didn't do nothing," James said. "Grant got too close to the mother goose and she didn't like it."

"All of yawl come in the house right now."

That's what they get, we thought, as we snickered into the house.

Grampa Ellis and Pappa were engaged in conversation on the front porch with most everyone else either sitting, listening, or talking among themselves in the front yard. This time Grampa Ellis spoke. I heard him say,

"Daddy, I was very focused on your prophetic word today. Did God reveal to you the person for whom the message was intended?"

"Yes, but I am not released to say yet. That person was in the church and he heard it." Pappa said.

Then Grampa Ellis said, "I am convinced that he heard it, too. In fact, I received a continuation of that word. It is welling up in me now."

He continued, "My son, I'm making you like a rubber band. I'm going to stretch you like you've never been stretched before. Not just double. Not triple. But a hundred times. You're going to be stretched. So, step forth and step out. And, go. Go. Listen. Speak. But, you must listen first. Listen well. I made you with two ears and one mouth. So listen twice as much as you speak. Then follow Me. As you follow, you will spread the seeds of truth to both groups of people. And, you're going to fight battles. Listen intently to what others are saying. You are to intercede for them. You have a sword in your hand with which to destroy strongholds. You will break chains. When you break those chains, you are going to loose the people from their bondages. The demons must flee. They will no longer deceive my people. I have a mighty work for you. And I'm not done with you yet."

I thought, "Here they go again. What in the world are they talking about?"

"It's getting late, Daddy, and I promised Doris that I would get the boys home early. I had better go," my Daddy said to Grampa Ellis.

"I'm going to leave too, Daddy," said Uncle Money.

Both cars full of kids took off at the same time. Daddy and Uncle Money were pretty close brothers. They were less than two years apart in age. They hung out a lot together as kids growing up. They continued throughout their teenage years into adults. Uncle Money really missed Daddy when he moved to California. One of the favorite things they had grown to do together was race cars. They raced everywhere they went. They raced to Raeford. They raced to Lake Fontana on fishing trips. And, yes, they raced to Morehead City. I am sure that's where Ralph got the itch for speed. How quickly we forget.

"Bo, when we get to Sparta and the roads get a little straighter, I'll race you to Greenville."

"You're on."

"TJ Come on. You have all the kids in the car," complained Ms. Marilyn.

"No problem. It's just a short 10-mile run. Then, we'll take it easy the rest of the way to Fayetteville."

I was really nervous when they took off. But I didn't dare say a word. I remembered Ralph. I remembered my dream before his death. I just sat in the back seat cramped up with four other kids and kept my mouth shut.

"I got you now!" yelled Uncle Money out his window.

"Not yet, you don't!"

About halfway to Greenville, we approached a train whose tracks were running parallel to Highway 69, the highway on which we were speeding. Daddy picked up speed.

"Now don't start racing the train, too. You'd better slow this car down. And slow it down now!" Ms. Marilyn was yelling at the top of her voice, "Now!"

Daddy slowed while Uncle Money sped off in the distance.

And I was going to tell Mamma……………………………….

4

Walking With The One Who Has Power

Growing up in Lincoln Grove Village was a lot of fun and excitement. It was a community of about 180 families. It had six courts each with about 30 units of the same size. The two-bedroom apartments in each court circumscribed an open grassy area that was well manicured. The sidewalks were wide with light poles about every forty yards. The builders included a rent office, barber shop, liquor store, record shop, Laundromat, grocery store, and beer joint along a circular drive that marked the 'Front' of Lincoln Grove. It was one of many 'housing projects' built around the United States at that time. The early inhabitants of Lincoln Grove were two parent families with respectable jobs. In Calvin Court, our court, the Blackburns worked at the Post office and Fire Station. Both of the Allens were schoolteachers as were the Prices and Mrs. Glover. Mr. Coleman owned a construction company like my dad and his wife stayed at home like my mother. Mr. Ford, Mr. Drummer, Mr. Baker, and Mr. Harris worked at the refinery.

Then there was Mr. Taylor. He was the local 'numbers' man. It amazed me that a man in the public projects would be allowed to build a patio with imported Palm trees in his back yard. Yet, he did. He was related to Grampa Ellis in some way. I never got it straight. I do know that Aunt Ethel, one of Grampa Ellis's sisters, was married to a Taylor. That could have been the link. In any event, because of the connection, I was able to go inside his house and on his patio. I felt like a big shot. Mr. Taylor, the most influential man in Lincoln Grove allowed us on his property. We witnessed a couple of amazing things, too. He would actually light his cigars with $5, $10, and $20 bills. He also burned money, including coins in a small incinerator. Later, I understood that he did it because the money was either marked in some way or counterfeit. At the time though, it was impressive.

Lincoln Grove was a stable environment for the first few years. Then families started to break up. Mr. Ford and Mr. Drummer left their families. Mr. Price and Mr. Blackburn died. Mr. Baker and Mr. Harris moved their families to the Greenspoint neighborhood. Then the most damaging blow of all to me was that my dad left us, and moved to California. Yet, the six children and my mother established a special bond. We learned to depend on each other. We also established some life-long friends in the neighborhood. Lincoln Grove took on the character of the second part of its name. It became the Village. The children of these single parent homes found fathers and additional mothers in every court of Lincoln Grove Village. We were no exception.

There was a patch of trees in the back of Lincoln Grove where kids from elementary school through JR High School would play. We would build camps and hideouts based on which court we lived in. The clever ones would either build a hideout in the tops of trees or beneath the ground. We were ingenious in the ways we would ring our campsites with thin wire and bells to warn of intruders. When an enemy approached, the weapons of our warfare were slingshots made with wire clothes hangers and thick rubber bands. We cut other wire clothes hangers into smaller pieces then bent the pieces to form sling shot bullets. Other weapons included BB guns and bamboo shoots used as spears. We bent soda pop bottle tops into arrow tips for the spears. Even if the base camp was underground, it would not be unusual to find one of us in the top of a tree around which the camp was strategically built. This watchman would call down on the phone made of aluminum cans and wire to summon the troops for any battle that was necessary. Inside the camp, we would play marbles, tops, and various other games. Most of the time, we would join forces with the kids from Lawndale court. They were our buddies.

High school students and those no longer in schools would hang out on the 'Front'. That's where the big boys were. As time passed, Lincoln Grove got the reputation of being a tough neighborhood. It was debatably one of, if not the toughest neighborhood in Fayetteville. It was its own kingdom. And it had a king. His name was Floyd. As you know, a king dominates his domain. Well, Floyd dominated Lincoln Grove. Nobody messed with Floyd. In fact if you joined in with Floyd, nobody messed with you. He who has an ear, let him hear the word of the Spirit.

The enemy (other neighborhoods) did not come into Lincoln Grove without Floyd's permission. If they did, Floyd would gather his boys, beat up on the enemy, and then run them out of Lincoln Grove. We had both some 'loose' and some 'respectable' girls in Lincoln Grove too. If one of them wanted to hang out with one of the guys from another neighborhood, they had to leave Lincoln Grove to do so. Nobody came to visit either of our women inside Lincoln Grove without some resistance. If somehow they came in without notice and Floyd found out about it, he would gather his boys, wait for the guy to come out of the house, beat up on him, and then run him out of Lincoln Grove. Sometimes Floyd would even go up to the girl's house and call the enemy out, and then run him out of Lincoln Grove. Floyd was a bad boy.

We had a rivalry with another High School in Fayetteville that played its home football games across the railroad track from Lincoln Grove. It was the enemy's camp and it was walking distance from Lincoln Grove. Sometimes, usually under the leadership of Floyd, we would go into the enemy's camp and beat up on him. At half time, we would walk to the dividing line at either the 110-yard or 330-yard mark on the 440-yard track that encircled the football field. Floyd would protect our side of the field. He would dare the enemy to cross the line. If they did, he would beat up on them. Even if they didn't cross the line, Floyd would cross the line, go on the enemy's side of the field and beat up on him. And we went with him. Most of the time, we never had to throw a punch. Either they ran off when they saw Floyd, or he knocked one of them out with one punch. Many times, Floyd would just speak something like "Get out of here" and the enemy would run. I remember some of the guys repeating what Floyd had said. That included me too! Floyd would say, 'Get out of here.' Then I would say it. It had the same power as it did when Floyd said it, as long as I was with Floyd.

Now, I was not the toughest guy in Lincoln Grove. Not even close. But whenever I was in Floyd's presence, I felt like I could beat up on anybody who was around. With Floyd as my backup, I could. From the time I was about five years old until I entered high school, I had a fistfight every day. Most of the time, Floyd and other big boys on the Front orchestrated these fights. These fights were challenges. They were a test of my development. They were used to determine the pecking order (I now see in Floyd's army). Floyd or one of the big boys would pick someone near my age and say fight that one. I had to fight. If I didn't, I would get beat up anyway. I lost many of these fights. And I won quite a few. It got to the point that if I lost a fight with my fists, many times I would go looking for a weapon. It didn't matter to me what the weapon was. Knives, a bowling pin, a stick, a BB gun, a rope, or just about anything else would do. Some came to know me as that crazy Willie. 'He'll use any weapon he can put his hands on.'

I led a double life of smart kid and wanna be thug. In the classroom, my grades were nearly always an 'A'. It didn't take much effort for me to excel, either. I didn't spend much time at home doing schoolwork. Since I was almost always outside playing and trying to be tough with everybody else, not many of my friends knew that I had any intelligence. It only became evident at school assemblies when honors were being distributed. Then my Lincoln Grove friends would see that I had some sense. I can remember in high school, I would sit in the back of the gymnasium with those from Lincoln Grove instead of up front with the rest of the respectable students. When I received an award, I would take the long walk from the back to the stage and return to my seat. During the entire time, the thugs would be yelling "Lincoln Grove!! Lincoln Grove!! Lincoln Grove!!" It made them, and me feel good about living in this tough neighborhood.

I allowed myself to frequently get caught up in questionable activities. For example, the back entrance to Olympia Motors adjourned the side entrance to Lincoln Grove. During the sales day, the manager of this car lot would leave the keys to each car in the driver side door. I can't tell you on how many occasions a car from that lot would end up missing over night only to be returned in the wee hours of the next morning. That is, if it didn't run out of gas first. In that case, it was left where the gas ran out.

The summers were always the most fun. During my early years, almost as soon as school was out, we would head for Raeford. As we got older, the summer vacation in Raeford would come later and later in the summer until as teenagers we only went for the Homecoming.

****

Chrissie was now married and starting her own family. Jessie had gone off to the war. Tommie and I were working most of the summer with Daddy. James stayed with neighbors in the Village until either Mamma or we got home.

Working construction with our dad was not one of the fun parts of summer. Construction in the hot summer sun was difficult work to say the least. Plus, our Daddy was testing us just as he did Jesse. I believe that is one of the reasons Jesse quit school and joined the Army. He saw no future in school or working construction with Daddy. Frankly, I didn't see much future in construction work either.

My dad loved Tommie. He was teaching him everything about the business. Me? I was simply a laborer. Tommie learned how to read blueprints. He could survey open land and determine the correct placement of forms for building the foundations. He learned schedules, contacts, pay rates, and multiple job skills. I remember the day Tommie got his nickname, DZ.
Daddy smoked big fat cigars. He always had one of them hanging out of the side of his mouth. He hardly ever took it out. Sometimes when he talked, it was difficult to understand exactly what he said because of that cigar. Tommie was really learning the business well. So Daddy started calling him Top Cat. He shortened that name to TC. When he would call Tommie, he would call him by the short name TC.

"TC, bring me that blueprint," he would say. "TC, take my car and fill it up with gas."

Because he had that cigar hanging out of his mouth, many of Daddy's laborers, including me thought that he was saying DZ. No one ever challenged my dad. So no one ever got any clarity on what he was saying. Eventually, other people started calling Tommie by his short name. But, instead of calling him TC as Daddy intended, we called him DZ as we heard it. That name stuck with him especially because of the story behind it. Daddy became fond of the name DZ and just stuck to calling Tommie DZ, just like everyone else!

That same summer, Daddy promoted me from digging dirt trenches in the middle of foundations to working the cement. This was still primarily labor. But working cement required a little more skill and a lot more muscle.

"DZ, I want you to take Willie, Shot Gun, and Limbo on that foundation next door. We have to pour 20 loads of concrete on two slabs today. We need everybody raking that mud as quickly as they can," Daddy told him.

"I got it, Daddy."

"Hey, Willie, are you ready?" he asked me.

"Yes sir." I replied. I was unsure though. I had never raked concrete before. I had seen them do it. It looked simple enough. All I had to do was stand at the end of the chute that was attached to the concrete truck with a shovel in hand. As the concrete came down the chute, my job was to rake it as far as I could away from the chute. In that way, the concrete would not pile up and I would be assisting in getting it to the intended location. It was a job that required quickness and muscle. If the concrete piled up, it could start to harden and create a real problem for the finishers. The good news was that both of the foundations were adjacent to each other. If anything happened, the work could be suspended on one while laborers teamed to complete the job on the other.

"Let her rip!" DZ yelled.

The engine on that concrete truck went from a slow hum to a roar. The concrete began flowing like water down the chute. I started raking and raking and raking. For the first few minutes, I kept up pretty good. Then my muscles started to ache. I didn't say a word. I wanted to impress my Daddy and DZ. My muscles started to burn. Still, I said nothing. I just raked and raked. My arms now felt like lead. My knees started to buckle. I could hardly lift the shovel.

"Somebody better come get him!" DZ yelled.

"Get out of there Willie and get out now!" Daddy yelled.

But I could not move. My legs were weak. The concrete was piling up around my feet. It was harder to lift my knees as the seconds passed.

"Cut it off! Cut it off!" Daddy yelled. "DZ get that boy out of there. He's not ready yet. Get him out of there. We're going to lose this slab if we don't hurry."

DZ and Shot Gun were on me in a flash. They grabbed me by each arm and dragged me out of the concrete. Then they rushed back to the job and finished the work. I was tired, embarrassed, hurt, and disappointed. After sitting on a log for quite a while, I turned on the water hose to wash off my rubber boots. I took them off, took off the polyethylene from around my feet, put on my work boots and then walked slowly to the truck. I watched everybody else working both of those slabs until all 20 loads were dumped and laying smoothly across both foundations. I had tried but I just couldn't do it.

Then there was the time that Daddy told DZ to drop me by myself in the deep woods of Oak Lawn, North Carolina to spread the dirt for a foundation. Oak Lawn was one of the most racist cities in the United States of America. Generally, it was OK for a black man to work in a labor job during the day. But by nightfall, you had better be gone.

Building the foundation of a home without a basement was usually a four-day process. The first day was dedicated to setting up the forms. Dump trucks of dirt came on the second day while a crew spread the dirt. The foundation was made ready for the concrete on the third day. That is, trenches were dug, polyethylene was laid, and then rods and wire was properly placed. The fourth day was dedicated to pouring concrete and finishing the work. On this occasion, the forms had already been set the day before. My job was to direct the dump trucks so that all of the dirt would fall inside those wooden forms. I was then to spread the dirt. If I directed the trucks just right, it would only take me a couple of hours to do this job.

The first three trucks dumped all of its dirt inside the forms beginning at the very back of the foundation. Things were going smoothly. "Back it up. Back it up. Whoa! Get ahead. Whoa! Get ahead. Whoa!" Such were my instructions to the first trucks. Each time I told the driver to get ahead, he dumped a small load of dirt. Each pile was even and just barely above the height of the foundation. Perfect. Then the fourth and fifth trucks came at the same time.

"Back it up. Wait! Wait! Wait!" It was too late. The truck had crashed into the wooden forms. Then, without me telling him to dump it out, he opened the tailgate of the truck and let the entire load out in one spot. Half of it was outside the foundation. This was a mess. The driver left. The fifth truck did slightly better. At least he didn't crash into the forms. Yet, his piles were uneven and much higher than the foundation. This two-hour job was now a full day's work. The foundation had to be repaired. The dirt on the outside had to be spread to the inside. Each of the piles had to be leveled to about four inches below the tops of the wooden forms. What a job.

"What in the world happened here?"

"I tried to tell him to stop, Daddy but I don't think he heard me."

"I trusted you to do a simple job of spreading dirt and look at what happened. You're going to have to finish this job yourself. Today! I'll be back later."

I felt bad. Not only did I have a big job on my hands now. Daddy was angry with me and he left me in Oak Lawn. I worked all day mending the foundation and spreading dirt. 3:00pm. 4:00pm. 5:00pm. Finally I was done at 6:15pm. Yet Daddy was not back. The typical workday started at 5:30am. The men usually knocked off work around 2:00pm. He should have been here a long time ago. 7:00pm arrived and no Daddy. 7:30pm, no Daddy. It was getting late. It would be dark at 8:30 or 8:45pm and this was Oak Lawn! Surely he did not forget me in the middle of these woods. Then, at 7:45pm I saw his car turn down the construction road. Whew!

I knew at that point that I would never work another day in construction once I left high school.

****

The second week in August did not come fast enough for me that summer. As soon as I got off from work on Friday, I was headed to Raeford. Grampa Ellis was going up early this year so James and I rode with him. I stayed with Uncle Eddie. I was now old enough to go to the Cave. After Ralph died, all the stories of his wild driving and sneaking to get keys were shared amongst the family. As a result, Uncle Eddie was well aware of my ability to quietly steal car keys and a car. For the last couple of years, he took no chances. The car keys were always put away safely every night. There was no way that I could go anywhere except next door to the Cave.

There were plenty of girl cousins my age still living in Raeford. In fact, most of the girls there that night were cousins. There was about twenty or more of them. I could not flirt with anybody. No one I knew was there. None-the-less, it was fun dancing and clowning around with family. It was just good for me to get away and relax for a couple of days. I didn't stay late. In fact I was back at Uncle Eddie's around 11:00pm. Grampa Ellis was still there. He had plans to spend the night with Pappa. He just had not made it up the hill yet. Uncle Eddie and he were talking about the War and Jesse. Grampa Ellis did not like this war and really did not like Jesse quitting high school to sign up. I wasn't that interested in joining them. I said goodnight and went to bed.

I slept late but woke up to scrambled eggs, bacon, pancakes, syrup, and buttermilk. Aunt Hattie and the girls were making breakfast for Uncle Eddie, James, and me. The only plans we had for the day was horseback riding. We would then visit Aunt Helen after the Saturday night singing.

"Let's take the horses for a walk along Cow Creek then out in the open pasture for a good run," I told James. James was a very good rider. We had lots of fun racing the horses when we got off by ourselves. Uncle Eddie would let us ride just about anywhere we wanted. All of Raeford was one, big countryside. One cousin's property ran into another. So riding for great distances was no problem. The only thing to worry about was avoiding the seed ticks. These little insects would position themselves on the edges of branches or sagebrush. As you passed by, they would attach themselves to you in the crevices of your body. They were bloodsuckers. You hardly felt them. We had grown accustomed to one of our Aunts, Grandparents, Chrissie, or Mamma looking us over real good when we came back from a ride. It would be no surprise to find one or two of them in an armpit or other private areas where body parts formed crevices.

James chose Lady Luck, a big white horse with a flowing mane. Lady Luck was young and spunky. She was known to throw riders who were not very experienced. She was no problem for James. I chose Thunder. He was just as big as Lady Luck. He was a gray stallion that loved to run. Since it was a hot day, we decided to trot the horses in the shade of the trees along the fence line. The cows must have had the same idea, as many of them were either chewing cud near the fence or walking toward it. I paid no attention to the cow with his head sticking through the fence. Both of our horses sure did though. First, Lady Luck was startled. She rose up then bolted toward the creek. Thunder was surprised and broke out in a fast run, too. We were holding on for dear life. After about 60 or 70 yards, James got Lady Luck under control but kept riding pretty fast. I was soon able to get control of Thunder as well and tried to catch him. James was moving out. I could see that his feet were firmly in the stirrups and his back was hunched over Lady Luck's head.

"Yeeee. Hiiiii!" I could hear him yell.

"I'm coming after you," I shouted as I whipped Thunder's hindquarters with the long end of the bridle. He just kept yelling, "Yeeee. Hiiiii!" We jumped fallen logs and ducked under low branches. I braced myself in the stirrups and pushed Thunder as fast as I could. The wind felt good in my face and the scenery was as beautiful as ever. The pine trees stood tall, and red dirt peaked ever so often from the tops of mounds. We could hear the creek gurgling in the distance. My mind was on nothing but running with the wind.

I never did catch James. I was close but I never caught him. After we rode hard for about a half-mile, the horses were pretty sweaty and getting tired. We eased up and brought them to a trot then a walk again.

"That was fun," James said.

"I always did like coming up here just to do that," I said.

We walked the horses over to Cow Creek and let them have a drink. We even walked them down to the crossing that was shallow enough for them to wade across with us on their backs. The afternoon was lazy and we enjoyed it. We dismounted and continued walking the horses while we talked.

"I miss Jesse. Don't you?" I asked.

"Yep. I wonder when he will be back."

"I don't know but I heard Grampa Ellis and Uncle Eddie talking about it last night."

"I know. They had been at it quite a while by the time you got back from the Cave. They were keeping me awake," James said.

"It really bothered Grampa Ellis that Jesse left like he did, didn't it?" I thought out loud.

"Yeah, and it bothers him even more since his dream. He told Uncle Eddie that he saw Jesse and his unit pinned down in an ambush," James said.

"Uh, Oh! When Grampa Ellis gets visions, you can bank on much of it being true."

"What are we supposed to do?"

"Pray I guess. I don't know," I told him.

****

Tommie came up on Saturday night with Chrissie and Aunt Dorothy. Since they were staying at Aunt Helen's, we were all going to meet them over there after the singing. We got dressed at Uncle Eddie's and went directly to the church. It was a good time of singing that night. The Simpson Quartet from Sanford, North Carolina brought the house down that night. They sang 'Two Wings', 'The Blood of Jesus', 'Going Up Yonder', and 'My Soul Is Anchored In The Lord.' There was standing room only in that little country church. I didn't see Tommie, Aunt Dorothy, or Chrissie at any time before, during or after the singing. After the service, we went to Aunt Helen's as planned.

"What yawl doing here?" Grampa Ellis asked. "We were looking for you at the church."

"We just got here ten minutes ago. We were running late. Since we were not going to make much of the singing, we decided to come straight here," said Aunt Dorothy.

"Yawl miss some good singing," I said.

"I wish we didn't have to miss it. I also wish we could have missed what we did see," Chrissie said.

"What did you see daughter?" asked Grampa Ellis.

"You wouldn't believe it. Then again Daddy, maybe you would," said Aunt Dorothy.

"Believe what?"

"After we left Sparta and turned onto the Raeford road, the lights dimmed in the car. They didn't go out. They just dimmed. I figured there was a shortage somewhere. They were bright enough to see. But it was evident that they had dimmed. So, we kept going. Besides, what were we going to do? It is too dark in these woods to stop or turn the lights completely off."

"OK?"

"We drove until we came past Oak Hill Cemetery. We had gone beyond the front entrance but were not passed the back entrance when the lights went completely out. At that point, there was a ruckus all around every window. There was beating on the front window, beating on the back window, and beating on the side widows too.'

"We were scared Grampa Ellis. What was that all about?" Tommie asked.

"We started screaming. All I could do was keep driving," Aunt Dorothy continued.

"I saw it and heard it too," Chrissie said.

"Now calm down. There is no reason to be frightened. These or no other spirits can do you any physical harm," Grampa Ellis said.

"But what was that?" Aunt Dorothy asked.

"First of all, God did not give you a spirit of fear. But of power, love, and a sound mind. And, greater is He that is in you than he that is in the world. So do not be afraid. There are demonic spirits who would have you believe that they are disembodied spirits of the dead. But know that they are not the spirits of your loved ones. They are demons posing as such. Their intent is to get you to focus on them instead of focusing on God. Do not be afraid of them. Take your stand with the belt of truth buckled around your waist. Know God's word and know that it is true. It is that truth that will free you of fear."

All the while Grampa Ellis was talking; I was thinking that I was glad that I didn't see it. He may have been right in what he was saying but I was just glad that I didn't see it. I might have 'peed' on myself.

The next day was another one of the sad days in our family's life. In the middle of the Homecoming Service, two white men in army uniforms walked into the back of the church. Talk about sticking out like a sore thumb. They waited until the end of the service before asking for Doris Johnson. Immediately Mamma started crying.

"Not again. Not again. God. No. No. I can't take anymore!" she wailed.

Daddy pulled them aside while Christine, Big Mamma, and other women of the church surrounded Mamma.

'What happened?" Daddy asked.

"Sir, your son and his platoon were on a routine scouting mission. They had been gone two days without meeting any enemy resistance. They were less than 5 miles from base camp when the enemy ambushed them. They didn't see it coming. They were trapped on all sides. They were hit with everything. Grenades, mortar shells, and machine gun fire. Your son got off a call for air support but it was too late. Our reinforcements arrived in time to take your son and two others who were wounded back to the camp. The wounds were just too severe. He died within minutes of getting to the camp."

"How about the other guys?"

"They didn't make it either. No one survived."

I couldn't help but think about the conversation between Uncle Eddie and Grampa Ellis the night before. In all likelihood, he saw this in his vision as it was unfolding…………

****

I have a word of encouragement for you. You have a King with power and when you walk with Him you have that same power. He who has an ear, let him hear the word of the Spirit. I want you to listen with spiritual ears to the word of God in this life experience. Every kingdom has a king. God's Kingdom has one too. His name is Jesus. Hallelujah! The good news is that Jesus is alive. Better yet, He lives in you. I believe that by faith you can receive a fresh impartation of the Holy Spirit's power while reading this book that will catapult you to a new level in Christ Jesus. By faith, you can receive Jesus Christ as Lord and Savior. By faith, you can receive the baptism of the Holy Spirit. By faith, you can walk in the power of prophetic intercession. By faith, you can stop the enemy at the gate and run him out of town. By faith you can protect your home and environment from the enemy. By faith, men of God, you can call the enemy out of your wife or loved one. By faith you can go into the enemy's camp and knock him out. By faith, you can receive your God given authority to overcome all the power of the enemy. By faith you can receive power, love, and a sound mind. By faith you can speak love, joy, and peace into the atmosphere. By faith, you can impart spiritual gifts into your seed and your seed's seed.

    It was Lincoln Grove for me. Maybe your old kingdom was the Bronx, Southend, Northend, Westside, Southside, Englewood, Harlem, Plateau, or another neighborhood. Maybe your old king had a different name. In any case, by faith you now have all the power of a new king, Christ Jesus, as long as you walk with Him and live in His kingdom. Do you know that you are as holy as Jesus, as long as you walk with Him? If you believe this word, receive this word, and act on this word, your life will never be the same from this moment on. Hallelujah!! Hallelujah!! Hallelujah!! Glory, Hallelujah!!!

5

Marriage

The lives of two people that God has placed together in the bonds of marriage are very important to His kingdom. That life and every aspect of it is a witness. What kind of witness have you been? What kind will you be? Consider letting your marriage be a service to God. Commend yourselves in every way. '... in great endurance; in troubles, hardships and distresses; in beatings, imprisonments and riots; in hard work, sleepless nights and hunger; in purity, understanding, patience and kindness; in the Holy Spirit and in sincere love; in truthful speech and in the power of God; with weapons of righteousness in the right hand and in the left; through glory and dishonor, bad report and good report; genuine, yet regarded as impostors; known, yet regarded as unknown; dying, and yet we live on; beaten, and yet not killed; sorrowful, yet always rejoicing; poor, yet making many rich; having nothing, and yet possessing everything.' When you commend yourselves to the service of God through your marriage, can you see the honor that it brings to His kingdom? Help me to pray for restored relationships and a new intimacy with each other and our God.

Those of you who are not married, I pray that you call upon your anointing as an intercessor and see God answering your prayer of agreement as you stand in the gap for marriages in your family.

****

Jesse was everybody's friend. From early childhood, he had always admired our oldest brother, Ralph. Although he and Tommie were twins, it was Jesse who followed Ralph everywhere. As he got older, he wanted to be like Ralph in everything. However, he lacked the athletic ability needed to be a superstar. He was pretty good at basketball. He was just not the star of the team.

In fact, Tommie was slightly taller, could handle the ball better, shoot better, and pass better. Those things bothered Jesse quite a bit. To top it off, his younger brothers, James and me were showing signs of academic prowess that he didn't have. He wondered where he fitted.

The one arena in which Jesse received attention was with the girls. He was the spitting image of Daddy. Tall, handsome, yellow skin, and wavy hair. He went through puberty early. The resulting deep voice had been with him for a long time. Jesse was one of the few males in our family who could sing with the best of them. The Christmas after Daddy returned, Jesse began to ignore school all together. His focus was girls and singing. The more Mamma pushed him to stay in school, the more he would hang out with singing groups and girls. One evening when Mamma got home from work, he had some news for her.

"Mamma, read this."

"What is it, Jesse?"

"Just read it."

"It looks like some kind of contract. Did you sign up with that singing group from Washington D.C.?"

"Mamma! Just read it."

"All right. All right. What? What?"

It was army volunteer papers. Jesse had joined the army on his eighteenth birthday. It was just a few months before graduation. Well graduation date, anyway. It was doubtful that Jesse would have graduated given the distance he had fallen behind in classes. In all likelihood, he would have had to return for at least another semester before the school district would have allowed him to get a diploma. He was having nothing to do with that. He dropped out of school to join the army.

It had been about fifteen months since we last saw Jesse. He was deployed to the war from Washington D. C. We all drove Caravan style as usual, to the army base to see him off. He looked so strong and good in his uniform. That would be the last time that any of us saw him alive.

"May day!! May day!! May day!! This is Bravo Company. PFC Johnson. Come in. Over."

"We read you Bravo. Over."

"We're under heavy fire, Captain. The enemy is on all sides. We're pinned down. We need some help. Over"

"What's your position Johnson?"

"WhiskyBravo89237466. Bullets are flying everywhere. You gotta get here in a hurry."

"Stay calm soldier. Any casualties?"

"I can't tell how many. Blood is all over the place. There's mortar, grenades, and bullets from trees. We're getting hit pretty badly. Ahhhhhh!"

"Help is on the way. You all right?"

"I've been hit. My, my, my side. I'm bleeding."

"Hold on, Johnson. Where's SGT Booker?"

"Ahhhhhh! I don't, don't know. I think dead, sir."

"Boooom! Booom!"

"Johnson!!! Johnson!!! Come in, Bravo company. Johnson!!!"

The helicopters arrived with reinforcements in time to pull Jesse, SGT Booker, and PFC J. Stone out of there. They took care of the enemy but could not save the rest of Bravo Company. PFC Stone was dead before they landed back at base camp. Sgt. Booker never regained consciousness.

"Hang in there Johnson. You're going to make it," the Medic said.

"Tell my Mamma I'm coming home," Jesse said.

"Will do, soldier. You'll be home soon."

Jesse came home but not as he or anyone else wanted. His funeral was a military one but Mamma insisted that he be buried in Raeford. She wanted to be able to remember him and Ralph each year at the Homecoming. This was a pretty difficult time for our family. Ever since Daddy came back, all kinds of bad things seemed to be happening. And, Mamma was blaming him for much of it. She was even angry with him about Jesse. She complained that he didn't pay enough attention to Jesse. Daddy was always trying to win Ralph's favor. Christine was his sweetheart. Tommie stayed under his feet. He had a new family. James was the baby of our family. Jesse decided to just go his own way and Daddy didn't seem to pursue him. I had some of the same feelings but told no one.

Mamma was a very strong woman with strong family roots. Her father, Big Daddy, had passed before I was born. Big Mamma was a pillar of strength for all of her kids. Mamma especially leaned on her. This time was no different. For months, Mamma would go to Big Mamma's house every weekend while Tommie, James, and I visited Daddy. This was a time of restoration for her as she was back to her old self in about six months. She even seemed to forgive Daddy for whatever wrongs she thought he had done. She was reminded by Big

Mamma that God's word says in Matthew 6:14 – 15, "For if you forgive men when they sin against you, your heavenly Father will also forgive you. But if you do not forgive men their sins, your Father will not forgive your sins."

****

By the time I was a senior in high school, life for me was pretty good. I had been elected Class President by a landslide. I had mastered hanging with both the thugs of Lincoln Grove and my intelligent friends from two parent homes. Charming the teachers on a daily basis was duck soup. Classroom academics continued to be easy requiring very little study time. I even had a girl friend, Joyce Moore, who was the president of the Math Club.

This was the first year of desegregation in North Carolina but few of the schools had actually integrated. This first step was to send a group of ten students from each of the five public high schools in town to one of the white high schools to participate in a technology and engineering class. Two of the high schools were predominately black. There would be class rankings posted on a weekly basis. The expectation was that it would take all semester if ever for the black students to match the academic skills of the white students.

"Look at this. Look at this. The first rankings are out," a participating student said.

"Alright! We got eight of the top ten spots. And the first four are all from our school," she exclaimed.

And who was number one? You got it. I held the top spot every week for the entire semester. There were never fewer than seven of the top spots occupied by a black student. Our teachers and administrators felt vindicated by the years of segregation and oppression in the school system. We felt pretty good, too.

The end of the year came quickly. Senior Prom, Senior Week, Honors Day, and then, finally, Graduation Day. Because we were now integrated with the larger North Carolina School System, there would no longer be a valedictorian and a salutatorian. Instead, the honor students would be grouped as Magna Cum Laude and Cum Laude without public rankings. What a rip off. We all wanted to know who was number one just as students from previous years knew.

"I have asked you ten students to come to my office to discuss this year's graduation program," our Principal started. "As you know, we no longer have a valedictorian. We had to devise a means by which we could choose individual students to speak at different times on the program. The best process that we could devise without getting too subjective was to look at your class grades over the years."

"You mean you ranked us?" One of the ten asked.

"This is not a public ranking. But, yes we did calculate grade averages and ordered them in an effort to fairly select the student who would give the diploma acceptance speech for your class. These rankings will not be published and I encourage each of you to keep them in this room, only."

Yeah, right, I thought. I now just wanted him to say what the rankings were. He was wasting too much time.

"We will only reveal the top six spots because there will only be six of you speaking. Since the only reason for ordering you, is to select the speakers, there is no need to reveal the list any further."

By now, we're all thinking, "Come On, Come On!"

"I want our school's Vice Principal to reveal the process so that you all know that it was fair."

"We took every final grade for each course for each year that you were here. Two of you were transfers this year. We took the liberty of getting your grades from your previous school. We did not give any weights to classes that were honor classes over those that were not since most of you only took honors classes. The exception is that we allowed final grades that were higher than 100 to be included in the calculations because they reflected bonus work. And, many of you did bonus work in honors classes nearly every year."

How long is she going to drag this out?

"First, let me tell you the scores to show you how close you are to each other. The top six averages are 98.985, 98.984, 98.983, 98.982, 97.5, and 97.45. There is only about one and a half points separating the top six. You should all commend yourselves."

Clap. Clap. Clap. Clap.

"I'll even tell you that the average for the tenth person is 95.75. Less than three and a half points separate all ten. You all did a marvelous job."

Clap. Clap. Clap. Clap.

"The top six students are Chris Reed, Joyce Moore, Carol Mitchell,

William Johnson, Gary Conley, and Andy Wilson," our Principal announced.

Clap. Clap. Clap. Clap.

"That means that Chris Reed will give the diploma acceptance speech," he said.

"Excuse me, sir. I really don't feel right about giving the speech. I am honored. But, I just got here this year. The students hardly know me. Shouldn't someone else do it?" Chris said.

"Chris, you earned it, son. The process was fair and objective. No rankings will be public. You are just the chosen one."

"I know. But I still don't feel right. I wish you would choose someone else."

"We don't have a fair process for choosing anyone else other than what we have done."

"May I make a recommendation?"

"Sure."

"What about Willie Johnson? He's the class president and an honor student. I think the students would accept him a lot better than me."

I was shocked. I didn't even like Chris Reed. He had come in at the beginning of this year from Spring High School because his father transferred to Jones High School to coach football. While he was smart, everyone knew that he was not nearly as smart as either Joyce or Carol. I bet if they looked at his grades since coming to our school, he wouldn't even be in the room. He was a four-eyed tattletale. He had few friends and he brown-nosed up to the Vice Principal all the time.

"What do you think?" He asked.

"Well, let's ask the other students in here."

"Yeah. Yeah. Yeah. Willie! Willie! Willie! Willie!" They all yelled.

They had selected me to give the speech before I had a chance to say anything. I liked the idea. But, I thought that either Joyce or Carol should do it. I did not have any problem accepting that they had higher grade point averages than me. I knew that they were really smart. So, if it were one of them, it would have been OK with me. The two of them, however, were the biggest proponents of the idea. I graciously accepted.

"Can you believe that they said Chris Reed was number one?" Gary said.

"No way," said Andy. "It's just because his dad is the head football coach and we won the state championship this year."

"Plus, grades from Spring High School? You got to be kidding me. The hardest class they have over there is basket weaving," Gary remarked.

"Chris was not even chosen to participate in the technology and engineering class. That should tell you something," Andy declared.

"Both of you guys know that I agree with you. But, at least he had the sense and guts to know that nobody would have liked him giving the speech. If somebody would have asked me though, I would have said either Joyce or Carol Mitchell."

"Nah! I mean, either one would have been OK. But, it is right that you do it. They even said so themselves," Gary said.

By the time I got home, everybody in Lincoln Grove knew the rankings. Although Chris was gracious about the speech, he couldn't keep his mouth shut at the end of his dad's spring football practice. He spoke loud enough for everyone on the team to hear when he told his dad the results. Half of the team was from Lincoln Grove. Most of them didn't know Joyce or Carol Mitchell nor did they like Chris. They thought I should have been number one.

The Honors Program was just a few days later and I sat in the back with Lincoln Grove as usual. I was blessed to go to that stage about ten times for a science award, math award, scholarships, Magna Cum Laude award, and just about every other award one can think of. Each time I made the long walk going and coming, the thugs in Lincoln Grove would chant alternately. "Lincoln Grove! Number One! Lincoln Grove! Number One! Lincoln Grove! Number One!" I just smiled and pumped my fists as I walked in both directions.

Graduation day and the party afterwards was a time to remember. My classmates and I were very happy. Our parents, brothers, and sisters were happy too. Daddy and Mamma sat on different sides of the auditorium. While I looked at Daddy a few times when I gave the speech, I focused most of the time on Mamma. She was very proud.

After the ceremony it was party time. Joyce and I joined our friends at Hector's In Crowd. This was a teenage party place in Lake Washington that allowed us to sneak alcohol in to our tables. As long as we were discrete in drinking it, he looked the other way. My favorite wines were Annie Green Springs Strawberry Hill and MD 20/20. I would start with Strawberry Hill then finish with the Mad Dog 20/20. Before too long, my head was swimming.

"It's time to go home, baby!" I was full of it.

"It's past time for both of us," Joyce said. She had a little too much herself.

"Let's go. I want to stop at our favorite spot on Pine Bluff Road," I told her.

"I don't know about that. Let's just go," she said.

I could drive OK. I definitely could feel the liquor. And these were dark North Carolina roads with very few cars. The police were especially few and far in between. It is sometimes said that the Lord looks out for children and fools. If that's true, He was looking out for the fool that I was this night.

"Let's stop in here for one kiss," I said.

"Just one kiss?"

"Yeah. Just one kiss. That's all. Then we can go."

"OK, that's enough. That's more than one kiss. Let's go."

"Come on. Not now. Just one more."

Pine Bluff Road was a very dark side road between Lake Washington and Fayetteville. It was used during the day by oil tankers traveling between the many plants. At night, no one used it. There were not even streetlights. In addition, it was a cloudy night with very little of the moon shining through. I had convinced Joyce to get into the back seat with me.

"Willie, you had better stop. You're loaded and so am I. We're going to get into trouble."

"Come on. You are going to visit your relatives in Philadelphia this summer. And, we are both leaving for college just a couple days after you get back. Let's do it, now. We may never get the chance again. I'll just do it one time. That's all. One time!"

****

St. Morris College was a small coed university situated in the middle of Bismarck, North Dakota. The first time that I ever saw the campus was the day that I arrived for freshman orientation. Getting to St. Morris from Fayetteville, North Carolina was an experience in and of itself. Gary, Andy, and I had bets on who got the best scholarship to college. The criteria were the distance from Fayetteville and the dollar value of the scholarship. I was determined to win. Since both Andy and I received scholarships to Morehouse, I was not going to accept mine. I couldn't win the bet going to Morehouse. I would have tied with Andy. Besides, a recruiter had come to my house from St. Morris with a full ride scholarship. Plus, it was in North Dakota. Perfect. If I accepted that scholarship, I would win. And I did. Now what did I win? Nothing materially but I had bragging rights that I went the farthest away from home. God had something else in mind.

I didn't know a soul on that campus of 3,500 students. I checked into my dorm, got my things settled, then ventured out onto the campus. There were not very many black students. In fact, the total population of black students including the twelve of us incoming freshman numbered only forty-five. So, it was not very difficult to spot the three young black students huddled near the cafeteria. The college was sponsoring a picnic on the lawn to allow students to get to know each other. I needed that event.

"Hey, brothers. My name is Willie. How yawl doing?" I introduced myself.

"Oh, no. Not another 'yawl' brother. My name is Scott Jupiter. You are from the south, aren't you? This is Archie and Glen. They are from the south, too."

"Really. Where are you from?" I asked.

"Quincy, Alabama," said Glen. "But call me Sonny."

"Birmingham, Alabama," Said Archie. "And call me Bubba."

"Where are you from Willie?" Scott asked.

"Fayetteville, North Carolina," I said.

"North Carolina and Alabama," said Scott. "You brothers came a long way. I hope you brought some heavy coats for these winters."

Scott was a native of Bismarck. His father was White and his mother was Black. I had not known any children of a racially mixed couple before meeting Scott. He was very high yellow with straight hair. He looked a little like Jesse but his skin was even whiter. He didn't look completely white, though. He had bubble red lips and walked with a pronounced swagger.

"Has anybody seen any women here yet?" Bubba asked.

"You mean our women, don't you?" said Sonny.

"You know what I mean man," was Bubba's reply.

"Just a couple of upper classmen who helped out over the summer," Scott said.

I had not yet thought very much about any women. Everything was so new to me. In addition, I had left Fayetteville without seeing or hearing from Joyce. She had gone to Philadelphia all summer. We wrote each other for the first month or so. Then by late July, I didn't hear from her again. Her sisters kept telling me that she was planning to write. But, I never heard from her. I didn't know what to expect. I assumed that she found a city slicker in Philadelphia. Besides, my interest had begun to wane.

"Who is that?" Bubba had his tongue hanging out.

The most beautiful woman that I had ever seen in my life was walking fast across the campus headed toward the library. She had long black wavy hair that came down below her waist. Her skin was a smooth caramel brown. Her eyes sparkled from the distance even as I looked at them from the side. She was about 5' 4" in high heels. Her legs were sculptured and she had a coke bottle shape. As she walked, her hair and a few other body parts bounced in unison. She paid no attention to us. She was on a mission.

"Forget about her," said Scott. "She's a sophomore and her boyfriend is a linebacker on the football team."

"Who cares?" said Sonny. "I'm headed for the library."

"I saw her first. So, back off!" rushed in Bubba.

'Both of you can just forget it. She's not going to say anything to either one of you," Scott said. "I tried already. She was here this summer and so was I. As soon as I said hello, I could see in her eyes that her response was not hello but rather Hell No! If she didn't give me a play, you don't have a chance."

"Man, please. She just has not been introduced to this southern charm," Said Bubba.

This lady was gorgeous. But, what could I do? She had a boyfriend. Sonny, Bubba, and Scott were already going crazy over her. I didn't want to add to the mix.

"What's her name?" I asked.

"You interested too?" Scott asked.

"Look I just want to know her name. Yawl are way ahead of me. I'm just trying to know people," I said.

"I bet you are. What, you not interested in girls?" Scott was curious.

I told them all about Joyce and the lack of communication with her recently. They were interested but not for long. This beautiful young lady was getting out of sight and Sonny was determined to catch her or end up where she was going.

"Come on, Scott. What's her name?" Sonny asked this time.

"It's Kimberly Andrews. But it won't do you any good. I already told you. She won't be interested. She's smart, studious, and popular. And, she's got sense enough to stay away from the likes of you," Scott added.

"Beauty, brains, and from what I see, butt. What a combination!" said Bubba.

"That's why you won't get anywhere with her, Bubba. You're crude. But, if you want to waste your time, go ahead. I'm trying to tell you!" Scott said.

Soon, Kim was out of sight. Her entrance to the library was quick. Even the way she opened the door was attractive. We gawked for a while then continued the conversation until it was time to eat. We purposely were hanging near the cafeteria so that we could be first in line. The food was very typical of a college campus. Mashed potatoes, green peas, fried chicken, and a slice of white bread. We ate it though. Not only that day but we also ate it many days thereafter.

St. Morris was a very good school academically. It was different from high school. I had to study in this place. When the classes started, I buckled down. It was tempting to skip classes with some of the other guys but I knew that I had better stay focused at least through this first year. Calculus, physics, macroeconomics, and English were all challenging. I spent many hours between classes and in the evening studying. Most of the time, I would study in my room. However, occasionally, and especially on the weekends, I would venture into the library.

"Hi. You're one of the new freshmen, aren't you?"

It was Kim. I never expected her to say anything to me. I had seen her often over the last few weeks. But I never even said as much as hello. I wasn't shy. I just had school on my mind and I still had not heard from Joyce.

"Yeah, I am. My name is Willie. And, you are Kim?"

"Kim, it is. There's a play by Shakespeare that I am looking for in this section. I just wanted to say hello. Have a good time with your studies."

And, she was gone. Just like that. She appeared then she disappeared. It was getting near Thanksgiving. I had heard that Joyce was back in Fayetteville. I wrote her three or four times. Still, there was no answer. I figured by now she must have another boyfriend. That wasn't a problem. I just had not heard from her. I wanted to communicate that we should each go our separate ways rather than just let it happen. Then, I got a phone call on the dorm's hallway phone.

"Willie, it's for you," yelled one of my classmates.

"Hello, this is Willie"

"Hi, this is Joyce."

"Joyce!!! Where have you been? I have written you a hundred times. You never wrote back. What's going on?"

"I've got some news for you."

Here come the 'Dear John' story, I thought. "What is it?" I asked boldly.

"I'm pregnant!!!"

"Huh? What?" My mind was racing. I wanted to ask for whom. I had not seen her since May. It was now October. What was she talking about? "What did you say?" I asked.

"I'm pregnant. And, the baby is due in about sixteen weeks."

"Sixteen weeks. Wait a minute! What are you talking about? Sixteen Weeks!!"

"Yeah, remember on our way home from Hector's In Crowd, we had too much to drink, and I told you to stop."

"You *told* me to stop. But, you didn't mean stop. I mean. You didn't stop. What are we going to do? Why didn't you tell me?"

"There's nothing to do. I wanted to tell you but I didn't know what you would think or do. So, my Mamma made me stay in Philadelphia until you left for school. I started night school at Fayetteville State about a week after you left. I figured you would be coming home for Thanksgiving. Therefore, I thought it would be best to tell you now."

"Thanks for telling me but what now?"

"Willie, let's be honest. I don't know what now. I'm going to have the baby and think about things. At first, I wanted you to share in the misery and embarrassment that I was suffering. Now, I don't know. I am not sure that I even love you. And, if you were honest, you don't know if you love me either. Let's just take it slow and talk about it when you get home."

Wow! This was a shock to my system. I was going to be a father. I didn't even know what that meant. I did not feel like I had much of a role model in my Daddy. He was gone half of my life. The time he was with me, I didn't feel close to him. Now, I was going to be a dad. Wow! Something had to change.

****

Thanksgiving came and went. My stay at home was stressed. I told Mamma about Joyce and Mamma wanted me to get married. That was the proper thing to do, she thought. While that was the social expectation, neither Joyce nor I felt like that was the right thing for either of us at the time. We didn't do it. I saw her again during the Christmas holiday. There was some bitterness and hurt feelings, initially. She and her family did not think that it was fair that I got an opportunity to go away to college while she had to stay at home with a child. Because I understood the sentiment, I continually encouraged her to continue with school.

"I understand and even agree that we won't be together, Joyce. But that doesn't mean that you can't go to school or that the baby can't have the best opportunities," I said.

"Of course, I can go to school. You have to admit that it will be a lot harder for me with a child, though."

"Harder? Yes. But not impossible. Many girls do it. You are not the first. And, I doubt that you will be the last. One of the keys will be to receive as much support as is offered to you. There are limited things that I can do from school. But, I'll do what I can. Mamma is there to help, too. When you take advantage of every bit of support that you can find, you will improve your chances of getting through this period and beyond with great success."

Evening classes continued until the baby, Audrey, was born on February 11th. But Joyce soon stopped going to school at all. In fact, when I called during the spring break to check on the progress of the baby, Joyce had left Fayetteville. Her mother would not tell me where she and Audrey had gone. No one in my family knew either. My immediate assumption was that she was back with her aunt in Philadelphia. I had no means of getting in touch with her there.

Mamma maintained contact with her family throughout the year. As a result, she would occasionally get reports that Audrey was doing well and growing. Of course she would pass the information on to me. I did not go home again for quite a while. The stress and circumstances of Audrey's birth made my freshman year very difficult both socially and academically. Then, Scott introduced me to marijuana.

"Try this man," he said.

"What is it? I asked.

"Ganja. The best."

I had heard about marijuana from some of the 'big boys' in Lincoln Grove who had gone off to the War and come back. In addition, a few of my high school classmates were smoking it on graduation night at Hector's In Crowd. I just didn't have any urges before now to indulge.

"Go ahead. Take a puff and hold it in. That's the way to do it."

"Cough. Cough. Cough." I nearly died on the first puff when I held it in. My lungs were on fire. Scott and Bubba were laughing up a storm. They thought it was very funny.

"Try it again. This time don't take such a big drag. Just a little puff is all you need to get started," Bubba said.

"OK." Cough. Cough. It still caused me to choke but it didn't burn as much this time. And, it didn't take long for me to feel the effects, either.

"I think I've had enough," I said.

"Try some more," Bubba said.

"I don't think so. I'm getting blind already. I don't need any more. You guys go ahead. I'll stay here with you."

Little did I know at the time that as long as I stayed in the room, the marijuana would continue to have an effect. Stupid me. I didn't consider that I would still be breathing it in. With that introduction, I started smoking on weekends about once a month for the rest of the semester. I didn't party very much. But I did my fair share. It was just too cold for me to be out all the time. The warmest winter coat I had was good for North Carolina but was at best a spring jacket in Bismarck. My blood was still too thin to venture outside a lot. I was snow bound, stressed, and starting a very bad habit. Yet I was able to finish the school year with a 3.0 grade point average. I stayed in North Dakota for the summer working the same program that Scott attended the year before.

My job was essentially to help the incoming underprivileged freshman get acclimated to college life. I assisted with developing study habits. High on the list of priorities was how to develop the discipline of going to class, doing homework, studying, and experiencing the freedom of college life. I had to draw on my experiences of the first semester because the second semester was no role model for anyone to follow. The month of June was dedicated to our training as counselors so that when the students arrived in July we would be ready. We role-played and prepared scripts.

Both during the counselor training and after the students arrived, there was plenty of opportunity to reflect on my life experiences. There was only about six hours each day that I was required to be either in a group session or private tutoring with students. The remainder of the day was free time. I reflected on my early years in Lincoln Grove Village and summers in Raeford. I envisioned The Shade Tree. I thought about Pappa, Grampa Ellis, Daddy, Mamma, my sister and brothers, high school, and the Homecomings. The Homecomings! I had not been to one since Jesse died. That was three or four years previous. I missed the good times of the woods, the singing, nights on Pappa's front porch, and even honoring those gone home in the cemetery.

It was during this summer that God tried to get my attention. The seeds of the gospel had been planted many years before. I found a church home in Bismarck and attended most Sundays. It was still perfunctory, however. On several occasions I was asked to participate in one ministry or another of the church. I always had a convenient excuse not to do it. When the Pastor became aware of my counselor training, he encouraged me to lead a youth group. I declined citing the lack of time. God was pressing in. I knew there was something more. But, I didn't want to surrender to it.

****

"Hey Scott, I'm glad to see you back," I told him.

"I wish I could say that I am glad to be back. In a sense, I am because it's good to see you and the rest of the fellas. But, this school thing is getting tiring."

"They say the first year is the worse. And, it is behind us," I encouraged him.

"That's a good thing because if it got any worse, I don't know if I could make it."

"You'll make it. You just want to have something to complain about. You seen the boys from Alabama?"

"Sonny and Bubba? Not yet. My guess is that they will be here any day now."

Scott and I headed toward the student union. The pool hall, bookstore, student lounge, snack bar, and mailroom were there. It was a good place to just hang out. Most everyone did so between classes, in the evenings, and on weekends.

Nearly all of the student activities were held there also. As we entered the front door, we noticed posters advertising the Religion of Black People would be coming to the campus. One of their young ministers, Thad Davidson would be speaking in three weeks. I had heard very little about them. I knew that they were based in Los Angeles and had a growing following. In addition, there had been news a couple of years ago about Thad Davidson and Mahmoud Two X. I had not kept up with the details. So I didn't know very much.

"The Religion of Black People is coming to St. Morris. Imagine that!" Scott said.

"You know about them?" I asked.

"A little. I know that they are not very high on Christianity. Since I can't get into the church thing and they sound interesting to me."

"What are you saying?"

"Let's check them out when they get here in a couple of weeks."

"No problem. I'll go."

"Hey, here's a poster of the first Fall Mixer. It's that same weekend."

"Sounds like a fun weekend."

I was prepared this time for both the beginning of class and the North Dakota winters. Jokes had been going around that North Dakota had only two seasons, winter and the first week of July. I was beginning to think that was no joke. It got cold early in the fall and stayed cold late into the spring. I bought a real North Dakota winter coat with some of the money that I earned over the summer. I also got my books for class early and began to study before classes actually started. That was a big boost. It kept me about a week ahead for the first couple of months.

"Willie, you going to the Fall Mixer this weekend?" Sonny asked.

"I think so. It should be a good break from studies. It will also give us a chance to meet the new freshmen and hang out with some of the upper classmen. We're upperclassmen now, too, you know."

"Have you seen any of them? The freshmen, I mean? There's a bunch this year. St. Morris started an Equal Educational Opportunity Program this year," Bubba said.

"Yeah. There are about 30 new black freshmen. And half of them are women," Sonny said.

"I know. I saw most of them this summer. Given what I have seen and my interaction with them, that's about all I want to do - see them. And even that I want to do from a distance!"

"They are not all as bad as you make it sound. How about Dianne Caesar?" Sonny questioned.

"Not bad. I think she's mixed with something though," I said.

"So? What you got against mixed people?" Sonny asked.

"Nothing! I just thought you were asking about the black freshmen."

"She is black. At least, half black," Sonny said.

"Anyway, she's not my type. But I'll be at the Mixer none-the-less," I said.

Every fall and spring St. Morris would sponsor a dance for the students. They were called 'Mixers'. The intent was to allow the students to mix with each other. While most of the students were from the Midwest, there were students from across the U.S., a fairly large population of international students, and a growing number of black students. So these mixers were important in getting the students acclimated to each other. The results generally showed the success of the mixers. There were many interracial couples on campus. Most involved an international student and a white student from the United States but many were black students and white students, as well. The number of black females available was even smaller.

"Look who's here, Sonny," said Bubba.

"You have not learned your lesson yet," declared Scott.

It was Kim. She had her hair hanging down below her waist as usual. But, it was cut in a style that I had not seen before. It looked like layers of hair perfectly placed on top of each other. The bangs in the front kind of swirled across her forehead. Her dress had spaghetti straps and was cut modestly low in the front but very low in the back. It was short with flowing pleats at the bottom. When she walked, it flapped in the front and swished in the back. And, to watch her dance in those high heels was just too much. When she 'swung out', her hair, dress, and arms made perfect circles around her dance partner.

"Is that her new boyfriend?" I asked.

"Nah. That's just Daryl McWhite. They went to high school together then decided to come here to St. Morris together. As far as I know, they're just friends," Scott said.

"That's not what the linebacker thought. Daryl is why he and Kim broke up you know," Bubba said. "Every time he had a date with Kim, she insisted that it would be a double date with Daryl and some other girl."

"I bet he thought Daryl was just blocking, if you know what I mean," Sonny said.

"Either way, it's too bad for him. Kim is free," Bubba said.

"I wouldn't go that far. But, she is available for anybody who is brave enough," Scott said.

Kim was now off the dance floor and standing with two of her friends, Barbara and Pamela. Now was a good opportunity to walk over and reintroduce myself. The whole male student body must have had the same idea. While I was thinking, it seemed everybody else moved in quickly on her, including Scott, Bubba, and Sonny. Scott was talking to her, Bubba was talking to Barbara, and Sonny was talking to Pamela. When the music started up again, all three couples were on the dance floor. Kim was a very good dancer who loved to dance. Scott could dance, too. I watched her the entire time. It was as if I was in a trance. I heard no one and saw no one; not even Scott who was cheezing like an alley cat. When the music stopped, they all walked back in my direction. My heart started to pump 'dish water'. I was nervous. I didn't know why. The music started again. It was a slow record. I darted toward her and asked for the dance. Was I crazy? Supposed she said no. I would be embarrassed. It was now out of my control. I was already reaching for her hand.

She gave a simple nod and walked back out onto the floor with me. Now what? Her back was out and glistening in the soft light. Her eyelashes were very long. I had not been close enough to notice that before. She was walking gracefully with the back of that dress swishing. Where would I put my hands? Do I hold her close? What would I say while we danced?

Before I knew it, she had her arms around my neck. I had to fake not being impressed. So, I put my hands low on her back trying to avoid touching her skin. It was impossible. My thumbs were on her. I could feel the blood flow up and down the softness of her back. I could smell the sweet perfume. I'll never forget that it was Shalimar. My feet were like five-ton bricks. I couldn't move them. I was trying to think of something witty to say. My mind was putty. It was blank. Here was my chance and I could not think of a single thing to say. Interestingly enough, she didn't say anything either. She just kept her head looking basically at my shoulder and followed my slow moving steps.

"The dude from Fayetteville, North Carolina got lucky, huh?" Scott was teasing me. "What did you have to say to her?"

"Wouldn't you like to know?" I said.

"Probably nothing," laughed Bubba.

"And, I could have driven a Mac truck between the two of them. What were you thinking, boy?" Sonny laughed.

"Yawl just jealous cause you're not cool like that," I said.

"If that was cool you can keep it," Sonny said.

"Who was dancing with her and who was watching? Just think about that!" I quipped. "Enough of that. Yawl going to the Religion of Black People speech tomorrow at the Chapel?"

"You know I am going to be there," said Scott. "Where do you want to meet?"

"How about 30 minutes before on the steps of the Chapel?"

"Sounds good to me."

For the remainder of the evening, I couldn't keep my eyes off her. I did not dance with her again, though. She was just too popular. Guys were lining up. I danced with a few of the other ladies, hung out with the fellas, and then headed for the dorm.

****

The four of us were all on the Chapel steps on time. The Religion of Black People was an institution that preached separation and independence for black Americans. Their founder was Michael Mahmoud. Kim thought he was a self-proclaimed messiah. Thad Davidson was a fast rising minister whose mission was to establish mosques across the United States. His appearance was clean shaven and neatly pressed. Bodyguards surrounded the podium from which he spoke and along the aisles of the Chapel. Since college campuses were identified as ripe arenas for nurturing converts, he and his entourage was on a ten-campus tour. He spoke for nearly an hour on Jews, white America, black America, separation of the races into sovereign territories, and his god.

Scott was very impressed. I was repulsed while Bubba and Sonny were inquisitive. There were about a half dozen new black staff member at St. Morris as a result of the influx of new black students. They were in attendance at this meeting as well. This speech created quite a stir among this multi-racial campus. Three of the staff members and about a half dozen students including Scott became converts immediately.

"What are you guys waiting for? Didn't you hear him? This is the black man's religion. That Christianity stuff is for the white man. It is used only to suppress black America," Scott preached.

"I don't know, Scott," Bubba said.

"I know. That doesn't sound anything like the God that I have been taught about," I said. "I don't buy it."

But, what did I buy. I had been baptized years before in Raeford. Yet, I really did not have a relationship with Jesus Christ. I surely was not living like I had one but I knew something was wrong with this Religion of Black People.

****

It was late January and the snow had been piling up for a couple of months. The sidewalks on campus were clean. The staff kept this campus beautiful all the time. They were always prepared to handle whatever weather came. Two feet of snow was definitely not a problem. The piles on each side of the walkways must have been at least double that and the wind was blowing fiercely. Classes were starting that week and it was a good thing that the campus was relatively small. I learned to walk fast and surefooted. I had fallen one too many times during my freshman year. My first class was microeconomics.

As I walked into the back of the auditorium, I noticed that long pretty hair right away. She was seated on the front row on the left side next to the aisle. I didn't want her to see me. I sat directly behind her about five rows up. In that way, I could both look at her and the professor at the same time. Looking at the back of her hair like that reminded me of when I was in the fourth grade. I liked one of the little girls but she didn't like me. The good news for me was that she sat directly in front of me. The back of her chair touched the front of my desk. The bad news for her was that one-day in order to get her attention I took a pair of scissors and cut off one of her braids. Actually, that turned out to be bad news for me. I got at least three whippings that day. Maybe four. The teacher, the principal, Chrissie, and my Mamma. What a mistake. Needless to say, that girl never liked me and my butt was sore for weeks. Kim didn't have to worry about me making that mistake. I was getting very attracted to her and I wasn't going to mess it up by cutting her hair.

"Your homework for Thursday is to read through chapter 5 and answer all 30 of the questions for the Unit," the professor said while closing the first day.

"Hey, Kim. How was the Christmas holiday? I am sure glad to see you taking this class," I said as I waited for her to come out of the auditorium.

"The holiday was the usual stuff. I went home with family. Did the Christmas thing. Ate too much. Then relaxed. How about yours?"

"Pretty much the same. Except I was in North Carolina, you know, so I didn't have a white Christmas like you probably did."

"Yeah, I did. We always have a white Christmas in New York. That's one of the things I like about it," she said. "I didn't know that you were into economics."

"Well, I'm trying to decide whether I will major in it or Math. Maybe both."

"You trying to impress me, little boy?" Now, she was putting me down. But, I could tell she really was getting impressed. So, I pushed a little.

"I took Macroeconomics last year along with Advanced Calculus and Integral Calculus. I liked all of them. I thought I would try microeconomics this semester."

"Why didn't you take it last semester?"

"I couldn't get in. It was full."

"The same thing happened to me. Maybe, this is fate, huh?"

"Maybe so. This professor is kinda tough, isn't he? Five chapters and thirty problems in two days? When are you going to study?" I asked.

"Why do you want to know?" she pushed back.

"Just curious. I thought maybe we could get some study time in together."

"I'm kind of busy but I'll let you know."

I let her get away without pressing when she would let me know. Then again, I thought that I might have pressed too far already. Who could tell? I was just glad that I was in the same class with her.

Half of the semester went by without us doing much other that seeing each other in class. She never found the time to study with me nor did she seem to need it. She did quite well on her own. I asked one other time and she declined again. She was never rude and she always made her way to speak to me both before and after class. I wondered if I was making too much out of a small thing. But, she still didn't have a boyfriend either. That was good. When the Spring Mixer came around, I decided I would be bold.

"Kim, are you going to the mixer this weekend?" I asked.

"I don't know. Probably. Why?"

Now was my chance to press a little more. At least, I would know if there was ever going to be anything more that classmates who didn't study together.

"I thought we could go together. I'd drive by to pick you up at 7:30 but I left my Cadillac in North Carolina!" I joked.

"Funny. I tell you what, why don't you meet me in the library tomorrow night at 7:00pm? We can study for the mid-term. I'll have a chance to think about it and let you know."

I did all that I could to keep from shouting for joy right there in the middle of the campus. I had a study date with Kim Andrews. I didn't tell anybody. I didn't want to mess up anything. I was at that library at 6:15pm. I was not going to be late. I started studying too, because I sure didn't want to look dumb to her. She had no idea of whether or not I had any intelligence except when I tried to impress her with the classes I had taken. By the time she arrived, I had made a cursory review of the chapters for the test. If the truth were told, I really could use some help in more than a couple of areas.

"I'm so glad that you are already here, Willie. Something has come up." She said.

'Oh. Can I help in any way?"

"No, it's one of the freshman girls. I'm a dorm counselor. I have to go back and take care of it. I am so sorry. I can't study with you tonight." She started to walk out of the library.

"Wait a minute, how about the mixer?"

"Oh, yeah. That's all right with me. Will you come by the dorm at 7:00 in your Cadillac?"

Ah, yes. She was joking back with me, now. Although I needed help with the mid-term, getting a date for the mixer was even better. Plus, I'm glad I didn't tell anybody about tonight's date. I could hear Scott, Bubba, and Sonny now. I wouldn't hear the end of the razing.

This dance turned my life around. It is one of the milestones that led to my current life in Christ. I would get to know Kim better. I almost blew it though. I was so excited that I did tell Bubba and Sonny. Scott had gone to Los Angeles to attend a Religion of Black People conference. They convinced me to smoke a joint before picking her up just to be cool. I thought that I had sprayed the smell away with cologne. There was still a trace left. She asked about the smell and told me that she was not into drugs and did not care for people who were. I lied and told her that some guys in my dorm were smoking and I guess the smell got into my clothes. She accepted the lie but informed me that drugs were the reason she and the linebacker didn't make it.

The dance was a lot of fun. She was finely dressed as usual. We danced the night away. I had learned the New York Bop from Scott. It was one of her favorites. I twirled, spun, and swung. She laughed and smiled and so did I. We only danced on the fast songs. During the slow ones, we just stood along the wall and talked and talked. She told me all about her family of twelve brothers and sisters. I got the low down on Daryl McWhite who was truly just a friend. Whew! And, I heard about her freshman year when there were less than thirty black students on campus. Now there were more than seventy.

I told her about my family and about Joyce. I had to get that out of the way right away. If there was going to be a problem, it was best that I know from the beginning. I told her about Ralph and Jesse and a little about Raeford. I didn't get into much discussion about Daddy, however.

****

Kim and I started hanging out more often a couple of weeks after the Spring Mixer. Most of the time, it was in the library. She was very studious and an avid reader. I didn't like to read as much but I knew that I had to study. So, the library was not a problem for me. By the end of that semester, I was calling her my girlfriend and she didn't object. Again, I stayed for the summer session and convinced her to stay as well. Since she had done it two summers before and I did it last summer, the two of us were among the senior counselors. That gave us even more time together.

As the summer ended, I knew that I was smitten. My heart was mush. I wanted to be with her all the time. If I could have taken every class with her, I would have. But, her major was business law while I was focusing on both Math and Economics but on the way to class, after class, in between classes, on the weekends, and holidays, I was by her side. She was now a senior and thinking about graduation. I was thinking about her graduation too, except I was thinking that she would be gone if I didn't do something soon. I couldn't let her go back to New York without me. What if she found some old high school flame, who was a war hero or something waiting for her?

"Kim, you know that I joined the black theater group this year?"

"You said that you were going to do that. What's the name of the group?"

"Black Arts of the North."

"Cool. When's the first performance?"

"In a couple of weeks. I have reserved seats for you down front."

"You didn't have to do that."

"I know. But, I have the lead role in the play titled, 'The First Man'. I wanted you to get a close up view of what an original man looks like (smile)."

"You ain't that funny, you know. But keep trying."

I had other ideas for that play. I knew that I wanted to marry Kim. We had talked about the idea briefly but not seriously. I did not want to scare her off. I tested the waters over the summer with questions about the ideal marriage with her. She told me of her desires for a small family and a devoted husband. She planned to work in a field where she could use her college degree. She was not too particular about which area of the country she lived but New York was most attractive because it was home.

The last scene of the play has the First Man alone on stage admiring the universe that he now dominates once again. He kneels before the Father and raises his hands in praise as the lights dim then go completely dark.

I purposely had Kim sit on the front row in the middle of the audience. As the lights went dark, I kneeled directly in front of her and raised my hands. It became completely dark and silent. When there was complete silence over the audience and on the stage, I spoke out of the darkness in a loud voice for all to hear.

"KIM!!! WILL YOU MARRY ME?"

The spotlights came up. One shined only on her. One shined only on me. I was offering her an engagement ring!

6

What Is Your Character

Kim and I were married the summer following her graduation from St. Morris. It was a beautiful wedding. DZ stood as my best man. Pamela was her maid of honor. Everything was purple and white. Purple was her favorite color. I even had on a White Tuxedo with a purple shirt and purple shoes. What a man would do for the one he loves! Actually, I thought I was cool with those purple shoes. The guys had on traditional black tuxedos with purple shirts and black shoes while the girls had purple chiffon dresses and white flowers in their hair. Kim's dress was a two-piece silk Corset gown with Spaghetti straps, a full skirt, matching stole, and a chapel train that seemed ten feet long. The top piece was purple with crystals and beads intermixed. The headpiece was white silk that flowed from the middle of her head to below her waist. The tiara was the color of rubies and sparkled like diamonds.

The wedding was held on the Westside of New York and attended by a large number of family and friends from New York, North Carolina, and North Dakota. I was glad that many in my family came up from North Carolina. Mamma, Chrissie, DZ, James, Big Mamma, Grampa Ellis, Gramma, Aunt Alice, Uncle Eddie, and many of my cousins. The one person who was missing was Daddy.

"That was a wonderful wedding Kim and Willie," Mamma said.

"Thank you," Kim responded.

At the reception, all that I heard continually was "Congratulations. Congratulations. Congratulations." It was one of the happiest days of my life.

"When are you getting back from your honeymoon in Jamaica?" Sonny asked.

"Around the 1st of July. Then, we are headed back to North Dakota. Kim is starting a job at one of the banks while I work the summer EEOP session again," I told him. "I'm looking forward to our senior year. School has been fun but this is better."

"See you in a couple of months," he said.

Sonny was going home to Quincy for the summer. He had a job with his uncle at one of the pig farms. He made good money at that job every summer. So, in spite of our teasing, he always went back to it. Bubba went back to Birmingham to work in a cotton factory. And Scott? Well, Scott left school after the first semester last year to join the Religion of Black People in Los Angeles full time. There were plans to start a mosque in Bismarck and Scott wanted to be in on the ground floor. We stayed in touch, as he would often come back home to Bismarck. But the contacts were getting fewer and farther in between.

School took on a completely different meaning during my last year. Now there were more than one hundred and fifty black students on campus including the additional fifty-five that were freshman that year. I hardly knew any of them. Since Kim and I were married, I would rush home after my last class to be with her. Married life was different. I was finding out things about her and she was finding out things about me that frankly were sometimes irritating. For example, I could not believe that she just squeezed her toothpaste tube in the palm of her hands. I would squeeze the toothpaste by rolling it from the bottom. That made the most sense to me. We would get most of the toothpaste out of the tube that way, I thought. It didn't matter to her. That bugged me. The bigger problem for her was my growing habit of smoking marijuana. It had gone from one weekend a month to just about every weekend now.

At one point on our honeymoon, I thought the marriage would be over before it got started. In Jamaica, marijuana was everywhere. It was the most powerful 'weed' that I had ever smoked. I came out of the closet with my habit and joined the locals frequently. Kim was livid. I didn't see the problem. Two of the first three days of our two weeks were spent not talking to each other very much. Then, I promised two lies. First, I would stop when we got back to North Dakota. Second, I would only smoke on the middle weekend of our stay in Jamaica. Instead, I got up in the middle of the night after she was asleep to smoke on the balcony or on the beach. I don't think she was fooled, though. Since I did not take away time from the daily activities of the honeymoon, I think she tolerated me. She also expected that it would stop once we got home. I didn't and the situation was getting worse.

After the Fall Mixer, Kim put her foot down. Either I would change or she was leaving. I didn't want that so initially I stopped. But at this point, I was hooked. I had to do it out of the house during the day or sneak away on the weekends.

"Sonny, you have to help me sneak out of the house this coming Friday. T-Bone is going to leave some of his cocaine with me while he goes away for the weekend. I told him that I would sell some in return for a pound of marijuana. If you help me get out and sell the coke, I will split the marijuana with you."

T-Bone was the nickname of an older student from Bismarck. His background was close to the thugs that I knew from Lincoln Grove Village. While he and I got along well, I had resisted his offers of snorting cocaine in the past. He was only asking me to sell it this time. So, what was the harm?

The plan was to tell Kim that we would be going night fishing at Canyon Lake north of Bismarck. We had often done that in the past. It would not be an unusual request. Bubba would gather a few friends in his room where I would sell them the cocaine. After hanging out a few hours, I would leave the remainder of the unsold cocaine with Sonny, and then go home with Kim being none the wiser.

"This is wild stuff, man. We should have been doing this a long time ago," Bubba said.

"Willie, you can have this line. Try it for once." Sonny suggested.

Sonny had chopped a pile of cocaine with a razor blade on top of a mirror then separated the drug into several lines. I had a pocket full of individually aluminum-wrapped white cocaine powder remaining. In addition, I had already smoked a couple of joints. I was feeling pretty good. I also felt very safe in Bubba's room with friends.

"What the heck? I can try one line, one time. What can it hurt? I am out of here in a few minutes, anyway," I said. I rolled a one-dollar bill as tight as I could get it. I stuffed it in one nostril while holding the other nostril closed with my finger. I had watched T-Bone, Bubba, Sonny, and others do this over the last few weeks. I had the process down. I just had not done it before. I completely exhaled away from the lines then turned and in one deep breath snorted from left to right. There was no coughing, no choking, or apparent ill effects. Yet, the combination of the two drugs and the amount of cocaine that I sniffed sent me almost immediately into a stupor. I spoke and acted very incoherently for a while then fell into a deep sleep.

"What time is it?" I asked.

"About 6:00am," Bubba said.

"What! I gotta go. Kim is going to be really mad. I should have left around 10:00pm last night. What happened?"

"After that coke, man, you were out like a light."

I got up to wash my face and leave when I noticed that all of the cocaine that I had in my pocket was gone. I assumed that Sonny had taken it to sell since I was in no condition to do so. Before leaving Bubba's, I called him in his dorm room.

"Sonny, wake up. I'm still at Bubba's. You got the coke?"

"No. I left right after you fell asleep."

"Something strange is going on. All of the coke is gone and I have no money. Somebody must have clipped me!"

"What are you talking about? Nobody clipped you. Didn't you say you slept at Bubba's?"

I asked Bubba what happened after Sonny left. He told me that he remembered very little. All he knew was that Germane Bartelson had asked for some coke. He told Germane that I had some but he didn't know about anything after that.

I was angry. Someone had clipped me. In addition, T-Bone would be back the next day looking for either his money or his drugs. I had neither. I was determined to get one or the other before T-Bone returned. If not, who knew what would happen. Drug dealers didn't play. They were going to ask T-Bone for one or the other. He was going to ask me. If they came after him, would they come after me? I wasn't taking any chances!

"Willie, where have you been? Do you realize what time it is? It's 7:00am in the morning!!" Kim screamed.

"Not now, baby. I got something to do," I said as I reached for my 38-caliber pistol in the bedroom drawer.

"What are you doing? Put that gun back! Talk to me. What's going on? Put that gun back!" she continued to scream.

"I'll tell you later. I'll be back in a little while."

I left and went to Sonny's dorm room. I wanted him and Bubba to help me recreate the events from the night before. Reluctantly, Sonny came with me. He and I smoked a joint then went to the field house where Germane Bartelson was running in a track meet. Now, I was angry, high and had a gun. When I approached Germane with the gun pointed in his side, he did not hesitate to join Sonny and me. On the way to Bubba's room, the three of us smoked another joint. Bubba was smoking when we arrived.

"Now, after I did that line of cocaine I fell asleep. Each one of you must tell me what you did after that!" I started.

"Are you accusing me of stealing from you?" Bubba blurted out.

"I am not accusing anybody. I just need to know what happened. I was in your room. My friends were with me. Now, cocaine and money is gone."

"Sounds to me like to you are accusing me," Bubba said.

"What are you getting so upset about? You got something to hide?"

"Get out of my room! I thought we were friends. If you think I stole from you, you can get out now," Bubba continued.

"I am not going anywhere until I get some answers. And neither are you."

Bubba then rushed me. I backed away and pulled my 38 from my pocket. We tussled around the room then fell. I got the better position and rolled on top of him with my gun hand free.

"Don't do it, Willie!! Don't do it!!" yelled Sonny.

Bam! Bam! Bam!

Bubba was bleeding from his leg. I had pointed the gun to his head but heard a voice tell me to lower the gun and put it down. I lowered the gun but I didn't put it down. Instead, I shot Bubba in the leg.

The campus was in an uproar. By now, students were in the hallway and outside the dorm. In a panic, I gave Sonny the gun then went home. I tried telling Kim the story from the initial lie about Canyon Lake until the time I shot Bubba. The phone kept ringing. Most of the time, it was Sonny. An ambulance had come to take Bubba to the hospital. Police were asking questions. They wanted to know who had shot him. Neither Bubba nor anyone else told them. Sonny had called one of the black student counselors, who had arrived a couple of years earlier with the first infusion of EEOP students. He arranged to have Kim and I stay in a local hotel and assured me that he would take care of everything. The next afternoon, he and Sonny came to visit us.

"Willie, you will have to turn yourself in tonight as close to midnight as you can." The counselor started. "I have talked to both the school officials and the police. They are trusting that I will take care of things. Bubba is not pressing charges. But, the school feels that something must be done about discharging a firearm on the campus. That will be the charge when you are arraigned tomorrow morning. You will have a school attorney representing you. I recommend that you plead guilty to the charge. Then, plead mercy from the court. The judge will likely fine you then give you a sentence of thirty days."

"This sounds all so scary to me. I know that I've messed up. I don't have any money for a fine. And, if I spend thirty days in jail, I will not be able to graduate."

"Look. I will pay the fine for you. And, you will be able to attend classes during the day. You will only be locked up at night during the week and for the weekends. You'll be out before Christmas."

"I guess that's OK."

"You don't have much of a choice under the circumstances. You are blessed that Bubba is not pressing charges or the school is not suspending you."

"I know you're right."

"Yes, I am. I will be back around 11:30pm tonight to pick you up and take you to the police station."

It was all Kim could do to prevent herself saying I told you so. She had warned that the drugs were going to get me in trouble in more ways than one. I had a habit that must be broken. I had shot a friend. My graduation was threatened. I would spend time in jail thus getting a record. My marriage was suffering. And, Christ was nowhere in my current thinking.

I did my time in the Burleigh County Work Release program. At night I slept in a county jail work detention location. During the day, I was released to attend classes at St. Morris while the other prisoners worked in the farm fields, on the roadsides, or on the grounds doing various odd jobs. There were no hardened criminals there. No murderers, rapists, bank robbers, or big time drug dealers. Most of the inmates committed fairly minor infractions such as multiple traffic violations or civil disobedience.

However, very few of them were allowed back into the 'normal' world during the day as I was. Some resented it. Others tried to take advantage of it by offering incentives to bring back drugs or information from friends and relatives. I resisted the drugs but frequently made contacts on the outside for them. I primarily kept my nose clean, if you know what I mean. I saw Kim between classes then made a beeline for the county jail to be in by 7:00pm because one of the rules required it. For every day that I reported in late, a day was added to my time. I was never late. Best of all Kim both stayed with me and prayed for me. It was during this 30-day period that Christ spoke once again to me. He told me how much He loved me and wanted me to join Him in eternity. I knew that I was in trouble but I still did not accept the call. I figured that if I could just quit smoking and stay away from cocaine, things would be fine.

I never got to the bottom of what happened to the cocaine or the money. Drug dealers came after T-Bone who paid them the money. He allowed me to pay him back over the remainder of my time at St. Morris.

After I got out of the county jail and by sheer will power, I persisted in staying away from drugs for the remainder of my last semester. My focus on class work and Kim improved. We attended church on a regular basis and God continued to call. Since I was not involved in drugs, I thought that I would be OK.

"Kim, graduation is in two weeks. Can you believe it? I'll be done."

"Thank God."

"I am so glad that you put up with me. It helped me to get things back on course. My grades are good and I will graduate with about a 3.4 average. Can you believe it?

"I knew that you could do it. It just took focus."

"Focus and a wakeup call. Something or somebody is looking out for me."

"What do you mean something or somebody? You know that it is God. It's not like you have never heard of God before!"

"Don't start on me again. Just be glad that I have made it thus far."

"I am glad. But, I will be happier when you accept the call of God on your life. I'll keep praying for you."

****

After graduation I accepted a job with CBS. I had options to live in Omaha, Nebraska; Kansas City, Missouri; Dallas, Texas; or Manhattan, New York. Dallas was the most appealing option to me but Kim promised that if I moved to New York for just five years then she would follow me anywhere. That sounded like a good proposition to me. So, off to New York we went.

My first year at CBS was devoted to training. The program called for a month of studies in the local office followed by a month away at classes in Upstate, New York, and Dallas, Texas. While I was away in training sessions, my marijuana use started again. This time, it was more intense than ever. Along with other new recruits, I smoked quite a bit in the evenings after class. I learned where to find it in each city and how to hide it on my body to take it through the airports. When I returned for my month of local office study, the intensity seemed to grow even more. I was desperate to hide it from Kim. But, the inevitable happened.

"What is this I found in your suit pocket?" I was busted. I had to play it now as if I was in control.

"It's what you think it is! I only do it when I am away from you just to have something to do. It is better than getting bored at night or getting into other kinds of trouble."

"You can study or start reading the bible. What's wrong with either one of them?"

This was a no win conversation and I knew it. She was right but I didn't want to admit it. I promised her that I could stop anytime that I wanted. Didn't I stop once before? I could stop again. Yet, I couldn't. It had gotten so bad that I was smoking multiple times during the week. Six months after I started, Kim dropped another bomb on me. She called during the last week of my stay in Upstate New York.

"Hey, honey. How are you doing tonight?" She asked.

"I'm doing fine. I'll be glad when this week is over, though. I'll be home Friday. The plane lands about 8:00pm."

"Good. Make sure you come straight home. I've got some news for you." I could see the smile on her face through the phone.

"I hope it's good news. I could use some. This has been a tough month for me here. Classes are getting a lot more difficult. So, what's the news?"

"I'll tell you when you get here." She was giggling as she talked.

"You can't hold it. I can tell. You are busting to tell me. What is it?"

"OK. I'm pregnant!!!!" she blurted.

"Oh yeah! Really? I mean, Oh Yeaaaahhh!! That is good news."

"My doctor told me today."

"Alright. Now I feel a lot better. I'll see you Friday."

Then, I got worried. This marijuana thing was really bothering me. I had lied to Kim about the time I was getting home. The truth was that the plane was landing at 6:00pm. I was leaving enough time to make my usual first run when I arrived at home. I knew that unless something drastic happened, I would head straight for the drug house once the plane landed. I didn't want to do it anymore. But, I was unable to stop. I had tried on many occasions. Each time the result was the same. I ended up at the drug house then felt guilty until I did it again and again and again. I still had three days before Friday. What was I going to do this time?

      That night, I had a dream. In the dream I am in a line of people who are about to enter Heaven. Actually, I am watching this line in an out of body experience. I see myself in the line. The person does not look like me but it is me. In reality, this line is a judgment line. Most are going to Heaven but some will go to hell. I am near the front of the line. I have been moving up in this line until I am about the fifth person. I am pretty certain that I am going to Heaven but suddenly there is a diversion. I find myself walking down in the pit of a cave. This cave has fire jumping out around the edges. I can tell that I am going toward the pit of hell. I can see a large serpent behind an entrance to one of the adjacent caves. I also see through myself in the cave that if I continue on this path, I will end up in hell. I must turn around and go back to Heaven. I saw a bird fly into the cave where the serpent was. But, a cat not the serpent ate the bird. It was symbolic of what would happen to me if I did not turn around. I turned and went back out of the cave. I started back toward the line to Heaven. End of dream.

      I woke up in the middle of the night and called DZ.

      "DZ, I need your help." He was now a young Deacon at his church in Raleigh.

      "What's up?"

      "This marijuana is really getting to me. I can't stop and to top it off, Kim called and told me that she is pregnant. What's more, I just had a terrible nightmare. I saw in a vision that I was headed for hell."

      "Hold on. The pregnancy is good news. Congratulations! And, you know that God has been speaking to you especially through dreams for some time. He's talking to you now. You just don't want to accept it. So, what are you going to do about the drugs, now?"

      "I don't know. All I know is that if I don't get some help soon, I going to lose my mind, my family, and go to hell."

"What can I do to help you?"

"I'm glad you asked. I am in Upstate New York right now. I was hoping that you could meet me at LaGuardia when I land this Friday."

"What time does your plane land?"

"6:00pm."

"Let me check it out. My plan is to be there. If I can't make it, I'll call you."

DZ was the only one other than Mamma that I could trust to stop me from going to the drug house. I would argue with Kim, fight with my Daddy, and ignore just anybody else. Plus, I was too embarrassed to tell Mamma. It was very short notice in calling him but I needed help and I needed it right away!

By the time I left for the airport on Friday, I had not heard from DZ. He had said that he would call me if he couldn't make it. Now I wished that I had asked for a positive confirmation. I had gone a couple of days without smoking weed. My flesh was calling for it big time. On the plane, I prayed as I had never prayed before.

"God, I know that I have not been very good. But I need you. I need my brother to be at LaGuardia when I land. Please let him be there."

As the plane landed and rolled down the runway, I pressed my face to the window. I was looking for him in the terminal. When we pulled into the gate, I recognized a familiar figure. But, it wasn't him. It was Kim with her face pressed to the glass waving at the plane. I was glad to see her but wondered if DZ made it. Kim was the first to greet me when I came through the doorway at the gate. DZ was right behind her.

"Man, am I glad to see the two of you."

"We're glad to see you, too," Kim said.

"I thought it would be best if both of us were here when you stepped off the plane," DZ said. "I got in earlier today and went to your house. Kim and I then drove back here to get you."

We went straight to our house, put away the luggage, and then went into the Den to talk and pray. Kim told me all about her doctor visit. We wondered if it was a boy or a girl. DZ told me that I could prepare for a wonderful life with my expanded family by giving my life to Christ. As guided by the Holy Spirit, he took me through the Romans Road of scripture then led me in a sinner's prayer.

(Romans 3:23 NIV)   for all have sinned and fall short of the glory of God,

(Romans 6:23 NIV)   For the wages of sin is death, but the gift of God is eternal life in Christ Jesus our Lord.

(Hebrews 9:27 NIV)   Just as man is destined to die once, and after that to face judgment.

(Rom 5:8 NIV)   But God demonstrates his own love for us in this: While we were still sinners, Christ died for us.

(Ephesians 2:8 NIV) For it is by grace you have been saved, through faith--and this not from yourselves, it is the gift of God.

(Ephesians 2:9 NIV) not by works, so that no one can boast.

(John 1:12 NIV)   Yet to all who received him, to those who believed in his name, he gave the right to become children of God.

(Romans 10:9 NIV)   That if you confess with your mouth, "Jesus is Lord," and believe in your heart that God raised him from the dead, you will be saved.

(Romans 10:10 NIV)   For it is with your heart that you believe and are justified, and it is with your mouth that you confess and are saved

(Romans 10:13 NIV)   for, everyone who calls on the name of the Lord will be saved

MY PRAYER FOR SALVATION

God, I praise You for who You are. You are the Lord God Almighty. I know that I have been a sinner all the days of my life. I don't want to live like that anymore. I have come to see You and know You for who You truly are. I now know who I am, a sinner.

I am so sorry for the sins that I have committed against You. I repent and turn from them. I renounce my past life with Satan and close the door to all of his devices. Forgive me God. Jesus, come into my life. Be the Lord of my life. Direct my every thought and action. I trust You and accept the blood that You shed at Calvary for the redemption of my sin.

I confess that Jesus Christ is my Lord. I know that You raised Him from the dead and that He sits at Your right hand in heaven. From this moment forward, my life belongs to You, Jesus, and You alone. Thank You for Your grace and mercy. Amen.

At the end of that prayer, I cried like a baby. The weight that was lifted from me was like ten tons of bricks. The three of us sat up until the wee hours of the morning reading God's word, praying, praising, thanking, and worshipping my new found Lord and Savior, Jesus Christ. The entire weekend, DZ and Kim followed me everywhere I went. I had an eye doctor's appointment. They went. I stopped in the office to pick up material. They went. We had lunch together. I went to a movie in the afternoon. They went. We went to dinner together. We went to church the next day together. We watched a football game on television together. There was not a single minute when Kim, DZ or both were not at my side. It was just what God ordered.

I asked God what I must do now. He told me to read His word. I asked him where I should start. He told me that it didn't matter since I did not know any of it. So, while riding the train to and from work each day, I started with Genesis and read straight through until I ended up with, "The grace of the Lord Jesus be with God's people. Amen." (Revelation 22:21- NIV). That took the better part of one entire year.

In the intervening months, Kim gave birth to a beautiful, chocolate chip baby girl. She had long black hair like her mother but everything else was the spitting image of me. We were joyful that God demonstrated His grace by bringing Tiffany to this world free of the effects of my drug use. She was healthy and full of energy.

While looking into her big brown eyes one day, I could see a reflection of myself. It was then that I realized that constantly reading the Word of God was like a mirror. It showed me more of who I was. It showed me more dirt. Then it cleansed me of all the filth. I thought I only needed deliverance from drugs but the Word of God revealed pride, lust, lying, and money worship as major areas of my life that needed blood washing. He worked on those areas and gave me opportunities to serve Him during the next couple of years. Kim and I joined Rock of Ages Baptist Church and studied for seven months in their new members' class. Then, I taught in Vacation Bible School before joining the Christian Education Department. I taught Youth Sunday School and an occasional adult mid-week bible class.

"Kim, I had a dream-vision last night."

"Now, you know that you should pay attention to your dreams. What was it?"

"Weird as usual. In the dream I committed some kind of minor infraction against the law. However, I was judged to receive the death penalty. There were about five of us who received the same penalty. Sonny was one of them. Aunt Alice was around but not involved in the infractions or penalties. It appeared that she was larger than anyone else and was hovering over the courtroom. You had driven me to the courthouse around 10:00am. It was in the afternoon when I received the judgment. I wanted to go and say goodbye. But, the person who was to carry out the judgment wouldn't let me. The others and I were to die by lethal injection.

Sonny and I were going in at the same time but I lost track of him. Aunt Alice seemed to be hanging in the shadows around the room where I was. When it was time for me to receive the injection, I remember not being afraid. I didn't know why such a minor infraction deserved the death penalty. But, I was not afraid. I knew I would see Jesus. I just didn't know what death was all about. I was imagining it was something like going to sleep.

The injection was given in my upper lip. Two others had previously received their injection and were either dying or dead. When I received mine, my lip started to go numb. My body started to weaken. But, I did not die. I started to think. Man, if I don't die, they can't try me for the same infraction and judge me again. But, I was wrong. The lady who gave me the injection saw that I was not dead. She came back, shook me, and then told me to leave for a while. But, she would give me another injection later.

I left thinking now is my chance to say goodbye to Kim. But, I couldn't find you. While looking for you, 'character' came up. What is my character? Do I exhibit the fruit of the Spirit? That was most important. If my life exhibited the fruit of the Spirit then God is pleased.

Before I knew it, while thinking about character, I received a second lethal injection in my upper lip again. I did not die again. Character kept coming up. Is there love, joy, peace, patience, faithfulness, gentleness, goodness, kindness, and self-control in my life? There is some fruit in my life but there needs to be much more. I woke up. End of dream."

"Boy, you have some really weird dreams. I notice some things, though. First, you are being held to a higher standard. Second, Aunt Alice is looking over you in this dream. I also notice that you did not die from the injections. Could God be talking to you about eternal life with him?"

"I don't know what it means but I do know that I must pay closer attention to the things that God shows me."

Two years later, Kim gave birth to our son, William Jesse Louis Johnson, Jr. (aka Billy) He too was a very healthy baby. The only problem I had was that he looked just like his mother. I wanted him to look like me. However, over the years, both he and Tiffany developed features that were a good combination of the both of us. Whenever either one of them was alone with me, strangers would say that they were the spitting image of me. On the other hand, if either were alone with Kim, strangers would say that they were the spitting image of her. So, both Kim and I were pleased that the best of both of us physically came out in them. God was now working on us and especially me to be the best spiritual father that I could be to the both of them.

I remembered that I did not have much of a father figure to emulate. To make matters worse, I had pretty much lost contact with Audrey. Joyce and Audrey's grandparents had taken her to another part of the country and shielded my family from any contact with her. But, God was gracious to me. He led me to the men's ministry where by example and His word God taught me to be a decent parent. I learned to spend time with Tiffany and Billy on a daily basis. I helped with their nurturing and did my share of cleaning dirty diapers. When Billy was nine months old, I enrolled both of them in swimming lessons with the YMCA. The lessons required parental involvement in the pool and classroom. I volunteered for the duty. It got me even closer to both of them. As the years passed, I took them to piano lessons, dance lessons, and just about every other lesson in which Kim enrolled them.

God continued to prune and refine me with a deeper study of His Word. I reread and meditated on every book in the Bible. As I did so, God led me to write something about each chapter. I was learning to hear from Him. After about six years, God had allowed me to write over 1000 pages of notes based on His Rhema words to me while I read. Along the way, God gave me experiences in the stewardship ministry, pastoral care ministry, and prison ministry. He was preparing me and using me for works of service.

"Willie, I was just thinking. You know we have not been to the Homecoming since Tiffany was born. How would you like to go down there this summer? It is only January. So, we have plenty of time to plan."

"I like that idea. Let's go."

****

This subject of character has come up both in general conversation and my personal reflections over the last couple of weeks. I believe there is a word for all of us about character. Here it is.

My character and my personality are two different things. My personality is embodied in my emotions, intellect, and will. My character is my distinctive way of looking at and reacting to things. Let me say it this way. My personality is who God made me to be. My character is who I choose to be. It is how I choose to respond to life.

My character has been undergoing tremendous change over the past few years. Mind you, my personality has not changed. My soul is who God made me to be. I had to look at it this way. Character is a conscious choice to accept and obey the transformation that God gave me upon accepting Jesus Christ as Lord and Savior. His transformation was to make me innocent before Him. Now, my choices turn that innocence into holy character. This character is based on the moral choices that I make. Do I choose to let my old nature dominate me? Or, do I choose a life of faith? What are your choices? Some of you can handle the spoken word very well. Do you use it to cut like a thief? Or, do you use it to cut like a skilled surgeon? Your character determines how you use what God has given you.

This transformation that God gave you by grace occurred when He gave you the Holy Spirit. He also gave you faith. As you applied your faith to receive his grace, your character transformation began. This character change does not come easy. It is a constant fight. We must determine to demolish all arguments and pretenses that come up against the knowledge of God. (2 Corinthians 10:4 – 6) It is these strongholds that attempt to keep us tied to our old character. God's word helps us. To our faith we are to add goodness, then knowledge, then self-control, then perseverance, then godliness, then brotherly kindness, then love. 2 Peter 1:5. (It all comes back to love, doesn't it?) Our character transformation then continues. The sign that God is at work in transforming our character is that He is destroying our confidence in the natural virtues that we hold dearly.

Your character must continually transform so that God can use you at higher levels in the building of His kingdom. Your character must become a tested and true faith built on your reliance in the Holy Spirit. You must risk everything and leap by faith into what He says. As you do so, God will reveal more to you. That revelation comes in the form of greater spiritual requirements on your life. If you take a look back over the last year and can see greater spiritual requirements on your life then it is likely that your character is changing. If not, then you must review the choices that you are making. You must change them and let your character change.

Hallelujah!!

7

Gold in the Hill

As so many of us are going through some test, trial, or attack, I am reminded of the encouraging life of Christ. Everything that He did is a reminder of how we should live. Take a careful look at John 18:1. If you meditate on it a while, seek revelation knowledge and understanding, then you see your life in that one verse. Jesus went from the Garden of Gethsemane through the Kidron Valley to the Mount of Olives. And, He did this on purpose. Was He showing you something? Was He showing you that there is gold on the other side? The Garden of Gethsemane was a place of rest and refreshing. It was generally a place of calm. Jesus left there then went through the Kidron Valley.

The Kidron Valley has a history of being a place of death and the grave. Jesus went through the valley on purpose. He placed it beneath His feet. If you are like me, at some point, you have left a place of rest and journeyed through a valley of death. Look at where Jesus ended up on the other side of the valley. He came to the Mount of Olives. Do you remember what significant event happened on the Mount of Olives? Yes, Jesus ascended into Heaven from this point. Hallelujah! In this one verse, Jesus is showing by His actions that if we journey through the Kidron Valley placing death beneath our feet, we end up in a place of glory. Hallelujah! Hallelujah!! Hallelujah!!!

****

"Kim, I was just thinking, I cannot ever remember going to a Johnson family reunion."

"What about homecoming?"

"That is a reunion of sorts to be sure. But, it is basically a reunion of everyone who has ever lived in Raeford."

"Well!"

"It is true that in one way or another many if not most of those who live there are related. But, I am talking about a reunion of the descendants of Harvey and Asia Johnson."

"That's pretty narrow."

"I don't know about that. Pappa was one of seventeen children. He had fourteen children himself. I don't know much about any of his brothers or sisters except Uncle Simon who had at least five children. I suspect that the number of descendants from Harvey and Asia number in the hundreds. If I can find most of them, it would be a very large reunion."

Kim agreed that would be an interesting and fun reunion. Getting it together though could be a daunting task. I had to start somewhere. But, whom would I go to for information? The natural choice would have been Daddy. However, two years before, he had died of a heart attack. It was a surprise to everyone. It happened like this.

"I'm going to the Safeway grocery store to pick up some milk and bread," I told Kim that day as I walked out the back door. I was only gone about twenty-five minutes. When I reentered the house, Kim had a sorrowful look on her face.

"What's wrong? Where are Tiffany and Billy?"

"They're upstairs playing. Chrissie called as soon as you pulled out of the driveway."

"Oh, yeah. Is she doing alright?"

"Not too well. It's your dad. He died of a heart attack about an hour ago. He was in his bedroom at home when a massive heart attack suddenly came upon him. He was gone before the ambulance could get to him."

I was numb. I really did not know how to feel. I tried to hold my composure. But, as soon as Kim hugged me to console me, tears welled up in me then came streaming down my face. I did not make a sound but the tears kept flowing. She just held me for as long as I wanted to be held.

"When do you want to go home?"

"I don't know yet. I guess I should go soon."

Since I was not needed to help make the arrangements, I waited until the day before the wake. The funeral was in Fayetteville. He was buried at Oak Hill cemetery in Raeford. I would miss him more than I ever dreamed. He was my dad. There was so much that I wanted to talk to him about. And, now I couldn't. This stage in my life would have been the perfect opportunity to talk to him about his family and his life. But, it wasn't to be.

I went to Mamma as my next step in getting names and addresses. She told me the names of two of Pappa's brothers and all of Grampa Ellis's brothers and sisters. The two brothers were Uncle Simon and Uncle Calvin. Grampa Ellis's siblings were Helen, Ethel, Bernice, Nathan, Rachael, Martha, Joseph, Alice, Anna, Hannah, Felix, Jethro, and Eddie. I visited with Grampa Ellis who then told me a great deal about the children of his sisters and brothers. What he could not remember, Aunt Alice and Uncle Eddie filled in enough to start making phone calls. My dad's two sisters, Aunt Dorothy and Aunt Jean were a big help as they maintained contact with several of their first cousins.

Over the next couple of weeks, I solicited two cousins to assist with phone calls that were now numbering in the tens per day. Along the way, we created a spreadsheet of names and addresses that grew exponentially. When a new relative was contacted, we gave them the then current version of the spreadsheet. That encouraged them to assist with obtaining more names and addresses. Finally, we had reached nearly 500 relatives who lived all across the United States and in South America. We were elated that nearly all of them responded that they would attend a reunion to be held in July of that year.

The reunion was now becoming a reality. It would be held during the first week of July. My two cousins would coordinate the program, location, and food. I would coordinate the communications. It was early spring and I was planning to attend my first Apostolic and Prophetic conference in Texas in April. While time and schedules were tight, there was just enough time to plan. Then Kim and I got an unexpected phone call.

"Hello, this is Willie."

"Hi, Willie. This is Joyce."

"Joyce!! What a surprise!! I would have never guessed that I would receive a call from you. What's going on? How's Audrey? Where is she?" I had a ton of questions. "It's Joyce," I whispered to Kim. Kim sat straight up in her chair and looked intently at me. She shrugged her shoulders and opened her hands as if to ask, 'what does Joyce want now?' I put my finger to my lips and shook my head.

"I didn't want to bother you or surprise you but I need your help."

"What is it?"

"I don't know where else I can turn in the short run. My mother insisted that I call you. She got your number from Mrs. Doris."

"No problem. Is Audrey OK?"

"Actually, that is the reason that I am calling. Things are not OK. I am not sure what is going on but Audrey may need to stay with you for a couple of months."

I nearly dropped the phone and hit the floor. "What?" I asked in a loud voice. Now Kim was standing right next to me reaching to pull the phone next to both of our ears.

"I mean, sure. This is rather sudden, though. What's going on?"

"If it is a problem for you and your wife, just let me know. I'll find another solution."

"Look, Joyce, I don't even know what you are talking about. Of course, I will have to discuss it with Kim. But, tell me what's going on. I need to know and so will Kim."

"Can she stay with you or not? That's all I want to know."

"Yes, she can stay. But, not until you tell me more."

"I'll make it brief."

I could tell that she was distraught. Her voice was shaky. She was clearly uncomfortable yet there was no anger. She could hardly get the words out. She forced it.

"Audrey has claimed to my mother and the police that her step-father touched her in an inappropriate way."

There was silence on the phone. I wanted to interrupt but did not yield to the temptation. Although hesitant, she continued,

"According to the authorities while the investigation is going on, Audrey has to stay in a neutral place."

"What makes you think that I would be neutral with such a charge?" I now blurted.

"Because you don't know any of us! You don't know me. You don't know Audrey, really. And, you surely don't know my husband."

There was now anger in this tone. She did not have to say much. I knew where she was coming from. I had not been a part of Audrey's life up to this point. That was going to be a discussion to be held at some point in the future. But, for now, Joyce just wanted some peace between her husband and her daughter. Since I could be a part of that solution for her, she decided to call.

"OK. There's no need to get excited. Audrey can stay here. But, we obviously need to talk a great deal more."

"We do. But, not now. The sooner we can make arrangements for Audrey to leave, the better."

I got off the phone and told Kim what I knew. She was supportive given the nature of the situation. She would have been supportive of Audrey living with us even if things were not as drastic as they seemed.

Joyce had married a year after Audrey was born. They had moved to Kansas City, Mo. to allow her husband to take a job with AT&T Long Lines. During the ensuing years, Joyce had given birth to two boys and two girls. Her husband started showing signs of favoritism almost immediately with the birth of his first son. Now at age 10, Audrey was accusing him of fondling her. Since the accusations included repeated offenses, the authorities gave Joyce two choices. Audrey would become a temporary ward of the court or Audrey could live with her natural father. Joyce would have preferred Audrey to live with her mother or any of her siblings. But, the court system disapproved based on the potential that those who knew her so closely could influence Audrey. To her chagrin and at her mother's recommendation, Joyce was left with the choice to send Audrey to live with me.

Audrey arrived about a month before I was scheduled to leave for the conference in Texas. She looked just like her mother. She was not very tall, round, and dark skinned with short-cropped hair. Her smile showed the most beautiful white teeth I had seen on a ten year old in quite a while. Kim and I had prepared Tiffany and Billy for Audrey's arrival. They were excited to finally meet her. The three of them hit it off right away. Kim enrolled her at Lincoln Elementary School where Tiffany attended kindergarten. Although the school was walking distance from the house, Kim usually drove the two of them.

This was a great situation for me. I was finally getting a chance to know the daughter that was taken away from me so many years before. She seemed happy. Kim was happy. Tiffany and Billy were happy, too. Audrey was quick to make friends. She had a bubbly personality and talked a mile a minute. It was not difficult to get her to take dance lessons, piano lessons, and swim lessons. In addition, she talked regularly with her mother. That, of course, helped to ease the transition. Things were great until the week before I left.

"Audrey, I will be leaving for Texas next Sunday, you know."

"Already? I just got here."

"I know sweetheart. We talked about this trip before you got here and again just about every week since. Remember?"

"Yeah. But, I didn't think it would come so fast."

"Well, we still have another week. I'll only be gone a week. Besides, Kim, Tiffany, Billy, and all of your new friends will be here. You'll hardly know that I am gone."

Beginning with that conversation, Audrey started to withdraw day by day. She was not as excited about school, lessons, family, or friends. There was nothing serious that she either did or said. There was no violent or drastic behavior change. With each passing day, she was simply less bubbly. She continued with all of her activities and continued to talk with her mother. I thought that maybe it was something that had occurred during one or more of those conversations that had slightly upset her. However, according to Joyce, they never spoke of the accusations.

Kim and I talked about it and agreed that it was just an adjustment period. She would be back to her initial self in a day or so. When Sunday arrived, the family took me to the airport without incident. I hugged and kissed everyone then said goodbye.

****

This Apostolic and Prophetic conference had been introduced to many of us by a good friend. The previous year, he participated in the first module of an eleven module training session. It so impressed him that he raved about it for months. Somewhere in the bowels of my soul and spirit, I was attracted to what he talked about. I decided to participate in the next offering. This first module focused on the spiritual gifts as Paul describes them in 1 Corinthians chapter 12. Disciples Globally, the conference sponsors, had a decided focus on prophecy. I believed in the gifts of the Spirit and had seen some in operation like speaking in tongues. However, I knew very little about prophecy and nothing of the conference sponsors. I was unsure of what they were teaching. Would they read my palms? I certainly was having nothing to do with that kind of teaching.

With some research on Disciples Globally and assurances from our friend that they were legitimate, two others and I decided to attend the next conference. Our friend attended with us and took the module two training. My excitement grew, as the plane got closer to Texas. Each module assigned prerequisite reading. I calmed myself and passed the time by reading the concluding chapters of the book for the first module. We checked into the hotel then went directly to the conference center for the opening praise and worship session.

"This first session is a joint session for everyone attending the conference," we were told. "If it is like last year, we will want to be on time to get a good seat."

"Let's go," I declared.

There were about two thousand attendees. Most of them arrived fairly early. We ended up in the middle of the sanctuary. That was a good place. The session started on time with high praise music. There were live musicians with the typical drums, piano, guitars, cymbals, horns, and a curious instrument that looked like a ram's horn to me. Praise dancers and singers were leading the worship. I sat on the end so that I could step into the aisle if and when prompted by the Holy Spirit. And, it didn't take long. At about the second chorus of the first song, half the attendees and I were in the aisles and blanketing the front of the church. The praise continued at a fever pitch for nearly an hour before the first speaker, Bishop Carter, approached the microphone.

"Praise the Lord, everybody," he said.

"PRAISE THE LORD," was the response.

"I feel the presence of the Almighty God in here," the Bishop said. "I want someone to bring that young lady in the wheelchair from the back to the steps of this podium. The Lord has pointed her out to me as one He will use to demonstrate that He is still in the miracles business."

He was pointing to what looked like a relatively young lady in her mid-thirties who was sitting in a wheelchair opposite a short pew near the back row. There were four or five individuals in wheelchairs around the sanctuary. Yet, it was this particular lady that the Bishop was fixed on with Christ-like loving eyes. Everyone was in a roar and clapping loudly as she was slowly but steadily pushed toward the front.

"Do you believe that God heals and restores, today?"

"Yes, I believe."

"Do you believe Isaiah 55:3 that says, "But he was pierced for our transgressions, he was crushed for our iniquities; the punishment that brought us peace was upon him, and by his wounds we are healed?"

"Yes, I believe."

"Woman. Your faith has made you whole. Get up and walk."

I watched with amazement as this woman slowly pushed herself up by her arms and stood for about 15 seconds. No one said a word or made a move towards her.

"Walk!" The Bishop said.

She took a step, unaided. Then, she took another step, and another, and another. She started walking fast. Then, she took off in a run as fast as her legs could take her. She ran right by me and nearly knocked me over as she was smiling and focused on moving her legs. She paid no attention to anyone or anything else.

The shouts of joy and praise became nearly deafening. Clapping, shouting, dancing, singing, music, crying, and bodies bent over in worship continued for another thirty minutes. I could hardly believe what I had just witnessed or the sustained praise and worship. It was beyond any experience that I had encountered to that point in my Christian walk. I had been in high praise and worship before but not for that long. I had seen miracles of that type on television before. But, I had not witnessed it in person. I could hardly believe it all. There was no choice but to believe the praise. However, I wondered about the lady walking. Why hadn't he chosen the others either in addition to or instead of her? My mind was reeling.

When the praise session ended, we were sent to individual module training. The instructor had rightfully discerned that many of us in this first module had some questions about the miracle that we just witnessed.

"How many of you have previous experience in high praise and worship like we just concluded?" she asked. Only about fifty hands were raised out of nearly three hundred people.

"How many have witnessed firsthand the miracles of God as we were just now so honored?" This time, only about ten hands were raised. The rest of us were brand new babies to this kind of experience.

"I want you to know that I had the pleasure of walking with Mrs. Wiley for the last fifteen minutes of that session. Mrs. Wiley is the lady who came forward in the wheelchair but left running. She is from the Appalachian region of Kentucky. She and her husband were introduced to the prophetic last year when a prophet from Disciples Globally Ministries visited their home church," she continued.

"While she and her husband came here with high expectations of receiving an impartation of the Holy Spirit's anointing for the prophetic, they had no idea that Bishop would call her out. By the way, neither did he. It was not until he walked up to the podium that he received a Word from God to lay hands on someone to heal them. God then pointed her out. He doesn't know her. Nor, does she know him. He thought that he was going to add his welcome to this conference and introduce the agenda for the week. The Holy Spirit had something else in mind."

"Where is Mrs. Wiley now?" It was a question from one of our group.

"She is getting formally introduced to the Bishop. She wanted to thank him. He was gracious to oblige. Since this is her first time through the training, she will be joining this group. You'll get a chance to talk to her throughout the week, I'm sure."

That was the beginning of a tremendous week for me. I got a formal introduction to the prophetic. Every day, multiple times throughout the day, each of us was given an opportunity to activate the gift of prophecy. Through demonstrations, lectures, and activation exercises, I began to not only understand this gift but also to hear from God, as I had never listened before. The days were long. They began at 8:00am and concluded at 10:00pm or later.

I got the opportunity to speak with Mrs. Wiley throughout the week. That miracle was the real deal. She had been crippled from birth with polio. Therefore, she had grown to accept her condition. She often dreamed and prayed that she would one day walk. However, it was not her expectation that she would return home from this conference walking next to her husband. She had, of course, told everyone back at her home. A grand reception was being planned for her return. The whole conference was excited for and about her.

On the last night of the conference, another praise and worship session was scheduled for the entire group. It was every bit as exciting and God-honoring as the first. This time, though, there was about thirty of those ram's horns in the choir stand. Each one of them appeared to be about three or four feet in length. In addition, every seventh or eighth row seemed to have at least one person with a smaller version of the horn. The blares of those horns were both piercing and harmonious. After about forty-five minutes of praise and worship, we received a teaching on praise. God inhabits the praise of His people. When he does so, it is to exact judgment upon His enemies. According to Psalm 8:3, "From the lips of children and infants you have ordained praise because of your enemies, to silence the foe and the avenger." Scripture after scripture was used to show God taking vengeance upon His enemies in the midst of praise from His worshippers. Matthew 21:9 – 12 and Revelation 19:1 – 16 were among the many that shows exaltation followed by vengeance. For the first time, I truly received a spiritual understanding of why I should shout, sing, and dance during praise. There are spiritual warfare connections to each of these.

Shouting... "Clap your hands, all you nations; shout to God with cries of joy…. God has ascended amid shouts of joy, the LORD amid the sounding of trumpets."(Psalm 47:1, 5 NIV) "The LORD will march out like a mighty man, like a warrior he will stir up his zeal; with a shout he will raise the battle cry and will triumph over his enemies." (Isaiah 42:13 NIV) In both of these scriptures, we see that through the shout God ascends, releases, and raises the battle cry. The Hebrew word for shout is ruwa. Its primitive root means; to mar (especially by breaking); to split the ears (with sound). So, you can see that we are breaking up the enemy's kingdom and splitting his ears with shouts of praise.

Singing... In 2 Chronicles chapter 20, we see that King Jehoshaphat recognize the power of singing in spiritual warfare. He was told that the battle was not his. It was the Lord's. After fasting and inquiring of the Lord, Jehoshaphat appointed men to go ahead of the army singing, 'Give thanks to the LORD, for his love endures forever.' Singing praises to the Lord caused confusion in the enemy's camp then and it causes confusion in his camp, now.

Dancing... "But for you who revere my name, the sun of righteousness will rise with healing in its wings. And you will go out and leap like calves released from the stall. Then you will trample down the wicked; they will be ashes under the soles of your feet on the day when I do these things," says the LORD Almighty.'" (Malachi 4:2–3 NIV) "Let them praise his name with dancing …" (Psalm 149:3 NIV) Here we see a prophecy by Malachi that as we leap in dance before the Lord, we will trample the wicked beneath our feet. David says to praise God in dance.

Then, I received a teaching on the ram's horns. They are called shofars. The Holman Bible dictionary defines it as the Hebrew word for the ceremonial ram's horn used to call the people of Israel together (Ex. 19:16). The shofar was to be blown on the Day of Atonement in the jubilee year to signal the release of slaves and debt. It also was used as a trumpet of war as the Israelites were campaigning against their enemies. Now, I understood why it was blown so loudly at the beginning of each worship service. The sponsors were calling the people together. I also understood the spiritual connection with canceling debt and calling the saints together for spiritual warfare.

The last day of the conference was reserved for delivering a personal prophecy to each person participating in the first module. By then, I was ready to hear a Word from the Lord that would edify and build me up.

'My son. I bless you My son. I have given you eyes to see through the darkness. I have given you courage to go where few men would go for you are one of My Mighty Men. And, I have given you strength. I have given you the assignment and the ability to tread upon unholy spirits. You will be walking in places that are hot. But, you are going to be protected because I am with you. You are being prepared and have been given all that you need to do this job. You have a willing heart, strength, courage, intensity, endurance, a caring spirit, and strong shoulders. This is a heavy spiritual load. Yet, I, your God have faith that you can do this mighty work for Me.

Son. I've made you a man of valor, a man of war. I have called you to this because you are mighty. You are going in to possess the lands. And, you will possess it. Fear not because I will always be with you. I will send forth angels. I will send forth praisers. I will place My full armor upon you. You're a warrior. But, I need you to listen very carefully to my Spirit. You've done the right thing thus far. You have opened the door into a new realm of hearing, seeing, and sensing. You are never going to be the same, again. Your life has changed. You have a new direction. I am drawing you to walk closer and closer to Me. When you hear Me speak, remember that the mouth of two or more witnesses will establish My word. So, listen to My word. Listen to My spirit. And, go where I send you. Hallelujah!!'

****

I returned from that conference on fire. I had a greater understanding of the prophetic. I had actually heard with assurance an edifying word from God and through the activations spoke it into the life of another individual. I finally understood the spiritual significance of praise and worship including the use of a shofar. To top it all off, I had received a personal prophesy. While I did not yet fully understand the seed that had been planted, I knew in my spirit that a connection was made with this word.

On the plane ride home, my mind replayed each day. Every activation, every demonstration, every lecture, every praise and worship session, and every spoken word reverberated like the sounds of a tuning fork in a closed-in cave. Because the days were so long, I only had the opportunity to speak with Kim twice. The first time was the middle of the week. The second was the morning that I left Texas. So, I was very excited to tell her all about the conference once I got home. She and the kids picked me up at the airport late on Friday.

"Daddy!! Daddy!! Daddy!!" shouted Audrey, Tiffany, and Billy.

"Give me a hug," I said to all three of them. We had a group hug then I hugged and kissed them one by one.

"Hey, honey. I missed you," I told Kim as I gave her a hug and a kiss.

"We missed you, too. Boy, did we miss you!!" she said with her head tilted to one side.

"I have so much to tell yawl," I said

"Tell us. Tell us," Audrey and Tiffany said excitedly. Billy just continued to smile and hold my hand.

"I have a lot to tell you too," Kim said with a different tone. Something was on her mind. But, she was willing to wait as I began with my arrival in Texas. By the time we got home, I had summarized everything up to and including my personal prophecy. The kids were still fairly young. So, I didn't get into a lot of detail or application for them. I just shared my excitement. Then, they told me about their week. Most of it was the typical lessons and schoolwork. Softball season started while I was away. Tiffany played T Ball and Audrey played Mustang League. Both of them shared the fun they had at practices; mistakes, homeruns, and all. After they went to bed, it was Kim's turn.

"How did the week go for you?" I asked.

"What a week. Are you ready for this?"

"Tell me about it."

"On the way home from taking you to the airport last Sunday, Audrey and Tiffany got into a verbal fight."

"That's to be expected with kids, though, isn't it?"

"Well, we knew it would happen one day. After all, Tiffany and Billy get into it all the time. Audrey had not had so much as a cross word with anyone since she arrived."

"OK."

"It started when Tiffany tried to sit in the front seat. Audrey pulled her back and told her to get in the back. She was going to sit up front. Before it got out of hand, I told the both of them to get in the back seat and buckle up."

"That's good."

"Then, Audrey started picking at Tiffany. She called her a spoiled brat who always got her way. According to her, it was Tiffany's fault that she had to sit in the back crowded up with the two of them. Tiffany told her that she was not spoiled. Audrey insisted that she always gets her way. She claimed that I always take Tiffany to her classroom first, I take her to lessons first, I take her to baseball practice first."

"What do you think is going on?"

"I am not exactly sure. But, you will recall that she started to act a little strange the week before you left."

"You think it has something to do with me being gone?"

"It may be. Why don't you have a talk with her tomorrow? I know that you are excited about your trip. But, put that aside for a while and see if you can get her to talk."

"Consider it done."

I had been so excited before, during and after the conference week that I failed to pay much attention to the sudden change that was occurring with Audrey. Kim had correctly discerned that a deeper issue needed to be addressed. It didn't take long for it to be identified. The next morning, Kim was up early making breakfast. Billy usually was up before the girls and hanging in the kitchen with his mother. She would take out a pot and close the cabinet. He would open the cabinet and take out another pot. She would open the dishwasher to put in a dish. He would open the dishwasher and take the dish out. He had a ball following her around trying to do what he saw her do. She would eventually get him to help her with something. Most of the time, it was something like putting silverware or juice on the table. His favorite, pancakes were on the menu. So that morning, Kim had no trouble getting him seated.

"Breakfast is ready. Everybody get washed up and come to the table," Kim called.

Audrey, Tiffany, and I were just waiting on the call.

"I want everyone to bless his or her food out loud. I will start. Then, Mamma. Then Audrey. Then Tiffany. And then you, Billy. OK?"

Billy concluded with "Thank You, Jesus"

"I am glad that you are home, Daddy," Audrey said.

"I am glad to be home," I told her.

"I didn't think you were coming back," she said. Kim and I looked at each other.

"Why would you think that, honey?"

"I don't know. I just thought you wouldn't come back."

"There was no way that I would not come back to all of you. I love you, Tiffany, Billy and Mamma."

"How far away is Texas?" she asked.

"Several hundred miles. It was too far for me to drive on this trip. So, I had to take a plane."

Now, Kim and I had a clue to Audrey's change in behavior. It had something to do with me leaving and her thoughts that I was not coming back. Neither of us understood why she would think such a thing. But, we knew that it had to be addressed and soon. We agreed to take a counseling approach with a pastor at the church. Since Audrey's addition was a sudden change for all of us, the pastor recommended that all of us in different combinations spend some time every week talking it out.

She started with the entire family. Then, Audrey and me. Kim and me. Kim, Tiffany, Billy and me. Audrey and Tiffany. Finally, Audrey alone. Each session was a little different. However, everything pointed to discussions about life before Audrey and life since Audrey arrived. The pastor called Kim and I into her office for a final assessment.

"Willie and Kim, the situation is not as bad as you might have thought. It is not pretty. But, it could be a lot worse."

"That's good to know," Kim said.

"There are things that need to be addressed. But, with a lot of love, I believe that your family will be fine."

"What can you tell us?" I asked.

"Audrey has moved from family to family quite a bit since her birth. She lived with her mother and grandmother until her mother was married. After living with her mother and stepfather for a month, they brought her back to her grandmother and left her there. Audrey's grandmother raised her until she was three. At that time, she moved back with her mother and stepfather. By this time, her mother had given birth to another child, a boy. At age five, she and her family visited relatives in Marion, North Carolina over the summer. Her mother and stepfather unwisely left her in Marion without talking to her. She looked up one day and they were gone. A year later, she was back living with them again. Now, another child, a girl, had been born."

"It appears that each time Joyce had a child, she would take Audrey to live with her mother," Kim said.

"It appears that way to me, also. But, there might have been other reasons. It is hard to imagine. Again when Audrey was age eight just before the birth of another brother, her mother took Audrey back to Marion. She had only returned to live with her parents nine months before she came to live with the two of you," the pastor said.

"Did she talk much about the accusations of fondling by her stepfather?" I asked.

"I was surprised at how freely she talked about it, actually. She described several incidents dating back to when she was five years old," she said.

"Really!" Kim exclaimed.

"The timing of these incidents appeared to be just after she returned to live with them each time."

"Do you believe that they occurred?" Kim asked.

"The more important question is does her mother believe that they occurred. It was in conversation with her mother just before you left for your conference that Audrey realized that her mother did not believe her."

"So, that's what started the mood swing. By the way, I asked her mother about that. She denied bringing up the incident," Kim said.

"She was likely telling you the truth. In one of the conversations, her mother was extolling the virtues of her husband and his devotion to the children. It could be that she was trying to paint him in a positive light to Audrey. However, Audrey perceived those comments to mean that her mother did not believe her."

"What do you believe?" I asked.

"I honestly don't know, yet. It is a bit more complicated than that."

"How so?" Kim asked.

"Each time she was left with her grandmother, Audrey felt abandoned. There was little or no conversation with her prior to the events. It is entirely possible that upon her return to the family, she could have been seeking revenge. The stepfather was clearly affectionate with his natural children. And, of course, he never left any of them with the grandmother."

"So, she thought that I was leaving her with Kim," I said.

"I believe in combination with the comments from her mother that is what had her upset. With you now at home, things should be better."

"What do you recommend?" I asked.

"Plenty of love and plenty of conversation. Especially if you are going to be away for any length of time. She also may be feeling that she doesn't belong anywhere. It is important that the two of you show her that you want her to be with you forever, if that were possible."

We thanked the pastor and agreed with her to bring Audrey back once a month for a while. In the meantime, Kim and I made a special effort to include Audrey in everything that the family did. Tiffany and Billy were, of course, included too. We were becoming a family. All the kids received the same training and instructions in the Lord. Both reward and punishment were meted out with good, sound judgment and reasoning. As the end of the school year approached, things got much better.

Audrey continued to talk with her mother on a weekly basis. The investigation into the accusations was proceeding very slowly. It was basically Audrey's word against the stepfather's. No one had witnessed any of the claims. The basic question was whom had Audrey told of the incidents in the past and under what circumstances. That explained why Audrey was not allowed to live with a close relative. The courts did not want any influence to come from either party. While the investigations continued, Audrey became more and more comfortable with the new family. I even encouraged her to help with planning the Johnson family reunion. She would get to know more of her relatives even before she physically met them.

"Who are we going to call tonight, Daddy?"

"Let's try some of Aunt Anna's children in California."

"Who is Aunt Anna, again?"

"She is one of Grampa Ellis's sisters. She and her husband moved to California from Raeford many years ago. That is where she raised most of her children. The oldest of them, Benjamin who we called Shot Gun, remained in Raeford. After her husband died, she moved back to Raeford where she now lives next door to Aunt Alice."

I started with her oldest son and continued until I had reached more than ten different relatives in California. I reminded each of them that the Johnson family reunion was being held in July in Raeford. Since we had not met in this way as a family for as long as anyone could remember, there was a confirmed commitment to attend from nearly everyone that I called. Cousins had been diligently working on the program and location since the earlier part of the year. Things were coming together. The months turned into weeks. Then the weeks turned into days.

It finally arrived. The reunion began on a Friday night with a reception at a hall rented in Greensboro. One by one, family members arrived from all over North Carolina; Fayetteville, Charlotte, Winston Salem, Wilmington, Henderson, Greenville, Sparta, Mt. Airy, and Marion. Families came from Florida, Colorado, North Carolina, Michigan, California, Illinois, Virginia, Oklahoma, Louisiana, Hawaii, Oregon, Washington, and Paraguay, South America. We had a terrific time just getting to know one another. It was one big hug fest. Smiles and laughs were everywhere.

"Who are you? And, who are you?"

"What's your daddy's name? What's your mamma's name?"

"Where do you live? How long have you lived there?"

"How many children do you have? What are their names?"

"Did everybody come?"

There were questions and answers galore. Nothing special was planned for this day. The food was light and gospel music was played on tapes. Some people had not seen each other in years. Others had not ever seen each other. The children especially got a kick out of meeting so many relatives. The Saturday activities were scheduled to begin at 10:00am with a picnic. I decided to leave fairly early, 10:30pm. However, many stayed around until well past midnight.

****

The picnic was scheduled for 10:00am until 3:00pm. Since the evening program got started at 7:00pm, the late afternoon was left open for family home visitations, walks in the woods, and trips to the cemetery. The picnic had both indoor and outdoor games for kids, games for adults, plenty of food, and more reminiscing than any one person could handle. During the evening program, the musical, poetic, comical, and verbal talents in the family were on grand display. The committee had done an excellent job of coordinating a live band composed of Johnson family members, gospel singing, reading original poems, and comic relief with reciting family history by the elders in the family. While all of it was fun, the most captivating of all the events was when Grampa Ellis told the history of his grandparents, Harvey Johnson and Asia McMann.

"They were slaves brought to Raeford in 1860 as teenagers from Georgia," he started. "Granddaddy Harvey's mother was African but his father was the white slave owner. Grandma Sissy's (Asia) mother was Native American and her father was a different white slave owner. She was purchased by Granddaddy Harvey's father and brought to live in the big house along with Granddaddy Harvey. Since they were not field 'hands', they were taught how to read. The favorite book for the both of them became God's Word, the Bible. After a while, they took a liking to each other. He was eighteen and she was seventeen when they got married in the back yard. To them was born Abraham, Amos, Simon, Calvin, Adam, Margaret, Reba, Lucy, and nine more children. They taught all of their children about God and had them to memorize scripture. ………"

He continued on until he had named all of his brothers and sisters, all of his and their grandchildren, and all of Uncle Simon's children and grandchildren. He told us how the rest of Pappa's brothers and sisters passed for 'white' and virtually hid from the rest of the family. Aunt Margaret was caught after she had married a white guy and was placed in prison. He didn't know much about the others. He spent most of the time talking about his father, Pappa Abraham. Pappa had a deep conviction of Jesus Christ and devoted much of his life to studying God's word and His gifts to the body of Christ.

Grampa Ellis ended the evening with a prayer that all would seek God's purpose in this reunion. He prayed that we would do justice, show mercy, be kind, and compassionate to each other. It was his petition that we would all not only get to know each other but to know Christ in a much deeper way. He decreed that among us were men and women who either were or would carry the mantles of the five-fold ministry of Christ. He asked God to reveal to us those things about which the family should fast and pray. He released angels to fight with arrows dipped in the blood of Jesus to protect every child that was among us and those who could not be there. He acknowledged that it was not his words or thoughts that mattered but rather God's words. He prayed for spiritual ears throughout the family to be opened and eyes to be opened to the work of God that weekend. He closed with a praise shout of Hallelujah and Amen.

That Sunday was a day of worship at the Oak Hill Church. With food spread around the Shade Tree, it resembled a Homecoming Sunday. The difference was that the only family present on that day was descendants of Harvey and Asia Johnson. Again, Grampa Ellis gave the message from God, 'Family Unity'. He spoke of both old and new pains. Integrity, relationships, and reconciliation with each other were necessary to keep family unity. In agreement, he led the family to bind pride and loose love. All barriers were destroyed and hostilities renounced. He showed in God's word that repentance must go with forgiveness. It is our character from the inside out that matters. And living responsibly means having the courage to face opposition, building relationships to form one body and one spirit, and engaging in spiritual warfare.

The family was uplifted. It was a wonderful way to end a great weekend. After the worship service, we remembered family members who were buried in the cemetery and visited individual homes before departing to our own homes. I went by to see Aunt Alice on my way to the airport.

"Willie, you and the girls did a wonderful job in pulling this reunion together."

"Thank you, Aunt Alice. But, it was your daughters who did most of the work."

"All of you did your part. But, I have something else to talk to you about."

"Yes, Maam."

"I have been watching you over the years and watched you throughout this weekend.'

"You have?"

"Yes, I have. Did you hear your grandfather talk about the five-fold ministry of Christ?"

"Yes, Maam."

"Well, I want you to study what God's word has to say about that. And you and I will talk about it over the next few months. What do you think?"

"I guess so. I mean, Yes, Maam."

"I know that your grandfather and Doris have been teaching you. But, I want to tell you some special things. I'd like to become one of your mentors if you would like."

"I would like that a lot. When do we get started? What do you want me to do?"

"Slow down. Actually, we've already started. We don't need to do anything more, now. Just get to know God's word on the five-fold ministry. Then, we'll talk some more."

On the drive to the airport, I told Kim everything that Aunt Alice and I talked about. She found it both interesting and intriguing. Audrey, Tiffany, and Billy were sound asleep in the back seat. They had worn themselves out from so much fun over the weekend. Now, it was time to enjoy the plane ride back home while thinking about things to come.

8

BE A TRUE GODLY FRIEND

There will be times in your life when it appears that the best thing to do for your friend is to rescue him from the pains of his current trials. However, unless we have God's direction on the matter, we could be actually preventing God's best. We are perfected by our trials. Notice what Romans 5:3 - 5 says. "Not only so, but we also rejoice in our sufferings, because we know that suffering produces perseverance; perseverance, character; and character, hope. And hope does not disappoint us, because God has poured out his love into our hearts by the Holy Spirit, whom he has given us."

Each time we rescue a friend, they become just a little more dependent upon us. Shouldn't they become more dependent upon God rather than on us? It is only when our help points the friend to our Lord and Savior that our help produces the fruit that God desires. James 1:2 - 4 describes the desired fruit. "Consider it pure joy, my brothers, whenever you face trials of many kinds, because you know that the testing of your faith develops perseverance. Perseverance must finish its work so that you may be mature and complete, not lacking anything." Being kind and compassionate is a good thing. But, do not let your sympathy get in the way of God's methods for developing character. Be a true Godly friend.

****

School started one week after we returned from one of the best summers that any of us had experienced in many years. The kids had fun in the woods. They met many new relatives. Kim always had a soft spot for the plants in nature. This time, she developed a fondness for the wildlife too. I got a spiritual mentor in Aunt Alice. The excitement flowed over into the first couple of weeks of classes. 'My Summer Vacation' reports had plenty of substance.

Audrey was especially excited. While Tiffany and Billy knew many of the relatives at the family reunion, virtually every one of them was new to Audrey. She found more cousins than you could shake a stick at. She told of her adventures and some of theirs. In addition, Audrey separately had a wonderful visit with her mother and other siblings. Her report was filled with all kinds of stories about a really fun summer.

In early October, Joyce called. She and Audrey had their usual weekly conversation about things. To my surprise, Joyce asked to speak to me.

"Hello, Joyce."

"Hi, Willie, how are you, Kim, and the kids?"

"Everyone's doing fine. How's your family?"

"Other than missing Audrey, we're doing OK as well. I have something important that I would like to talk to you about."

"What is it?"

"The child molestation case against Audrey's stepfather has come to a close."

"Oh. What's the verdict?"

"He was found guilty. This has been very difficult for me. I didn't want it to be true because he is the father of my other kids and I love him. But, I also didn't want Audrey to be hurt."

"Is there anything that I can do?"

"Well, I told Audrey that I would like to come visit her later this month. It would just be me coming. If it is OK with you and Kim, I would like to talk to you about Audrey coming home."

"Did you mention that to Audrey?"

"No. I wanted to talk to the two of you first."

"Good. I don't know about Audrey going back, Joyce. However, I am willing to talk about it. When can you be here?"

"I am thinking the last week of the month. Is that OK with you?"

"That's probably a good time. I'll check with Kim and let you know if there is a conflict. Otherwise, we will plan to see you then. I know Audrey would like to see you."

"And I would like to see her. I will talk to you later. Bye."

I told Kim about the conversation. There was just so much to consider. How could we, if at all, support Audrey moving one more time? How could we help Joyce face the dilemma of supporting her husband versus supporting Audrey? How should we pray for him? We had about three weeks to come up with some answers. We began in prayer.

"Father God. We thank you for being the Almighty God that You are. We bless and praise your Holy Name. Forgive us God for our acts and thoughts of unrighteousness this day. This situation that has been placed before us by Joyce is one that only you can resolve. We accept you working through us as vessels on this earth. Without You, we are unable to answer these questions. Neither are we able to give proper counsel to these your children. So Father, in the name of Jesus Christ, we seek your Spirit of Wisdom and Revelation. Give us the knowledge God so that we may honor you in the choices that we make. Then, give us wisdom to execute those choices such that you are glorified. We pray for peace and unity in this family in the name of Jesus. Hallelujah! Amen."

Kim and I decided to contact our pastor to get her insight. We understood that the people and circumstances surrounding it made each situation like this one different. There was not one solution that would fit all. After much prayer and wise counsel, God guided Kim and I to agree with Joyce to take Audrey back to be with her mother, brothers, and sister in North Carolina. That was the place where the spirit of abandonment first entered. It was there that Audrey would get loosed through a tighter bond with her mother and siblings. We also knew that Joyce would need encouragement, a listening ear, faith, and the anointing of God. We did not know her husband at all. Without a supernatural word of knowledge about him, we would have to trust Joyce's comments so that we could pray for him.

When the time came, Joyce arrived on a late Friday afternoon for a weekend visit. The kids, Kim, and I picked her up at the airport. Although Kim offered our home to her, she insisted on staying at a local hotel. Besides, she wanted to spend some private time with Audrey. We agreed with the understanding that we would all have dinner together at a restaurant tonight and breakfast at our home in the morning. In addition, Kim, Joyce, and I would have dinner on Saturday evening. After Friday's dinner, we dropped Joyce and Audrey at the hotel and went home.

"Dad, Audrey looks just like her mother, doesn't she?" Tiffany said.

"Yeah, she does. But, you and Billy look just like a combination of me and your mother."

"I know. I love you, Dad." Tiffany said. "Me too," Billy added. "Me three!" Kim smiled.

The next day, Joyce and Audrey took a cab to the house. They arrived early enough to join us in devotion and to help Kim with preparations. After devotion, Billy and I just cooled out watching cartoons while the women cooked and got to know each other in the kitchen. Every now and then I would peek in without them knowing. I was pleasantly surprised to see them getting along well. I wasn't sure how Kim and Joyce would mix. But, the Christ in them brought them close. Hallelujah!

Breakfast and the remainder of the day went fairly well. Joyce and Audrey spent some more private time together at lunch before joining the rest of the family in the afternoon for a stroll in a nature preserve. It was the Fall of the year and a good time to see the leaves turn to the magnificent colors of God's imagination. As we walked quietly along, I could not help but reflect on God's wisdom. He knows and plans every detail of every life. He planned every detail of every tree, tilt of the earth, sunrise, wind, and shape of every leaf on the planet. How could I have ever missed that God is real? No one but God could plan the earth, the seasons, and universe as it is. All of this an accident? I don't think so. On the way home, Kim reminded the kids that they would spend time with Kim's mother while she, Joyce, and I went to dinner. That was a good idea to them because Kim's mother always had a house full of kids.

Because of the nature of our dinner conversation, Kim chose a restaurant that offered private booths. It was an Italian restaurant in a well-established neighborhood of descendants from Italy. It was heavily rumored that the majority of the homeowners had connections at one time or another to organized crime. While these rumors had not been proven, some things were evident. The neighborhood was quiet, had a nearly nonexistent crime rate, and great Italian restaurants. We ordered our food and settled in to talk about Audrey, Joyce, her husband, and us. We all agreed that the focus and most important consideration was Audrey.

"Joyce, Kim and I have prayed and talked quite a bit about this conversation that we are about to start," I said.

"I have thought about it a lot, too."

"As you know, Audrey has moved about quite a bit. That was a concern of ours," I said.

"I know that better than you could ever imagine. It has long been a concern of mine, too. I am afraid that I have not protected Audrey well enough over the years. The best thing that I knew to do was to let her live with my mother whenever a conflict arose."

"Now all of us have an opportunity to do what is best for Audrey," Kim added.

"Are you saying that you don't want her to come home with me?"

"Not at all," I interjected. "We love Audrey and would want very much for her to live with us for the rest of her adolescent life. But, God has revealed that it would be best for her to rejoin you in North Carolina. The only question is how to tell her that. She is finally getting comfortable with us and her position in this family. It's a delicate situation."

"So what do we do?" Joyce asked. "It was my hope that I could tell her tonight or tomorrow morning then start making arrangements to get her in school before this semester was over," she said.

"I suggest that we start with agreeing on the date that she will be with you. We can then back up to when we tell her, how we tell her, and making plans for her move," I said.

"We're already at the end of October. Wouldn't it make the most sense to let her finish this semester here then move to North Carolina?" Kim reasoned.

"That does make some sense," Joyce agreed.

"And, let's not rush into telling Audrey. If you agree, Joyce, let's give it a couple of days or so after you leave to tell her. Since she will not be leaving with you tomorrow, it may be a little confusing to make the announcement to her and then you leave. What do you think?" Kim continued.

"Again, that makes a lot of sense. So, we've agreed that Audrey will come at the end of the semester. Let's agree to talk a couple of days after I get back," Joyce said.

"Agreed. Now, tell us about you. We know that this must be very difficult."

"It is. But honestly, I have not thought about me very much. I have been thinking mostly about Audrey and her siblings in North Carolina. Will they get along as well as they did prior to this confusion? My husband received a sentence of 20 years. So this is serious. They will be grown with their own kids by the time he is released. When we visit him, I obviously won't take Audrey? What will she or the kids think?"

"Before you get too far down the road, let's focus on you for a minute," Kim counseled. "It is in times like these that you need the direction of the Holy Spirit more than ever before. You always need Him. But, deep valley experiences such as this one is usually when it becomes clear to us that we need His help most. Can I pray for you now?"

"Please do."

Kim started, "Please don't take this the wrong way, but have you accepted Jesus Christ as your Lord and Savior?"

"I have and thank you for asking."

"Glory to God. Father, in the name of Jesus Christ of Nazareth, we come boldly before Your throne of grace expressing our love for You. You are a wonderful God and we exalt Your Holy Name. We lift up our sister, Joyce, to You, God. We plead the blood of Jesus over her mind, body, soul, and spirit. I pray that the anointing falls upon her during this season of seeking direction from You. According to Your word, the yokes of guilt, oppression, and sexual immorality surrounding this situation are destroyed because of the anointing."

While Kim was praying, Joyce began to weep and praise God uncontrollably. God's presence consumed that booth. Kim was crying. I stood, raised my hands, looked toward heaven, and worshipped God. In the midst of the worship, God gave me a word of knowledge concerning her husband.

"Joyce, God has revealed to me that your husband has a demonic spirit of a pedophile. He wants to repent but he does not know how. In fact, God says that he was molested by his stepfather."

"How did you know that? My husband never told anybody that. It never came up in the trial and he didn't volunteer it. But, it is true. He told me that many years ago."

"I didn't know it but the Holy Spirit did. He revealed it to me. Such revelations are not to be judgmental, however. Now that we know it, we must help him as best we can. When he admits that he needs and wants help, we can help him. You can help him."

"Can we pray for him now?"

"Yes. Lord God, we lift up our brother to You in the name of Jesus. Our prayer is that You remove the scales from his eyes so that he can see. Encourage him, Lord, to seek You. I pray that You place someone in his path that will reveal the truth of Your grace and mercy to him. Show him Your mercy,

God. Direct him to Your word. Teach him repentance. I pray that whenever Joyce opens her mouth to him that You give her words that fearlessly proclaim Your mysteries. I pray that his ears are opened to hear You speak through all that You place in his path. It is in the name of Jesus Christ that I pray. Amen."

We left that restaurant super excited. There was no doubt in our minds that if anyone went into that booth after we left, the anointing of God would immediately arrest them. That same anointing went with us as a fire by night as we picked up the kids and went home for the evening.

Joyce left the next day. That weekend was a turning point in the relationship amongst all of us. Bonding became stronger between Joyce and the kids, Joyce and us, and us and the kids. Within a couple of days, we were on the phone to each other. However, since Thanksgiving was only a couple of weeks away, we agreed that Joyce would give Audrey the news when she visited for that holiday. She had not yet told Audrey of the verdict, either. That would give the two of them plenty of time to talk about all of those things.

Audrey was on a plane immediately after school on the Wednesday before Thanksgiving. She arrived in time to help her mother with the next day's dinner. Joyce wasted no time talking to Audrey. She wisely wanted as much time as she could get over the remaining few days to talk. "Audrey, the trial ended a couple of weeks ago."

"Really. What happened? Did they let him go?"

"No. They found him guilty. The jury agreed that you were telling the truth. They carefully reviewed your video testimony and your documents as key evidence. They also found several inconsistencies in his testimony. His attorney's cross examination of you on video also helped to convince the jury of the truth."

"Yippee!!!! Does that mean I can come home, now? Can I, Mom? Can I? Can I? Please!!"

"Of course, you can. Don't you want to know more about the trial?"

"Nope. I just want to come home. I don't care as long as he won't be around me."

"You will not have to worry about that for a very long time. He will be in prison for 20 years."

"Yippee!!! When can I come home?"

"We'll have to talk to your Dad. But, I think very soon."

"You think Dad will mind? I like living with Dad and Kim probably better than any place that I have lived except with you."

"I know that he will understand. In fact, we talked about the possibility very recently. If you want it, I bet you could be here by the end of this semester."

"I want it. I want it. Yippee!"

It was a bittersweet time when Audrey left at the end of the semester. However, everyone understood it was best. The kids were especially sad. After a rough start, Tiffany and Audrey had grown close. Although Billy didn't like having two big sisters to boss him around, he had grown very fond of Audrey, too. Kim and I would miss settling disputes between the girls and Audrey's great big smile. Yet, we knew that a bond had been established that could now never be broken.

About a month after Audrey left, Kim and I saw our pastor after a Sunday Service.

"How are you guys doing now that Audrey has been gone for a while?"

An entirely unexpected lump came into my throat as I opened my mouth to respond. I wanted to say fine. However, the silence prompted her to invite us to stop by to see her during the following week. When we did, it was obvious that Audrey's leaving was affecting all of us but especially me much more than I initially thought. I was feeling like I had found a lost possession only to lose it again. Pastor agreed that allowing her to go back to Joyce was the best thing for all concerned. Her recommendation was to recognize the sovereignty of God and let go. Then, turn our focus to worship and completing his preordained assignments for us.

****

During this season at school, Billy was playing basketball while Tiffany ran indoor track. Kim and I both got involved in their activities. I coached Billy's YMCA team while Kim was a scorekeeper. For Tiffany's track meets, Kim clocked the races while I judged the lanes. One Saturday was incredible. We knew something special was about to happen when during our morning devotion at home; the Holy Spirit's presence was so strong that all of us could only sit completely quiet for about twenty minutes. Afterward, I prayed for supernatural protection and divine revelation. I covered us with the full armor of God and asked for His divine favor. Then, things happened.

The rules at the YMCA required all participants and spectators to leave their winter coats in the locker rooms due to a shortage of space in the upstairs gym. This day, one of the spectators challenged the rule and drew the attention of one of the coaches.

"Hey. You with the coat! Son, the rules state that you should leave your coat down stairs in the locker room. You know better. Now take that coat back down stairs."

The young man was about thirteen years old and wearing a heavy three quarters length jacket. It was one of those athletic team jackets with a hood that both zipped and buttoned in the front. When the coach got his attention, the young man unzipped his jacket. As he stood facing the coach, the scorer's table, and the team benches, with his left hand he pulled his jacket back to reveal a 45-caliber pistol tucked into his left waistband. With his right hand, he pulled his jacket back to reveal a 9mm pistol tucked into his right waistband. He told the coach,

"If you want me to take off this jacket, come and make me."

People started to scatter as soon as he revealed the 45. They ran out the front door, the back exit, and through the adjacent gym. The floor was crowded with players, parents, and friends. I grabbed Billy and Kim and pushed them toward the adjacent gym. Two of the coaches who were behind the teenager rushed him in an attempt to disarm him.

He pulled out the 9mm before they could stop him. He got off two shots.

"Bam. Bam."

One grazed the left shoulder of the coach while the other hit the ceiling. They wrestled him down to the floor and took the guns away. There was pandemonium. Kids were screaming. Chairs and balls were everywhere. And, who knows why the fire alarm went off. Within minutes, the paramedics and police officers were on the scene. They handcuffed the teenager and took him away. The coach was bandaged and taken to the hospital.

"Kim, Billy. Are you guys alright?"

"We're shaken up pretty badly. But, physically, we are OK. What happened in there?" She asked.

"The best I can tell is that the young man was apparently high on drugs. In addition, he was upset with another teenager whom he suspected would be at the gym today. When the coach confronted him about the rules for coats, the kid went off." I told her.

"That was scary. It is just another example of what drugs are doing to our young generation. When you mix the drugs with anger and guns, death is lurking ever so near," she said.

"Are you OK, Billy?" I asked.

"Yes sir! But, why was he so angry?"

"It is difficult to know the full story. It was clear that drugs were involved. A lesson for you is to steer clear of drugs and anyone who is involved with drugs. Nothing good ever comes from those who get trapped in that life style."

Kim then said, "Let's go to the track meet. I would rather go home. But we committed to Tiffany and her coach that we would help out today."

The track meet at the high school was only about three miles away. It didn't take us very long to get there. All of us were still shaken. We decided not to mention any of the activity from the YMCA until after the meet. Since the basketball games were cancelled, we arrived at the track meet earlier than planned. Tiffany didn't ask any questions, though. She was just happy to see us.

It was nearing the end of the track season. The runners were peaking as they prepared for the upcoming State track meet. Intensity grew with each passing weekend. This meet was no different. It was a big one with over twenty schools competing from across the state. Tiffany competed in the 200 Meter Dash, 400 Meter Dash, and ran anchor legs on the 4 x 200 meter relay, and 4 x 400 meter relay teams. In her first meet as a Freshman in high school, she established the school record in the 200 meters at 25.4. She had been running great all season. She felt good and was favored in both the 200 meters and the 400 meters. However, runners from Cooley High and Stamford West had been closing in on her. The three of them had finished 1, 2, and 3 in both events in the last three meets with Tiffany taking first twice and coming in second once.

The finals of the 200 meters came first.

"Runners on your mark......" The starter's gun was up.

"Set....."

"Bang"

Those eight young girls came flying out the blocks and around the curve. Tiffany was in lane 4 flanked by Cooley High in lane 3 and Stamford West in lane

5. She had a good start but the other two girls came out quicker. Tiffany was pressing on the backstretch to catch Stamford West while Cooley High was on her left shoulder in a flash. I could see her relax her face at the top of the second curve. I knew she was about to switch into another gear.

"Pump…. Pump… Pump…." I yelled. The stadium was in an uproar. Everyone was on their feet as the three of them rounded the curve and headed for the tape. Cooley High had edged ahead of Tiffany coming out of the curve while Stamford West maintained her stagger. Then, Tiffany kicked it into another gear. Her knees seemed to lift higher and her legs turned over quicker. It was like she turned on booster rockets.

"Ooooooh….. Oooooh." The crowd buzzed. She surged ahead a meter, then three, then five and broke the tape at 24.8 seconds!

"Wow, look at this time!!" Kim said while jumping like a jackrabbit. "Can this be right?"

It was right. Tiffany had just run the fastest time in the state not only this year but ever. It was a new state record. She was excited. The team was excited. The fans were excited. There were cheers everywhere as she took a victory lap around the track. This race set the stage for an incredible day.

The girls from Cooley High and Stamford West were happy for her but they were determined more than ever now to beat her in the 400 meters. It was just that kind of competition that made for a very exciting track meet. In the 400 meters, the three girls were stacked in the same three lanes except Tiffany was now in lane 3. On this 200-meter oval track, they ran the first lap in their lanes before breaking to the pole on the second lap. Again, Cooley High held the pole position at the sound of the gun on the second lap. The split time was 26.5. They were cooking. Stamford West who was in the third position quickly ran around both of the other two girls to take the lead down the backstretch. Tiffany tried to come back but she was boxed in. These girls were moving with each determined to win. Tiffany was forced to run wide in the last curve but pulled even at the top of the home stretch. She was running strong but so were the girls from Cooley High and Stamford West. Nor was there going to be a burst this time like it was in the 200 meters. Running wide took care of that. The three were running neck and neck. All three were relaxed. So, you could tell they were running a very fast time. With 40 meters to go, Tiffany began to inch ahead. The crowd was screaming so loud that I could hardly hear myself yell my typical "Pump…. Pump… Pump," to Tiffany. Stamford West drew back even. Cooley High was barely a step behind. The stadium was yelling madly for their favorite runners. At 20 meters, the positions didn't change. "Pump… Pump… Pump…!" At 10 meters, Cooley High drew at little closer. "Pump… Pump… Pump…!" At 5 meters all three girls started to lean. All were running strong. All three ran through the tape. No one pulled up short or faltered in their stride.

The judges had clocked the winner at 54.5 seconds, a new state record. The other two received identical times of 54.6 seconds. It took reviewing the pictures from this photo finish to determine that Tiffany had done it again. She now had two state records in one meet with a couple of relays to go. The girls from Cooley High and Stamford West had incredible days, too. All three had pushed each other to personal bests.

In the 2 x 200 meter relay, the team from Cooley High took first place with a time of 1:45.1. Stamford West won the 4 x 400 meter relay with a time of 3:54.5. Tiffany's team finished second in both races.

What a day this had been. We were caught up in the excitement of both the activity at the YMCA and the track meet. It wasn't until we had time to relax that we reflected on the morning's time in devotion. God had done as we asked. He provided both supernatural protection and divine favor.

About three months previous to these events, God had favored Kim and me with teaching a 7th and 8th grade Sunday school class. This age group was both fun and a challenge. These transition years were difficult for both sexes. However, the boys seemed to be in greater danger of physical violence. As God would have it, the lesson that Sunday was on the beatitudes. The eight groups of blessed people from Matthew chapter 5 generated a lively discussion. The boys were especially interested in the meek, merciful, and peacemakers. How could they really be blessed?

As Kim began explaining the scriptures, I couldn't help but reflect on how similar the shooting had been to my own personal experiences with drugs while in college. As I looked back on that experience, it became crystal clear to me just how much God had divinely intervened to protect me from myself. He shielded me from what could have been a heinous crime. He shook me yet kept me for a greater work in His kingdom. What a blessing! Kim and I prayed for the young man at the YMCA to receive God's blessings. We also received greater insight into just how important it was that these young souls understood at an early age that a focus on Jesus Christ was of paramount importance.

9

God Hears You

What a wonderful God we serve. Just think about it. He knew your trials before the foundations of the earth were established. He prepared you to deal with them. He opened a channel to allow you to communicate directly with Him. Let me encourage you that He hears you. Just listen to some of His promises.

- 1 Peter 3:12- "For the eyes of the Lord are on the righteous and his ears are attentive to their prayer, but the face of the Lord is against those who do evil."

- Proverbs 15:29- "The LORD is far from the wicked but he hears the prayer of the righteous."

- Job 22:27-"You will pray to him, and he will hear you, and you will fulfill your vows."

- Psalm 55:17-"Evening, morning and noon I cry out in distress, and he hears my voice."

- 1 John 5:14 – 15- "This is the confidence we have in approaching God: that if we ask anything according to his will, he hears us. And if we know that he hears us—whatever we ask—we know that we have what we asked of him.

- Jeremiah 29:12-"Then you will call upon me and come and pray to me, and I will listen to you."

Isn't it comforting to know that our God hears us? While it may appear at times that He has not heard us, we have His word on it that He does. He even hears us before we call to Him. When you are thinking about calling on God, He hears you. He answers before you are aware of His answer. (Isaiah 65:24 - "Before they call I will answer; while they are still speaking I will hear.") What a wonderful God we serve.

****

Later the following year, I attended another session of Apostolic and Prophetic training. I was not sure why I was so interested in the prophetic. After the last session, I had developed a yearning to receive more. I went to Texas again. However this time seven members of our church, including Kim and I attended.

"Get ready for an awe inspiring time with the Lord," I told her.

"I'm ready," she said.

I was prepared this time for just about anything from God. My expectations of high praise and worship were met to excess. Kim's expectations matched mine. She too was infused with the glory of God throughout this session. God had impressed upon me to join Kim in module one. That meant retaking the first session, but I had no qualms.

God continued to show us through activations that when you are in the company of prophets, it is a great deal easier to hear from God and speak His word. The format for the week was pretty much the same as before. High praise and worship was followed by training and activations. Kim and the other five participants were able to experience firsthand what I had tried to explain to them from my earlier trip. It was now real to them. The session on the spiritual significance of praise and worship again captivated most of the first time participants. Our group was no different. They were exuberant about the teaching. While I was refreshed and renewed, my focus this time was on those horns. The more I heard them blow, the more I knew that I had to have one.

"Kim, I want one of those horns."

"That would be great. But Willie, you have never played an instrument of any kind in your life. How do you expect to blow that ram's horn?"

"I don't know. I just know that I have to get one. God will take care of teaching me."

By the end of the week, I had secured all the information that I needed to get me a horn. I couldn't wait until I got home to order it. On the last day of the week, Kim and I received our prophecies together. It focused not only on continued unity in our marriage but also unity in our ministry to God. The spoken word challenged us to get our house in order as God was releasing us to minister together in unexpected ways.

Kim and I returned from the apostolic and prophetic conference with a renewed zeal and inspiration to press on. Our life was full of changes. God was at work in some very powerful ways. But what was the full meaning of what was going on? We shared with the other five participants of the conference and with others at the church. We had been stretched but felt very good about it.

"Kim what did you really think about the conference?"

"Now I understand why you were so pumped up the first time you came back. God has given me a greater insight into His word, His character and His ways. I did not give much thought to the prophetic before. But now I see God at work in the prophetic. There is so much more to learn."

"Yeah, there is and I am drawn to know it!"

****

Summer seemed to come early that year. The New York oceanfront was teaming with activity as usual. It was one of the favorite places that our family visited on hot days. On any given day, there was music, sidewalk minstrels, art shows, fireworks, picnics, or a multitude of other things to do. Nearly all of it was fun. But, I can remember one Saturday afternoon when I took the family to the park for a picnic. There must have been tens of thousands in the park that day because of an annual food fest. Tiffany and Billy had just returned from picking up a variety of foods when we heard a rumbling.

"What's that?" Kim asked.

"I can feel the ground shaking," Billy exclaimed.

The sound and the shaking grew louder and louder. Then we heard screams. We all sat up on the blanket and looked around to see where the noise was coming from. It grew louder and louder. The ground was trembling now like an earthquake. The screams were getting closer. We stood up anxiously scanning the horizon. People all around us were now standing looking in the direction of the screams. Then in a flash, we saw it. There was a stampede of people coming directly toward us. We could not see what was causing them to run so fast and wildly. We just knew that we had to get out of the way or be trampled.

"Run Tiffany and Billy, Run!!" shouted Kim.

"Wait a minute!" I yelled as I grabbed the two of them by the shoulders. "This way!"

Rather than run straight ahead in front of the stampeding crowd, I rushed Kim and the kids across the path and away from the mass of rolling humanity. Most of the people ran straight ahead as the crowd continued to build like a snowball rolling down the side of a hill. We got far enough away to stop and look back at what was going on. Then, as suddenly as it started, the stampede stopped. There was nothing in pursuit of the people. No earthquake was happening. No automobile was out of control. No mad dog. Nothing.

I could see a few of the people in the front of the crowd stooped over in laughter. Then it dawned on me that this was all a dangerous prank. Some youngsters stood, took off running while screaming stampede, and others joined them until there was a great rush of people running across the park. This kind of prank had been sweeping the country this particular summer. We never dreamed that we might be caught up in the middle of one. Thank God that no one was hurt.

The event upset us enough, however, to pack our belongings and leave for the day. The initial focus of our conversation during the drive home was this silly and dangerous prank of stampeding the crowd. However, before long we had turned our attention to another family outing planned for a couple of weeks from that weekend. We were going horse-back riding. This was a favorite of mine since my childhood. I reminisced riding with my brothers and cousins. The kids listened intently as I told of daring rides across the countryside and an occasional wild ride as a result of startled horses.

"Where are we going to ride this time, Dad?" Billy asked.

"I believe we'll go to Connecticut. There is plenty of open space out there and the owners will usually let experienced riders leave the trail for some adventure."

"Good. Then we can race Dad," said Billy. "I bet I can beat you, now!"

"Maybe so. But not if I get a good horse. I have been riding a long time and I know all the tricks," I told him.

"Yeah, but your tricks can't beat me. I'm going to ask the owner for his fastest horse."

"We'll see what happens in a couple of days."

Over the course of the remaining drive home, the family continued in conversation while I drifted into thoughts about them. I had always enjoyed family outings of any sort. The interactions with the kids were especially important to me. I am sure that the absence of my father in my early childhood had an influence on my desire to spend time with my children. I am just as sure that as I grew in Christ, the importance of family became clearer to me. I was learning that I am the priest of my home. As such, I am to teach my children of the atoning sacrifice of Jesus Christ. I am to bring them up in the training and instruction of the Lord. In addition, as father and husband, one of my key responsibilities is to provide for their sustenance and safety.

So, in the midst of the sounds, I was caught up in a day vision. I could see our family living in modest but very comfortable surroundings. There was a red fence around the property that seemed to extend for miles. It was about twenty feet tall with seven gates. Each of three sides of the property had two gates while the front of the property had a huge gate with marble pillars on each side. It was arched with a trellis full of roses. Each of the side gates was identical in size. They were rather narrow and looked like French paneled doors from a distance. Yet, they were separate gates. The pathway leading to the house from each gate was made of individual stones. Each stone was of a different size and color. They were all beautiful and bright. The grass was a lush green and manicured. There were trees along the pathways and surrounding the house. The rest of the property was an open field. At the back was a barn and corral with seven gorgeous white stallions. The house was relatively small given the boundary size of the property. However, it was sufficiently spacious. There was plenty of room for us to come together as a family or enjoy quiet times in a closet of our own. The furniture was conventional with a sprinkling of soft desert colors.

While we were at peace within our home, we could see that outside of the gates, storms of different kinds were brewing all over the place. There were snowstorms, rainstorms, hailstorms, windstorms, and lightning storms. But, none came near our gates.

"Willie!! Willie!! Did you hear me?" Kim asked as she awakened me from my day-dream.

"Yeah. Yeah. I was just thinking. That's all," I responded.

"I want you to stop at the grocery store on the way home."

"OK. No problem."

All of us went in to the shop. Kim only needed to pick up a few items but going in was better than just sitting in the car waiting on her. So, away we went. Once inside, Billy noticed a large poster advertising a raffle from one of the food companies whose first prize was a free trip for the family to Disney World. He wouldn't rest until Kim picked up items that qualified her to enter the drawing. She filled out the raffle, dropped it in the box, and then forgot about it.

Two weekends later, we all drove out to Connecticut to ride horses. As we drove up to the gate, I could hardly believe my eyes. It was a huge arching gate with broad stone pillars on each side. The driveway curved around a small grove of trees through which we could see a relatively small ranch house. There was a huge open field surrounding the house with a herd of horses roaming freely. The stables were in back with several horses already saddled. While it was not exactly what I saw in the day vision, it was close enough to confirm in my spirit that this was the place I had seen in my dream.

I now tried to remember as much of that dream as I could for I knew that God was trying to tell me something about this trip before we got here. I vaguely remembered beauty, peace, and storms outside the gates.

The owner checked us in then gave us instructions. He would go out with us so that we would know where the trails were. However, there were relatively few restrictions for those who knew how to ride. We each were required to wear helmets. But other than that, once the trails were pointed out, we were free to ride. One word of caution was that if we chose to run the horses in the direction of the ranch, it was likely that their speed would pick up and stopping them could be a challenge.

Tiffany and Kim opted to stay close to the owner and ride slowly on the trails soaking in nature. Billy wanted to make good on his challenge to beat me in a race. As soon as we cleared the initial grove of trees, he was ready.

"You ready, Dad?"

"Yeah. There is another grove of trees about three hundred yards to the north. The first one over the ridge just in front of them wins. Ready?"

"I'm ready," he said.

"Go!"

I kicked my horse in his back legs then pulled tight on the reigns to make him rise up. Billy took off pushing his horse as fast as he could. I knew that I could catch him. And, I wanted it to be both competitive and fun for him. I let him take a slight lead. While the experience of the riders mattered, the strength, savvy, and hearts of the horses would determine much of the outcome. So I couldn't let him get too far ahead.

"I'm on top of you now, son. You had better run!"

"No way you're gonna catch me this time, Dad."

At about one hundred and fifty yards, I could see a small black stream of smoke rising just above the treetops in the distance.

"Slow up Billy."

"Not this time Dad. I got you this time."

"I mean it son. Slow up. There's trouble. Look ahead."

He looked up to see the same black smoke as I did. We brought the horses to a slow trot then a walk. We came to a full stop and took a good look at the smoke. I could tell that a fire had broken out. The only question was whether or not it was under control. I told Billy to turn around and go find the others. He should get his mother and sister back to the ranch house and send the owner out here to me. I would ride a little closer to see if I could determine the nature of the fire.

My horse was a little nervous as I trotted him toward the smoke. At about fifty yards out, he started to prance. I was able to maintain a tight rein and walk him a little closer. I could now see through the trees that a wild fire was burning in the underbrush.

I whipped my horse around and took off for the ranch house. As I did so, that horse sped like he was in the Kentucky derby. I remembered the caution from earlier. The horse would run extremely fast in this direction and stopping him would be a challenge. Nonetheless, at this point, I was not concerned about stopping him. I wanted to get to a phone as fast as I could to call the fire department. As I approached the trees surrounding the ranch house, the owner was racing toward me from one of the side gates. He was motioning for me to slow down.

I pulled as hard as I could to stop that horse. Initially, he was having none of that.

"Whoa! Whoa!" I yelled as I pulled back even harder. About this time, the owner had reached me. He rode in my direction and grabbed the reins, too. Between the two of us, we were able to stop the horse although he remained a little anxious.

"I got the word from your son," he said. "My wife has called the fire department. I suggest that you get back to the ranch house with your family and stay put. You'll be safe there. I have already called some of my neighbors who will help me to contain the fire until the fire department gets here. We are familiar with this sort of thing. Don't you worry. Just go be with your family."

I was comforted by his words. Yet, I knew there was even greater comfort in the foreknowledge that God had provided in the daydream from a few days earlier. Inside that gate would be safe. No storm on the outside of it would harm us.

Fortunately, we saw this fire early enough to prevent a catastrophe. The ranchers had contained it to only a few acres by the time the fire department arrived. During the whole time, we prayed with the owner's wife for minimal damage to wild life and property. We pleaded the blood of Jesus over the firefighters and the owner. We were at peace when the anointing of the Holy Spirit came over us. We watched and prayed to see the miracle of God's work.

The underbrush was gone and the land was scorched. A few trees were destroyed. But, not a single animal was lost and no one was hurt. We sat on the front porch and thanked God for His hedge of protection around the ranch house. Nothing came near us.

****

Several months later, Kim got terrific news. We had won the trip to Disney World. The kids, of course, were elated. Tiffany called Audrey right away with the good news.

"Get ready, girl. We're going to Disney World!" Tiffany told her.

"Really? We won? I don't believe it."

"Well, you can just start believing because we won."

"When are we leaving?" Audrey asked.

"I don't know yet. We have a year to take the trip. I think Mom and Dad want to take some time to plan it."

"You think that they would want to go around Thanksgiving or Christmas? I hear it is a lot of fun at that time."

"Who knows? I'd like to check it out though. But honestly, I'll go at anytime. Wouldn't you?"

"Yep. I just hope it's during a holiday when I am supposed to be with Dad anyway. You know. So there won't be any problems."

"Girl, there will not be any problems. Dad will figure it out. You'll see."

Audrey told us of her desire to go during the time she was scheduled to visit us. And, Kim took that into consideration when planning the trip. We decided to go during Thanksgiving holiday. We coordinated flights such that Audrey would meet us at the airport in Florida. The five of us rode in the rental car along the tree-lined roads toward our hotel. The usual excitement of giggles, shouts, pushing, and fussing accompanied our journey. Many of the trees were still green. Billy pressed his nose to the window to both enjoy the scenery and ignore the female chatter between Tiffany and Audrey. What a wonderful time to be both in the warm climate of Florida and to get away with each other.

The drive to the hotel was short but full of images both real and imagined along the way. It seemed as if we saw the advertisements for every theme park, water slide, and resort in the state. Each billboard was more exotic that the others. Three-dimensional graphics of animals and attractions filled the skies. With just a little imagination, you could envision our automobile as one of the cars on an adventure ride in one of the theme parks.

We were greeted at the hotel by a host of attendants. One opened the car doors while another got luggage from the trunk. Still another opened the huge doors to the hotel while yet another asked if I wanted the car to be valet parked. Since parking was included in the award, I gladly flipped the keys to him.

After checking in, we found ourselves in a beautiful two-bedroom suite with a pullout couch. The girls claimed the room with two double beds. Billy had no problem accepting the queen-sized pullout. With their clothes barely in closets and drawers, the three of them rushed out to the pool. Kim and I took our time getting things put away then joined them at poolside. As we sat there just soaking in the sun and relaxing, I noticed that the kids were dunking each other in the water. I wasn't concerned because all of them were very good swimmers. Kim had made a point to enroll them in swimming classes at a very early age. Each could easily swim a few hundred yards without much effort.

At one point, however, both Tiffany and Audrey got out of the pool and walked toward where Billy was treading water in the deep end of the pool. While still playing, they both decided to simultaneously jump in the pool on top of Billy. They were laughing but he had a panicked look on his face. He was surprised as they jumped in on each side of him and thrust him under. They swam away thinking that he would retaliate. But, I could see beneath the water that Billy was in trouble. He was flapping uncontrollably. I immediately dove into the water, went beneath him, grabbed him by his waist, swam to the surface then pushed him to the edge of the pool.

It all happened so quickly that the girls did not know why I had come into the water. They initially thought that I was joining them in play until they got a good look at Billy's face. He and I climbed out of the pool and sat on the side while he gathered his composure.

"What happened?" they asked.

"I don't think Billy was ready for your double attack. Your jumps surprised him and he panicked."

"We're sorry Billy. We didn't mean it."

Billy was still recovering. He shook his head acknowledging and accepting their apology. They sat next to him and hugged and petted until they got a big smile from him. When he got his breath, he stood up to walk toward the diving board. As they followed, he quickly turned and pushed the both of them into the water then ran to the shallow end of the pool laughing all the way.

Of course, Kim who was beside herself took this as a teaching opportunity. She called them all together for the lecture.

"I am glad that all of you are OK. But, I want to share something with you. I want you to see some important lessons in what just happened. First, it is OK to have fun in the water. Actually, it is OK to have fun in many places. But, in the water, you want to be careful how you play. Audrey and Tiffany, you surprised Billy. Had he been looking, he would have been prepared and been able to handle both of you coming at him. The two of you should learn that those to whom you mean no harm should clearly know that no harm is meant before you take an action. Billy, it is wise to be alert especially if you are in a potentially dangerous area like the deep end of the swimming pool. In such places, you may need all of your resources to get you to safety. You don't want any of your resources like your emotions to be compromised. Notice that your Dad took immediate action. When you are in a position to help someone who may be in serious trouble, respond quickly. He could see the danger. There was no question. Therefore, there was no need to ponder an action. He took the action right away. Each of you should learn all of these lessons. We are going to be in Florida for a few days. On some occasions, we may not be with the three of you. A good example of that is when you first came out to the pool. We are relying on you to take care of each other and to take care of yourselves. Will you do that?"

"Yes Maam."

The rest of the trip was wonderful. We visited all of the amusement parks, Sea World, the beach, and a couple of water parks. We took pictures galore. On one occasion we visited a nature park where the majority of the activity was taking pictures. There were beautiful hibiscus plants, palms trees, cypress trees, spider lilies, spring lilies, azaleas, crepe myrtle, philodendron, dieffenbachia, ferns, corn plants, bamboo, bonsai, bromeliads, orchids, blooming violets, mums, roses, begonias, kalanchoe, spathiphyllum, and much, much more. The place was a sea of green with colors everywhere. While focusing on the captivating surroundings, we nearly walked into two precious little three-year-old curly headed children. They were twins.

"Excuse us, Honey," Kim said.

"Hi." "Hi." They both responded.

We looked up to see that their parents were not far away. They had settled onto a public bench and were enjoying the scenery. The twins scampered back to their side.

"You guys enjoying the park?" They asked.

"It is beautiful. Isn't it?" Kim asked.

The parents were in their mid-twenties. They were very casually dressed in contrast to our very obvious tourist attire of shorts, gym shoes, polo shirts, and cameras around our necks. In fact, they looked more like a throw-back to the 'hippie' dress of the mid-1960's. She had on bell bottomed pants with a peasant blouse and flowers in her hair. He had on bell-bottoms, too. He was also wearing a tunic shirt with a leather headband. Both had moccasins on their feet.

"It sure is. You been here on vacation long?" The mother asked.

It was obvious that they were friendly and desired some conversation.

So we strolled over to them. That was fine with Audrey, Tiffany, and Billy for the twins now captivated them.

"Not long. Just a few days. My name is Kim. This is my husband Willie, and our children Audrey, Tiffany, and Billy," Kim continued.

"My name is Bonnie. This is Richard. You have already met the twins, Kelly and Richie."

"We're glad to meet you. You been here long?" Kim asked.

"Actually, we live near here. We like to come to this park. It is so beautiful. It gets us so close to nature."

"I bet it is great to be so close. How far away do you live?"

"Not far. We are just up the road. We park our van on the beach most nights. Every now and then, we rent a spot in a trailer park for a week or two."

Kim and I took quick looks at each other. We knew in our spirits that this encounter was going to be out of the ordinary.

"Richard and I are immensely concerned about the conservation of wildlife and preservation of the environment. So, living here in Florida is a dream for us."

"Are there any particular issues that you and Richard are focused on at the moment?"

"No. We just know that nature is good. Animals are good. Everything and everyone is good. Being in an environment like this is nourishing to our souls."

"I am so glad to hear that. Willie and I are interested in improving world conditions, battling injustices, and proclaiming the truth, too." Kim answered.

"Really? Then we are kindred spirits," she said.

"Well, I pray that is so. May I ask you a question?" Kim was now on a mission.

"Sure. Go right ahead."

"Who is Jesus Christ to you?"

"Richard and I know all about God. God is everywhere. He is in nature. He is in us. He is in you, too. Don't you think?"

"It is true that I have a personal relationship with God. But, if you don't mind, I am still interested in who Jesus Christ is to you. Who is He?"

"Look there are several religions that speak very well of Jesus. We are familiar with many of them. Jesus was a very good person. We don't have any problems with Jesus."

"Have you accepted Him as your personal Lord and Savior?"

"What do you mean?"

"Do you believe that He died on the cross for our sins? Do you believe in your heart that God raised Him from the dead as the propitiation for our sins? And have you proclaimed out of your mouth that Jesus is your Lord?"

"I don't know about all that. I mean, we don't hurt anyone. We basically mind our own business. Other than taking a stand for the rights of nature, we generally leave other people alone. We sort of believe that if we just keep doing good, God will understand."

"Bonnie, do you have a Bible?" Kim pressed.

"I don't think so. We use to have one. But I haven't seen it in a while."

"I want to give you some encouragement. First, we have a bible back in our car. Once we are finished with our conversation, if you would like to have it, I welcome you to it. Next, God is a Holy God. Do you know what that means?"

"I think so. He's good, right?"

"It's more than that. To be Holy is to be sacred, undefiled, consecrated, and pure. In the context of our daily lives, it means to be without sin. It is to be blameless. So a Holy God, our God will not live in the midst of any amount of sin. He is Holy."

"OK. But, we don't sin. We don't lie or steal or cheat or kill people. We're good people."

"When you get the Bible, I want you to read a few scriptures. The first is Romans 3:23. It says for all have sinned and fall short of the glory of God."

"Everybody?"

"Everybody! You see sin means to miss the perfect standard of holiness that God has set for us. No matter how good we try to be, we have inherent in us a sinful nature."

"How can that be?"

"In Genesis is the account of Adam and Eve who chose to disobey God. When they did, these perfectly created beings became corrupt with sin. This corruption became a part of their nature. This nature was passed on to their children through their blood. Then to their children's children and so on, throughout all generations."

"Yeah. But, I still don't see the sin in us. Surely little Kelly and Richie don't sin."

"While I believe God has a special concern and place for innocent children like Kelly and Richard who may die in their innocence, remember that sin is missing the perfect standard of holiness that God set. That means any rebellion, gossip, sexual sins, placing other things before God, swearing, using God's name improperly, hatred, discord, jealousy, fits of rage, selfish ambition, dissensions, factions, envy, drunkenness, orgies, and much, much more are sins committed against God. Anyone who has ever committed a sin is tainted and cannot live in eternity with a Holy God."

"Nobody can be that perfect."

"That's my point. Romans 6:23 says, "For the wages of sin is death, but the gift of God is eternal life in Christ Jesus our Lord.""

"What does that mean?"

"It means that God made a way for your sins and mine to be forgiven. God requires a sinless perfect sacrifice for our sins. The Holy Spirit conceived Jesus who is not a bloodline descendant of Adam. So the tainted blood of Adam was not passed on to Him. Jesus Christ was sent here by God to be executed on a cross, that is, to die in your place and mine. By accepting Jesus Christ as Lord, we can have eternal life with God. Another confirming scripture is Romans 5:8. "But God demonstrates his own love for us in this: While we were still sinners, Christ died for us.""

I could see that both Bonnie and Richard were very interested in what Kim was telling them. Both looked very intently at her while she continued.

"There is hope for all of us as a result of what Jesus Christ did on that cross and His subsequent ascension into heaven. That is why I asked you who Jesus Christ was to you. It is essential that you decide who will pay for your sins. Will you do it? Or will you allow Jesus Christ to do it for you?"

"So, what must we do to allow Jesus to pay for our sins?" They both asked.

"I am going to give you a series of key scriptures. Afterwards, I have a life giving question to ask you."

Kim then quoted Ephesians 2:8 – 9, John 1:12, Romans 10:9 – 10, and Romans 10:13.

Ephesians 2:8 – 9 - "For it is by grace you have been saved, through faith—and this not from yourselves, it is the gift of God - not by works, so that no one can boast."

John 1:12 - "Yet to all who received him, to those who believed in his name, he gave the right to become children of God."

Romans 10:9–10 - "That if you confess with your mouth, "Jesus is Lord," and believe in your heart that God raised him from the dead, you will be saved. For it is with your heart that you believe and are justified, and it is with your mouth that you confess and are saved.""

Romans 10:13 - "For everyone who calls on the name of the Lord will be saved."

"Now, I have to ask you. Do you both want to accept Jesus Christ as your Lord and Savior?"

"Yes, we do!"

"Hallelujah!!! If the following prayer confesses the desires in your heart, then repeat it aloud right now. Oh, God, I know I am a sinner. I believe Jesus was my substitute when He died on the cross at Calvary. I believe His shed blood, death, burial, and resurrection were for me. I repent of my sins. I now receive Him as my Lord and Savior. I know without a doubt that you raised Him from the dead. I thank you for the forgiveness of my sins, the gift of salvation and everlasting life. I am a new creature in Christ Jesus. It is all because of Your merciful grace. Amen."

"Is that it? Is it that simple?" they asked.

"It is that simple," Kim said. "If you meant what you prayed, then you are saved. You may not feel much different yet, but God has now forgiven all of your past sins. He sees you through the blood of Christ."

"Now what do we do?"

"Let's go get that Bible. The both of you must read it, meditate on the words, pray and ask God to give you wisdom and revelation knowledge concerning what you have read. A good place to start is the book of John. Then, ask God to lead you to the right local church where you can fellowship with others who believe as you now do. Finally, tell others about God's saving grace and forgiveness through Jesus Christ."

****

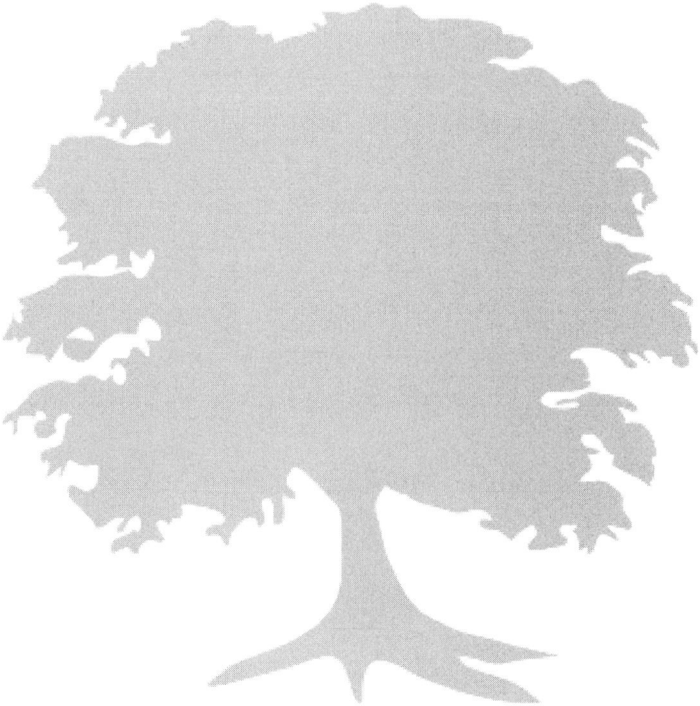

10

Enter The Most Holy Place

I have an encouraging word for you today. It is a reminder that you can enter the Most Holy Place. You have God's word on it. Check out Hebrews 10:19 - 25. "Therefore, brothers, since we have confidence to enter the Most Holy Place by the blood of Jesus, by a new and living way opened for us through the curtain, that is, his body, and since we have a great priest over the house of God, let us draw near to God with a sincere heart in full assurance of faith, having our hearts sprinkled to cleanse us from a guilty conscience and having our bodies washed with pure water. Let us hold unswervingly to the hope we profess, for he who promised is faithful. And let us consider how we may spur one another on toward love and good deeds. Let us not give up meeting together, as some are in the habit of doing, but let us encourage one another—and all the more as you see the Day approaching."

As with all of God's word, these verses are full of divine messages. There are three of you who need the following separate but related messages.

To the first person. You can go directly into the throne room yourself. The blood of Jesus covers your sin. Appropriate the blood, confess the sin, repent of it, seek forgiveness, turn from it then go to the Master's throne room.

To the second person. You are at odds with a relative. Rather than brood, stir her up. Encourage her to be all that God has planned for her. Neither you nor she is destined to sit on your gifts. You be the encourager.

To the third person. Your church assembly has turned you momentarily sour. Do not forsake the assembly. You can find both encouragement and give encouragement in that place. Remember the final words of this section of God's Holy Word. The final days are approaching.

****

Over the next few years, Kim and I were honored to visit many states and several different countries around the world. God had prospered us financially. Kim's financial training combined with her excellent discernment positioned our family to take advantage of growth in the financial markets. Her wise investments in growth stocks and mutual funds catapulted our portfolio beyond our wildest dreams. She didn't stop there. She made real estate investments that seemed to grow exponentially. Commercial property was her specialty. In addition, we both were scaling the corporate ladders with our respective employers.

We were in a position to take a major trip at least once a year. We visited Hawaii, the Caribbean Islands, Mexico, Canada, Germany, Scotland, Australia, Japan, Italy, Ghana, Cote d'Ivoire, Ethiopia, and South Africa. We were planning a trip to Jerusalem when fighting broke out in the Middle East. So, we accepted wise counsel to delay the visit until another time. With each trip, God opened our spiritual eyes to see His mighty hand at work. God was giving us a holy boldness to speak His word wherever we went. We were growing in God's grace and others could see it in our lives. It was amazing to many of my high school and college classmates that my zeal for life was now directed toward telling the world about Christ. There was a point in time, however, when I was not as careful in watching and praying as I should have been. Pride started to seep in.

I remember the occasion when we were returning home from South Africa. Kim and I were seated in a middle row of five seats across. The gentleman sitting next to us had his Bible opened to the book of Acts. It is important to point out here that while God had been maturing us by his glorious grace; neither Kim nor I had yet received the baptism of the Holy Spirit with the evidence of speaking in tongues.

"I see that you are enjoying God's word from the book of Acts." I spoke.

"Oh, yes. It is a refreshing account of the move of God in the early days of the church,"
He replied.

"It sounds as if you are a child of God. May I ask you a question?"

"Of course," he said.

"Who is Jesus Christ to you?"

"Jesus Christ is the Son of the living God. He is the Messiah. He is my Lord and Savior. He is my rock. He is my salvation. He is my bread of life, my sustenance. Jesus is my all in all. Thank you for asking. Have you and your wife accepted Jesus Christ as your Lord and Savior."

"Yes, we have. And, thank you for asking us," I responded.

"Let me ask you another question. Have you received the baptism of Holy Spirit with the evidence of speaking in tongues?" he asked.

"Well, no. You see, speaking in tongues is not really for today. It was given to the early apostles so that the gospel could be spread. It ceased when the church started to grow," I said confidently.

"Are you sure? Can you show me that in the Bible?" he asked.

"Not right now. I mean, I have not studied the topic very much. But, my wife and I have an intimate relationship with Christ and He has not seen fit to give us any other revelation on it."

"It may be a wise thing for you to study God's word. If you don't have the evidence of speaking in tongues, there may be a question of whether or not you are saved," he said.

When this conversation initially turned to speaking in tongues, I felt a little embarrassed. But, now I was getting offended. This man was questioning my salvation because I did not speak in tongues.

"Look, I can agree to the study of God's word on the subject but your doctrine is way off regarding salvation. Ephesians 2:8 tells me that it is by God's grace and Romans 10:9-10 tells me the conditions under which I can know my salvation. Neither one of them mention salvation by speaking in tongues." I was starting to get testy.

"Let me be honest with you," he said. "The reason that I am studying the book of Acts is to get clarity on the topic. I speak or rather pray in tongues but my wife does not. Given my concern for her, I thought I had better review God's word."

"Good for you," I quipped.

"May I make a suggestion to you?" he asked.

"Sure."

"There are several New Testament verses that address this topic. They are Mark 16:17, Acts 2:2,3,11; Acts 10:46; Acts 19:6; Romans 3:13; Romans 8:26; 1 Corinthians 12:10,28,30; 1 Corinthians 13:1,8; 1 Corinthians chapter 14; Ephesians 6:18; and Jude 17-20. You will also find many more related scriptures that are cross-referenced should you embark on an intensified study. I am just getting started. You may want to take advantage of the long ride home to begin a study of your own."

"Thank you for your suggestion. I will consider it."

I excused myself and turned to Kim. She had heard the conversation and looked at me as if to ask 'What are you going to do now?' I had to think about this. I got up to go to the washroom and stretch my legs a bit.

As I walked the aisles, Holy Spirit worked on me. He convicted me with pride. I did not speak in tongues and my pride did not allow any fresh insight into the topic. Then came offense followed by rebellion. I knew that this was a moment of truth for me but I didn't want to yield. Kim and I had discussed speaking or praying in tongues on several occasions. Our conclusions were based largely on word of mouth and the lack of evidence in our own lives. The implication that I was not saved because I did not pray in tongues really took me overboard. Yet, I knew in my spirit that I had to yield to the suggestion to study God's word. I went back to my seat. As I approached it, I noticed that the gentleman had moved to another row so that he could take a nap. When I sat next to Kim, I told her what I was thinking.

"You know, his suggestion to study what God has to say about tongues is actually a good suggestion," I said.

"Yeah, it really is. If we are as honest as he is, then we have to admit that we have never really looked at the word for ourselves either," she said.

"Let's start now. Do you remember the scriptures?" I asked.

"I am a step ahead of you. I wrote most of them down while he was talking. I looked up the others in the concordance in the back of my bible."

We began with Mark 16:17 and shared the word with each other. We had been traveling for some time now with a laptop computer with several reference books and commentaries that were helpful in our studies. I pulled it out and looked at several bible translations of each scripture. As each scripture contributed a different piece of the puzzle, the picture that was emerging was in stark contrast to our beliefs. This was very difficult to accept. But, here are some of the truths that emerged. Jesus said that every believer would speak in a new tongue.

In the book of Acts, every time a new convert was filled with the Holy Spirit, he spoke in tongues while praising God. No one in Acts spoke to other people in tongues. Rather, the speaking was done to God. There appeared to be two circumstances under which individuals could or would speak in tongues. In one circumstance, Paul describes speaking in tongues to an assembly of believers as a spiritual gift. He also spoke of praying and singing in tongues as a form of communing with God. By the time the plane landed, Kim and I were feeling pretty convicted.

"Well, what do you think now Willie?"

"The evidence is pretty clear that praying or speaking in tongues is both for today, and a gift from God. But, I am still not so sure."

"NOT SURE? What more evidence do you need?"

"I need the evidence of actually doing it. I would like to receive this gift and speak in tongues."

"Me too."

****

After that experience on the plane, it seemed as if the subject of speaking in tongues came up everywhere. Whenever we turned on a Christian television or radio show, the minister of the hour either had a message concerning tongues or pointed the listeners to some study material on speaking in tongues. Both Kim and I continued to listen intently and study the topic. Then, it happened. I had joined the leaders of our church on a Boy Scout camping trip to the woods of Vermont. It was my habit to end my day with reading the scripture and praying. On the second night of the trip after the boys had gone to sleep, I studied 1 Corinthians chapters 12 through 14. I kept hearing in my spirit to covet the best gifts as we are told in 1 Corinthians 12:31.

"God, what are the best gifts?" I prayed.

I meditated on all of chapter 14. My desire for the baptism in the Holy Spirit with the evidence of speaking in tongues had not subsided. I prayed then drifted off to sleep well past midnight without anything happening.

At 3:00am I was awakened with a start. My eyes popped open but I heard no sounds nor saw anything unusual. However, I was wide-awake. I knew that I had to pray about something. But, what was it? There were more than 50 boys and 10 adults with us at the camp. For whom should I pray? About what should I pray? There were about ten tents encircling a burned out campfire. I walked outside with my bible to see if anyone or anything might be there. Nothing!!

I quietly approached a log near the campfire, sat down, and turned on my reading flashlight. There was something that I must pray about, and I still did not know what. As I opened my bible, I remembered Romans 8:26-27. So, I began to pray those scriptures.

"Father God, in the name of Jesus Christ of Nazareth, I give you praise and honor your Holy Name. I stand on your promise God, that the Holy Spirit helps me in my weakness. I hear You God that I am to pray. Yet, I do not know what I ought to pray. I believe that the Holy Spirit knows and intercedes for me now with groans that words cannot express. He searches my heart and knows Your mind. As the Holy Spirit prays and intercedes for me, He prays in accordance with Your perfect will. Hallelujah! Hallelujah! Hallelujah! Hallelujah! Hallelujah! Hallelujah! Hallelujah!"

Then, all of a sudden, bam!!! I started speaking sounds that I could not understand. It shocked me, at first. My mind did not understand what I had said. I stopped for an instant. When I opened my mouth to continue in prayer, the sounds came out again. This time I let it flow. For nearly thirty minutes, all I spoke were words that came out of my spirit. I did not understand a single one of them. Yet I knew that I was now praying God's perfect will. I was praying in a language that He understood. While I didn't understand the words with my mind, the sounds were beautiful. It was a bubbling that came out of me with inflections and tones that were evidence of speaking to God.

When I finished, I knew that my reason for praying had been satisfied. I still did not know what it was. But, I felt an assurance in my spirit that it was done. I was at peace. I went back to my tent, crawled into my sleeping bag, and fell sound asleep with a smile on my face.

The next morning, immediately after breakfast, I had to tell someone. I found my deacon who had come along on the trip and told him all about the previous night. He was as happy for me as I was. I couldn't wait to get home to tell Kim. The rest of this camping trip was an absolute delight for me. We had three more days and nights. Each time I had a private moment to pray, I prayed in this unknown tongue. Although the sounds were not consistent with any foreign language that I knew, I could tell that there was some uniformity in the words. So, I freed my mind and let my spirit pray.

While I was at the camp praying, Kim was at home praying with her mind.

"Willie, I am so glad to hear that you have received praying in tongues," she said.

"Me, too. It was a glorious moment that night and has been wonderful ever since," I responded.

"You know, I have been praying and asking God for the same manifestation of the Holy Spirit in my life. But, it hasn't happened yet."

"I wish I could explain it," I responded. "But, I can't. I just believe in my heart that as you persevere, God will in His own time bless you in this way, too."

As Kim and I continued in conversation, I could not help but to reflect on our plane ride from South Africa. I wondered if our friend's wife had now received the gift of speaking in tongues. If I could see him now, I would thank him for encouraging me to study God's word on the subject.

In the meantime, and about two weeks later, Kim and I were attending a prayer meeting when the subject came up again. As we shared both the excitement of my new gift and our expectation that Kim's would arrive soon, one of the elders pointed out to us that in the book of Acts the baptism of Holy Spirit with the evidence of speaking in tongues often happened when one of the apostles laid hands upon the individuals. He reminded us that not everyone receives the gift in the same way.

"Kim would you like to receive the gift of speaking in tongues?" he asked.

"I sure would," she answered excitedly.

"Then all of us present will pray in agreement that God has released that gift to you. When I lay my hands upon you, I will impart that gift. You will activate it by faith by opening your heart, closing your mind, and speaking with your spirit," he told her.

The elder led us in prayer while we agreed. He praised God and acknowledged Him as the One and Only true God. We agreed. He thanked God for all of His blessings from times past and even now. We agreed. He confessed our corporate sins and repented. We agreed. He acknowledged that Kim was a child of God who had accepted Jesus Christ as Lord and Savior by faith. We agreed. He acknowledged that Kim had heard His word and knew the truth of His word regarding the gift of tongues. We agreed. He declared that Kim believed in her heart and had bypassed her head knowledge regarding the gift of tongues. We agreed. He asked Kim to confess with her own mouth that she had received the gift of tongues. She did so and we agreed with her confession. He then laid hands on Kim and decreed that she had the gift. We agreed. Kim then opened her mouth and out poured a new tongue as Jesus Christ declared in Mark 16:17.

"Hallelujah!" Kim shouted.

We all shouted "Hallelujah. Glory to God. Praise His Holy Name!"

Kim and I went home full of joy. Now both of us had a new spiritual weapon. We use it often to build ourselves up in our most holy faith, to pray the perfect will of God, to receive wisdom, to speak the mysteries of God, and by the power of the Holy Spirit go beyond what our minds could ask or imagine.

****

God's timing is always perfect. His time for both of us to receive this gift was in line with the Annual Prayer Ministry Retreat to be held in the fall of that year. As God would have it, Kim and I were designated to lead the group in entering God's presence according to the pattern God gave to Moses. That is, we were to teach the Tabernacle of Moses as God's plan to enter his presence throughout the Old and New Testament. As we prepared for this vital teaching, we found ourselves constantly praying in the Spirit or praying in tongues. We were encouraging ourselves and each other that God was using us to take many to the next level in Him. We received wisdom and His insight into scriptures such as Hebrews 9:1–8 and Hebrews 8:5–6 that revealed the Holy Spirit's plan for entering the Most Holy Place, God's presence. There were things God did in us and through us that were beyond what we could have ever imagined.

The retreat started on a Friday evening with praise and worship. Kim and I were not scheduled to teach until the following day. Yet, we knew that as facilitators our mission was not to teach as much as it was to lead the group into the Holy of Holies. We asked for permission on Friday to speak so that everyone would know what to expect the next day. While the worship music was playing softly, Kim began.

"Do you remember the stories when you were younger, about kings and queens? The king was often stately. The queen was beautiful. There was always a darling princess. And of course, they were rich. Super rich. There was gold, plenty of gold and diamonds and rubies stashed away in the king's treasury. There were knights on white horses fighting battles. Some of those battles were for the neighboring king's treasures. If won, those treasures would be taken back to the winning king's throne room. Now, close your eyes and imagine with me what a king's throne room looks like. Look back on the textbook pages from elementary or junior high school. Others of you will remember scenes from movies that you have seen. Can you see the richness of the settings? Think back on the trips you made to museums that depicted a king's throne with the huge halls leading to it. As you walk into this very large room, imagine all of the people who are lined on both sides of the red carpet leading to the throne. They are all worshipping the king. Harps are playing. People are dancing. See the steps made of gold leading up to the throne itself. It is a grand setting. Do you see it?"

"Now, keep your eyes closed and imagine what God's throne room must look like. This is the throne room of the Master of the Universe. It must be thousands upon thousands of times bigger than what you just imagined. It has millions or billions of angels from the entrance right up to His mercy seat. Can you see them flying around? Can you see them walking about? The beauty has got be something to behold. How majestic it must be. How inspiring? It must be huge, expansive, and awesome. This place, God's throne room, is where He wants us to come into when we enter His presence. He wants everybody here to come to that place, His throne room."

"Tomorrow, we will all walk into God's throne room. We will enter the Holy of Holies by the grace of God and through the power of the Holy Spirit. It is God's greatest desire to be with us. And, we want to be with Him. Therefore, as you prepare for our journey tomorrow, Willie and I want you to literally see yourself in that room. Build up your faith by praying in the Spirit. Elevate yourself until you can see yourself seated with Christ Jesus at the right hand of the Father."

All of the Prayer Warriors left the Friday night session with high expectations for the next day. Most went to their respective rooms and went to sleep. Others stayed up with their roommates and continued in fellowship. I roomed with two other brothers who decided to stay up a while. Not me. I headed straight for bed. As I drifted off to sleep, I remember starting to dream. In this dream, all of the Prayer Warriors were in one very large room with the door opened. As we were praising and worshipping, some noticed a foul odor coming into the room. Believing it was coming from the opened door, I rose to shut the door. However, a black log was wedged into the top of the door so that it could not be closed tightly. In addition, there were several large black birds perched on the roof where we were praising. Then suddenly, the birds changed to gargoyles and flew en mass directly at me. I yelled Jesus. Jesus. Jesus! Some of the prayer warriors rushed to help me close the door while others climbed a ladder to remove the wedged log. The gargoyles did not enter the room and immediately vanished. Eventually, we closed the door and returned to praise and worship.

The next morning, my roommates asked what my dream was all about. I had been dreaming while they were still up talking. When they heard me yell Jesus in my sleep, they came to my bedside and began praying for me. After a few minutes of prayer, I seemed to be restful to them. I told them of the dream. We agreed that their prayers were Jesus' answer to my cry for help. It was the prayers of those righteous men that closed the door and allowed for a restful sleep.

****

Later that day, Kim and I reminded everyone that the Israelites approached the tabernacle while singing. They were getting themselves ready to enter His presence. It was important that we did the same thing. So, as we began this awesome journey, we sang songs of joy. We filled our hearts with thanksgiving. Kim taught and led the group in prayers of thanksgiving according to Psalms 100:4. We thanked God for what he had already done. We were specific. As we thanked Him on credit for what He was going to manifest, our faith began to rise. Some within the group were thanking God this way for the very first time. Others were simply extending the offers of thanks that they began in their early morning devotion. Each minister thanked God for salvation, healing, deliverance, and financial support. Some stood. Others kneeled. Some sat while some walked around. We thanked God for baptizing us in the Holy Spirit. We thanked God for granting mercy when we had no identification in Him. Some shouted the thanks. Still others thanked him quietly. Most of all, we thanked Him from our hearts.

I then took us to the Brazen Altar where we confessed our sins and made a decision to change. Each minister was encouraged to go into his or her inner closet. No one considered who was around him or her as each one pressed in to God. It was necessary to confess specific sins.

"Did you lie, curse, gossip, worship an idol, dwell on evil thoughts, lust in your heart until your lust was spiritually satisfied, show arrogance, deceive, display a lack of faith, or in any specific way displease God? Pray that God searches you and shows you the sin."

Everyone was taught to plead the blood of Jesus over his or her lives. They acknowledged that their sins crucified Christ and His blood redeemed them. Kim and I joined them in declaring that we all are living sacrifices on this altar. As a part of this dedication, we anointed our ears, hands, and feet.

There was a moment when I became so overcome with the Holy Spirit that all I could do was lay on the floor, travailing in prayer for me, my family, and those present at that retreat. Before I knew it, there was not a dry eye in the place. Cries and moans abounded.

It took every ounce of strength that Kim had left to make her way back to the front of the group in order to lead us in the next step, the Brazen Laver. She explained that it was here that we cleansed ourselves before going into the Holy Place. We listened to a moving worship song about God's word that directed us to meditate on His word and get the word to abide in us. Kim then had several of the Prayer Warriors to read scripture from both the Old Testament and the New Testament. Some of them were John 15:7, Exodus 15:26, Matthew 7:7, Isaiah 41:13, Psalms 4:8, and Proverbs 3:24. We were reminded that God's word is the standard for our lives. Jesus Himself is the Word of God. When we have God's written word in our hands, we should remember that it is akin to having Jesus Himself in our hands. The word is spirit. It is alive. We are to hide it in our hearts through memorizing it. It then becomes real to us. It shows us who we are and who God is in our lives. The word becomes precious to us. Our faith was increased as we heard the word of God spoken into our ears.

Since Kim and I were alternately leading the group through each step, it was now my turn to enter His courts with praise. We had previously come into the gates with thanksgiving. Now I encouraged everyone to get his or her praise on. We were to uplift God for who He is. Magnify His character. Make a joyful noise. Raise our hands and raise our voices. We called Him by His names as we magnified His character. Adonai. Elohim. El Elyon. El Olam. El Shaddai. Jehovah. Jehovah Jireh. Jehovah Mekaddesh. Jehovah Nissi. Jehovah Raah. Jehovah Rapha. Jehovah Shalom. Jehovah Tsidkenu. We declared God to be the fruit of the spirit. We danced and blessed the Lord. We got our eyes off ourselves and onto God. We cried Hallelujah! Hallelujah!! Hallelujah!!! There were shouts of Glory to God! Glory to God!! Glory to God!!! I blew the shophar much to my surprise like I had heard it blown at the conferences. A refreshing spirit came upon us where there was laughter to no end. We had each made independent decisions to praise God no matter what anyone else did. As a result, the cumulative praise reached tremendous heights.

As we had now entered the Holy Place, Kim took us to the Table of Shewbread. It was there that we submitted our will to God. The will is the strongest element of our soul. So, it was necessary to completely surrender to God. We submitted our decisions and declared our obedience to God. Our very souls were laid bare for God to see. We pressed until nothing was left of our carnal nature. All that remained was God. We were consumed by the will of God and felt crucified with Christ.

When it was time to approach the Golden Candlestick, I had all of the natural lights turned off. Every window was covered with black construction paper. All cracks around the doors were sealed until it was completely dark in the room. There was to be no natural light and no natural thinking. We got ready to deal with our minds. Every thought that exalted itself against the knowledge of God was captured and submitted to Christ Jesus. We knew that our natural minds and our natural eyes could not see the good things that God has planned for our lives. We depended on the Holy Spirit to give us illumination by releasing our minds to Him.

At this point, every person with a heavenly language began to pray in tongues. God had prepared Kim and me for this experience by previously honoring us with the precious gift of tongues. Now, we understood His timing. Some prayed for the interpretation of speaking in tongues. We spoke out loud and obeyed what the Holy Spirit gave us. As I was declaring Jesus to be the light of the world, God led me to actually light the physical golden candlestick that was present in the room. As these candles were lit, many received revelation about many things that had been occurring in their lives. It was not the candles. It was the Holy Spirit flowing in each person. Things were being spiritually discerned.

We had committed our wills at the Table of Shewbread and renewed our minds at the Golden Candlestick. Now, Kim taught us to release our emotions. It was only at this point that we could now trust our emotions. Our love for God was then expressed at the Golden Altar. We brought the awareness of the work of the blood with us to this altar. We brought the love that had been offered in praise and worship. We became spiritually intimate with God. In the spirit, we hugged God; we kissed Him, and longed for Him. We told God of our intense desire to be in His presence. The barriers fell down as we paid homage to God. Out of a contrite heart that was on fire for God, we lifted up our love and adoration for God. We gave our hearts to Him.

A spiritual 'explosion' occurred as we entered the Holy of Holies. There was absolutely nothing left of us. The teaching I had planned was totally unnecessary. While now in His presence, all anyone could do was worship Him. No one could help it. The expressions of worship were as varied as the number of people present. We recognized that worship was an individual matter. Many warriors bowed down, laid prostrate, stood with arms lifted, stooped, sat, adored, paid respect, gave honor, along with a multitude of other expressions. We were free, humble, and broken in the worship. Fresh embers of sacrifice and meditation were presented to our God. Worship produced an abundance of faith and peace as we experienced His power and love.

Since anything was possible in God's presence, Kim reminded us to write down those things that we desired of Him once in His presence. Otherwise, we might not be in a state of mind to remember them. Some of the warriors were obedient to write them down. They pulled out their sheet of paper and prayed those things into existence that had been recorded. Many had been slain in the spirit and could only lay before God in blissful rest.

Throughout the entire experience, worship music was playing softly and incense was burning. We now quieted our spirits and soaked in God's presence. We listened to the music and imagined our prayers and worship to God being a pleasing aroma to His nostrils as the incense was to ours. When the music stopped, all was quiet for what seemed like hours. My face was drenched with tears. My body was limp but my mind was clear. I had no desire to speak. I only wanted to listen to God.

****

One of the things that I had written on my sheet of paper was to ask God how to become debt free. While our income from investments and employment was relatively high, so were our expenses. I especially, had little restraint in purchasing just about what ever came to my mind. Over the years, we had accumulated a lot of stuff including a nice home, nice cars, and clothes. I charged diamonds, gold, pearls, rubies, and plenty of other jewelry for every one of Kim's birthdays, or holidays, and days when I just felt like it. We acquired a mortgage for ten acres of undeveloped land in the mountains of Vermont with the intention of building another home there someday. We added two time-share units to the mortgage. Both Tiffany's and Audrey's wedding was expensive and paid with credit cards. The only thing that was paid for with cash was the college tuition of all three children at private institutions. We frequently lent (gave) money to family members who needed it or on many occasions just wanted it.

Kim agreed that we should listen to God's instructions to become debt free. We started with taking some cash and paying off the terms on the two time sharing units. By combining those payments with additional income, we paid the principal balance on the two luxury cars. With the help of a Christian financial advisor, we continued in this manner until all of our debts were paid over a four-year period. All of them were paid including the mortgage on our home. We were debt free with no kids at home.

We enjoyed this freedom in many ways. Although I had not yet mastered my impulse buying, at least now I was doing it all with cash. Our physical health was pretty good at that time, too. In fact, I jogged three times a week and went to the gym on two additional days. My favorite place to jog was Central Park. It was a huge 100-acre Forest Preserve with loads of trees. The jogging path curved around a small lake then into a fairly dense mixture of underbrush, oak, spruce, dogwood, maple, purple ash, and black cherry trees. It was there that I often meditated on God's work and word as I ran. I had gone out early one Saturday morning after devotion. While in the midst of this forest, I could hear God speak clearly.

The Lord said, "Son, I am calling you to a higher place. You must be tested in many areas. I will not tempt you as I cannot tempt you. But, I will allow the tempter to do so. As you come through that temptation without sin, as I know that you will, I am pleased to take you to a higher level in Me. I will test you as you rise. But, with each test I will give you greater confidence in Me." The Lord continued to say, "Peace, be at peace. My peace I give to you as none other you have known. Do not let the trials and tribulations cause you to sin. Be calm and assess the situation with the knowledge of Me that is within you. Stay on course with Kim. Continue to love her and grow with her. Feed her the word as I feed you. Then, the two of you will walk in My light. You will walk in the light of My Son, Jesus."

The Lord said, "Son, go on with Me. There will be times when you will be tested beyond what you think that you can bear. But, faint not. I have prepared you and expect that you will pass the test. This is not a test of your honor but a test of My honor living through you. Man does not reject you. He rejects the light, Me, that shines through you. In sickness, in disappointments, in financial troubles, and confusion keep your eyes fixed on Me. I am the Author and Finisher of your faith. What I have promised, I will deliver. So, wait on Me. Persevere and see the glory of the Lord."

The Spirit of the Lord said, "Son give up all that is within you and follow Me. There are areas that I still need to clean up. I will show them to you as you progress in Me. They are little things but important things to Me. I am using you now in ways that you cannot see. Continue to walk in My word. Continue to study and meditate on My word. I am pleased that you are developing an ear to hear clearly from Me. There are coming times when you must know that it is My voice. This is good preparation. For there will come a time when I say go and you must go immediately. Listen my son with your heart and you will hear Me. I am not difficult to hear," says the Lord.

It was only a five-mile run. But in moments like this, my attention was so focused that the run seemed to be over before it got started. After coasting to a stop, I panted over to the car and cruised back home. I wanted to share with Kim what I just heard. I wanted to get her view on what it meant.

I was barely in the door when the phone rang. I walked to the kitchen phone and answered it.

"Hello, this is Willie," I said.

"Hi son, this is Ray. I have some news for you."

"What is it?"

"It's your mother. We lost her this morning. She's gone home to be with the Lord."

I was silent. I couldn't speak. Kim had walked into the kitchen and saw me standing, holding the phone and not saying a word.

"Willie? What is it?"

"It's Mamma. She's dead!"

****

11

Are You Receiving Your Preparation?

Now fifty years old, I have witnessed much of God's sovereignty. In fact, I have been seeing and hearing God speak quite a bit lately on surrendering and suffering. At bible studies, ministry meetings, worship services, personal devotion times, and counseling with others. Have you? If so, what is it that God is saying to us? Are we receiving that for which we are being prepared? God never promised that He would reveal His entire plan for us. However, He did promise that He would never leave us or forsake us. He made it clear that He knows the plans that He has for us. Saints, these are plans to prosper you.

So, what is this suffering all about? Listen to what God tells us in 1 Peter 4:12-13. "Dear friends, do not be surprised at the painful trial you are suffering, as though something strange were happening to you. But rejoice that you participate in the sufferings of Christ, so that you may be overjoyed when his glory is revealed." If you are like me then you know that these sufferings are not sin-based. You are participating in the sufferings of Christ. I saw something recently that just lifted my spirit. His word says that I will be overjoyed when His glory is revealed. Well, John 2:11 state that Jesus revealed His glory when He performed His first miracle in Cana. Jesus has miracle(s) for you that will reveal His glory to you. And, you will be overjoyed, Hallelujah!! There is even more than that. As a result, you will place even greater faith in Christ Jesus. The word says the disciples did just that (John 2:11b).

Check out Mark 10:29 -30. God tells us that when we surrender all that is dear to us for His sake and the gospel, we will surely receive a hundred times as much in this present age. The key is that it is for His sake just like the suffering is for His sake. See the connection? When we surrender in this way, we can stand on the full promise of Jeremiah 29:11–14. "For I know the plans I have for you," declares the LORD, "plans to prosper you and not to harm you, plans to give you hope and a future. Then you will call upon Me and come and pray to Me, and I will listen to you. You will seek Me and find Me when you seek Me with all your heart. I will be found by you," declares the LORD, "and will bring you back from captivity. I will gather you from all the nations and places where I have banished you," declare the LORD, "and will bring you back to the place from which I carried you into exile."

****

Thursday (The First Day)

"Jeremiah, that's a mighty big piece of luggage that you have for just two days," I said.

"You know Jeremiah. He has to have two or three outfits for each day. A different pair of pajamas each night. Exercise clothes with matching gym shoes. Walking shoes. Dress shoes for the events. Slippers. Raincoat. Umbrella. And, a different outfit for the plane both going and coming," laughed Bobbie.

"Come on, guys. Its two and a half days. Plus, my wife packed for me. Who knows what she has in here," answered Jeremiah.

"Yeah, sure. The wife packed," continued Bobbie.

"You still on your honeymoon after nine months?" I asked.

"You got that right!" Jeremiah smiled.

Bobbie and Jeremiah, two good friends and fellow members of the Prayer Ministry at Rock of Ages Baptist Church sponsored me to attend the Strong Men conference in San Francisco with them. We had been anticipating the event for six months. The year before, the three of us plus five more friends of ours attended a different Men's Conference in Los Angeles. Jeremiah got married the day after we returned from that event. A couple of weeks later, the eight of us formed a small men's group that had been meeting for the previous nine months. We met every Thursday evening at alternating locations. The results had been tremendous. As expected, these men bonded very well. We were accountable for each other. If one was not at the meeting, nearly every man called to find out what happened. That was not only true for the Thursday meetings but also for Sunday worship services. We shared successes and sorrows. We counseled and received counseling from each other. The praise, worship, and prayer times in the Thursday meetings were off the hook. I looked forward to these meetings nearly as much as I look forwarded to the Sunday services.

One of the firemen at the firehouse where Bobbie was a Captain told him about this men's conference. Bobbie told Jeremiah and the two of them invited me to join them. Since my plastics manufacturing business was not doing so well, it did not appear that I was going to be able to join them. But, by the grace of God, the business closed at the end of July on the very day the conference started. Now I had the time and they helped me with the finances. Thank God for good friends.

Of course, that was all in God's plans for **I was now beginning the most incredible twelve days of my entire life.**

"Hey, Jeremiah, isn't that Pastor Watts over there?" I asked.

"Sure is. I believe that crowd around him is from Memorial Baptist," was his response.

"I see some brothers from Macedonia Baptist over there too," Bobbie added.

It seemed like everyone in the baggage claim area was headed to the conference. A few we knew, but by far most of them were complete strangers in the natural. Through both detection and discernment, God let me know that they were going to the same conference. We smiled, shook hands, or in some way acknowledged each other. This was going to be a good time for many. For some like me, it was going to be a time of death. I was going to die to the current state of my life. God's mission for me began this day. By the time it was done, I was never the same.

"Willie!!" This call came from across the way. It was Luke Jackson, a member of Rock of Ages.

"Hey, man. What are you doing here?" I asked.

"Same as you!"

"Why didn't you let me know you were coming?"

"I didn't know that you were coming. For that matter, I didn't know that these two rascals, Jeremiah and Bobbie, were coming either. I had planned to come with a partner of mine. At the last minute, he had to stay home with his father who took ill. So, I came on my own."

"Where you staying?" I asked.

"The Vacation Inn Express on Cypress Blvd. How about you guys?"

"We're at the International Club Downtown. We got a suite. Want to join us?" Bobbie asked.

"Why not?" said Luke. "Anybody else here from Rock of Ages?"

"Just the four of us," said Jeremiah.

Luke had been the head of the Men's Ministry at Rock of Ages for the first four years of its existence. However, he had missed quite a few of the meetings just prior to this conference. Seeing him in San Francisco was quite a pleasant surprise.

God was up to something.

"This is a nice sized room," Luke exclaimed.

"Works for me," I said. "I got the couch."

"I'll take the roll-away," said Luke.

"Bobbie, I guess that leaves the King size bed for you and me," said Jeremiah.

"Don't get any ideas over here, friend (smile). You told us a little while ago that your honeymoon is not over yet. And, my legs are too hard to be your wife's. I'm putting a line of pillows between us!" Bobbie was quick to answer.

"Hey Luke, I don't believe in coincidences, and I know you don't either. So, I am real interested in your story for coming down here," I said.

"Well, I was planning to come with Patrick Wolff. You know Pat, don't you?"

"Of course. He is a Scout Master at the church."

"He and I planned this trip about two months ago. You guys may have noticed that I had not been at many of the Men's meetings lately."

"We noticed."

"Pat was planning to drive and I was going to help him drive. Well, Pat's father took ill suddenly and was rushed to the hospital a couple of days ago."

"What happened"?

"He doesn't know yet. The doctors are still giving him every test under the sun. They thought it was a stroke for a minute. But, the tests were inconclusive.'

"Wow."

"They are keeping him for a while for observation and more tests. Pat is staying with him as you would expect."

"I understand that. So, you decided to drive yourself?"

"No way! I don't think that I could have made the drive by myself safely and get here on time. I booked a last minute plane reservation."

"That must have cost a fortune with only two days before the flight."

"You wouldn't believe it but it only cost me $212.50."

"You got to be kidding me. What did it cost us, Bobbie?"

"$235 each," Bobbie responded.

"How did that happen?" Jeremiah asked. "You paid less than we did and we made our reservations six months in advance."

"Favor ain't fair," Luke said. "It had to be God!"

"Now, I know God is up to something. He made provisions for you like that so, I know he also made preparations. What are the things that led up to you deciding to come?" I asked.

"Well, I've gotten in this deep. I might as well talk about it. I stopped coming to the Men's meetings because I was feeling guilty about the constant sin in my life. I was hooked on pornography. It was mostly magazine stuff, you know. But, it had gotten to the point that my wife did not interest me anymore. If she wasn't looking like the women in the books or acting like them, I preferred the books. This, of course, led to further problems in our relationship. I started hanging out at topless and bottomless bars. Look, I never did anything. None-the-less, it was creating a big problem in my life and I had no control over it."

"Go on," I said.

"I was feeling like a hypocrite. So, I came less and less to the meetings. What would a leader in the church look like with this huge problem of mine? I went to God and asked for help. I still had the problem but He started working on me. Everywhere I read in the bible, God was pointing out sexual immorality as a sin condition that was intolerable. In Matthew, Mark, Acts, Romans, 1 Corinthians, Ephesians, Colossians, Galatians, 1 Thessalonians, Jude, and Revelation. Everywhere. He was getting my attention.

So, in a private session with God and my wife, I confessed my sin against God, to God. I asked His forgiveness. I then asked my wife to forgive me. Both did. We prayed for the desire to be removed. We agreed that the demonic spirit behind the pornography was bound. Freedom to love my wife was loosed. We asked for deliverance. God did it. It was like ten tons of bricks were lifted from my shoulder."

"Your wife forgave you too?" Jeremiah asked.

"Yeah, isn't God good? He had prepared her heart for forgiveness. His love is wide, long, high, and deep. I repented by turning away from the pornography. I threw away every magazine, video, and book. I invited my wife to travel with me everywhere I went. It didn't matter if I was only going to the store. She was welcomed."

"Did she go?" I asked.

"In a heart-beat! At every opportunity, she was at my side. If she couldn't go for some reason, I asked her to monitor me by checking up."

"God is faithful and just to not only forgive sin but also to clean us up. How were you cleansed?" Bobbie asked.

"God first made me accountable to Him. Then, my wife held me accountable. He gave me another accountability partner in Patrick Wolff. I bought books on deliverance. God told me to go to this conference and get dipped in his word seven times then I would be clean."

"Have you noticed that there are seven sessions between today and the time we go home on Saturday?" asked Jeremiah.

"I sure have and I am not missing a one of them. Plus …." Luke hesitated.

"After hearing about your preparation and provision, I don't blame you. I'm sorry. I interrupted. Was there more?" I asked.

"Well, we'll see. I mean. Well, we'll see," said Luke.

Luke had more to say but stopped short of saying it all. What was it? We could tell there was more but we didn't press him. We now understood why Luke was here. But, why did God allow us in particular to meet him at baggage claim when we landed?

"Luke, I have already told Bobbie and Jeremiah that this is the first day of a twelve day journey for me. After getting back home on Saturday, I will then be with Kim's side of the family at the amusement park on Sunday. On Monday, I leave for eight days on a mission in North Carolina."

"It sounds like God is working with you too," he said.

"He is. I don't know all that He is doing. He has given me partial instructions. But, I can tell you this. He told me to memorize the entire book of Ephesians before I go. I just began chapter four. Three of them are done. I will be taking some time here and there on this trip to make sure that I have all six chapters done by Sunday night."

"Need help practicing out loud?" Luke asked.

"I'm glad that you asked. I would like that. But first, I want to review before I speak it out," I responded.

"That gives us time to go get a quick sandwich before tonight's session. Want us to bring you something back?" Jeremiah asked.

"No thanks. I'm OK."

Jeremiah, Bobbie, and Luke headed to the Hamburger stand that we saw on the corner about six blocks from the hotel. It was a warm evening in San Francisco. They decided to walk. I got immersed in Ephesians right away. I reviewed the words then studied their meaning. I was so focused that it seemed like they were only gone 5 minutes. In actuality, it was nearly an hour. They decided to eat there in order to give me a little more time.

"You guys got back quick," I stated.

"Not really. But, the question is - are you ready to recite?" Bobbie responded.

"I believe I am!" I declared.

"Let's hear it," Jeremiah said.

"From the NIV, Chapters 1 through 3: "Paul, an apostle of Christ Jesus by the will of God, To the saints in Ephesus, the faithful in Christ Jesus: Grace and peace to you from God our Father and the Lord Jesus Christ. Praise be to the God and Father of our Lord Jesus Christ, who has blessed us in the heavenly realms with every spiritual blessing in Christ. ….."

"Now to him who is able to do immeasurably more than all we ask or imagine, according to his power that is at work within us, to him be glory in the church and in Christ Jesus throughout all generations, forever and ever! Amen.'"

"Amen. Amen. Amen!" they all echoed.

****

It was time to head to the dome for the first of two sessions that night. As we drove the three miles, Luke thanked Bobbie and Jeremiah for keeping him focused when they walked to the Hamburger stand. As it turned out, the blocks between the hotel and the restaurant were lined with prostitutes. Luke's flesh started to rise as soon as they left the hotel. It was as if he could smell the sexual aroma the moment the front door opened. After only a couple of blocks, they were being approached from all sides.

"Don't worry. We got your back, man," Bobbie assured him.

Then the three of them interlocked arms and strutted on past the line-up. They gave no thought to the onlookers who were driving by tooting their horns. Those three knew they were manly men and simply ignored the sneers. Coming back was void of any incidents. I guess the hookers took their cue from them walking past the first time. Luke was grateful and knew that was why God had hooked him up with us at the airport.

****

We got there only thirty minutes before everything started. We had guaranteed seating in the Partners section so we were not concerned about the more than 40,000 men who had already filed in before us. Methodically, we made our way to our seats. We had great seats in the center section about halfway back but directly in front of the podium. The California Dome is huge. It seats well over 70,000 people. And, it was filling quickly. As the hour to get started approached, the men broke out in a shout,

"JESUS!! JESUS!! JESUS!! JESUS!! JESUS!! JESUS!!"

It went on for 5 or 10 minutes. The atmosphere was electric. I could sense the Holy Spirit's presence already. The psalmist brought the men to a higher level in praise and worship. Men were crying, hugging, sitting quietly, singing, and clapping. Then R.J. McWaters, the Key Note Speaker, took the microphone. You could tell that he had been in the presence of God. He wasted no time.

"Everything is Against Me, is the title of this message tonight. It is based on Genesis Chapter 42 verse 36 in the NIV. Jacob's favorite wife, Rachael, had died. His daughter had been raped. The kids got in trouble. There was a famine in the land. He thought Joseph was dead. Simeon could have been dead as far as he knew. And now, his other sons wanted to take Benjamin to a foreign land. Jacob feared that he might not see Benjamin again…

"There are times in our lives when by all outward appearances, things are going extremely well. But, you of all people know the trials and tribulations that you went through to get there. Things ended up well in Jacob's life. He became the father of the twelve tribes of Israel. Yet, along the way there were some very rough spots.

But, by faith, we can overcome life challenges. Jesus said that if we have faith the size of a mustard seed, we can tell mountains to throw themselves into the sea and it will be done. We can do all things in Christ Jesus who strengthens us. God is strengthening us. So, keep on pressing. Keep on running. Hang in there. Weeping may endure for a night. But joy comes in the morning…"

By now, nearly every man in that Dome was doing a 'David dance.' The aisles were filled. Men were running around the stadium. At one point, R.J. McWaters, who was in the midst of his own David dance by then, stopped and said to the men.

"Touch the brother next to you. Tell him that if he does not want to dance, get out of your way!"

At that point, a young man who was seated in our row but about ten seats to the right came running across the top of the chairs to the aisle where we were dancing. The second he touched the floor, space opened up all around him. He was dancing with great fervor. He was bent at his waist with his arms spread wide. He bobbed up and down like a Native American or African warrior. He would spin, jump, and kick his legs out like a pair of scissors. He could not stand in one place. Occasionally his movements would slow down long enough for him to engage in high stepping like the drum major of a college band. He touched one brother. Blam! Down he went; slain in the spirit. He touched another brother. Blam! Down he went. He was on fire for the Lord. I was dancing about 10 feet from where he was. All of a sudden, he was upon me. He grabbed me around the waist and the two of us started dancing. I'm telling you that I could feel the power surging in him. I was not slain but to hear Jeremiah, Bobbie, and Luke tell it, I was jumping around like I was in electric shock. It wasn't electric shock. It was the power of Holy Spirit.

When he let me go, I looked at R.J. McWaters.

"Jeremiah!! Do you see what I see? There's fire coming from R.J. McWaters' eyes."

"Yeah, I see it. You see it, Bobbie?" said Jeremiah

"Nawh. What yawl talking about?" said Bobbie.

"Me neither," chimed in Luke.

"There's literal fire coming from his eyes," I said. "Revelations 19:12a is being manifested for us to see. This is what the fire in Jesus' eyes will look like. Do you see it?"

****

It was very difficult to get to sleep that night. We talked for a couple of hours about the night's events. After R.J. McWaters, it was Rev. Smith who spoke. God used him just as powerfully to talk about "Getting A Fresh Revelation." At the end of Rev. Smith's message, he asked all the men who had wives with an ailment to come to the altar. He would pray for healing for the wives, with the husbands standing in the gap for them. I joined several hundred other men who ran to the altar. I placed my hand on my back because of the pains Kim had been having for the last twenty years. When Rev. Smith was done, I had an assurance in my spirit that Kim was healed. Hallelujah!!! If the rest of the sessions were going to be like tonight, we would all be changed men for sure.

As the night wore on, we got ready for bed. Luke was out like a light, first. Then, Bobbie and Jeremiah drifted off. I stayed up another 30 minutes or so studying Chapter 4 of Ephesians before I too fell asleep.

****

"Bobbie, you up already?" I heard Jeremiah ask.

"It's the fireman in me. I can't stay asleep too long. But, I'm fresh and ready to go," said Bobbie.

"If we are going to beat the crowd, we'd better get Willie and Luke up," Jeremiah whispered.

"I heard that. I'm getting up, now." I gagged.

"Uhhhhh! Me, too." It was Luke.

Three powerful men of God were scheduled to speak that Friday. Each had their own ministries with 'sons in the gospel' who had received both training and ordination from their respective 'fathers'. Rev. Smith spoke first on the topic 'Sexual Purity'. God got directly to the point that morning with not only Luke but also with all of us who have some measure of trouble with this issue. If the truth were told, most men have an issue of one kind or another with sex at some point in their life. Rev. Smith had no problem getting the men's attention. Praise and worship music filled the dome after Rev. Smith was finished. Then, Rev. Storm took the podium.

"Hold up you Bible. This is my Bible. I am what it says I am. I can do what it says I can do. I can have what it says I can have. As a result of this anointed word from this Bible, I will never be the same again…

You have been empowered by the word of God in Deuteronomy 8:18 with the ability to produce wealth. However, do not forget God, His commandments, or His decrees. Never serve anything more than you serve God…

Declare with me. I will never be sick another day in my life. I will never be lonely another day in my life. I will never be broke another day in my life. I will lack nothing another day in my life. My God is sufficient. In Him, I will not have one single thing missing or broken in my life."

Rev. Storm made an altar call just before closing. In the midst of it, he asked the men to look at their shoes. The cost of his shoes would be the amount of the offering that each man should consider giving. The instructions were to reach in our pockets, ball up the cash or check, and then literally throw it on the stage. These instructions were not just to the men who came up for the altar call. It was for all 70, 000 men in that dome. The men at the very top of the dome were to throw their money as well. Obviously, they could not throw their money all the way to the stage. So, the further instructions were to pick up any money that hit you and throw it forward. It was fairly easy for me to throw my money on the stage since I was one of the men who responded to the altar call. When the final instruction came to throw the money, I reached the stage with my first throw. But, money was hitting me in the back of the head, on my shoulders, and in my back. I turned around to pick it up to throw it on the stage as instructed.

"Oh, my God, look at this!" I was given another manifestation in the natural of one of God's verses from His Bible. "This is what Malachi 3:10 looks like when God says that He will open up the floodgates of heaven and pour out so much blessing that you will not have room enough for it."

Money was raining from the top of that dome. You have to see this with me in your sanctified imagination. It was a steady downpour of money from the top of that dome. It was like a literal storm of money. This was not a drizzle. It was a storm. And, it kept coming and coming and coming. It didn't seem like it was going to stop. When I turned to throw the money that I picked up to the stage, I saw the steady downpour of money being washed upon the stage like huge waves of water upon the beach. This was incredible. God was not only letting us hear His word. He was allowing us to see it in action.

****

The afternoon break for dinner was lengthy but needed. We had about two and a half hours before the evening session with R.J. McWaters began at 7:00pm. I especially needed the time to get back to my study of Ephesians. God was gracious to me. He allowed me to finish chapter 4 and begin chapter 5. My friends took a short nap. By the time they woke up, I was well into chapter 5.

"How are you coming with Ephesians?" Jeremiah asked.

"I'm getting there. With time tonight before bed and time on the plane tomorrow, maybe I can have chapters 4 and 5 done."

"God sure is moving you along!!" said Luke.

"Glory to God!" I declared.

The evening session began in much the same way as the others. There was high praise and worship. The shouts of "JESUS!! JESUS!! JESUS!! JESUS!! JESUS!! JESUS!!" was constant throughout all of the sessions. This session was no different. Like the night before, R.J. McWaters would be the final speaker of the day. The same would be true of tomorrow.

His message was 'The God of Glory!" based on 2 Thessalonians 2:14. At the end of the message he made this statement.

"Now this message is for all of the Pastors and Preachers who are with us this weekend. I want all of you to stand up."

To all of our surprise, Luke Jackson stood up. Jeremiah, Bobbie, and I all looked at each other. We were astonished. Luke is a Pastor or Preacher? So, that's what he did not want to talk about yesterday!! We knew something was up. Now, it was revealed.

"OK, Luke. You have to tell us - what was that about tonight?" Bobbie asked.

"What do you mean?"

"You know what we mean," Bobbie said. "You stood up when R.J. McWaters asked all the Pastors and Preachers to stand. What was that all about?"

"OK. I told you guys about how God is cleaning me up. He also turned me around and placed my feet on solid ground."

"He called you to preach?" I asked.

"Yep. I have not been ordained yet. I start seminary in the Fall. But, I could not deny what God has already accomplished in the spiritual realm. When R.J. McWaters asked all Preachers to stand, I had to be obedient. I had to claim what God had already prepared in advance for me to do."

"Hallelujahhh!!!"

"Gloryyyy!!!"

"Hallelujahhh!!!"

We couldn't stop shouting and praising God for the work that He was doing in Luke. We felt honored to be a witness to his stand. That, of course, was the topic of the night until our eyes got too heavy to keep open. I tried to study some of Ephesians but the excitement of the day and night had been too much. I was asleep in 5 minutes.

****

Bishop Carlos Short and R.J. McWaters were to speak on the final day of the conference. As we were making our way to our seats, I felt like someone was watching me. I kept looking around but I didn't see a familiar face other than the three guys that I was with. I thought that maybe we would have seen Rev. Watts, some of the guys from Salem, or someone from Macedonia by now. Interestingly enough, we had not. Since there were seventy thousand men and we had been so engrossed in each day's events, I simply had not given it much thought. But, somebody was watching me. I shook it off as we made our way to our seats. We were there about an hour early so I opened my bible to Ephesians to do a little studying. About 5 minutes later I heard, "Willie Johnson!" It was Rev. Ira Brown.

He and I had worked together at CBS before I left to open the plastics company. I had heard that he was planted as Pastor of a new congregation in the Bronx. I had not seen him since I left CBS.

"How you doing, man," he said.

"I'm doing great. I am doing even better now that I see you. I didn't know that you were here," I responded.

"I knew you were here. I've been looking for you the last two days."

"Is that right? How did you know I was here?"

"I am rooming with Rev. Watts. He told me he saw you at the airport."

"I saw him too. But, I didn't get an opportunity to shake his hand. Too many people. Not enough time. Plus, I thought that I would see him again. Do you know Jeremiah, Luke and Bobbie?"

"I do now. Glad to meet you brothers. You mind if we join you guys?"

"Not at all. Whooaaa! Who're all these men?"

"God is so good, Willie. These are twenty-five brothers who came with me from the new church. I saw you down on the floor when we first walked in. It took me all this time to make it over here to you!"

"So, that is what I felt. Just as I was about to sit, I felt eyes were watching me. I now see that twenty-five sets of eyes were watching me!"

"Look. I heard that you are the chair of the Prayer Ministry at Rock of Ages," he said.

I felt a little strange when Rev. Brown made that statement. It was true enough but I felt a little strange none-the-less. I closed my bible and fellowshipped with him, his men, Jeremiah, Bobbie, and Luke. Poof! The lights went out in the Dome. It was pitch black in there. The shout went out, "JESUS!! JESUS!! JESUS!! JESUS!! JESUS!! JESUS!!" I didn't know what was going on. Was this planned? There was no announcement. There were no other sounds except "JESUS!! JESUS!! JESUS!! JESUS!! JESUS!! JESUS!!" I was compelled to join in. We all joined in. Still, no lights. No announcements. This went on for about 10 or 15 minutes before a makeshift lamp was shining on the stage. R.J. McWaters came out to the roar of the men. We all thought that this was a part of the event. It wasn't.

"Brothers, you just continue to have a good time praising God," he said only with the aid of his own vocal cords. "There's a yet unexplained power outage in the Dome. I am as convinced as you are that as we continue to praise God and pray, the lights will be restored. But, even if they are not, we're going to praise our Lord and Savior anyhow!"

"JESUS!! JESUS!! JESUS!! JESUS!! JESUS!! JESUS!!" "Just give us a few minutes; we'll be back to you one way or another."

"JESUS!! JESUS!! JESUS!! JESUS!! JESUS!! JESUS!!"

Only those of us who were seated near the stage could hear him. We now knew that this was not a part of the plan. The other 70,000 men had no idea nor did they care. It was a high time of praise. The dome just boomed with the shouts of "JESUS." The crescendo rose as each minute passed.

A few minutes later, as quickly as the lights went out, they were back on again. There was a message in there somewhere. I could not help but reflect on the recently memorized sections of Ephesians chapter 5. "For you were once darkness, but now you are light in the Lord. Live as children of light (for the fruit of the light consists in all goodness, righteousness and truth) and find out what pleases the Lord. Have nothing to do with the fruitless deeds of darkness, but rather expose them. For it is shameful even to mention what the disobedient do in secret. But everything exposed by the light becomes visible, for it is light that makes everything visible. This is why it is said: "Wake up, O sleeper, rise from the dead, and Christ will shine on you."

The men did not get an explanation. The session just continued as if nothing happened. Bishop Carlos Short got right into his message. R.J. Mc-Waters followed with the culminating message of the whole conference for me. This was the one that nailed the coffin shut on the state that I was in before coming to the conference. God had been preparing me for the next season of my spiritual walk with him for quite a while. In March of that year, I felt like my life had been completely destroyed. Relationships were in a shambles, death seemed on the horizon for family members, money was gone, and my self-esteem was shattered. What was God doing to me? Now, I knew.

"Open your bibles to Mark 9:2-8. God wants to kill you then restore you to a new day. I want to talk to some men today who are tired of yesterday. You have drawn a line in the sand and declared that this day is the beginning of a new season. You have made a conscientious decision to follow Christ and Christ alone…

Yesterday, August 1st, you stepped into a new beginning. On July 31st, God finished something in your life. That was the last day of the seventh month. It's over. It's done with…

It is also, after six days for you. Six is the number of man. You have done everything and tried everything that a man knows. You are at the end of depending on self. God has led you through all of the hell that you have endured. He wants to take you to a height in Him where no temptations of your flesh could bother you. He had to kill you so that He could qualify you to be His ambassador, for real. Take a good look. According to 1 John 3:2, see Christ and be like Christ. Exercise your spiritual vision so that you become what you see in Christ. Let yesterday go. The best is yet to come. It is your new day. Hallelujah!!!

****

On the plane ride back home, I could hardly contain myself. God had given me two instructions over the last two and a half days. It was clear to me that one of them was that I must step down as the chair of the Prayer Ministry for he had a greater work for me. That is why I felt so strange when Rev. Brown addressed me as the chairperson. The second instruction was just as clear. Yet, I did not acknowledge hearing it. Kim and I had been wavering in our commitment to participate in the Apostolic and Prophetic training that was coming up in September of that year. I knew that I was being drawn to go but I wanted to talk to Kim first.

I relaxed in my plane seat and opened the bible to Ephesians. With the grace of God, I was able to complete chapter 5 by the time we landed. "… However, each one of you also must love his wife as he loves himself and the wife must respect her husband."

Kim was a welcomed sight. This had been a good time but I was glad to get home.

"How was your trip?"

"There is so much to tell."

"From the time we arrived in San Francisco until the last message today, God has been speaking loudly. Guess who we met at the baggage claim in San Francisco. Luke Jackson. Then…"

I told her as much as I could get out in one breath. I talked without stopping from the time we pulled out from the airport until we were in the house. I told her everything. She listened intently as we walked in the house.

She turned on the 10:00 o'clock news and there was a report from San Francisco.

"Earlier today, a member of a white supremacist group was caught trying to sabotage the annual Strong Men conference. The irony is that this conference while attended by a large number of African Americans is not exclusive to black men. The attacker was successful in cutting the main power wires but was caught red handed in the act of trying to cut the wires to the back-up generator…!

12

ON WHAT DOES YOUR FAITH REST?

I have an encouraging word for you, today.1 Faith is REAL. And, you have it. God's word says so. Look it up for yourself. The Bible says that God hath dealt to every man the measure of faith. The foundation of your faith is built on what? God's word has an answer for that question too.

But first I must share a reminder with you that I heard just a couple of days ago. God's word already declares that you have faith. That is established, forever. It is irrefutable. You have faith. Yet, the Word also describes great faith, little faith, weak faith, strong faith, full of faith, sincere faith, shipwrecked faith, wavering faith, rich faith, perfect faith, world overcoming faith, and exceedingly growing faith. How can that be? How does this spectrum of faith from weak to strong, little to great, and wavering to perfect come to pass?

I have faith that God will come against everything that contradicts Him. This faith encourages a person to remain true to God's character whatever He may do. Well, how do we know what contradicts God? His Word tells us. The Word tells of His character and His ways. We must be rooted and grounded in His Word. That is the foundation of faith. When we have that foundation, when we feed our faith with the Word and exercise that faith by our works then we find ourselves at the upper end of the spectrum of faith.

When we feed and exercise our faith, what happens? Signs, wonders, and miracles become evident. We no longer stand on the empty words of a man. Rather, our faith stands on the power of God. Notice God's confirmation. "That your faith should not stand in the wisdom of men but in the power of God." (1 Corinthians 2:5)

Here is the conclusion of the matter. You already have faith if you are a child of God. Feed your faith and exercise your faith. Watch it grow. Walk by faith. Live by faith. See the manifestation of God's Holy Ghost power in your life. Hallelujah!!!

****

Monday (Day 5)

Beep! Beep! "Have you been waiting long?" Philip asked as I stood at the curb.

"Not long. Maybe 10 minutes. The plane was a little late."

"Thank God. I was running late, myself. Let me help you with your luggage."

"Philip, I really appreciate you picking me up like this."

"No problem, man of God. Once you told me of your mission, I knew that God wanted me to be the first one to provide transportation."

"Thank you. I am trusting God for several things on this trip. I know that He is faithful. I am not surprised that He is providing as He said that He would. I am just thankful that you are obedient to what he gave you to do."

Philip is a long time family friend. His mother and father, Deloris and Howard, attended high school with me. They raised their family of three boys across the street from Chrissie's house in Fayetteville. I had seen Philip occasionally over the years but he was much younger than me. It wasn't until he became an adult that I started personal communications with him. I added Philip to my Prayer Ministry email distribution list when I found out that he was a freelance writer for a community newspaper. Philip's writing style and insight into a wide range of issues attracted large numbers of readers. Since he was not shy about voicing Christian truths, his constituents were often interested in things like prayer, fasting, worship, deliverance, and salvation. As a result, he became the focal point for a prayer circle in Raleigh. In one of my frequent family directed emails, Chrissie asked me to include Philip. Over the ensuing months, we communicated frequently and shared prayer requests of our respective warriors. In addition, because of the closeness of the family, Philip had come to call my mother, Grandmother, and my stepfather, Grandpa.

"I am excited for you. I am especially honored that you chose to share a little of this trip's mission with me," said Philip.

"No problem, Philip. There is so much that God has told me to do. I am not yet allowed to share it all. He has released me to share some of it with some of the people. Other portions are just for me," I responded.

"I understand. I don't want you to tell me what God has not released you to tell. That would cause you to be disobedient and may risk canceling a blessing along the way," Philip replied.

"I can tell you this, however. I am to stay with DZ tonight then on to Fayetteville tomorrow and stay with Ray."

"Cool. I will drop you there, come back later with Ashley, and fellowship with you and his family."

"That would be fine if he were home. He is in Miami with Regina and Allison. Allison made it to the Jr. Olympics this year running both the 800 meters and the third leg of her mile relay team. He told me where I could find his house key. I will stay there tonight then head to Fayetteville tomorrow."

Philip and I left the airport and headed for Raleigh. I had not traveled along this stretch of Interstate 95 in quite a while. The scenery is uniquely North Carolina. Lake Fontana was to the west and the Atlantic Ocean on the east. Much of the land there is below sea level. There are bridges everywhere. There is one bridge that stretches about 10 miles south of Washington D. C. It spans a swamp. As we crossed it, I could see an occasional alligator resting on the bank of an island of water logged trees. Cranes were swooping down to catch a few fish and steam seemed to rise from the water in the distance. The air was heavy with moisture. The humidity must have been 96.

As we looked out upon the landscape, a sense of serenity came upon us. We sat quietly for a while. Then, we talked about the geography. Inevitably, we began talking about Christ. At one point, Philip wanted to know my testimony.

"Philip, I grew up in a family with a strong belief in God. My grandfathers on both sides of my family were ministers of the gospel. Big Mamma, my mother's mother was a Deaconess for many years in a sanctified church until her health began to fail. I was in church by habit all the time. I was even baptized as a young teenager. However, that baptism was without truly accepting Christ. I did it because it was my chronological time to do it and I wanted to please my mother."

"Everyone in our family was baptized somewhere between 11 and 13 years of age. It wasn't until I was much older that I asked Jesus Christ into my heart. I confessed Him as my Lord and Savior and by faith believed without a doubt that God raised Him from the dead. DZ was instrumental in getting me to fall on my knees in the den of our home, in the early morning hours that day to accept Christ. I have not been the same since."

"I can tell by your emails that you love the Lord," Philip observed.

"If I could only love Him as much as He loves me. How did you come to know Christ, Philip?"

"You know my mom and dad. So, you know that I did not grow up with a strong Christian influence. Oh, I knew about God. I would say that I even knew there was a God. But, I sure did not have a personal relationship with Him."

"Sounds familiar."

"After graduation from college, I got a pretty good job in Winston-Salem writing for one of the local papers. The economy turned sour and I was a casualty of downsizing. It depressed me quite a bit. For about a year, I did nothing but accept unemployment checks, drink, and party. Along the way, I met Ashley. She had not accepted Christ either. We got married and I found a job in Raleigh. One of my fellow coworkers kept insisting that I come to church with him. Eventually I did."

"That was a good thing," I said.

"It was there that God got my attention. During the altar call, they sang a simple song of "Come to Jesus. Come to Jesus. Come to Jesus right now." It was as if God was calling me personally.'"

"He was," I told Philip.

"Before I knew it, I was in the front of the church accepting God's gift of salvation."

"Hallelujah!"

"But, Ashley did not come right away. Eventually, we started to verbally fight and argue about attending church together. She stopped going all together. By the grace of God and with wise counsel, I told Ashley one day that I was going on with Christ. She was welcomed to follow. But, I was not going back to Egypt. Neither was I going to send her away. She was upset. After about a week, she committed to Christ. We have been steadily growing in grace and the love of God ever since. I became a mentor to many young men and she taught Sunday School."

As we pulled into the driveway at DZ's house, I noticed the unexpected. His car was parked there. He told me that he and Brenda, his wife, were planning to drive to Florida. So, what was his car doing in the driveway? Maybe they decided to fly. Or, maybe they rode with someone else.

My plans were to retrieve the keys from the secret place, say goodbye to Philip, then review Ephesians chapter 1 through 6. God again displayed His sovereignty by changing both my plans and my brother's plans.

Knock. Knock. Knock. DZ answered the door. He gave me a bear hug and I hugged back.

"I thought you were going to be in Miami!" I exclaimed.

"We were. I'll tell you about that in a minute. How are you, Philip?"

"I am blessed, Uncle Tommie." Since childhood, Philip called him Uncle Tommie. We were not really his uncles. It was just a sign of respect and was indicative of the closeness of the family.

"We were all planning to drive together. Regina, Allison, Brenda, and me. Then, I noticed some wood rot on the back of the house. When I called the inspector, the worse expectation was confirmed. Termites. That was about a week ago. "

"Termites!!!!"

"Yeah. I had them taken care of, though. I called the exterminators right away. It took a couple of applications of bug spray. Eventually, the termites were eliminated. So now, I am remodeling. I will extend the master bedroom toward the back of the house. I have already had contractors to tear out the portion of the house where the termites were discovered. My house is now wide open. I can't go anywhere. For sure, I could not go as far as Miami with the house in this condition. We put Regina and Allison on the plane. We also decided to baby-sit Regina's other two children, Sophia and Caleb. We expect Regina and Allison to return to Charlotte tomorrow then come over to pick up these two. How long you going to be here?

"My plans haven't changed. I will stay with you tonight then head to Fayetteville tomorrow."

"How are you getting there?" DZ asked.

"I don't know yet. I'll have to see what God plans. I just know that I must be in Fayetteville, tomorrow."

Philip could only stay a few minutes. He talked a short while with us, said hello to Brenda then left with a promise to return that evening with his wife. Given the unexpected nature of my visit with DZ and Brenda, I knew that I had to have my spiritual eyes open. God had orchestrated this divine appointment. Since activities for the day had begun, I joined in. Brenda went to a doctor's appointment with Caleb. He had been complaining of a stomach ache for the last few days. In addition, his throat had been sore and the pain from his stomach had intensified.

I traveled with DZ to get corrections made on his building permit. We then checked on one of his cars that was being repaired and spoke with an attorney regarding a personal matter. The afternoon went by pretty uneventfully until we got home. Brenda had returned with a report that Caleb had contracted mononucleosis probably from a drinking fountain at the soccer field. The mono had led to an infection that caused his appendix to be enlarged. It was a serious problem that would require Caleb to sit very still for at least two months. This five year old would not be able to run, jump, or otherwise do things that kids his age, love to do.

"Tommie, what are we going to do? The doctor said that Caleb has to sit in a chair with a ball held closely to his stomach for two months. He's only five. He can't do that," Brenda worried.

"The doctor told you what he was trained to tell you. He was as accurate as he could be given his training. And, we must seriously consider his recommendations," DZ replied.

"Look at him over there, Tommie. He looks so sad. He's holding that ball so tight. You can tell that he wants to get up. Go talk to him." she said.

As I listened to their conversation, I received an inner witness from the Holy Spirit to point them to His word. Given that both had strong Christian foundations, it did not take long to get their attention. God reminded all of us of who we were in Christ Jesus. We are children of God. We are heirs to the Kingdom. We are ambassadors and witnesses of His miraculous powers. We have a covenant relationship with God. He has seated us in the heavenly realms with Christ Jesus high above all rule and authority, power and dominion, and every title that can be given not only in the present age but also in the one to come.

We have the authority to trample on snakes and scorpions and overcome all the power of the enemy. We received miracle-working power when the Holy Spirit came upon us at the moment we accepted Christ. He gave us the charge to lay hands on the sick, cast out demons, raise the dead, bind and loose on earth, and speak in new tongues. He has assured us that if we have faith, we will do what Christ did while on the earth. We will do even greater things than that. It became clear to us that God wanted Caleb healed. He wanted us to be His vessels.

"Caleb. Cheer up, man. Everything is going to be all right. I know what the doctor told you. So, I want you to be sure to do just what he says unless we get a different instruction from God. OK?" Tommie told him.

"Yes sir."

"Now, I want to ask you something. Do you believe that God can heal you just like he healed in the bible stories that you have been reading?"

"Yes sir."

"Then, I want you to follow my instructions very carefully. I am going to ask your MeMe (Brenda), Sophia, and your Uncle Willie to join us over here to pray for you."

"Okaay."

"Uncle Willie is going to pray and lay his hands on your stomach."

"Okaay."

"While he is praying, I just want you to repeat these words. God, I receive your healing."

"Okaay."

We all gathered around Caleb. DZ told him to put the ball down for just a minute and lift his arms in the receiving position. Then, I prayed.

> "God, You have promised that Your word will not return void. Jesus has born Caleb's infirmities and bears his sickness. Caleb is redeemed from the curse of sickness."

"God, I receive your healing."

> "We submit Caleb and ourselves to You, God. We surrender to You and resist the devil. We fight this spirit of sickness with the divine power of the Holy Spirit.
> Caleb dwells in Your secret place with Your hedge of protection around him and under the shadow of You, the Almighty God. Neither he nor do we fear this sickness. We pray that You command Your angels to guard Caleb, to protect Caleb, give Caleb comfort, and relief, yea complete healing from this sickness. We are assured of this by Your word."

"God, I receive your healing."

> "We confess the word of God gives us power, Your power to boldly claim healing in the name of Jesus, to the glory of God. That power heals Caleb's body and spirit even to the deepest parts of his

bones and marrow. We hold firmly to this confessed faith."

"God, I receive your healing."

"Your word is medication to Caleb's life. It gives health to his whole body and makes him free from the law of sin and death."

"God, I receive your healing."

"We dress Caleb in the whole armor of God to fight the rulers, authorities, powers, and spiritual forces of this evil world. We give him Your shield of faith and pray that he takes it up boldly with Your word's of assurance that the darts of the evil one will be deflected."

"God, I receive your healing."

"We praise You Father and seek Your blessing on Caleb. We have no fear of bad news. We trust in You. Thank You God that this sickness is bound and that Your healing is loosed. Glory to Your Name. Hallelujah! Hallelujah! Hallelujah! Forever and ever. Amen"

"God, I receive your healing."

"Now, MeMe is going to put you to bed. The whole time you are sleeping, I want you to keep repeating, "God, I receive your healing," DZ told him.

"Okaay!"

Sophia was focused and praying during the entire time that prayer went forth. So, when I finished praying, she was ready to go to bed too. It was still early but Brenda put both of them in the bed. DZ had a financial business meeting at the church which began at 7:30pm. He rushed out the door as soon as they were snug under the sheets. Brenda and I talked about the events with assurance that God would do the miraculous. There was no doubt in my spirit that God had this under control. We did not cancel our faith, the faith of the children or DZ's faith by going backwards in the discussion. We just simply agreed that God had healed Caleb in the heavenly realms. We were to wait on the manifestation in the natural.

Within a half hour of DZ's departure, there was a knock at the door. It was Philip and Ashley. Ashley was a fair skinned, 5'4" native of Washington D.C. While Raleigh was an acceptable environment for her, her heart longed for D.C. She and Philip had frequently talked about moving back to D.C at some point. But, the opportunity had not yet presented itself. We talked about the positive attributes of both states. In fact, the culture of Raleigh was very similar to that of the area south of D.C. where she grew up. So, she was content to remain in Raleigh until an opportunity was presented to move back.

At one point in the conversation, Ashley pulled out a newspaper article that challenged the reader to see an image of a mermaid in a collage of mosaic art. As it turned out, it was a good game to pass the time until DZ returned.

"Uncle Tommie, how was the meeting?" Philip asked.

"Just a typical church business meeting. Nothing unusual. Just a review of numbers mostly. Brenda, how's Caleb?"

"Sleeping like a baby. I could hear him saying, "God, I receive your healing" for a few minutes. Then, he was fast asleep.'"

"What are you guys talking about?" asked Ashley.

Brenda then told her and Philip of the events of the day. She went back to when Caleb first complained of a sore throat. It started right after Regina dropped him and Sophia off before leaving for Miami. Brenda had taken him to a soccer field where young boys his age were playing. At the end of the day, he cooled off with a drink of water from the fountain at the north end of the field. Brenda thought nothing of it. When he started to complain of a stomach ache, she initially thought it was just something that he ate. As both the sore throat and the stomach ache persisted and intensified, she took him to the doctor's office.

"How did he receive the prayer?" Philip asked.

"Very well, I think. I just believe that God is gracious enough to heal him," I added.

"If we have as much faith as Caleb demonstrated, there is no doubt of what God has done," DZ concluded.

"Speaking of faith," I interrupted, "I'd like to take this opportunity to share with all of you some background on this mission trip."

I told them all about the Strong Men's conference in San Francisco. I also shared with them that before leaving New York, God had given me some fairly specific instructions. He told me:

- With whom to stay
- On what days to stay with them
- Not to go back the way I came (Don't go back to a house once I left there)
- Depend on Him for my transportation from city to city and around the city

- I was warned that I would be tempted with sexual lust
- Pray with DZ and his family
- Pray with my High School classmates
- Pray with the family in Raeford

"I heard from God both in San Francisco and New York. Now, I have seen God provide transportation to Raleigh and arrange to have me spend some unexpected time with my brother. He had me participate in a healing session with my grandnephew and fellowship with a long time family friend," I continued.

"Ashley and I have some more good news for you," Philip chimed in. "We prayed about driving you to Fayetteville tomorrow. We heard, "yes, drive him.""

"Glory to God! By faith, I believe that He will do everything that He said He would," I continued.

"Actually, I don't have to be on the job until 7:30pm tomorrow night. Ashley has to punch the clock at 8:00am in the morning. So, I will drive you there then return," said Philip.

"I'm looking forward to it. By the way, God also told me that the primary purposes of this mission were to reconcile with Christine and break generational curses in Raeford."

"You are going to stay with Chrissie when you get to Fayetteville?" DZ asked.

"I am not sure what is going to happen. I am to stay tomorrow night with Ray. When I told Chrissie that was my first stop, she didn't like it. She told me to skip staying with her. I told her that I couldn't do that. God told me to go to her house on Wednesday and Thursday. So, I will show up on her doorstep. We'll see what happens then."

"God will work it out," Ashley tried to comfort me.

"I know that He will do His part. We all just have to do our part," I told them.

****

Perseverance is not just endurance. It has its base in the grace of God. When we persevere, we maintain a consistent course of action. When our purpose is grounded in God's direction, we press on toward His high calling. It keeps us moving despite life's failures. When we persevere, we do more than just hang on. We have high expectations of success. Negative physical manifestations mean little to the one who perseveres. There is hope in God no matter what we see, hear, touch, taste, or smell. So, in what will *you* persevere? What is your hope? My hope is in stronger relationships steeped in supreme love for each other. A season of trial in our relationships WILL result not only in peace but also magnifies God.

...And we[a] boast in the hope of the glory of God.3 Not only so, but we[b] also glory in our sufferings, because we know that suffering produces perseverance; 4 perseverance, character; and character, hope.5 And hope does not put us to shame, because God's love has been poured out into our hearts through the Holy Spirit, who has been given to us. (Romans 5:2 – 5)

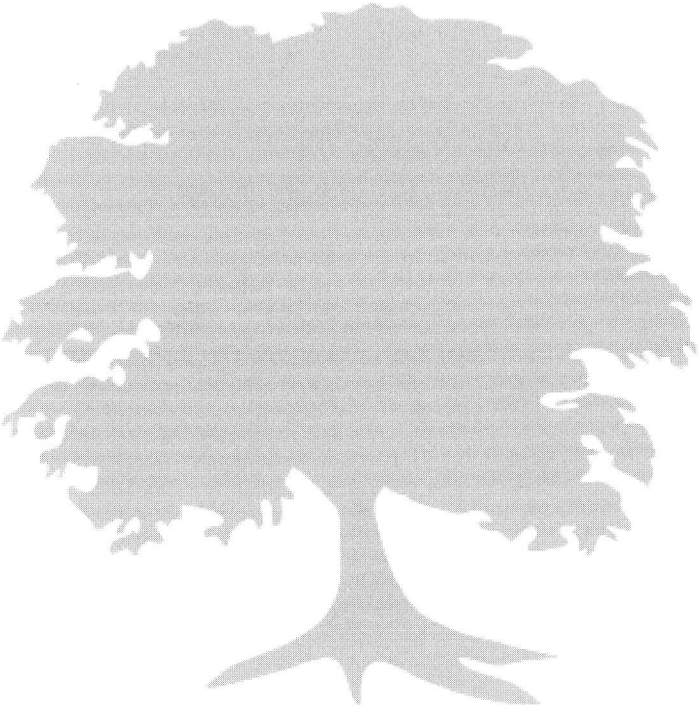

13

Who Made You The Judge?

Tuesday (Day 6)

I was up at 6:30am. "Father, I thank you for another glorious day. You are the Lord God Almighty, the Great God Jehovah. You are my God and there is none other," I prayed. "Thank You for the blood of Jesus that has cleansed me of my sins and bestowed upon me the righteousness of Christ. I lift up this family who has so graciously extended their home to me. I plead the blood of Jesus over them, Philip and Ashley. It is in the name of Jesus Christ of Nazareth that I pray. Amen."

The early morning hours have proven to be the best time for my prayer, devotion, bible study, and memory work. This particular morning in Raleigh was especially peaceful. The final dewdrops were evaporating. The sun was casting a shadow through the branches of the Oak tree that stood tall in DZ's back yard. Prince, their 130 lb Rottweiler dog was meandering toward me as I slid open the patio door. He was a fierce and protective guard dog. Yet, he had come to know me over the seven years since he was a puppy. Therefore, I felt safe relaxing in the patio chair to begin my work.

I opened the bible to the book of Ephesians. By this time, I had memorized Chapters 1 through 5. I began to memorize chapter 6. As soon as I got comfortable, DZ, Brenda, Sophia, and Caleb got up and came into the kitchen.

"MeMe, my stomach don't hurt no more," I heard Caleb say in an unsure voice.

"Let me see," Brenda said as she pushed ever so lightly on his stomach. She pushed in the middle, on each side, at the top of the stomach, at the bottom, and in particular where the appendix would be.

"Does any of that hurt?" she asked.

"No Maam," he now smiled.

"Glory to God! Tommie, I believe that God has healed Caleb!" She said.

"Hallelujah! Praise the Lord!"

"Should we take him to the doctor's office and have him checked?"

"Of course. But, I have no doubts as to what the doctor will find. The swelling will be gone and the pain eliminated. Nothing is too big for our God. Willie!! Come in. We got something to tell you."

"I heard. Thank God. In fact, let's do just that. "Father God, we thank you for showing yourself as Jehovah Rapha in the life of this young warrior. I declare this healing to be sealed not only in his body but also in his memory forever as a testimony to Your grace and mercy. The power of the Holy Spirit has touched Caleb in his body, soul, and spirit. Thank You for building his faith. Thank You for building our faith. And it is so in the name of Jesus. Hallelujah!! Amen.'"

Caleb's smile beamed as brightly as the morning sun. He was healed and he knew it. Sophia knew it, too. She was soaking in every bit of the glory of God. She was a witness of God's power. Her life would never be the same, either.

Tommie and Brenda had diligently taught their children and now their grandchildren of God's abundant grace and mercy. Unlike me, Tommie actually accepted Christ when he was baptized in Raeford at the age of 13. Brenda accepted Christ as a teenager, too. They were married during their last year of school at North Carolina Southern University then moved to Raleigh when their fifth child, Solomon, was born. The years in Raleigh had been good to them. The elementary, JR High, and High schools were all within five blocks of their home. So, the two of them were pretty involved in their children's education. Brenda was always on one school board or another. And, it was a must for them to find a church home that was fairly close to their home too. The Pilgrim Rest Church of God In Christ was the first and only church they have attended in over thirty years. Tommie' first ministry opportunity was as a Sunday School teacher. It was not long after that God called him to be a Deacon. Later, he became the Assistant Pastor.

All six of his children were grown and living in Charlotte. They missed the children being around the house. Yet, they knew that all of them had accepted Christ and were growing in His grace. That is, all except one.

"Brenda is going to prepare breakfast then make plans to take Caleb back to the doctor's office," he said.

"It's still early. Is there someone at his office this time of the morning?"

"Only his answering service but that is all that she needs to make an appointment. I am sure that it will not be before next week at the earliest. By then, Regina will be here. She can decide then if she wants to wait for the appointment here or take him back to Charlotte."

I had my digital camera with me as usual. For years, I had taken photos everywhere I went. It started when I was in college. I had amassed over a hundred albums of photographs. Now, with the digital camera, the collection was growing even faster. Regina was scheduled to arrive in Raleigh that evening based on conversations Brenda had with her the day before. I couldn't wait until she got there before I began to take pictures. I started with Sophia and Caleb right after breakfast. I took individual pictures and pictures with them together. Then, it was time to snap photos of Brenda and DZ.

"Willie, you are always taking pictures. You know I don't like to take pictures. And, you like to get them natural without a pose. At least let me change out of this house coat!"

While she was getting ready, I took pictures of DZ with and without each of the grandchildren. I snapped successive pictures of Brenda as she walked down their hallway from the bedroom. "Here comes Miss America," as I turned the camera to different angles. I squatted, tip toed, and took them from the side and from the back.

"See, you should have just let me take one or two quick ones. Now, I have a whole section just for you."

"You ought to quit it!"

It wasn't until I asked the family to step outside on the patio for more pictures that I remembered that my bible was still open. I had not taken the time to memorize any more of Ephesians. At that point, I simply closed the book and waited for a more opportune time to focus my attention on the Word.

However, after seeing it, I received a nudge from the Holy Spirit to pray for DZ and Brenda before Philip arrived to take me to Fayetteville. Back inside, they sat together on the couch while I prayed. The power of the Holy Spirit came upon me to anoint DZ with the same anointing that Samuel received in the Old Testament. Afterwards, DZ was to anoint his grandchildren not only that day but also often with specific blessings and consecrations. God poured out His Spirit upon them as I prayed and poured oil upon both of their heads. With outstretched arms both DZ and Brenda received God's offering.

Brenda broke down in tears. She proclaimed that the words God spoke were right on-time for the season that they were in. God spoke of unity between the two of them and a requirement placed on them to intercede for their children. Brenda requested further prayer for Solomon and his wife, Lisa, in particular. Neither had yet accepted Christ as Lord and Savior. It was evident in their lives. It was full of confusion, misunderstanding, verbal fights, and Lisa frequently leaving to go stay with her mother. The Holy Spirit led me to pray again not for Solomon and Lisa but for Brenda and DZ. It was God's desire that these parents would intercede for the children. Both Lisa and Solomon had received plenty of the seeds of Christ throughout their lives. The seeds had been watered and nurtured. However, the ground of their hearts was hard. The intercessory prayer was that the fallow ground is broken up in both of their lives. The parents were to pray for receptive hearts, hearts of flesh to replace the hearts of stone.

"Pray that the scales are removed from their eyes such that they cease to engage in any kind of impurity." "Based on a study of Mark 4:15, the two of them should stop running from the gospel, receive what is preached, forgive others, and avoid distractions." "Amen."

****

Philip arrived at 10:00am sharp. Since we needed to get on the road right away in order to give him time to get back, we said our goodbyes then got on the way to Fayetteville. I told Philip about my assignment to memorize Ephesians and that I wanted to spend some of the three-hour drive studying the word. He understood. We talked for just a little while. Then, I got into the Word and began memorizing Chapter 6 of Ephesians.
When I finished, we talked some more about his twin brothers, Brandon and Bryce.

"When was the last time that you talked with either of your brothers?" I asked.

"I am ashamed to say that I have not talked to either one of them in several months."

"Why is that?"

"As you may know, both were outstanding athletes in high school. Brandon excelled in football and basketball. Bryce, like Brandon, excelled in football. But, his love was baseball. Bryce was a High School All American pitcher and center fielder."

"That's great."

"Well, last year, Brandon accepted a football scholarship to Fayetteville State. Midway through the football season, he tore his ACL and was out for the season."

"Ouch."

"Brandon went through surgery and rehabilitation well for the first few months. However he rushed things by trying to play spring football and reinjured himself. It was devastating to him. He dropped out of classes, turned to drugs, separated from the family, and last I heard followed a girl to Chicago. No one has heard from him since May."

"And Bryce?"

"While his story is different in details, the lessons we all can learn from both of them are about the same."

"What do you mean?"

"Bryce was good enough to get both a scholarship to Fayetteville State and a professional baseball contract offer. The five-figure bonus and six-figure salary was just too good for Bryce to pass up. Immediately after High School, he went to the Pittsburgh Pirates Triple A team in Charlotte."

"How old is Bryce?"

"He just turned nineteen on July 2nd. He was seventeen when he was drafted and turned eighteen last summer."

"That is pretty young to be handling so much money."

"And that is the problem. You see, Bryce paid cash for a car for mom and dad. He then put a sizable down payment on a home and a new car for himself."

"That would take most of the bonus money."

"Yep. He then proceeded to spend the salary on parties nearly every weekend that he was not playing out of town. He sponsored trips to Charlotte for many of his High School buddies. In fact, he invited a couple of them to move in with him. And he paid all their living expenses."

"What did your mom and dad say about that?"

"Bryce would not listen to them. He told them that they needed to be happy that he bought them a car. And, they should stay out of his business. He is a man now, he says."

"Have you been to see him?"

"No. Bryce sent a message by Mamma that I should not bother coming or calling. He claimed all that I wanted to do was interfere in his life. He was having fun and living his own life. He told her that I was just jealous because I was stuck with a miserable life of Jesus, Jesus, Jesus!"

"Wow!! So what now?"

"That was a couple of weeks ago after Mamma finally caught up with him. I don't quite know. I have been concerned about both of them. Willie, I can see similarities in the actions that all three of us brothers have taken. While it was for different reasons, all three of us left home after high school. None of us currently live in Fayetteville. At one point, I was depressed, drinking, and partying. Brandon is depressed about his injuries. Who knows what he is doing in Chicago. And you just heard Bryce's party life. God placed people in my path to direct me to Him. I know that He has done the same for Brandon and Bryce. My prayer is that they listen and respond to God's call before Satan takes them out."

"I hear another lesson in the story about you and your brothers. That is, as parents, we must teach our children early and often about God. We must be specific with His scriptures so that as they grow older, they will remember them. The parable of the Sower in Mark chapter 4 comes to mind. Ultimately, the soil of the heart must be tilled, fertilized, watered, and sifted until it is good soil. When God's word is planted in that soil, it yields a bountiful crop. And it is never too late, as long as Jesus Christ has not returned. Brandon and Bryce could get good soil just like you did through others. You received from a good wife and a co-worker. Let's pray that Brandon and Bryce will also receive the word in good soil."

****

Philip and I had been prayer partners for a while. Some weeks before this trip, he told me of a husband and wife in Oak Lawn, North Carolina. The husband whose name was Clarence had symptoms of cancer. Through prayer and medical treatments, he had shown some steady improvement. Yet, there were times of setback that brought about some grief. In the weeks before this trip, I had prayed with Philip for this family. He shared my prayers for them with both the husband and wife. On the morning that Philip was to drive me to Fayetteville, he had an occasion to talk to the wife (Amber). Upon hearing that Philip was driving me to Fayetteville, she asked if he would bring me by their home to meet them. It was of course fine with me as my spirit witnessed immediately to the visit. We would go on to Ray's house afterwards.

When I was growing up in Fayetteville, I knew of Oak Lawn. Yep, this is the same Oak Lawn that Daddy dropped me off in years ago to spread dirt! Like so many of the neighboring towns, there were just no black people who lived there. Tensions were high and conflict was often the result of almost any contact with a resident of Oak Lawn. Of course, times were changing and black people were moving to all kinds of places. So, I gave no thought to the race of this couple in spite of Oak Lawn's history. Therefore, I was surprised to see that Amber and her husband, Clarence, were white. However, the good news is that they were Christians. We immediately bonded.

Clarence was about 6'3" tall with a full head of low-cropped white hair. Amber was also tall. She was about 5' 10". Her face had remarkably few wrinkles for her age. They were very friendly and invited us into their home without hesitation. We sat and shared God's word principally around healing. One of their sons was visiting with them. Amber invited him to join us. He too was a Christian.

"Amber, I brought the anointing oil as promised," Philip told her.

"Very good. I also received some in the mail from a favorite ministry of mine," she responded. "As you know, I am not very familiar with the use of oil in the ministry of the gospel."

"If you don't mind, I asked Willie if he would share a few words with us on the biblical use of anointing oil," said Philip.

"Of course. By all means. Willie, do you have a word for us?"

I proceeded to reference them to James 5:13 through 16 where God teaches the sick to call upon the elders of the church who would anoint them with oil and pray. The prayer of the righteous is powerful and effective. I also explained that the anointing oil was used in consecration. When things or people were set apart for the exclusive worship or service to God, they were often anointed with oil.

God also used me to speak to Clarence about the spiritual authority that he possessed within his home. He had symptoms of cancer. Yet, he was the authority in that house. God used Ephesians chapters 1 and 2 to reveal to Clarence his position in the heavenly realms with Christ Jesus far above all rule and authority, power and dominion. Since Clarence is seated with God in Christ Jesus, Clarence was seated higher than any of those authorities. He received the teaching. I was beginning to get revelation of how God would use my study and memory of Ephesians to minister to others on this trip. It was becoming apparent that there would not be one long dissertation or regurgitation of the six chapters. Rather, as God led, I would minister out of one or more chapters.

Clarence's son was preparing to go for a job interview in Greensboro. Clarence had the authority to bless his son's trip and to ask for God's favor upon the job interview.

In both cases, God showed up mightily. After receiving the teaching on the anointing oil, Clarence took his authority to anoint his wife, son, and himself. He spoke life into his body and favor in his son's interview. As he spoke, Clarence's hands began to glow.

"Honey, do you see this? And my hands are hot. I can feel the Holy Spirit's power moving in me. I want to touch something or somebody!"

"Touch yourself," she said. "Place your hands everywhere the doctors told you that cancer tumors are present."

Immediately after touching his body Clarence sank into his couch in a prone position. He described warmth and a pull as if something was being sucked from the inside of him. We all prayed in agreement that Clarence was receiving healing from cancer. No one doubted. We just thanked God. The room was quiet as Clarence lay there peacefully.

God then showed me a vision and Word of Knowledge concerning the job interview.

"You are to arrive fifteen minutes early for the 1:00pm interview with an unopened bottle of water in hand," I told the son. "When you're called into the interview room, bring the water bottle and sit it visibly on the table. Be prepared to utilize your CPR training, as an emergency will arise. Offer the person the bottle of water when things calm down. Afterward, you will be offered the job without hesitation."

We sealed God's work in the lives of this family before leaving. They accepted all that He had done by faith to the praise of God's glory. Clarence, Amber, and their son's hearts burned with His presence. It was a blessed visitation with all of them.

****

After leaving Oak Lawn, Philip took me directly to Ray's house. He was expecting us and welcomed us in to some good home cooking. He had fried chicken, fish, okra, rice, gravy, and cornbread. It had been a year since I last saw Ray. He looked good. Weight had been a constant battle for him in the past. Yet, he seemed to have that under control.

"Philip Fisher. I see you brought my son home safe and sound. Thank you very much."

"No problem, Grandpa. It was all my pleasure."

Philip had to go to work that evening. He could only stay a short time. But, he asked if I would stop by his mother's house to pray with her sometime while I was in Fayetteville. For some God-known reason, that did not seem to fit with His mission plans for me at this time. I simply bid Philip goodbye with a promise to communicate with him upon my return to New York.

Ray and I had a good visit talking about general things. He had not rearranged much in the house. Everything looked pretty much the same. The mantle over the fireplace was still cluttered with family pictures in either 8 x10 or 5 x 7 frames. The kitchen was nice and neat. I did notice however, that he had replaced the Buffet. When asked, he told me that he gave the old one to James. The only thing missing from the three bedrooms was breathing equipment that Mamma used before she passed. Her clothes, shoes, jewelry, and perfumes all remained as she left them.

"Ray, you know it is time to change some of this stuff?"

"I would like to. But, I don't want to give her stuff to just anyone. Don't you want to take some of it back with you?"

"Actually, I took what I wanted last year. I don't think I want much else. But, I'll look."

As I looked around, I noticed a bible that I bought for Mamma a couple of years before. Ray said that I was welcomed to take it. I did.

Then I remembered that Tiffany had asked me to bring her a bottle of Biscuit Syrup that was only produced local to Fayetteville. The grocery store was just five blocks away. It wouldn't take very long for me to scoot over there and get it before I forgot. So, off I went. There were not very many people in the store. The checkout lines were short. At one point, I noticed one of my classmates, Rev. Eric Rhodes walking out of the store.

"Rev. Rhodes, remember me?"

"Of course. Who could forget Willie Johnson?"

"Thanks for the compliment, I think. How you been? You know about the class meeting on Thursday night?"

"I do now. Where's it going to be held?"

"At Jeff Thompson's house on Beach Street. It starts at 7:00pm. See you there?"

"Don't know, yet. Kind of short notice. But, I'll check schedules with my wife. Hopefully, things will work out."

"I hope so, too. I am looking forward to a time of prayer after the meeting."

Before leaving New York, the class president and I discussed the potential of prayer both at the class meeting and on Friday night, as well. The insertion of this prayer time was not clear to me. Because we all need prayer, I didn't think about it very much. Yet, I told Rev. Rhodes that I would call him if I received any further news.

I left the grocery store and headed toward the cleaners to drop off suitcase wrinkled pants. As I drove down the street, I kept looking for Christine. She lived just five blocks in the opposite direction. Given the proximity, she could have been at the grocery store, the cleaners, or any place in between. I secretly wished that I did not bump into her. I wanted to finish my visit with Ray before engaging in what I anticipated to be some difficult conversations. That was not my idea of a good way to finish the day. I did not see her. Whew!!

After returning to Ray's house, he asked if I wanted to visit Mamma's gravesite. That set well with me so we prepared to go. As we backed out of the driveway, Regina drove up.

"Hey Grandpa and Uncle Willie."

"Hey, honey," Ray said.

"Where yawl goin?"

"We are on our way to the graveyard. You want to come?" I asked.

"Not this time. Allison and I are on our way to pick up Sophia and Caleb. They've been in Raleigh for about two weeks, now, you know."

"Is that right?" Ray said.

"Yes sir. And, Mamma told me that Caleb had Mono. We'll probably stay a few days before going back to Charlotte."

"Have you talked to your Mamma, today?" I asked.

"No sir. We left home early. I stopped at Solomon and Lisa's house for a couple of hours before coming on here. Then, I visited with my Mamma's sisters for a while. I also stopped by Aunt Chrissie's. But, she was not home. One of her neighbors told me that she had gone out of town."

That's why I did not see her earlier, I thought. To avoid spoiling the surprise of Caleb's healing, I moved on to taking pictures. It was a good thing that she brought up Caleb because it caused me to remember my camera. Regina and Allison each posed with Ray. Then, I took a group picture.

The two of them then headed to Raleigh and we headed for the cemetery. Ray showed me the new headstone that had been put in place since I was there the year before. It was a two-person headstone featuring a picture of him and Mamma in the center. The gravesite next to her was already reserved for the day Ray would leave this earth. This cemetery was in the North end of Fayetteville. My brothers, sister, and I had mixed feeling about where Mamma's body would lay. The Johnson and Freeman family gravesite was in Raeford. Shouldn't she be buried up there? In the final analysis, we concluded that it should be left totally to Ray and her to choose the place for her body. They chose this spot. I was satisfied.

Ray raised the question of whether or not any of us would want a spot in that cemetery. I avoided a direct response. It hardly matters where this corruptible and degenerate body of mine lies after I am gone. However, I do understand the convenience it affords those who choose to show their respect and honored memories by visiting gravesites. I wasn't up for the potential controversy. I nodded at most of his comments until it was time to leave.

"You know your Uncle Robert lives just a mile away. You want to go visit him?"

I had the urge to pray for guidance before I responded. When I did, God told me it was OK to visit him. Yet, as we pulled in front of his house,

Uncle Robert was leaving. We blew our horn and he blew back as he continued on his way. I wondered why God would send me to his house then allow him to leave just as we arrived.

In the meantime, we went inside to visit Aunt Lois, his wife. Francis, her daughter, was there with her two children. We talked quite a while. I told Aunt Lois some of the reason I was traveling alone. I told her some of the mission. When I told her about the prophecy that I received saying that Satan was trying to stop my ministry just like he tried to stop my great-grandfather's ministry, she remarked that the prophecy might have been about Grampa Ellis, my grandfather.

She revealed that if Grampa Ellis spoke a word from the Lord you could bank on it happening. During their days growing up in Raeford, when he stood and gave a prophetic word, it came to pass. Although I remembered that, I told her no. The prophecy specifically said my great-grandfather. And, I told her that I had since received confirmation that Pappa Abraham, my great-grandfather, had a ministry of prayer. I believed the prophecy was talking about Pappa. She agreed that Pappa did have a ministry of prayer. In retrospect, her face looked like there was more to this prophecy.

None-the-less, we continued in conversation until Uncle Robert returned. He had Justin, Frances's husband, with him. Justin and Frances had been married about six years at that point. Over the years, we were primarily in each other's presence at the Homecoming or family visits like this one. However, I had never had a conversation with him. He initiated a hearty conversation this time. He started by wanting to know all kinds of things about New York. Is it really as cold as people say? Does the Mafia still rule the city? What happened to the Knicks? How is Tiffany handling teaching business law and practicing law?

"As a matter of fact," he said, "I was on my way home to study for an exam to be taken in a couple of days."

"Is that the North Carolina Bar Exam?" I asked.

"No, I took that last week."

"How did you do?"

"I don't have the score back yet, of course. But, I feel pretty good about it. Two of the three sections were no problem. It was that third section that has me wondering."

"What does your gut tell you that you did?"

"To tell you the truth … I prayed about this exam before taking it. In a dream the night before, God showed me a score of 830."

"Wow. That's a pretty high score, isn't it?"

"That's a very high score. There's more. I didn't want to believe that high of a score. Yet, as I was driving home from taking the test, I continued to pray. I was feeling OK. But, I told you about that third section. When I stopped at the traffic light, right before my eyes was North Carolina Highway 830. There were two or three roads signs. I could clearly see the one that told of the coming intersection, the one actually on the north end of Highway 830, and the one on the south end of Highway 830."

"You think God was telling you something?"

"There's more. What do you think of this? The very next day, I prayed throughout my devotion for God's favor on this test. When I retrieved the day's mail, there was an envelope addressed to me as Attorney Justin Bolin. That was the first and only piece of mail that I received addressed to me that way."

"Now, what do you think?"

I reminded Justin that things don't happen by chance. God has a reason for everything that occurs. If he believed his prayers were answered before he prayed, then they were. As long as he was first seeking God's Kingdom and righteousness then everything else including a high score on the North Carolina Bar would be given to him. In addition, Justin had felt uncomfortable even asking God for His favor for a passing score on a test. Wasn't this just too small to ask for?

"Oswald Chambers once wrote, Faith by its very nature must be tested and tried. And the real trial of faith is not that we find it difficult to trust God, but that God's character must be proven as trustworthy in our own minds. Faith being worked out into reality must experience times of unbroken isolation. Never confuse the trial of faith with the ordinary discipline of life, because a great deal of what we call the trial of faith is the inevitable result of being alive. Faith, as the Bible teaches it, is faith in God coming against everything that contradicts Him—a faith that says, "I will remain true to God's character whatever He may do." The highest and the greatest expression of faith in the whole Bible is— "Though He slay me, yet will I trust Him." (Job 13:15).

We talked quite a bit about prayer and faith. What it means. How do you know if you have faith? How do you build it? How do you show it? By the time we were done, his faith had been increased. His attention was focused. We opened God's Word and reviewed Matthew 7:7, Mark 11:24, Luke 11:9, John 15:15, and John 16:24. At the conclusion of our study, Justin believed and claimed that one of the reasons that I came to Uncle Robert' house was to have that conversation with him. I believed it, too.

****

On our way home, I asked Ray to stop by Rev. Brooks' church. I had not talked to him in over six months, which was unusual for us. He had not responded to phone calls or emails. I wondered what might be going on with him. He was not there. Instead, according to a couple of guys hanging out in the vacant lot next to his church, he was preaching at the revival across town. Given it was getting late, we just went home.

We had one more stop to make; the grocery store to get soda and other things for the fishing trip that Ray and I would take. Howard, Philip Fisher's father, was in the store. I didn't recognize him at first but Ray did. We stood in the checkout line together and talked about family. I asked about his sisters and told him that Philip had driven me to Fayetteville. He asked about Kim, DZ, and Brenda. Afterward, Ray told me that Howard had stopped disappearing on weekends for the last two or three years. That surprised me because Philip had complained on the way to Fayetteville that his father was still disappearing. I remembered Philip's request to visit his mother, so I asked Howie about Deloris.

"Willie, she has picked up a stranger and brought her home to live with us."

"Deloris has a good heart."

"I don't know about this one though. This lady's man is in the pen. Deloris met her on one of her prison ministry visits. The girl told her that she didn't have anywhere to stay. Deloris invited her and her baby to live with us."

"For how long?"

"That's the point. Indefinitely. You know where her man is going to come when he gets out of the 'joint'? Straight to our house. That's where."

"I wouldn't worry about it Howie. Just set some rules if you have not done it already. Help her to find a place of her own then help them to settle once he is out. Where was she staying before?"

"At a shelter."

"There you go. I am sure that the shelter would be willing to help now and later if need be." I told him. "And remember to take everything to God in prayer."

Howie did not seem convinced but he was willing to trust my advice. I would not see Deloris on this trip. However, this situation would come back to me in an unexpected way.

****

Who are you to pick and choose what God wants to hear from you? Who told you that your issue was too small for God? Who told you that this desire of yours was too big to ask of El Shaddai? Check out the source of those doubts when they come. And, if they have not yet come to you, they surely will. When they do, I want you to remember just a couple of encouraging words. "Do not be anxious about anything, but in everything, by prayer and petition, with thanksgiving, present your requests to God." Philippians 4:6 (NIV) "I can do all things through Christ which strengtheneth me." Philippians 4:13 (KJV)

There is absolutely no request that is too small or too big for God. If the truth be told, everything is small to God. I don't care how big the problem is to you. It is small to God. Yet, all of it is important because what concerns you, concerns Him. Please don't decide for God what He wants to hear. Surrender to the Holy Spirit within you. Let Him intercede on your behalf.

"And it shall come to pass, that before they call, I will answer; and while they are yet speaking, I will hear." Isaiah 65:24

Saints, Give it **all** to God in prayer.

14

Can God Find You?

Don't let your 'Jerusalem' be destroyed because you don't stand in the gap. When was the last time you interceded for those closest to you? Have you cried before God for your household, extended family, community, or city? Have you labored for your spouse or dear relative by the power of the Holy Spirit on behalf of their concerns? There was a time in the history of Jerusalem that God was going to destroy it for the lack of one man to stand in the gap for the people.

Ezekiel 22:30 – "I looked for a man among them who would build up the wall and stand before Me in the gap on behalf of the land so I would not have to destroy it, but I found none."

Don't let your 'Jerusalem' be destroyed because you don't stand in the gap. Some of you already know that God has called you to stand in the gap for a specific reason or season. Yet, you look for someone else to do it. No, God called you to do it. So, you do it. Here's the encouragement. You have the power of the Holy Ghost in you. You have God's word on it. If you have accepted Christ as Lord and Savior then you have received His authority to overcome all the power of the enemy. Meditate on Luke 10:19. This authority is not some magic potion or wand. It is no physical or spiritual 'object' that is placed at your disposal. It is unlike any other gift that you have ever or will ever receive. This authority, this power is none other than the Holy Spirit, Himself. And, you have Him. So you stand in the gap. Be a blessing to someone else.

Rest assured that God will hear you. Psalm 4:3 - "Know that the LORD has set apart the godly for Himself; the LORD will hear when I call to him." May God continue to richly bless you.

****

Wednesday (Day 7)

The early sunrise shined brightly through the shades of Ray's kitchen window. As I sat at the table reading Chapter 6 of Ephesians, I reflected on Mamma's smiles, as she would eat at this very spot every morning for years. She had been blind for the last eight years of her life due to the effects of glaucoma. So Ray would sit next to her while she ate to help if she needed it. When I was in town, I would sit in this very chair and read the word to her. We would talk about God's word and life for hours.

Actually, the last conversation that I had at that table was about death. Kim and I had taken a hospice training class eighteen months before Mamma passed. It was during this training that I received my release regarding her death. Her health had been failing for many years. Glaucoma was just one of the symptoms. Heart disease, pneumonia, and diabetes were three others that she had battled for twenty years or more.

I did not want to think about her death but each passing year brought the inevitable closer. During a question and answer session in the midst of the hospice training, I asked, "When there is grief prior to death, to what degree is it common to share your grief?" I could hardly get the question out before I broke down in tears. I was thinking of Mamma's death. None of the more than 40 participants in the class, except Kim, understood why I broke down in asking such a question. It was relevant to the training and had the outward appearance of being impersonal.

There was silence in the room while Kim comforted me. Sitting next to us on both sides were fellow members of the Prayer Ministry at Rock of Ages. They joined Kim in comforting me. After a few moments, the instructor answered.

"Willie, grief in many respects is a clinical term. Obviously there are some strong emotions tied to it."

"It's his mother," Kim explained. "She is getting older and her body is physically breaking down with many illnesses. He is trying to come to grips with her eventual death."

"I understand," The instructor responded. My tears had dried but I still could not speak. My mind was clear. I was ready to listen.

"Death is a transition," She continued. "It is a completion of the tasks that God has ordained for the person. It is the granting of our life's PHD. The stage that you and your mother are in is called a mini-transition. A meaningful question is how do we live in this mini-transition? I have found it helpful to talk to the person who is ill before the final days."

"Talk about what?" Kim asked.

"Ask them how they feel about death. What does it mean to them? What lessons have they learned on how to live? Is there anything that they would like to pass on?"

That was the best therapy for me that I could have received at that time. I took it to heart. One year prior to her death, I visited Mamma in Fayetteville and sat at that table early one morning talking to her about death. I asked the questions almost verbatim. Mamma surprised me with the relative ease with which she answered each one. Her answers flowed freely from her heart. She had known all along that I was concerned about her death. As it turned out, she was waiting just like me for an opportune time to talk.

"The bible speaks of the death of a child of God as sleep. You know that we are spirits who have a soul and live in a body," She said. "Death is the end of the body that has carried us on this earth. It is not the end of who we are. Since our bodies have been decaying since our birth, death in many cases is a relief. That's the case with my body."

"But I'll miss you."

"Of course you will. But, think of 1 Thessalonians 4:13 – 18. We grieve. But, we do not grieve as one who does not have hope. I know that when this body dies that I will be with the Lord. I want you to be convinced of that. Are you?"

"Yes mamma. I am."

"Then do not worry. Do not fret. I'll leave here one day. But, I'll leave with great memories of my family. I have seen all of you grow to be strong men and women of God. That is the best thing ever. One day, I will return with Christ at the sound of a trumpet. We'll see each other again."

"Hallelujah! Any other lessons Mamma?"

"There are plenty. Most, no, all of them are in God's word. So, get to know that word deeply within your heart. When you do, you will have all the lessons of life that are necessary."

I remembered those words. Now, I was left to focus quietly on this last chapter of Ephesians in which God speaks to children, parents, slaves, masters, and the church. I had not only memorized all six chapters but also gotten to intimately know God in a deeper way. The prayers of chapter 1 and 3 had increased my faith in the power of love and God's grace. I could feel His love for mankind and sense the urgency to teach His ways of life. This chapter was the crown of this teaching. It culminates with a focus on spiritual warfare against the rulers, against the authorities, against the powers of this dark world, and against the spiritual forces of evil in the heavenly realms. Now that I had fulfilled the charge of God that I should memorize the entire book, how was He going to use it?

I had begun at 5:30am with a review of the previous five chapters. The Holy Spirit then quickly instilled the words of this final chapter into my heart. As the last words of the final greeting sank in, I suddenly realized what God meant by enlightening the eyes of my heart way back in chapter one. The book of Ephesians has essentially three main sections. God defines His divine purpose. God fulfills His divine purpose. Then, God lays the foundation for living out His divine purpose. I could now see that this trip was about those same three things for God's purpose in my life. He was showing me in this trip that He had defined His purpose for my life; he was fulfilling His purpose for my life, and he was laying the foundation for me living out His purpose for my life. Glory to God. There was a great deal that had already happened on this trip. There was more to come. Much more.

****

Ray was sleeping soundly. It was curious to me that he had not been up at the wee hours of the morning. He was an avid fisherman and knew to leave early. In fact, we had talked about that the day before. He did seem a little hesitant, though. He had even suggested that we go another day until I told him that I only had one day with him. Then I must go on to the next destination. In addition, it was customary to go fishing in the early morning hours for two reasons. The fish usually fed at the high morning tide and it was a lot cooler. Going later in the day usually meant sitting in the hot North Carolina sun for hours and that was no fun. Nonetheless, I let the time pass. When he finally awoke at 9:00am I anticipated that he would suggest that we not go but the Holy Spirit had told me to go fishing. There had to be a reason for the fishing trip.

"Good morning, Ray. Sleep well?"

"I sure did. What time is it?"

"About 9 o'clock."

"That's a lot later than I thought. You still want to go fishing?"

"Yeah. Let's go. We've got an hour or so of high tide left and we could be back by early afternoon."

I could tell that something else was on his mind. Yet, he was willing. We packed to go. I picked out two of his fishing rods from the storage house out back. When he saw my choices, he insisted that I take one of his new ones. He took my other choice plus his favorite. We loaded the rods, tackle box, a net, two large coolers, cups, and a five-gallon jug for drinking water. We would pick up ice for the coolers and a fishing license for me when we got near the water. My preference was to go to an ocean inlet rather than a local stream or lake. We would fish from the bank in either case. But, the odds of getting a big one were higher near the ocean. Therefore, we headed to Morehead City.

"It has been a while since we have been fishing together, huh?" He remarked.

"It's been a while since I have been fishing period. I really don't go very often in New York. I can count on one hand the times that I have been. And, that has only been with my brother-in-law on the Hudson River."

"Is it good fishing up there?"

"I think so. But, I don't really know. I mean, I hear guys talking about fishing all the time. They even go ice fishing in the winter. That is too much for me!"

"Ice fishing? You ever did it?"

"Nope. I don't intend to either. Actually, fishing in the summer up there requires a jacket in the early morning. It is still cool."

"I see why you don't go. That takes getting use to, doesn't it?"

"Sure does."

We headed south out of town toward the refineries and the ocean. As we exited the expressway at Old Lake Washington Road, I reflected on traveling this way many times in years past. In high school this was a favorite route to Lake Washington for party time. Pine Bluff Road was in this direction. Two of the many beaches in the area were in this direction. And, Green Lake, an old swimming hole, was walking distance from this intersection. The air was heavy with moisture and smelled of oil.

It wasn't until I moved away and returned that this distinctive smell became obvious to me. It was noticeable but not distasteful. As we got closer to the ocean, it was replaced with the smell of the sea and the roar of the waves. I always enjoyed both that smell and the sound. They instilled a sense of peace.

"Ray, they have done a lot to improve these roads, haven't they?" I observed. "This used to be a two lane dark road. But, now it is a divided highway with four lanes of traffic and halogen lights."

"The refineries finally made them do a lot back here. The big tankers were forever creating potholes. Repairs were constant. It became difficult for the trucks to get their products to the distribution points in a timely manner. Timing is very important to the refineries. So the county transportation department had to do something."

"Didn't they also build a new correctional penal facility near here?"

"Two miles east of here."

"Now, I see. That's why Deloris can make the prison ministry visits so often."

'Good for her. She had a tough time with her boys. Now she just wants to give back to help wherever she can. And Howie wasn't much help. He needed help himself, you know."

"He looked OK last night."

The Holy Spirit brought chapter 6 of Ephesians to my memory "...With this in mind, be alert and always keep on praying for all the saints." I said a silent prayer for the Fisher family. They had endured so much. Yet, I knew God was working it out with Philip Fisher as His vessel. I lifted Philip to the Father and asked God to cover him and his wife.

Ray stopped at one of the many roadside bait shops. This one like so many others was a makeshift facility. It was an abandoned mobile home with the backdoors removed. The owners, who lived on their boat, had moved to the area from Viet Nam after the war a number of years ago and started this business. Daily, they would catch a supply of shrimp and place them on ice to sell to guys like Ray. As a result, the coolers stayed full of fresh shrimp. We purchased three dozen medium sized shrimp then continued on our way.

But, I was still in need of a license. The fishing industry in North Carolina is especially popular along the Atlantic Coast. The game wardens patrolled frequently to check the size of the catch, the quantity of the catch, and the existence of licenses. In an effort to control the abuses of illegal licenses, the number of locations allowed to issue licenses had been greatly reduced since the last time I visited. In addition, Ray as a senior citizen had not been required to purchase a license for nearly fifteen years. He had no need to know where to get them. We had to search along the coast until we found a place. Along the way, we stopped at one of his favorite fishing holes. An elderly lady and her grandson were there.

"Catch anything?" Ray asked her.

She kind of shrugged her shoulders while she paid close attention to the nibble on her grandson's line. "Hook 'em," she told him. But, the fish got away.

"My grandson caught two catfish. They're in the cooler. Want to see them?"

Ray nodded in agreement as I tagged along behind him. They were about fifteen inches each. These were good-sized fish.

"How long have you been here?" he asked her.

"Since early this morning. It's about time to go now, though. He's had fun. But, I haven't had much luck."

Ray noted that they were fishing with worms, which is why they were catching catfish. Seeing those two fish got him a little excited. He knew that fishing with shrimp would attract a different kind of fish. The fish were active at this hole. He was anxious to get back.

"Where can we get my son a one-day license around here?"

"Have you tried the park district at Ocean's Rim Park?"

"Is that the closest place?"

"I am afraid so. The wardens are getting tough on the convenience stores. You gotta go to the warden's office directly."

Ocean's Rim Park is one of the popular beaches in the area. However, it was a twelve-mile drive along the coast from that location. We had no choice. Neither of us wanted me to risk a fine for fishing without a license. So, away we went. Once we got there, I was reminded of the dangers of that beach. There were signs that warned of both alligators and snakes. What a combination! And, many people still swam at that beach. Imagine that!

"I would like a one day fishing license please," I told the clerk.

"Those are no longer available sir. You must now buy a five day license."

"Five days? But, I'll only use it one day. Actually, I am only going to use it for a couple of hours."

"Sorry, but you still need to buy a five day license. That will be $30.00."

I felt like I was being taken for a ride. But, what was I to do? I had to buy the five-day license. When I told Ray what just happened, he said the full year cost for a resident was only $36. I really felt 'taken' then. It wasn't until much later in the day that I realized what was happening in the spirit. God had some fishing for me to do and I need a license to do it. His license! This was on Wednesday. I would be on this trip for five more days. The license, His license was to cover those five days. I had to pick up my cross each of the remaining days and follow Him. As I did, my life would preach the gospel. Others would see it and seek the Kingdom for themselves. Such was the spiritual fishing on this trip.

We got back to Ray's spot. No one was there. Good. Our intent was to each fish with two rods. We would cast one and place it among the rocks then cast the other. However, as soon as we cast the first line, we each got a nibble. I set my hook, snatched the line, and reeled in. No fish. He got away. Ray's got away, too. We cast again. The results were the same. There were plenty of hungry fish out there. But, we were not doing something right. They nibbled and nibbled but did not swallow the bait.

"I know what's wrong. Our bait is too big." He said. "Cut the shrimp in half. Then, they will take the whole thing."

Sure enough when we did that we started catching fish. Most of them were either too small or the wrong kind, however. We had our sights set on 15lb to 20lb red fish. We kept throwing them back while we waited on the right ones. Ray was first to catch his. I heard the whine of his reel as the fish took the bait and ran. Ray snatched the line. As the pole doubled over, he started to reel him in. I could tell it was a good-sized fish. But, he met his match in Ray. In no time at all, the fish was lying on the bank. It weighed about 16 pounds. Ray scaled and gutted him on the spot. While he was placing the fish on ice in the cooler, a red fish took my bait and ran for the rocks. Ray heard the whine and ran back to help me. He saw the fish going toward the rocks and told me to walk with him. I had to run along the bank to keep him from getting deep within the rocks.

"Get on the bridge," Ray yelled. I ran up there and pulled the fish in the opposite direction of the bank. When I got him away from the rocks, I walked back down to the bank and slowly reeled him in. This one was about the same size as the one Ray caught. I followed Ray's lead and gutted the fish before putting it on ice.

At that point, another family began fishing on the opposite shore. There were three brothers and a sister-in-law. One of the brothers and his wife came to the area where Ray and I were enjoying some success. Immediately, the brother on the opposite bank hooked what was obviously a very big fish. The pole and his back were bent way over. The fishing line was running away from him. He could hardly hold it. He eventually was able to set the line and lock the reel. But, he was having great difficulty holding that fish. It was a big one.

"Hold him, baby bro. Hold him," His brother yelled. "I'm coming to help you."

His brother held and held. The pole bent further and further. This big fish crested the water just enough to see a small portion of his back.

"Man, that's a big sucker," He yelled as he ran across the bridge.

Another brother grabbed a net. The fish ran back out into the water. The one brother could not reel against the heavy pull of the fish. He tried to drag him in by walking backwards. The fish rushed in the opposite direction and broke the line. A big one got away.

Ray and I were excited to watch the other fisherman work. Ray claimed that had it been him that fish would have been landed. Ray is a very good fisherman. I respected what he had to say. There is something spiritual to his instructions, too. Ray said the way to get that big fish in would have been to slowly reel him in once he took the bait. Don't fight with him. Let him run until he gets tired. Give the fish more and more line. Let him jump, dart, and dive. Stay calm and allow the fish to get it out of his system. Then, lead him in with a slow steady crank. Once, the big fish gets close enough then lock the reel. Lift him high enough to get the net under him. Then, take him in. The spiritual lessons of this fishing trip were to become evident to me as the week progressed. God is the master of the universe. He has divine plans for it and for his children. Satan is the master deceiver. He will try to mimic what God does if he thinks he can get away with it. I must be ever aware. I must be alert.

On the way home, Ray quipped that we only caught two fish. So, we wouldn't have much of a meal. I was immediately reminded that Jesus fed more than five thousand with two fish and five loaves of bread. He smiled and acknowledged that God was able to do a lot more with less if we just have faith in Him.

When we got home, I noticed that James had come by. He left one of his lawn care business cards in the mailbox. I went in to call him but Ray reminded me that he was now at his part-time job with InstaCopy.

Cleaning the fish in preparation for dinner was a breeze given we had partially cleaned them on the fishpond. Ray got out the seasoning and the corn meal. I got the grease hot. We boiled a couple of ears of corn and steamed a pot of rice. This was a perfect way to top off the day. He and I sat in the cool of the carport eating fish, talking about the day, and remembering Mamma. She had kept every plant that anyone had ever given her either in pots or planted along the sides of the carport. Several were Mother's day gifts from Kim and me. He pointed them out and I recalled the year.

One of them reminded me of my sophomore year at St. Morris when Mamma married John Raymond Dupre. He now sat before me. I called him Ray. He was a native of Carolina Beach with two children from a previous marriage. At 5' 10", 180lbs, and dark skinned, he was just the opposite of Daddy. He had the customs of a Native American and a very big heart. All of us except Chrissie accepted him and got along fairly well with him. For unexplained reasons, she seemed to have several issues with him. Yet, the relationships were tolerated until the symptoms of glaucoma caused Mamma to be totally blind. It was then that Chrissie decided to overtly challenge Ray in all that he said and did. The relationship reached the point where both applied for and received legal injunctions against each other. Neither could step a foot on the other person's property. Imagine the difficulty that caused for Mamma. Her daughter could not come to her house. And her husband could not take her to her daughter's house. What a mess!!!

Evening was now approaching and it was time for me to move on to Chrissie's house. I remembered Regina's comment from yesterday and wondered if Chrissie was home. I thought about asking Ray to let me drive his truck by there just to check it out. However, the Holy Spirit convicted me right away. I wanted to know if she was home before I went but God had instructed me to go without knowing whether she was there or not. I had to trust that God knew what He was doing.

She only lived three blocks from Ray. I could walk. As I gathered my luggage to leave, Ray told me that he would take me. His plan was to drop me at her driveway then visit with Jack who lived only four houses down the street from Chrissie. Jack was the nickname of Jackson Durley who was the brother of DZ's wife, Brenda. Like Kim, Brenda was a sibling in a very large family of brothers and sisters. Jack was the middle brother of Brenda's eleven brothers and five sisters. He and Ray shared many things in common. One of them was their love for playing dominos. Every evening, the men in the neighborhood would gather at Jack's house for a lively game of dominoes. It pleased Ray to assist me in getting to Chrissie's while he satisfied a favorite pastime.

"Thanks for the ride Ray. It was great fishing and talking today."

"No problem, son. I just wish you had more time. We could go fishing again another day. Plus there is so much more to talk about."

"I know but not this trip. I'll be back. We can spend more time then."

He dropped me in front of Chrissie's then drove on to Jack's house. The guys had already gathered under the maple tree in his front yard. The games were always played there so that the men could see everything that happened in the neighborhood. In addition, other domino players could easily spot them. Jack waved and I waved back.

****

Upon arriving at Chrissie's, I rang the doorbell several times. There was no answer. Just in case she was avoiding me, I also knocked loudly on the door several times. Still no answer. I sat on her porch. It was about 7:00pm. In my flesh, I wanted to leave and go play dominos. But, God told me not to even step off the porch. I waited. In the midst of this waiting, I wondered why I was there. There was clear indication and a word from Regina that Christine was not home. She had demonstrated in her previous conversations that she was uncommitted to being there. But, I waited.

Three young men gathered across the street and started smoking marijuana. There was not even a hint of discretion on their part. I had not known this neighborhood to condone such blatant activity in the past. Yet here they were smoking in clear view of anyone who came by. The guys playing dominoes did not appear to give a second thought to these young men. So, what was I to do? Consideration was given to this being the reason that I was to be there. Was I to confront them? God said, "No. Just sit and read the word." I recited Ephesians Chapters 1 through 6 repeatedly while waiting. Still, no Christine.

I watched the young men while I recited. They heard and watched me.

Their activities did not change, however. I stretched out on the porch using my handbag as a pillow. Within minutes, a car drove into the driveway. The headlights blinded me such that I could not even determine the make and model of the car. Chrissie at last, I thought. But, no. Whoever it was, simply backed out of the driveway and headed in the opposite direction. Surely, this could not have been Chrissie. She wouldn't have seen me lying on her porch then back away. Would she?

Again and again, I recited the six chapters of Ephesians. Three hours later, around 10:00pm, the guys stopped playing dominoes. Ray drove by and stopped. God released me.

"Christine never showed up, huh?"

"No sir. I guess she must be out of town."

"Jack thought that she might have left a couple of days ago."

"That would be consistent with what Regina told us."

"You are welcomed to go back to my house."

"I know. But I can't. I am not to go back the way that I came. If it is OK with you, I would like to go on to James's house."

"That's alright with me. But, he may not be home from InstaCopy yet. You want to call him from my house, first?"

"I believe that is OK."

James was home when I called. Ray took me to his house in the north end of town. For the previous twelve years, James had lived in the old homestead of Grampa Ellis and Gramma. Our grandfather built this house when he and Gramma moved from Raeford. After Gramma's death, Grampa Ellis lived there until he could no longer take care of himself. Aunt Dorothy then moved him in with her and boarded up the house. Years later, James acquired then renovated the property. He and his family of two girls and three boys lived there for about ten years. He was now separated from his wife. There was plenty of room for me.

"Hey, brother. Good to see you!" I said after knocking on the door.

"It is good to see you, too. How are you, Ray?"

"Good, James," Ray answered. "I know that the two of you have lots to talk about. So, I am going to say good night. I hope to see you before you leave on Friday, Willie. How are you getting to Raeford?"

"I don't know yet."

"Well, if you need a ride, I am happy to take you. Just let me know."

"Thanks, Ray. I'll call you if I need to. Talk to you soon."

James showed me to one of the bedrooms then offered to make some coffee.

"No coffee for me," I said. "But if you have some hot tea, I'll take that."

"Do you have a preference for a particular brand?"

"Nope. I'll take whatever you have."

"That's good because I only have this one kind. I came by Ray's house earlier to let you know that I took Chrissie to the bus station on Monday. She took a trip to Winston-Salem." He said.

"It doesn't really surprise me. She gave plenty of signs that she was uncomfortable talking with me. When is she coming back?"

"I don't know. She did say that she was not ready to talk to you, though. So, who knows? Maybe she'll stay there until you leave."

"Maybe. I'm not concerned about it. I did what God told me to do. I went to her house. She wasn't there. It is in God's hands to complete His plans."

"And, what plans does God have?"

Starting with my thoughts from the spring season of that year until that very day, I discussed just about everything God had been revealing and doing with me. After listening attentively, James stated that while there were many tasks to accomplish and people to visit, he believed this mission trip was just for me. I initially took offense thinking that he may have been referring to selfish ambitions. But, without comment, I heard him out. The Holy Spirit let me see the truth of his insight. In fact, this mission trip was for me.

James then shared that he had been leaning away from so much study of the Bible in lieu of listening only to the Holy Spirit. I counseled him that it was unhealthy to only listen for the Holy Spirit without studying the word of God. We hear many voices. It is only through alignment with the word of God that we can know with certainty that the voice we hear is God's. After much study and conversation, he agreed. We talked about God's word until about 2:00am. However, before going to bed we agreed to intercede in prayer for our family. It was our siblings, however, that received the most attention in the prayer. I led us in prophetically praying.

"Father God, I bless and praise Your Holy Name. You are wonderful God. You are our Counselor. You are our strength. James and I receive your prophetic word right now, Father. Because of the precious blood of the Lamb, Jesus Christ, we have accepted one another just as Christ accepted us, in order to bring praise to God. Our thoughts are far from ourselves. They are focused on You. Each of us receives now the promised indwelling of the Holy Spirit and seek Your face, and Your face only. We are no longer cursed by the Law of the Old Testament. Your love for us, our love for You, and our love for each other is the fulfilling of the law.

We honor You, God. We receive Your love then love each other just as You have loved us. I pronounce my love for Chrissie, DZ, and James. James pronounces his love for Chrissie, DZ, and me. James and I proclaim the love that both Chrissie and DZ have for each other and for the both of us. We receive that love and walk in that love.

We have laid aside every weight that hinders our love for each other. We are kindly affectionate to one another with brotherly love. We honor and prefer to fill the needs of each other by serving one another in love. My brothers, sister, and I understand Lord God that all the law is fulfilled in Your word. We receive the fullness of Your word that says, "Love your neighbor as yourself. If you keep on biting and devouring each other, watch out or you will be destroyed by each other." In the Name of Jesus Christ of Nazareth, we bind the devourer and loose Your love here on earth in our body, soul, and spirit. We claim Your abundant love. And, love each other just as Christ loved us and gave Himself up for us as a fragrant offering and sacrifice to God.

James and I now claim that as the days, months, weeks, and years pass that our siblings and us have already been kind one to another, tenderhearted, forgiving one another, even as God for Christ's sake has forgiven us. Our hearts are comforted as they are knitted together in love. It is Your fingers of love that is doing and has done the knitting. We have done nothing in and of ourselves. Yet, we receive all of Your love and love for each other.

Lord, You are our Lord. We have opened our hearts and receive the promises of Your word. We receive the proclamations of Your word. Both now and forever more, all of us forbear each other and forgive each other. We show Your signs of growing up by putting on charity. We put on love and forgive each other just as Christ forgave us. Hallelujah!!

Christine, Tommie, Willie, and James receive Your increase and bountiful LOVE TOWARD EACH OTHER, and toward all men, even as we do toward You. We thank You for hearts of flesh that You have established as without blame in holiness before God, even our Father, at the coming of our Lord Jesus

Christ with all His saints. To each of us, grace has been given as You apportioned it. So, we receive these gifts and use them for Your glory. We use them for the sake of the gospel and the furtherance of Your kingdom. As we do so, Lord we honor You and each other. We esteem Your works in each other and are at peace among ourselves.

You know us and have known us before the creation of the world. We are honored that You chose us to be holy and blameless in Your sight. Seeing that You have purified our souls as we obeyed the truth through the Spirit, we receive Your unfeigned love for our siblings. Thank You for these pure hearts for now we can and do love each other fervently. Lord God, You are love. Love is of You. As Your children made in Your image, we receive the love that is You. We love one another because You first loved us and gave of Yourself to be in us.

God, You have called us to be free. We choose not to use our freedom to indulge the sinful nature. Rather, we choose to serve one another in love. It is because of Your grace and Your mercy that we live in Your love. We bless You now and receive Your Christ-like love right now in the Name of Jesus Christ of Nazareth. Hallelujah. Amen!!!"

We went to bed.

15

Solid Foundation

The Word (Jesus) is our solid and sure foundation. "For no one can lay any foundation other than the one already laid, which is Jesus Christ." 1 Corinthians 3:11. This scripture tells us that Jesus Christ is our foundation. As we build our lives, it must be upon this rock, upon this foundation. Of course you know that Jesus and the Word are one and the same. Jesus is the Word made flesh. "In the beginning was the Word, and the Word was with God, and the Word was God. He was with God in the beginning. ... The Word became flesh and made his dwelling among us. We have seen His glory, the glory of the One and Only, who came from the Father, full of grace and truth." John 1:1, 14.

As children of God, if we are going to lead either our current or future families as God has ordained, we must have a solid foundation in the Word. To live as Godly Priests, Protectors, and Providers, we must build this solid foundation. A foundation is necessary if you want secure footing. God said that if we want to go higher in Him then we **must build** a deeper foundation. Short buildings have shallow foundations. Most one-story ranch houses without a basement have a 26" foundation with only 18" of it required to be below ground. Fifty story buildings have foundation pillars that are driven hundreds of feet within the earth.

How high do you want to go in Christ? How mature do you want to become? The deeper your foundation is in Christ Jesus, the more mature you will become. We saw in 1 Corinthians 3:11 that Paul said no one can lay any foundation other than in Jesus Christ. How do we build our foundations in Jesus Christ? How do we gain a greater understanding of His character, His ways, His promises, and His commandments? God suggested to me four things that we must do to get to know Him better.

Meditate on His Word **Be Patient**

Build a Barnabas Relationship **Worship Him**

****

Thursday (Day 8)

The roar of the garbage truck woke me early. Quietly, I moved into the kitchen to both recite and study Ephesians Chapters 1 through 6 with a deeper understanding. I slowly reviewed each verse. As I meditated and read commentaries for about four hours, the Holy Spirit quickened my understanding. The foundation that God had been building in my life was now getting deeper. From my experiences as a teenager working with Daddy, I knew that the higher a structure was to be raised the deeper the foundation needed to be. God had been doing something in my life over the past few years. Now, He was both giving revelation to the work and securing the foundation.

In the mean time, James arose, noticed that I was in meditation, and then stepped outside to take care of some errands. One of them related to his newly created landscaping business. About a month before my arrival, he and Rev. Jerry, a minister of the gospel, formed a relationship to provide lawn service to both commercial and residential properties. Rev. Jerry's riding mower had broken down. Now, he needed to borrow one of James's push mowers. The two of them were outside working out the terms and conditions when the phone rang. It was James' estranged wife, Tracy.

"Hello. This is Willie."

"Willie!! Boy, what are you doing there? I was expecting James to answer."

"I'm in town for just a couple of days. You know that I couldn't miss spending some time with my brother."

"When did you get in?"

"I got to Fayetteville on Tuesday. I spent last night with James and I will be staying with him again tonight."

"Very good. Will the kids get a chance to see you?"

"I don't think so. That is, not unless they are going to the Homecoming this weekend. I am headed to Raeford tomorrow. From there I will be going back to Washington D.C. for a flight back to New York."

"That's too bad. I don't think they'll be going to the Homecoming. Maybe we'll see you the next time."

"There's a good chance of that. I am not quite sure when I am returning but let's plan on it."

"Is James available?"

"I think so. Hold on a minute."

James and Rev. Jerry were beginning to get into a heated conversation. It appeared that the proposed equal partnership was not working out as well as James thought it would. James and his equipment were helping Rev. Jerry whenever it was needed at no charge. However, Rev. Jerry seemed unwilling to help James with his time or equipment on a reciprocal basis. So, this phone call was a timely interruption. Both would have the opportunity to cool off and think clearly.

"Hey, Tracy."

"James, let me get straight to the point. Omar does not want your name on the emergency card at his school this year."

"I understand that Omar is still upset because of our separation. But, he doesn't get a vote in this matter."

"Why not? He's in high school."

"He may be in high school but he's not old enough or mature enough to decide that his father cannot be contacted in emergencies."

"Well, you are going to have to talk to him. And, you must go to the school yourself to sign the card. I am not going to do it for you."

"No problem on either point. I can go to the school today and see Omar anytime including today."

"He's not home now and will not be back until about 5:30pm."

"I'll call him at that time."

James and Tracy had been separated for about a year. During the previous school year, Omar got into an argument with another student that led to pushing in the hallway. A teacher broke it up and took Omar to the Principal's office. When the school could not reach Tracy, they called James who came to the school immediately. While James, Omar, and the Principal were discussing

241

the incident, Tracy arrived. She received the message from one of her coworkers. Omar then took the opportunity to vent his frustration over his parents' separation. In anger, Omar laid the blame for his problems at James's feet. The incident blew up and Omar requested that James not come to the school again. However, as time passed, calmer spirits prevailed and James continued to go to the school whenever there was a need.

"Willie, I'm going up to the high school after I finish my discussion with Rev. Jerry. You want to go?"

"Sure. What's going on?"

"Nothing too serious. It's Omar. I'll tell you about it on the way."

James then resumed his discussion with Rev. Jerry. Rev. Jerry prayed for peace, understanding, and unity while James was on the phone. God granted all three to both of them. They settled their differences by agreeing to form a corporation where both would contribute assets. The revenue and cost of the business would result in profits that would be shared equally. They would need legal documents and an attorney. James decided to stop at the library to research the requirements for incorporation in the state of North Carolina.

I rode with James on his errands. After stopping at the high school and the library, he visited with an attorney to discuss both incorporation and his visitation rights as he considered a divorce from Tracy. Both of us expected that he would be with the attorney for a while, so I dropped him off then proceeded to pick up clothes from the cleaners and take my shoes to be shined.

Neither of these two errands took very long. I was pleasantly surprised to find James waiting when I returned to the attorney's office to pick him up.

"That didn't take long," I said.

"The incorporation was fairly simple. I found all the right forms in the library. It was just a matter of verification. The divorce issue with Tracy could be lengthy depending on whether or not she contends."

"Oh, you are the one filing for divorce. I thought it was the other way around. Why are you filing?"

"We just can't get along. I've tried several times over the past few months to reconcile with Tracy. Nothing has worked."

"Really, what does God say about the matter?"

"I believe God is saying that it's OK."

"On what grounds?"

There was a long pause. Then he answered, "Well, Tracy and I fight all the time. Occasionally, it has gotten physical. It is best that we divorce before someone gets hurt."

"There are two things that I know about divorce according to the word of God. He hates it according to Malachi 2:16. And, he **allows** divorce when a spouse has been unfaithful according to Matthew 19:8."

"I know that you are not judging me!"

"Not at all. I just encourage you to continue to seek God on this vital matter. His word will always be a lamp unto your feet and a light unto your path. God hates divorce. He says so in Malachi 2:16. 1 Corinthians talks more about divorce. Life at times can be very difficult. In situations that could lead to divorce, life can be extremely difficult. There are several things that can happen in a marriage that could warrant a divorce in man's eyes. While they may look like obvious reasons to you and me, it is important to check with God to be sure it is His will. One example of a difficult situation is when a man constantly physically abuses a woman or vice versa. I don't believe that God wants either to remain in that home suffering the physical abuse. Now, divorce? God will have to give you the counsel on that."

We returned to his home for more discussions. In the mean time, we made arrangements to pick up my shoes and drop him at his part-time job while I attended my high school class reunion meeting that evening.

God had not initially told me to pray with my classmates. That was inserted after I got to San Francisco. The process and opportunity for prayer was not clear to me, either. I believed prayer as a class would occur on Friday night. However, I received word from the class president at the time that extended prayer could be offered after this Thursday evening's meeting. I went to the meeting fully expecting anything to happen.

'Rev. Rhodes, I see you made it.'

'Yes, Willie. I checked with my wife and family first. As it turned out, this evening was relatively free of planned activities. So I am able to attend this meeting. I am glad that we bumped into each other at the grocery store the other day.'

'Me, too!'

The meeting, held at Jeff Thompson's home, was rather perfunctory. Schedules, money, programs, and responsibilities were planned for the next Class

Reunion. I visited with classmates that I had not seen in a couple of years. I had communicated with most of them through email. So, they knew that I was coming. And, they knew that I requested prayer on Friday night. But, that prayer time was not going to happen. At the conclusion of the meeting, the chaplain (Matthew Miles) gave the closing prayer.

In the fellowship minutes that followed, God showed up. As I spoke with each person, God either gave me a word of knowledge or discerning of spirits. The insights were overwhelming. The Holy Spirit was evident in some. God's ministering spirits, angels, were all about the room. Spirits of depression, lack, infirmities, deception, pride, lust, idol worship, and witchcraft were attached to many of those present. However, there were at least twice as many angels as there were demonic spirits present in that room. And, the human spirit of some came forth at times.

I knew immediately that God was showing me not only what to pray for but also that there was more of those that were for us than those that were against us. Because the Holy Spirit was so evident in some, I also knew that victory was assured. Greater is He that is within us than He that is in the world.

"Jeff, do you mind if Rev. Rhodes and I pray to cover both this room and those of us who are now present?"

"Of course not. Please do."

Rev. Rhodes and I each prayed in unison as if we had practiced what each one would say. We, of course, had not. It was simply the Holy Spirit moving in each of us to pray as one.

"I bless Your name, God. For You are Holy. You are Almighty. You are our God and there is no other. You are our wise God. You are the awesome God. And, we love You. I plead the blood of Jesus over me and all those that belong to You in this room. Your people live in reverential fear of You. So, I declare that we are covered and protected by the blood.

Lord, in the name of Jesus Christ of Nazareth, I lift up this room and Your people to You. I pray that Your blood forms a hedge of protection all around us. I thank You, Father, that You are a wall of fire round about this room and that You have set Your angels in every corner and throughout this room. Lord, You are the glory within this room. We stand on Your promise of Psalm 34:7 that You are encamped all around us.

I thank You, God, that all who have entered this room dwells and will dwell in the secret place of the Most High and abides under the shadow of You, the Almighty. I say of You, Lord, You are the refuge and fortress of all who are present. In You only will we all trust. You cover this room with the presence of the Holy Spirit. No one in this room is afraid of the terror by night or the fiery dart that flies by day. For God, You did not give us a spirit of fear, but a spirit of power, of love and a sound mind. So, only with our eyes will we behold and see the reward of the wicked.

Because we have made You, Lord, our refuge and fortress, no evil shall come upon or remain attached to anyone who is in this room. No accident will overtake any of us within this room either now or on our travels from this place. Neither shall any plague or calamity come near or remain on those in this room. We stand on the promise that You give Your angels charge over Your children in this room, to keep us in all Your ways.

Lord God, because You have set Your love within us, You will deliver us. You have promised that when we call upon You, You will answer us. You will be with all in this room in trouble, and will satisfy those in this room with long life and show us Your salvation. Not a hair on the head of anyone in this room shall perish.

Father, I bind the spirits of depression, lack, infirmities, deception, pride, lust, idol worship, and witchcraft that are in this room. Evil spirits, in the name of Jesus, we send you to dry places. You must go to where Jesus Christ would send you. Leave now. We forbid you to divide, replicate, or hide in anyone or anything in this room. The blood of Jesus is against you. In the name of Jesus Christ of Nazareth, I loose the anointing of the Holy Spirit in this room. There will be peace, love, and joy in this room.

Hallelujah! Hallelujah! Hallelujah! Amen. So be it."

One by one those who had demonic spirits of depression, lack, infirmities, deception, pride, lust, idol worship, and witchcraft approached either Rev. Rhodes or me. We laid hands on them and anointed them with oil. We decreed freedom in their lives and loosed the abundant love of God within them. Many were slain in the spirit. Others cried. Some had the glow of Moses upon their faces. Praise and worship burst out among God's people. One of the females with a spirit of witchcraft fell face down, crying to God to be saved. Rev. Rhodes and I then led her in the prayer of salvation. We continued for at least a couple more hours before departing. It was an astonishing work of God that went forth. God not only demonstrated His love for His people but also showed both Rev. Rhodes and me that there are no coincidences in God's Kingdom. Our 'chance' meeting at the grocery store was actually God's divine intervention. It was His intention that we would operate as one in His work that night.

I had hoped that Rev. Brooks would be there given I missed him the day before when Ray and I stopped by his church. He was one of my classmates who grew up with me in Lincoln Grove Village. He usually was in attendance at such meetings. But, not this time. Before leaving, I asked one of my classmates who saw him frequently to tell Rev. Brooks that I was looking for him.

****

After the class meeting, God told me to go back to Christine's house. According to his instructions prior to leaving for North Carolina, I was supposed to be there on Thursday night. Now however, I knew she was in Winston-Salem. So, this didn't make sense in the natural. I went anyway. I got there and no one was home. I waited and waited. Finally, a car pulled into the driveway. It was Chrissie's youngest daughter, Elaine.

"Hey, Uncle Willie."

"Hey, Elaine."

"How ya doin? I heard that you were coming home for a couple of days."

"I am well in Jesus' name. I will only be in Fayetteville through tomorrow, though. Initially, I had planned to spend this night with your mother."

"She's in Winston-Salem at Aunt Dorothy's house."

"I heard. James told me yesterday. But, God led me to stop by tonight anyway."

"Then, come on in. I came by on my way home from work to pick up Yolanda's dress. Mamma told me that she finished sewing it before she left. And, you know kids. That girl has been driving me nuts over the last two days to come get the dress her grandma made for her."

"That's the way children are. They want what they want and they want it immediately."

We had been in the house only a minute or two when the phone rang. Because it was our custom to answer the phone in the homes of our family members, I answered it. It was Deloris, Philip Fisher's mother. She had been looking for Christine since yesterday. The young lady who was living with Deloris had gotten into an argument with Howie. He threatened to put her out on the street if she did not find another place to live by Friday at noon. I got her to calm down. I explained that Chrissie was not at home and I was in town only for a couple of days. But, I would do what I could to help.

"Where are you, the young lady and her baby, at this moment Deloris?' I asked.

"All of us are at my house. Howie, too. He is calm now. But, he has been drinking and acting a fool all day yesterday and today. I drove the young lady with me to Chrissie's house yesterday evening. But, someone was lurking on her porch that I didn't recognize. Plus, there was a group of young boys hanging out in the street doing who knows what. I thought maybe one of them had wandered onto Chrissie's porch. I quickly backed out and called her."

"That was me. I had been waiting for Chrissie. But, as I mentioned, she was in Winston-Salem and I wasn't sure of that at the time."

"Willie, I don't know what to do. We can't put this girl and her baby on the street."

"Deloris, I believe that God has already provided a solution. Did Howie tell you that I saw him at the grocery store the other day?"

"No."

"Ray and I were shopping for our fishing trip. When we got into the checkout line, there he was. He told me about this situation. I encouraged him to pray."

"Howie Pray? Please!!"

"In any case, God is in control. Howie told me that she came to your home from a shelter. Could that be a temporary solution in your mind?"

"Well, maybe. She is such a sweet person. I didn't want her and her baby to stay in a shelter."

"Sometimes Deloris, such solutions are best for all involved. Did you ask God whether or not you should take her into your home at first?"

"No. But, God would want the best for his children, too. Wouldn't he?"

"Of course He wants the best. But, the best as we know it may not be the best as God is planning it. You have a good heart, Deloris. Please keep it that way. However, sometimes our good gets in the way of God's best. This time, take this decision to God and get His word on it. I assure you that if you are open to God's leading you will find peace in the way He works it out."

"What about Howie?"

"Is everything still calm?"

"Yeah, because he is out drunk."

"I will believe with you that by the time he wakes up in the morning, God will have provided a way out that is best for you, the young family, and Howie. His drinking is another problem. It is obviously related to his reactions to your house guest. But, it is a separate issue. By the way, Philip drove me to Fayetteville from Raleigh."

"My Philip? He didn't stop by here!"

"I know. He was rushed to get me here then back for work. He and I had a good long conversation during the drive. Philip is a strong young man of prayer. Both he and I will continue to lift up both you and your husband. If you listen intently with your heart, you will hear the call of God for you in this situation, too. Deloris, you must let God work on Howie. And, let God use you where He sees fit to help Howie."

"Thank you, Willie. Oh, I almost forgot. Tell Elaine hello for me. And explain my phone calls to Chrissie when you see her."

Now, I knew why God sent me back to Chrissie's house. Much of what He tells us at times is only partial and progressive. Now, we know in part. Then, we shall know fully.

I told Elaine hello for Deloris, said my goodbyes, then left to pick James up from his job. Upon arriving at his home, we grabbed a cup of soup from the refrigerator then talked again into the early morning hours. Our focus this time was on prophets versus fortune tellers. James wondered why God's prophets didn't advertise on television like the fortune tellers do.

"It is clear that fortune tellers advertise for a profit. Their bottom line interest is to make money. The purpose of the prophetic word according to 1 Corinthians 14:3 is to edify, exhort, and comfort. The NIV edition of the bible uses the words strengthen, encourage, and comfort. In either case, we can see the positive nature of a prophetic word. A mature prophet of God will not seek material gain in prophesying. In fact, it is important to note that the desire of material gain is the very reason Balaam is called a false prophet in spite of the true nature of his prophetic word. Such can be said of fortune tellers," I explained to him.

"Do prophets of God ever speak in public arenas?"

"Sure, they do. You may have even seen one or two of them on television giving a prophetic message to the corporate body of Christ. A Prophet is fully capable of preaching the word of God. More often than not, you will find them ministering to God's people in that fashion. However, they clearly will also give a personal prophecy that is partial and progressive while meeting the criteria of 1 Corinthians."

"Can I ask a Prophet for a personal prophecy?"

"Sure. I suspect that depending on the circumstances, you will likely receive one when you ask. A circumstance that may be a challenge is when there are hundreds or thousands who are making that same request at the same time during an assembly of the saints."

"So, there is a proper time to seek a word from a Prophet?"

"There is no book of rules or regulations. But, as the Holy Spirit leads you or the Prophet, you can expect that the prophetic word will flow. One key for you is your motive. We must always be very careful of the motives of our heart. One thing that you don't want to do is have an idol set up in your heart for which you have a strong desire. If your motive is to have a Prophet to confirm that idol, beware. You may get what you ask for although the idol is an abomination to God. Read and meditate on Ezekiel 14:4 – "Therefore speak to them and tell them, 'This is what the Sovereign LORD says: When any Israelite sets up idols in his heart and puts a wicked stumbling block before his face and then goes to a prophet, I the LORD will answer him Myself in keeping with his great idolatry." So, be careful of your motives for seeking a word from a Prophet.'"

"You mean to tell me that God would allow a Prophet to prophesy my desire even if that desire is in conflict with God's will for my life? Why would He do that?"

"See the next verse in Ezekiel chapter 14. Verse 5 says, "I will do this to recapture the hearts of the people of Israel, who have all deserted Me for their idols." When that desire is fulfilled to the person's detriment, God intends to have the person realize that it was the wrong motive in his heart that is the cause. God wants to recapture that heart."

"I see. It is really important to know God's word. Isn't it?"

"Without a doubt, there is no substitute for having the word enlightened in your heart. It is important to receive the Spirit of Wisdom and Revelation so that we may know God better. We need a solid foundation in His word."

****

(Friday Morning)

"Rev. Brooks!!! Boy, I have been looking for you for days."

"So I heard."

"Where have you been?"

"I have been right here in town. But, Willie, the last couple of days has really been something."

"What do you mean?"

"Well. As you know, I preached a revival on Wednesday night. Then, on my way to the class meeting last night, I stopped by my church. When I walked into the sanctuary, I noticed that the microphones were out of place. Actually, I did not see them at all. As I approached the pulpit, I noticed the speakers were missing."

"Uh-Oh!"

"Yep. The microphones, speakers, tape player, CD, amplifier, and the rest of the audio equipment had been stolen. The mystery to me was how did the thieves get in? All the doors were locked. No windows were broken."

"Who else has keys? Don't you have an alarm system?"

"No one has keys but me and my wife. Our little church can't afford an alarm system."

"So, what did you do?"

"There was no doubt in my mind that the drug addicts that hang out in the vacant lot next to the church were involved or knew who were involved. So, with my pistol in hand, I marched over to that lot, patted my leg with my pistol, and demanded that they get my equipment back in my church before the weekend's service. If anyone of them did not steal it, they had better tell those who did to bring my stuff back or there would be trouble in that lot."

"Rev. Brooks, I may have seen them Wednesday night when I went by your church looking for you. You confronted them with your pistol?"

"Not only that. I went back into the church, turned all the lights out as if I had left, went into my office, and waited. As soon as it was dark, I heard a noise from the hallway. Someone was in the church. I kept quiet but remained in my office until the noise stopped."

"What then?"

"When I came out of the office, all of my equipment was left on the floor in the sanctuary. I rushed to the hallway but didn't see anyone. When I went into the men's washroom, I noticed the window was cracked. I looked out and saw the shadows of two guys running away."

"And?"

"I lifted the widow and shot a couple of rounds into the air just to scare them."

"You did what? What if they had weapons and would have shot back?"

"Not them. They are nothing but addicts. By shooting in the air, I let them know that no one had better come back in here again. They will not know if I am in there with my gun or not."

"Wouldn't it be safer for everyone if you just got an alarm system?"

"I know you're right. It just upset me that they would steal from the church. Plus, you know the neighborhood that the church is in. Getting police to respond to an alarm may take several hours at best."

"An alarm system is still better than waiting all night in the church with a gun in hand."

"Again, I know you are right. So, I am going to bring up the issue with the church. I am confident that after this incident, we will find enough money to buy a sufficient system. Keep us in prayer."

"I will keep the church and my pistol packing preacher friend in prayer too. You can count on that."

****

James had gotten up by the time Rev. Brooks and I finished praying. The discussion had gone longer than anyone of us anticipated. As a result, there was precious little time for James to drive me to Raeford as promised in time to return to Fayetteville for his part time job. I told him that Ray agreed to drive me if no one else was able to do so. But, he insisted on taking me so that we could talk some more. We eventually left Fayetteville, drove, talked, and arrived safely in Raeford, which was about an hour's drive away.

Peggy and her family were somewhat surprised by the time of our arrival. They knew that I was coming over the weekend. But, they were not sure if it would be Friday or Saturday. As I rang the doorbell, I heard scampering in the background.

"Mamma, it's cousin Willie."

"Open the door, girl!"

I had not talked to them in over a week. Since, I had not arrived earlier in the day they decided to go shopping in Greenville. They had just returned minutes before James and I showed up on their doorstep.

"Come in. My mamma is in the back room changing her clothes."

"Where do you want me to put this luggage?" I asked.

"Put it in Jessica's room. You will be sleeping in her room, just like the last time."

Peggy emerged from her bedroom and gave me a big hug and a kiss. "We've been waiting on you. Hey, James. Y'all sit down and rest your feet."

"I would," said James. "But I have to get back to Fayetteville."

"What's the hurry? You just got here."

"I know. But, it's already 5:00pm and I have to be at work at 6:00pm. I had better get out of here."

With that, James was out the door and on his way back to Fayetteville. Little did I know that would be the last time I would see him on this trip. Had I known that, I would have given him a bigger hug, insisted that he come back, or something. Instead, I only waved as he rushed out the door.

****

"Willie, where is your rental car? Is James coming back for the Homecoming on Sunday? Are you traveling alone? Where's Kim?"

"Well, this will take a little while. Some of it, I can explain. Some I can't. I just know that God is doing a great work. As I continue to be obedient to Him not only on this trip but also each day thereafter, I am convinced that He will reveal more and more to me. Let me explain."

Melissa, Peggy's daughter, sat on the floor while Peggy sat with her hands under her chin in the easy chair across from me. Her other two daughters, Jessica and Jennifer were not in. From the couch, I shared what God gave me to tell them.

"While I would like to believe that I just came home for a good family visit, I am now convinced that God sent me on this trip. He had other things in mind. As you know, it is my first trip back home since Mamma died in August of last year. During the spring of this year, I realized that I should go home in the summer. When I started receiving emails concerning my high school class reunion, I thought the visit would occur in June, the scheduled time of the class reunion. As the time approached, it was evident that June was not the month."

"The remainder of the summer was looking pretty shaky, too. I was in the midst of shutting down our business. The doors would be closed on July 1st and all functions stopped on July 31st. In addition, two good friends of mine had sponsored my participation with them in the Strong Men Convention in San Francisco from July 31st to August 2nd. Since the business was closing, I would have to get a job immediately upon my return from San Francisco in August. I was headed to Texas for the prophetic conference in September and the marriage retreat at Rock of Ages in October. Things were looking bleak for a summer visit to North Carolina."

Peggy intervened, "Do you remember when you called me early one morning in June to tell me to pray for a female family member? You did not know for whom I should pray. You told me that the Holy Spirit had awakened you at 3:00am with instructions to call me. I did what you told me. I lifted up all of my sisters and nieces. As it turned out, my sister Melanie was on her way to Raeford that morning for a visit. On the way, she had a stroke. I didn't know it at the time but I was praying as it was happening. The good news is that after driving herself to the hospital, she was released in a couple of days with very little evidence of the blood clot that caused the stroke. Glory to God. I am so glad you called."

"Hallelujah!!! I didn't know that. You should have called me. That's further testimony of the great work that He is doing. God knows how to weave events and people together to further His Kingdom work. You may remember that I also asked you about Pappa. Do you remember?"

"Yes, I sure do," Peggy replied.

"You reminded me of the good times that we use to have every summer playing around the store and visiting with him on Saturday nights. You brought back memories of sitting on Pappa's front porch and chasing his chickens. God chose that phone call to connect our spirits. As a result, my desire to come home was strengthened. As July came and in spite of all that was happening, I received a burning desire to get here. That desire never went away. Each day, it increased. Therefore, I made plans to be here during the week of July 21st. I thought that was the only time I could go before other things started to happen. I marked when I would leave and whom I would visit."

"You've been gone since the 21st of July?" Melissa asked.

"Be quiet girl, and listen," Peggy told Melissa.

"No, Melissa. That was the time that I thought that I would leave. When I finished my planning for the 21st, God asked me, "Whose plan is that?" Obviously, it was my plans. Not His! My plan was scrapped in lieu of one God prepared. He told me exactly what to do and when to do it. He told me to join my two friends in San Francisco, then fly into Washington D. C. on August 4th and visit with DZ in Raleigh on Monday. Go to Fayetteville on Tuesday. Stay with Ray. Go fishing with him on Wednesday. Visit with Christine on Wednesday night. Stay with her through Thursday. Visit with James on Friday. Go to Raeford on Friday night. Pray with the family on Saturday night. Go to the Homecoming on Sunday. Go back to Raleigh on Sunday night. Then fly home from Washington D. C. Monday."

Melissa just sat staring intently, holding on to every word. She seemed to taste each word that flowed from my mouth. At one point, she asked if I was a preacher. I told her that I was not. However, I was a child of God who was learning to hear from Him as I had never done before in my life.

I continued, "He gave me some specific instructions as the time approached. And He gave me some general ones, too. The two principal reasons for going on this trip were to reconcile with Chrissie and pray with the family in Raeford. He also told me some other things before I left. He told me to memorize the entire book of Ephesians. He later gave me grace to memorize it before any prayer meeting. He told me to walk the grounds of Pappa Abraham's homestead in Raeford. As the day for leaving approached, He told me more. A prayer meeting with my Jones High School classmates was inserted with the message "Jesus is real and He is coming". A prayer with DZ's family was to be on the return Sunday evening trip. Not all of the messages were clear. For example, He told me not to return the way that I came. Yet, I believe that I heard go back through Raleigh to pray with DZ and his family. After all was said, I made airline reservations to go. When I tried to reserve a rental car, however, the Spirit stopped me. He told me to go without renting a car and depend on those to whom He sends me to drive me to the next city. That would require some faith."

"You mean you memorized the whole book of Ephesians?" asked Melissa. "Man, I didn't know that you could do that. I can barely memorize my Sunday School verse."

"I can't in the natural. But, with the help of the Holy Spirit, all things are possible. He will give you everything that you need to complete the tasks that He sets before you."

"This is so unlike you," Peggy remarked. "Every time you have come, you have had the nicest rental cars or your own. Not only has Kim been with you but most of your family, too. Tiffany, Billy, and your daughter from Marion, Audrey, would be with you. Now, you are alone and without transportation. This must be God."

"As I know more and He releases me to tell you more, I'll fill you in." I couldn't yet tell her about the healing line that would take place during this visit to Raeford. Neither had I been released to tell her of the specific dress attire that God gave me for the Homecoming. He told me not to put on a suit. It was an unimaginable thought. I was to go to the family Homecoming worship service without a suit. Tradition had it that all males dressed in a suit no matter how hot it was. For me not to wear a suit that day would be as obvious as a donkey in a thoroughbred race.

I talked with Peggy and Melissa for a while longer. Then, we went across the street to Aunt Alice's. She was the 84-year-old sister of my grandfather, Grampa Ellis. He had a total of thirteen siblings. Grampa Ellis was the eldest. Aunt Alice was in the middle. All of her brothers and sisters had gone home to be with the Lord except the youngest brother, Uncle Eddie. Therefore, she was now the family matriarch and keeper of family memories. If you wanted to know anything about anybody, she knew it. She knew who had a calling and who did not. She knew who had secrets and who did not. She not only knew those things that were wonderful about our family but also those things that were not. Aunt Alice knew it all.

I greeted Aunt Alice and Uncle Karl, Aunt Alice's husband, with hugs and kisses. They were both confined to wheelchairs and in constant need of physical help. I responded to her questions about the family in Raleigh, Fayetteville, and New York before moving on to talk about Raeford. I told her as much of my mission as I told Peggy and Melissa. While Aunt Alice was quite interested in the events of the last few months, she had a greater focus on what God was doing in my life in general.

****

She began, "Willie, of all my 300 plus grand nieces and nephews, you have been on my mind more than anyone else, lately. As you know, we have had occasion to speak quite a bit since I became one of your mentors at the family reunion a few years back. But, I have been expecting you to come so that we could have this face-to-face conversation. When Peggy told me that you were coming, that confirmed what I already knew in my spirit. I have heard the Holy Spirit speak these past few months regarding spiritual gifts. In particular, He focused on prophecy and speaking in tongues. I must now reveal His words to you. I know that He has been speaking to you about the prophetic for some time. Hasn't He? But, you have not listened. I am charged, as a result, to encourage you to give serious consideration to the apostolic and prophetic training that He has taken you through."

She continued, "It is no accident that God has quickened His preparation in you over the last couple of years. There is a current move of the prophetic at your home church and in this family. As it comes into full bloom in God's time, it is necessary that you have been trained and prepared to stand beside your leaders, be a watchman, and be a good steward of the Holy Spirit's message to this family and your home congregation.

There have been many in this family who received this spiritual gift. While some have accepted the call, most have run from it because they did not clearly understand it. Now, you are faced this weekend with a decision. You have received training and there is more to come. May God's grace, peace, and love always abound in your heart Willie!"

I could only listen to her with amazement. It was as if she had lived with me for the last few years. Renae, another one of Aunt Alice's daughters, came in about this time and was surprised to see me. She didn't see a car. So, she did not think that I had arrived as yet.

"I don't have a rental car because God told me to travel completely dependent on those whom I visit," I told her.

Renae raised her eyebrows then blurted, "So, that's why I just filled that old car with gas! When I got home from work today I told Keith, my husband, that I would take that old Ford Pinto in for emission testing, service, and filling with gasoline. We don't have a daily need for it, really. It usually just sits around. We got a notice, weeks ago to take it in for emission testing. I have been procrastinating. Today, I felt in my spirit to take it in. Now, I know why. It is so that you can have transportation while you are here in Raeford. Here, take the keys."

I accepted and declared further that God's timing is always perfect. It was now time to head to Pappa's home site to walk the grounds. Peggy and Renae offered to drive while I sat in the back seat and meditated on Ephesians. Once we arrived, Peggy anointed me with oil. Then I walked and walked and walked. I thought a lot about the words Aunt Alice had just spoken over me. It was true that I had been to several conferences and training classes on the apostolic and prophetic. Something had been stirred in me. Yet, I had not fully comprehended what it was all about. I knew that I would speak with Aunt Alice some more. But, at this point, I had to be obedient to walk Pappa's old homestead not knowing exactly what God had in mind. I soon found out.

I wandered about Pappa's property for what seemed like hours. The grass crackled beneath my feet as I slowly walked, stopped, prayed, and reminisced. The sun was hot. The air was still. I could only hear an occasional bird chirp or a cow moo in the distance. There was a moment when the Holy Spirit identified and guided me to sit on the ground in the spot where Pappa would sit on his front porch. I had not been on Pappa's front porch in over twenty-five years. I had no idea where that was. The house was long gone. New trees had grown up and old ones had been cut down. I followed the Spirit and sat. Immediately, God showed me more. As fresh smells filled the air, He took me back to times gone by …..

16

Restoration For Your Soul

"In the name of Jesus Christ of Nazareth, I renounce any affiliation with spiritualism, false religions, pornography, any other form of sexual immorality, greed, idolatry, bloodshed, or the breaking of God's covenants or any occult activity that is or has been within this family. Lord Jesus, forgive us of our sins. From this day forward, You and You only are our God. I loose the love of Jesus in our hearts and a steadfast devotion to You. I bless Your Holy Name and declare it to be so. Amen."

****

The smell of fresh tomatoes, blue berry pies, fried chicken, okra, and watermelon filled the air. Mosquitoes and an occasional bee flew around me as I sat in the midst of the sun-parched underbrush. I felt the sun beating through the clothes on my back. The hot, humid wind brushed against my cheek. New sweat glistened on my forehead as I thought to myself that this trip was no ordinary visit. The significance of the God ordained twelve-day mission was coming into focus.

As usual, it was very quiet in those woods. No one was near me. As a result, I could almost hear myself think. My heart beat echoed in rhythm with my thoughts. A beat. A thought. A beat. A thought. Anxiety was building around the events of the next couple of days. The last few days had been an incredible journey. But there was more to come.

I sat alone in the grass where the old porch used to be. There was no doubt that this was the exact spot given the warm sensation that gripped my body at the very instant I sat on the ground. Memories of the stories that Pappa told from his rocking chair on that porch so many times, so many years ago reverberated in my mind as if they were just yesterday. There were stories about our family, about finding your path to Christ, and about Homecoming. Every Saturday evening, he would speak to the family gathered in his front yard then pray until the pines trees bowed.

Visions of The Shade Tree surfaced as the Homecoming came into mental view. On the second Sunday of every August, that tree, in the middle of Oak Hill Cemetery, was the meeting place for all the families from this small community. It was surrounded by nothing important. There was just sand, red dirt, an old, tired, worn-down church and headstones for family members gone to glory. That tree had watched generations of us gather annually for the Homecoming. This was a fun time of family communion. We worshipped together, ate and fellowshipped, visited gravesites, and generally had a good time enjoying each other's company. Yet, that year there was more in store for me. I would go to that tree again but I would leave with a different assignment. The mission would be accomplished.

Friday Afternoon (Day 9)

When the Holy Spirit released me, I arose from the grass and headed back to the car. Along the way, I was given the revelation that the generational curses of sexual lust, cancer, and glaucoma in this family had been broken. As I approached the car, Peggy asked if I knew that when I sat on the ground I was sitting in the very spot where Pappa used to sit on his front porch.

"I didn't know that at first. But as I walked, the Holy Spirit told me where to sit."

"I am hardly surprised but always amazed at the workings of Holy Spirit," Renae said.

"He is always so wonderful," added Peggy.
I told both of them that I received word that generational curses over our family had been broken. The curses of sexual lust, cancer, and glaucoma had been broken. Each of us now simply needed to take our stand in this victory.

Before going to Pappa's home site, I thought that I would walk the grounds then go back to Peggy's where I was staying. When I got in the car, Peggy asked, "Where is the Holy Spirit leading you to go?"

Before I knew it, the words, "To Peter's house," came out my mouth.

"I was thinking that just before Peggy asked you. But, I didn't want to say anything," Renae added. We went to Peter's.

The drive from Pappa's home site to Peter's took us past the old Post Office, around the curves, and past Aunt Alice's old store. Peter's Barber Shop now stood where the Cave used to be. Uncle Eddie's house had since burned down. He built a new one in Greensboro. The schoolyard across the highway from Aunt Alice's store was still there. There was no longer a tire at the end of the rope swing but pieces of string still hung from the tree limb. We turned right onto the dirt road next to Aunt Alice's store. A lot of old memories are on that dirt road. Many cousins including Aunt Ethel lived along this road.

Aunt Ethel is one of the sisters of Uncle Eddie, Aunt Alice, and Grampa Ellis. One of her grandsons, George, used to come up to the country at the same time during the summers as we did. I remembered one night walking from Aunt Alice's store to Aunt Ethel's house. It was pitch black. It was country black. I could not see my hand in front of my face. George, Tommie, Jesse, and I were walking together. Tommie, the prankster, talked Jesse and George into misleading me about how far we had to walk. They told me that we had a mile to go before we reached Aunt Ethel's house. Then, they took off running leaving me behind in the dark. Boy was I scared!

"Come back. Yawl come back," I cried.

"See you later, alligator," was all I heard from Tommie.

All I could do was run as fast as I could to try and catch up. After about 50 yards, I could see the lights in the front room of Aunt Ethel's house. It wasn't that far after all.

As we pulled up to Peter's house, we were greeted by two of his grandchildren, Brian and Sarah. Two more, Stephanie and Emily, were on the inside with Ruth, his wife. Brian, Sarah, and Stephanie were called the Foot Loose Crew, Jr. Their parents are the original Foot Loose Crew. That's all they lived for, fun. None had accepted Christ. Emily's parents, like Peter and Ruth, were children of God.

"Granddaddy, Aunt Peggy, and Aunt Renae are here. They got a man with them."

"Stop blocking the doorway, Brian," Renae told him.

"You can't make me," he said as he stood spread eagled in the doorway.

Brian was a tall kid for twelve years old. He reached to the top of the doorway with the palms of his hands and spread his feet from one corner to the other. Renae punched him lightly in the stomach and told him to get back. Brian doubled over then backed up like a crab. He sat on the couch and pretended that he was in severe pain. The adults, who knew him well, ignored him. The other kids were glad to see their Aunts and welcomed them in with hugs and kisses. Peter was sitting in his easy chair while Ruth was preparing supper in the kitchen.

"Yawl come on in. Pay no attention to Brian. He'll be all right," said Ruth.

"I think I've got a hole in my stomach."

"You're going to have a hole in your head if you don't act right," Peter told him.

Ruth was just about finished cooking and clearing the table. She invited us to eat with her family. They were eating a little later than usual because they had just returned from the clinic in Greensboro. Peter had severely sprained his ankle. He missed a step on the front porch while on his way out of the house to close the gate before any of the horses got out. It was the first step down from the porch, too. He took a very big fall.

Nothing was broken but the swelling had started. The doctor said that he should keep weight off it for about a week. He gave Peter crutches and told him the pain would last for the next couple of days. Peter and Ruth stopped on the way home to fill a pain pill prescription at the drug store.

"Willie, we heard you were on your way up here to the country. But, we didn't know you got here until GeeGee (Aunt Alice) called me a little while ago," said Peter.

"Where yawl been? You want to eat? You must be hungry," Ruth said.

"As a matter of fact, I could eat a little. I've been on the move since early this afternoon and have not given a thought to eating anything. I'll take whatever you have," I said.

"Yawl gonna eat Renae and Peggy?"

Renae had eaten before going over to Aunt Alice's but Peggy had not prepared her supper yet. She accepted a plate while Renae just drank a glass of juice.

"Peter, you stay where you are. I'll bring your plate to you. The rest of you kids, go get washed up then come to the table."

After we all gathered around the table, Peter blessed the food from where he sat. Peter was the oldest of Aunt Alice's kids. Like many of the men in our family, he stood tall. At 6'4 and 235 lbs, he was an imposing figure. By all outward appearances, he was as healthy as a horse. On the inside, though, he was ill. At his recent annual checkup, Peter was diagnosed with symptoms of prostate cancer. Because of the history of cancer in this family, it had frightened him. That was two months, ago. Since that time, his health had failed to the point of not being able to operate the barbershop. He could not stand for long periods of time. He and Ruth had agreed that the following week, they would travel to Charlotte for surgery to remove the cancer cells. His faith was wavering. Some days, he felt great. At other times, a bit of depression would set in.

Today he was feeling good. He had eaten well throughout the day and found rest in Christ Jesus. As he sat comfortably on the couch from about mid-morning through the early afternoon, he had opened the scriptures to his grandchildren. While they were fidgety at times, most of the time they sat, listened to Peter, and asked a few questions. This was all still very new to them.

"We've been up to Pappa's old home site just walking, praying, and sitting," I spoke up.

"There's nothing up there but trees and an empty lot," was Peter's response.

"I know. But, the Lord led me there to do those things. And, now I have a little better insight into why He sent me there."

"What's that?"

"He wanted to reveal some specific things for this family and some general things for me."

"Oh, yeah, what's that?"

Now all eyes were on me. It was as if the forks and spoons were suspended in mid air waiting for the response. Time stood still for just a second.

"Well, I am not yet released to talk about the things for me. But, for this family, I have been assured by God that the generational curses of lust, cancer, and glaucoma has been broken."

"I knew this family was cursed," said Brian.

"You don't know what you are talking about, son. Just be quite and listen," said Ruth.

"Yes, I do. Granddaddy sprained his ankle. And, I stepped in some cow doo doo right after we got through with the bible study today."

"Brian, if you don't be quiet, I'm going to pop you on the head with this spoon," Ruth quipped.

"That's OK, Ruth. He'll understand more as he is taught more. He just needs to hang around you and Peter more often. It'll come to him," I said.

"These curses have been broken in the spiritual realms. So, we need not fear them or claim them. The way we talk about them has changed. By faith, we simply must stand our ground and don't accept anything that leads to sexual lust, cancer in our bodies, or the lost of sight," I continued.

"We must ask God to show us what things in our lives are linked to these curses and rid ourselves of them. It doesn't matter if those things are physical like heirlooms, emotional like our tones in communication, what we eat, or what we look at. God will show you what to get rid of."

"One of the major things in this family is the practice of spiritualism which is the belief that the dead survive as spirits that can communicate with the living. In reality, it is a demonic familiar spirit who through deception makes one believe that he is communicating with a dead loved one. His intent is to get you to move your focus from God to the spirit. If you are doing it, stop it"

It was obvious by the looks on the faces that many, especially the children, still did not quite understand all that was being said. I encouraged Ruth, Peter, Renae, and Peggy to pick up several books on the topic, study some more, and then teach what they have learned. While all was not understood, it was clear that by faith they accepted what they heard. The curses were broken.

We retired from the supper table to the living room and continued talking. I had my anointing oil with me and the children wanted to know what it was all about. We talked about the reasons for anointing in the bible. We discussed sanctification, anointing kings, anointing in healing, and anointing those of honor. There is no magic in the oil. The anointing flows from the Holy Spirit. It was clear that we were approaching a time of prayer.

Peter asked each of the four children to line up and have me anoint them and pray over them. Brian, then Sarah, then Stephanie, and then Emily each came forward. Brian wanted to be free from temper tantrums. Sarah wanted to make better grades. Stephanie had pain in her knee. And, Emily wanted a rash to go away. I anointed and prayed for each one of them. God then turned my attention to Peter. He still suffered with his ankle and wanted peace as he considered the prostate surgery next week. God had other things in mind for this family tonight. I now knew that this was the healing line that God had previously revealed to me in the spirit.

"Peter, do you believe that God can and wants to heal both your ankle and prostate condition?"

"Yes, I believe."

"Then, it is your faith that has made you whole. "Father God, in the name of Jesus Christ of Nazareth, restore Peter to full health in both his ankle and his prostate glands. He is like Jesus Christ. Christ has nothing missing and nothing broken. I join Peter in declaring the same for his body. He is healed in Jesus' name. Amen.'"

As I prayed, I held onto Peter's waist. I could feel warmth all over his body. My arms were hot. My hands were hot. I couldn't move. I just held him for a while. My hands were interlocked like vice grips. I couldn't pull them apart if I wanted to. There was stillness in the room. It was completely quiet.

"Granddaddy!!! Look! Look! Look at my arms." Emily screamed. "The rash! The rash is going away. Look at it!"

Ruth had walked into the kitchen during the stillness. But, Emily's scream startled her. She swung around and knocked a pot off the stove. It made a loud noise and she jumped. Peter jumped. He ran into the kitchen to make sure that Ruth was OK. When he confirmed that everything was fine, he asked Emily,

"Baby, isn't God good?"

"Look at it, Brian. Look at it Sarah. Look Stephanie. It's going away." Renae and Peggy were gazing at Peter.

"Peter, you sure got over there in a hurry. What about your ankle?" asked Peggy.

"Oh, my God there is no pain! And, the swelling is gone, too!"

"Thank you, Lord," prayed Ruth.
Stephanie started jumping to test her knee. "My knee!! My knee!! I can jump," she exclaimed with joy.

There was happiness all over that house. Sarah said that she could not wait until school started so she could get better grades. Everyone watched Brian. Would his attitude change? Only time and a test would tell. And what about Peter's cancer? His surgery was scheduled for next week. But, his faith was sky high. He had peace and believed that everything would be just fine.

Peggy, Renae, Stephanie, and Ruth broke out in praise songs.

"Our Godddd is an awesome God, who reignnnnns from Heaven above, with wiiisdom, power and love, our God is an awesome God.

"No, sing it like this."

"Our Godddd is THE awesome God, who reignnnns from Heaven above, HE's wiiisdom, power and love, our God is THE awesome God."

"Our Godddd is THE awesome God, who reignnnns from Heaven above, HE's wiiisdom, power and love, our God is THE awesome God."

"Our Godddd is THE awesome God, who reignnnns from Heaven above, HE's wiiisdom, power and love, our God is THE awesome God."
"HALLELUJAH!! HALLELUJAH!! HALLELUJAH!! HALLELUJAH!! …..

****

I was awakened with a burden to encourage all of you to 'Live Rapture Ready'. God is real and He is coming. Reread 1 Thessalonians 4:15 – 18. "According to the Lord's own word, we tell you that we who are still alive, who are left till the coming of the Lord, will certainly not precede those who have fallen asleep. For the Lord himself will come down from heaven, with a loud command, with the voice of the archangel and with the trumpet call of God, and the dead in Christ will rise first. After that, we who are still alive and are left will be caught up together with them in the clouds to meet the Lord in the air. And so we will be with the Lord forever. Therefore encourage each other with these words."

This is good news and we are to be encouraged by it. Since God is real and by the above scripture we know that He is coming, we each must live ready for this rapture of Jesus Christ. Scripture also tells us how to do so. "Therefore, my dear brothers, stand firm. Let nothing move you. Always give yourselves fully to the work of the Lord, because you know that your labor in the Lord is not in vain." "The work of God is this: to believe in the one he has sent." (1 Corinthians 15:58 and John 6:29)

Finally, God gives us these instructions on living rapture ready. "Now we ask you, brothers, to respect those who work hard among you, who are over you in the Lord and who admonish you. Hold them in the highest regard in love because of their work. Live in peace with each other. And we urge you, brothers, warn those who are idle, encourage the timid, help the weak, and be patient with everyone. Make sure that nobody pays back wrong for wrong, but always try to be kind to each other and to everyone else. Be joyful always; pray continually; give thanks in all circumstances, for this is God's will for you in Christ Jesus. Do not put out the Spirit's fire; do not treat prophecies with contempt. Test everything. Hold on to the good. Avoid every kind of evil. May God himself, the God of peace, sanctify you through and through. May your whole spirit, soul and body be kept blameless at the coming of our Lord Jesus Christ. The one who calls you is faithful and He will do it. Live Rapture Ready, saints."

17

Why Pray?

In Colossians 4:2, God tells us, "Devote yourselves to prayer, being watchful and thankful." But, why should we do this? Why should we pray? I want to share a short testimony with you. I am a Tea drinker. But, we have been without Tea in our home for more than three weeks. Each morning, I go through the same routine. I search everywhere, high and low. I find no Tea. I reminded myself and God that He can do the miraculous. I really wanted a cup of Tea this morning. While I sat praying, He told me where to look. I put on my glasses. Got up. Got down on my knees to look in the bottom cabinet. Moved some syrup bottles from the back of the cabinet. You know what happened next, I found one Tea bag. Glory to God! Now, lest you think praying is about finding Tea bags, let me tell you what then happened.

When I settled in to start drinking the Tea, it hit me what had really just happened. Oh, I was happy about finding the Tea. But, listen to this. 1) I prayed 2) With spiritual ears, I heard instructions from God 3) I immediately responded, 4) In the response, I put on my glasses (my spiritual eyes), 5) I got on my knees (I know you hear me), 6) I took the action to look. 7) I moved some stuff out the way (Hallelujah), then 8) God showed up.

I was then directed to another reminder of why we should pray and found a close parallel to my testimony regarding the Tea. Here are some reasons to pray. Prayer empties my heart of its cares. Prayer acknowledges that the answer is beyond my human abilities. I cannot do it. Divine direction comes through prayer. Prayer strengthens your intimacy with God. Prayer changes you. All of these reasons were discussed in a sermon that I once heard. I won't give you the sermon. But, I will give you this challenge. See if you can relate these reasons in the Tea testimony. God related them for me. I know that He will give you the same insight and more. You will find ample opportunities to pray in these reasons if you let God have His way.

****

    Ray and Chrissie had been feuding ever since Mamma went blind from the effects of glaucoma six years hence. Things had gotten so bad that both refused to step a foot in the other's home. Therefore, when Mamma died, getting all of my siblings together with Ray for funeral decisions was somewhat awkward.

    Ray had decided not to make any decisions until I arrived in Fayetteville. I made preparations for Kim and me to get there quickly. The day I arrived, we gathered at Ray's home to make arrangements. Chrissie refused to participate. Once a draft of the program was put together, James, DZ, and I went to her home to review it with her. She refused to look at it.

    "So, where are you boys going to sleep tonight?" Chrissie asked.

    "I'm going to my house." said James.

    "Brenda and I are sleeping at her sister's house," DZ said.

    "Kim and I will be staying with Ray," I told her.

    Chrissie was so incensed that none of her brothers was spending the night with her that she left the following morning for Winston-Salem. In addition, she refused to participate in the funeral arrangements in any way. She would return on the day of the funeral and sit in the back of the church to make a point of being distant from the rest of the family.

    The funeral services were held at our home church with Mamma's Pastor of the last twenty-five years officiating. Many friends and family ministers of the gospel spoke encouraging words from the pulpit. Others spoke when remarks were opened to all who would speak. It was then that Chrissie took the microphone and read a tribute to Mamma. It was interesting that she made a point of identifying our dad and not Ray as the one who raised her. I simply shook my head and looked straight ahead.

    Robert Jr. sang mamma's favorite song, "My Soul Is Anchored In The Lord." She loved to hear him sing that song. Hearing it was yet another reminder of the good things in her life here on earth.

    After the funeral, Kim and I remained in Fayetteville only one more day. We returned to New York.

    "Kim, I am not sure that I want to go back to work," I told her.

    "What do you mean?" she asked.

    "Well. I've been thinking. We are doing fairly well. We have no debts. Maybe it is time to venture out on our own."

"Do you mean a business of our own?"

"Yeah. I think that we are both ready and capable."

"But, is it time?"

"Why not? It is as good a time as any. Don't you think?"

Without much more thought or prayer than that, we started to research what kind of business we might either purchase or initiate. We settled on purchasing an existing plastics manufacturing plant. Neither one of us knew very much about plastics. But, with Kim's financial background and my experience in Sales, we convinced ourselves that we could handle it.

After getting the legal papers in order, we agreed that Kim would be the Chief Executive Officer and I would be the Vice President of Sales. Most of the fifty or so existing employees remained. The key exceptions were the President and Chief Financial Officer. We filled the few open slots with friends and family members.

The entire acquisition was purchased debt free. We invested all of our liquid assets to purchase inventory, new equipment, repair un-maintained equipment, install new computing devices and processes, and establish an eighteen month operating fund to offset the negative cash flow that existed. We believed the purchase was a good deal primarily because the location and customer base were solid. There were two significant problems. The previous owners had not established an effective marketing and sales plan. In addition, there were un-managed processes that were causing customer dissatisfaction. I was convinced that I could handle the sales and marketing while Kim could surely overhaul the broken processes.

After two years of daily struggles, we still had not turned things around. The economy, personnel issues, unwise investments, and most of all my interfering with Kim's responsibility and authority to run the company kept us in a deep quagmire and sinking fast.

By the middle of the third year, things had taken a dramatic change in our lives. It was more than just the business difficulties. Things were so bad that one morning while driving to work I felt the pressure rise with each turn of the wheels on the car. When I reached the parking lot, all that I could do was park and cry. Tears rolled down my face, my chest heaved, and I buried my head into the steering wheel and just let go. I had known God's goodness, grace, and mercy for many years by this time. All I wanted from God was an assurance that

He had not turned His back on me. I knew that His word says that He would never leave me or forsake me. But, it sure felt like it.

Two months earlier, Tiffany had given birth to a 1lb 8-ounce baby girl born three months premature. She had an O Negative blood type. Within hours of her birth, she needed a blood transfusion and the hospital had a very limited supply. An urgent call went out to every friend and family member that we knew who could possibly donate blood. In addition, she developed a bacterial virus in her blood stream that required transfusions just about every day. She suffered from seizures and would occasionally stop breathing. The breathing disorder was later diagnosed as apnea. Finally, she was not eating thus losing weight uncontrollably. God had assured me that the baby would be fine. However, I received a call that morning that she had been rushed into the emergency room because she had stopped breathing again. This was actually the tenth or eleventh trip to the emergency room for that baby as she flat lined on each previous occasion. Fear tried to enter. If that were the only concern I had, that would be enough. But, there was more.

The business was now in a severe state of financial depression. The monthly deficit was $50,000 and growing. Payroll was due within a week and there was no money in the bank. No financial institution would even consider a loan request. The Sales Manager had given his resignation and production was late on our biggest order in months. Processes were still broken. We were scrambling daily to patch these gaping holes in our proverbial leaking dam. If that were the only concern I had, that would be enough. But, there was more.

Our personal finances were completely depleted. The house was sold to bail out the business several months earlier. Loans had been taken out on the cars. All assets had either been sold or had a lien placed on them to continue financing the business. The rent on the apartment we were forced to live in had not been paid the previous month and the current month's rent was due in two days. We were behind three months on the car notes and the bank threatened to pick them up in less than a week. The only asset with any equity was the 10 acres of land. But, it was locked in a legal battle with the State because of a planned airport in the area. I had 10 dollars in my pocket and an empty refrigerator at home. If that were the only concern I had, that would be enough. But, there was more.

I had an estranged relationship with my sister, Chrissie, for the last three years. Ever since Mamma died, Chrissie had been very cold. In years past, we would talk at least weekly no matter the geographical distance. We had shared such sibling closeness that we each could tell what the other was thinking. We would often finish each other sentences even when talking to a third party. Yet, after Mamma's death, she neither returned phone calls nor initiated them. If I was fortunate to reach her at home, her words were often brutal if not insensitive. The day prior to the cry in the parking lot, I called her. It was her birthday. It was worse than calling a complete stranger.

"What do you want?" she asked.

"I am calling to wish you a happy birthday!" I told her.

"You don't need to do that. You don't mean it. Besides, I don't want a birthday greeting from you. I am not going to ever give a greeting to you on your birthday. I could care less if you ever had another birthday. You're wasting your money and your time calling me anyway. You may as well call someone who would appreciate it. I don't."

"Well, Chrissie, Happy Birthday. I love you. Goodbye."

That conversation was one of the milder ones. They had been much more brutal than that. If that were the only concern I had, that would be enough. But, there was more.

Billy had graduated from a military academy and was now serving a tour of duty in the Middle East. His unit was under heavy attack by the enemy according to new reports. He had been there six months with no end in sight. We had not heard from him in more than three weeks. My mind frequently reflected on Jesse's death in a war many years before. I tried not to focus on the dangers that he was facing. Yet, whenever I considered that bullets, bombs, and rockets could be aimed at him at any moment, I could not help but to be concerned. If that were the only concern I had, that would be enough. But, there was more.

I had been honored to chair the Prayer Ministry at our church. There was no doubt that God had called me to that season of ministry. So much corporate prayer coverage was needed. Yet, the Elders turned aside every programmatic attempt. Prayer was an afterthought at every meeting and evangelism effort. The Elders publicly voiced support but their actions did not agree with their words. Frustration had set in. It did not appear that I was being a very effective leader. If that were the only concern I had, that would be enough. But, there was more.

This last situation is the one that likely pushed me to tears. All of those things that had been affecting me had overflowed into my relationship with Audry. As the years passed from her early twenties until now, I allowed physical distance to migrate into emotional distance. She had on many occasions reached out to me for advice or paternal support only to receive a shrug or delay in my response. When I did respond, it was hardly ever to her liking. She withdrew and unfortunately I let her. Tiffany called me one morning.

"Dad, have you talked to Audry lately?"

"Not in quite a while. Why, what's going on?"

"She called me a few minutes ago and told me that she was going to catch a train."

"To where?"

"She said it didn't matter. She was going to go as far as her money would take her. She would get off the train at that point and kill herself."

"What?"

"Dad, you need to call her."

I called Audry right away but got no answer. I called Kim, left work and went home to think. Kim arrived within minutes of me getting home. After calling Audry again, and Joyce neither of whom answered, I decided to call the police. I became extremely frustrated and a little irritated when they would not call her, call Joyce, contact her husband, or do anything for at least 48 hours.

"Don't you know she could be dead by then?" I screamed.

I strongly considered rushing to the airport to take a plane to North Carolina. But, what would I do there? Kim remained at my side providing both emotional support and wisdom as she always did. Two hours passed. Four hours passed. Eight hours passed. I was in a panic. Then, Tiffany called. Audry had called her from a hotel room in Greensboro. She had reconsidered killing herself and decided that she was going to take a train back to Fayetteville the next morning. She told Tiffany to ask me to call her.

"Audry, I am so glad to hear that you are OK," I said.

"Really? You didn't seem to care much about me over the last several months," she said.

"I know. I have been such a jerk. Can you find it in your heart to forgive me?"

"I don't know, Dad. I really need some time to myself to think about things."

"OK, I tell you what. Why don't you think while I pray and think, too? I am actually thinking it may be a good time for you to visit us in New York. You can think all the way on the plane ride then think some more when you get here."

She was not thrilled with the idea of coming to New York. But, I wasn't taking any chances. Once I knew where she was, there was nothing that was going to prevent me from getting her here. Although she agreed to come, there would be a delay. She did not want to come for at least a couple of weeks. I became anxious.

All of these things came upon me as I drove to work that unforgettable morning. After crying for a while, I asked God to show me what to do. He told me to go to the prayer room at the church and worship Him. I did. I prayed, praised, thanked, and worshipped God with every fiber of my being. I was there for hours. He sent me to the Potter's House to put me back together again.

****

The crying incident was in March of that year. When I reflected on it, I realized that God had stripped me of everything that had gotten in the way of my focus on Him. I had to totally depend on Him. In fact, moments before I got the news from Ray that Mamma was dead, God told me that I would be tested. It would be for His glory. For the next five months, I reluctantly but assuredly began to shut down operations at the plant. We sold it to pay off accumulated debts and found jobs for all personnel who did not follow the sell. Tiffany's baby slowly gained her health. Friends helped us with personal financial needs. Chrissie and I began a reconciliation dialogue. There was much more needed. But, the process had begun. Billy returned unharmed from the Middle East. The Prayer Ministry received full support from the church elders. Audry and I began restoring our relationship. Best of all, Kim and I had grown closer than before. Five months after crying in the parking lot, we closed the business and I went to San Francisco for the beginning of the most incredible twelve-day period of my spiritual life.

****

Saturday (Day 10)

It was Saturday morning. Chrissie called at 7:30am and woke me up. She had returned to Fayetteville. She said that she had a message on her recorder from Peggy who had been looking for me. Aunt Dorothy had driven her from Winston-Salem. Now the two of them were on their way to Raeford to clean the family gravesites before the Homecoming started on Sunday. But, they needed help and tools to clean the sites. She returned Peggy's call to both ask for help and let her know that she had not seen me. Peggy had tools and called one of our cousins to help Chrissie with the cleaning. I told her that I would come to the gravesite to help, too.

We all met at Aunt Alice's then drove to the cemetery. At the gravesite, we cleaned the entire Johnson line of graves. Pappa, ten of his children, their spouses, and many of his grandchildren including my dad were all buried there. Mamma wanted to be buried in Fayetteville. She was.

Uncle Eddie was at the cemetery with one of his helpers. The project went pretty quickly. Before he left, he told me that he was going to get a haircut.

"Where is that barbershop, Uncle Eddie?" I asked.

"It's in Greensboro next to the Library," he told me.

"I could use a haircut. I think I'll go over there when I am finished here."

"My barber would like that. And maybe I'll see you there," Uncle Eddie said.

I moved on to clean the Freeman's graves. There was Big Mamma's, Big Daddy's, Uncle Garrett's, and more. Chrissie soon followed. She did not have all the flowers she wanted to put on our father's grave. So, she asked me to take her to the general store. I did. I knew that this was our opportunity to talk. We had not communicated face to face in nearly three years. I opened by taking her back to our childhood in Lincoln Grove Village. She picked up the conversation without missing a beat. She talked on our way driving to the store, at the store, driving back from the store, placing the flowers on the gravesite, driving to Aunt Alice's, and parked in front of Aunt Alice's house. I listened but made few comments. I let her talk. We sat outside Aunt Alice's house for nearly an hour before going inside. The breaking point for us had been the incident when she told me that Mamma was dying but she wasn't. I had become really upset with Chrissie because she misled me. She knew it and had tried on several occasions over the years to tell me that she was sorry.

"I didn't know how to say the words," she said.

"What words?"

"You know. I'm sorry. Please forgive me."

I thought about the fishing trip with Ray from a couple of days earlier. There was the moment when the fisherman was trying to reel in a big fish. But, it got away. Now, God gave me a different view of that incident. He was telling me how to minister to Chrissie and let her minister to me. We had each allowed our hearts to harden in some areas. Therefore, I was not going to restore the relationship by 'fighting' with her. This situation was like the big fish. I must remember that the big fish broke the line when the fisherman fought with him. I had to be gentle so that the line of communication would not be broken. God told me to just let the light from within me shine. Let my presence speak. Not my words. Let her talk. I could tell from the moment that she called early that morning that she too was being gentle. When she had emptied herself, both she and I would be ready to eat the word of God. Then, at the right time, I was to let the Word lock us in and bring her closer to me, me to her, and us to Him. Now was that time.

I prayed, "I lift up the name of Jesus Christ. Forgive me, God, for I have sinned. I have ignored my sister's pleas and turned my back on You. My eyes are now opened to the error of my wicked ways. I lay them on the altar and seek restoration for my soul. You have promised that Your eyes are upon the righteous. Your ears are attentive to their cry. I am crying. She is crying for the pains we have inflicted upon each other. We cry for deliverance and healing. We cry for the salvation of our family. We cry for restored relationship with each other and with You.

I come before You, God, in the name of Jesus Christ of Nazareth for my sister in Christ who has poured out of her heart and soul. She loves and adores You. She is a witness of Your love, goodness, grace, and mercy. You have declared in Your word that You will comfort her as a mother comforts her child. Likewise, as a mother replenishes her child, so I pray that You replenish her. Refill her this day with Your Holy Spirit. Give her rest by the quiet waters and restore her soul. As Your ravens fed Elijah, feed her Father with manna from on high. Remind her that there are living waters deep within her. Those, including her, that drink of this water will never thirst. Open her heart to receive a renewal of Jesus Christ. Bring to her memory the excitement and joy of salvation.

Father, You know my sister's heart. Her heart is heavy for the lost and blind. She has comforted those in trouble with the comfort that she has received. She has been distressed for the comfort and salvation of others. Lord Jesus, Chrissie has patiently endured suffering so that another might live.

She, God, has thrown her body on others and wailed for them. She has given of her heart, soul, body, finances, and spiritual gifts. She now seeks rest in You. She desires a refilling of Your love. Help her to stand another day. Refit her, Lord, with Your armor. Show her Christ today. Where she hurts, apply the balm of Gilead. Where there is self-doubt, remind her that she can do all things in Christ Jesus who strengthens her. Give her revelation knowledge, understanding, spiritual wisdom, and divine discernment.

I plead the blood of Jesus over Chrissie and take my stand with others of a like heart to build a hedge of protection all about her. Bless her, Lord God, with the life giving abundance that You have promised. Guide her and restore comfort to her. Peace God, peace to all those who receive Your word whether far or near.

May our Lord Jesus Christ and God our Father, who loved us and by His grace gave us eternal encouragement and good hope, encourage her heart and strengthen her in every good deed and word."

We hugged each other and smiled. No other words were necessary. God had just demonstrated another miracle.

****

Peggy, Renae, Aunt Dorothy, Aunt Alice, Uncle Karl, and Melanie were inside talking. Most of the talk centered on Pappa, Grampa Ellis, and Aunt Helen. These three seemed to have the gift of Prophecy and intercessory prayer. There was an attempt by Satan to pervert that ministry, though. It was clear that Pappa was a strong man of prayer. He taught the family and led the family in weekly prayer. He also had a gift of Prophecy. He could foretell and forth tell. So did Grampa Ellis, and Aunt Helen. All could speak a word and that word would prove to be true. At one point, Aunt Alice said in a very serious tone that Aunt Helen had a spirit that she did not understand and neither did anyone else. Aunt Helen could look at you and tell if something good or evil was lurking around or within you.

Aunt Alice told of a time when Pappa lived with Aunt Helen and a strange incident occurred. Aunt Helen told Pappa that as she approached her house late one night she could see people on her roof. Pappa dismissed the idea by telling her that she probably ate something that did not agree with her. A couple of nights later, Pappa heard someone walking on the roof. When he went outside to check, no one was present. Yet, he continued to hear the footsteps. He confirmed that unknown spirits were present in her home. The two of them then took their authority to cast them out. They sent them to where Jesus would send them.

Aunt Alice told of a favorite cup from which Pappa drank. He reached a point where he claimed to see responses to questions in that cup. Someone would come to him with a question. He would ask God, look into the cup, and then tell them what he saw. It was kind of eerie listening to this. After he died, Aunt Helen offered the cup to Aunt Dorothy. After accepting it, she broke it into pieces then threw the cup away. We recognized that Pappa did not get into spiritism. He used the cup as a thinking mechanism much like one might stare into the air when thinking. However, we also recognized an attempt was made to pervert the gift.

Aunt Dorothy then declared that the generational curses over the family had been broken. Two months prior to that time, the Holy Spirit told her to come to New York to visit me. But, she did not do it. Yet, she could feel a spiritual connection between us regarding family curses. At that point, Peggy told the others of the incidents from Friday. She told them about my walk around Pappa's property. She recalled that it was there that I, also, declared that the generational curses had been broken. From the mouth of two witnesses God confirmed that it was done in Jesus' name.

Aunt Alice then asked me to lead the family in prayer.

"Father God, in the Name of Jesus Christ of Nazareth, we give You honor and praise. We bless Your Holy Name. Thank You for being our Lord. Thank You for being our God. Thank You for life and freedom to approach You. Father, we plead the blood of Jesus over our family. We declare and agree that all generational curses over this family have been broken. We are no longer bound to any demonic covenants, vows, agreements, and practices that were entered into by any of our ancestors. We renounce any known and unknown pledges that we have made to anyone or anything that is not of You. We declare that You and You alone are our God. You are the One and Only to whom we have devoted our lives. Our covenant with You is based on the blood of Jesus shed on the cross at Calvary. We bind all demonic spirits, spirits of backlash and retaliation. We forbid those sprits from replicating, dividing, or increasing in any way. You are loosed from your assignments against this family. Those assignments are cancelled and called null and void. We loose love in abundance across this family. We loose purity in the name of Jesus. We loose joy, faith, and peace in the name of Jesus."

Aunt Alice then joined in with "By the authority Jesus gave us in Matthew chapter 10, Mark chapter 16, and Luke chapter 10, we cast out demonic spirits of perversion, infirmities, and iniquities from within this family. Cancer, we command you to flee. Glaucoma, we command you to flee. Diabetes, we command you to flee. Heart disease and strokes, we command you to flee. The blood of Jesus is against you. We curse you at the roots and command that you die. Come out of this family now and go to where Jesus Christ would send you." "Lord, I seal this prayer with the blood of Jesus," I prayed. "We love You, God. We are seated with Christ Jesus in the heavenly realms observing with our spiritual eyes to see what the end will be. These things are completed in the heavens and we decree their manifestation here on earth. It is in the name, character, and nature of Jesus Christ, our Lord that we call it done. So be it. Amen."

When I reached out to hug Aunt Alice, she screamed.

"I see!! I see!!"

I shuddered. I had no idea what she was talking about. My mind raced. I thought she had seen something demonic in the spirit.

"What is it, Mamma?" Renae cried.

"You. Peggy. Chrissie. Everybody. I can see everybody!!"

"You can really see us?"

"Yesssss!! Hallelujah!!! I can see!! Thank you, Lord. Thank you, Lord."

We shouted so loud and hard that I thought we were going to shake the foundation from beneath the house. Aunt Alice touched everything in sight. She hugged everyone. She rolled herself into every room to touch things. She lifted her arms in gratitude.

"Glory to God. Glory to God!"

This was the family prayer that God told me would occur on Saturday. I had not conceived that it would come about in this way. But, God orchestrated it perfectly for His purposes.

****

Chrissie and Aunt Dorothy went back to Fayetteville to prepare for the evening's Homecoming service. Typically, several groups would come together for a night of worshipping God in song, on the Saturday evening before the Sunday service. I left to go get a haircut.

When I got to the barbershop, Uncle Eddie was in his barber's chair. They were engaged in typical barbershop talk like sports, family, and current events. I told Uncle Eddie about the miracles and prayers at Aunt Alice's. He nearly jumped out of the chair. His barber stopped cutting hair, as both were extremely attentive to what I was saying.

"Hurry up, man. I got to go over to Alice's. I want her to see me. And, make sure you do it right. I don't want my hair messed up, now."

As I looked at Uncle Eddie, I imagined I could see my dad sitting in that barber chair. The dream of my dad in a barber chair from many years earlier came into clear focus. Uncle Eddie was now in part giving the attention that I had cherished from him but never received.

Because Uncle Eddie was the youngest of Pappa's children, he and my dad were close in age. I had not talked to him about my dad before. I took the opportunity to ask him about growing up with him. He principally told me about their late teens and early twenties when the two of them and others sang together. The group sang gospels as they traveled from church to church on Friday, Saturday, and Sunday nights. He had a gleam in his eye as he told of my dad singing the lead in 'Two Wings'. He had visited Daddy in California when he was a young man. He recalled that Daddy regretted not being able to raise us. Uncle Eddie told me that Daddy had seen something special in me. In particular, Daddy in remorse told Uncle Eddie that one of his biggest regrets was not being able to watch me grow into a child of God.

Tears welled up in me as I listened to Uncle Eddie talk about Daddy. I had no idea that he even knew that I existed half of the time. I never thought that Daddy actually wanted to be with me.

The barber finished Uncle Eddie then started my hair. It was getting late and Uncle Eddie was excited to go visit Aunt Alice. He told me that he would be happy to talk again whenever I desired. Uncle Eddie told his barber that he would see him the next morning. Then, he was gone in a flash.

The barber and I continued in conversation about Aunt Alice, my Daddy, and God's word. At the conclusion, he invited me to attend the Men's Sunday School class at his church. I told him that I would pray about it because I knew that the Homecoming service also included Sunday School. I was a little confused. Based on Uncle Eddie's comment, I assumed that he would be at the Homecoming's Sunday School service. But, this barber invited me to his church. When I asked him for an explanation, he told me that he and Uncle Eddie were members of the same church. And Uncle Eddie planned to go to Sunday School at his home church before going to the Homecoming.

I left the barbershop in Greensboro and headed back to Raeford. On the way, God told me to go to Sunday School with Uncle Eddie the next morning. When I arrived at Aunt Alice's house, everyone was still excited. Many family members came to Aunt Alice's house to see her. The house was packed. Peggy decided to go across the street to her home for a little while. I joined her. When I asked her about Uncle Eddie's affiliation with a church in Greensboro, she told me that several family members attended about five or six different churches. That also surprised me.

I had assumed that most of the family attended one church in Raeford. But, for a variety of reasons they had ventured off to other churches. Now, many in the family were not happy with their current church affiliations. For example, Peggy had concerns about the conduct of her membership at special church functions. Many times alcohol was served, members got intoxicated, and worldly activities were entertained. She was not sure what to do about it. We opened God's word to Ephesians chapters 4 and 5, which explained how we should imitate God in true righteousness and holiness. I encouraged her to seek God's counsel and guidance in addressing each specific circumstance. But, it was clear to us that she had a responsibility to discuss such activities with the Elders of that congregation. God would direct her actions following that conversation. I then took a nap for about 3 hours, got up, and prepared to go to the Saturday evening service. I traveled by myself but met the family at the church. The roots of this service go back quite a ways. Given that so many of the towns in this geography hosted similar Homecoming services, it was typical for many of them to come together on a Saturday night for fellowship before the Sunday services. Several groups from neighboring churches were there also. Each sang at least two selections. The songs were typically very traditional. Most were worship songs with a blues beat. While the intent was to fellowship in song, the atmosphere was more indicative of a competitive songfest.

I sat next to Robert Jr., who was now a Pastor. We talked between songs about family matters. He had received the news about Aunt Alice. We talked quite a bit about her. God then gave me a word of knowledge.

"The Lord says that you are to get a complete physical from your Doctor as soon as you can. He has shown me an attack to the lower parts of your body. You are not to be concerned, however. God has healed this condition as long as you are obedient to follow His directions."

"Willie, you won't believe this but my wife and I were just talking about that this afternoon. I had been feeling a little discomfort for the past few days. I wasn't sure that I would make it tonight. She encouraged me to press on. Now, I see that it was to receive this confirmation to get checked out."

"Glory to God!"

For the remainder of the evening, he and I enjoyed the music. I constantly kept looking for Chrissie and Aunt Dorothy. But, they did not return. So I went back to Peggy's house. It was very late.

Saturday Night

I dreamed that a young person was about to stab a baby in the stomach with a sharp instrument like a knife or a pair of scissors. I got up and interceded in the Spirit. I did not know what this dream was about. I just knew that I needed to pray.

****

18

Jesus Christ Is Real And He Is Coming

In the name of Jesus Christ of Nazareth, I bless your seed and the seed of your seed. I plead the blood of Jesus over your children and your children's children. A scripture that gives me solace when I think of my posterity is Isaiah 54:13-"All your sons will be taught by the LORD and great will be your children's peace." Isn't it wonderful to know that God has a plan for your children just as He has a plan for you? Great will be their peace. I pray that the greatness of their peace begins and extends this day. Their walk or ride to school, work, or play will be guarded by God's ministering spirits. Great will be their peace. No calamities, hurt, harm, or danger will come nigh them, today. Great will be their peace. They shall come out of the darkness into His wonderful light. Great will be their peace.

****

Sunday (Day 11)

I was up reciting Ephesians Chapters 1 through 6. Again, Chrissie called early. She could not find Aunt Dorothy. She was expecting Aunt Dorothy to come get her on Saturday night for the trip back to Raeford. But, she didn't show up. In addition, Aunt Dorothy's luggage was gone. It appeared that she might have gone back to Winston-Salem. But, since Aunt Dorothy was aware that Chrissie planned to go back with her, it didn't seem reasonable that she would leave without telling Chrissie. It could have been that Aunt Dorothy spent the night with one of our other relatives in Fayetteville. However, after a considerable telephone search, no one could find her. By all appearances, she had gone back to Winston-Salem with no explanation.

I asked Chrissie if she had spoken to James.

"I talked to him this morning. He told me that he did not make it back to Raeford last night, either," she said.

"No he didn't. I did not see him at the church," I told her.

"Well, if we don't catch up with Aunt Dorothy, he and I will return for today's Homecoming service," she responded.

"That would be good. By the way, before I left Raleigh, DZ mentioned that he might come up for the Homecoming," I said.

"Was he planning to come by himself?"

"I don't think so. Brenda was planning to come with him also."

Since both my brothers and sister would be in Raeford, I concluded that God was going to use one of them to drive me back to Raleigh. In addition, Rev. Brooks had implied on Friday that he would come to Raeford. If so, there would be many options available to me for my return trip.

It was getting close to the time to leave for Sunday School. I finished cleaning myself up and sat down for a little breakfast. Peggy joined me.

"While praying this morning Willie, I got a nudge in my spirit to be the one to drive you to Raleigh," she said.

"That would be great. But, are you sure?"

"Yeah, I am. If I can get Jessica to ride with me, I would consider it done."

"Then, let us wait and see how God works it out," I said.

As we talked, she had several questions. The subject of dreams came up. I told her about my dream during the previous night of a young child stabbing a baby. She got very quiet, reached behind her, and removed an ice pick from her drawer. A few days earlier, Aunt Alice told her of a dream that someone was going to be killed with a sharp instrument like an ice pick. Peggy had an ice pick in her kitchen drawer. Aunt Alice told her to remove it. Peggy was not obedient, thinking her mother had a food induced dream.

But, when she heard my dream, she decided to immediately obey.

"I understand now why you removed the ice pick so quickly. God is good. Whatever the connection was between your mother's dream and mine has now been taken care of," I told her.

"What do you mean?" she asked.

"You see, when I was awakened from the dream last night, I prayed in tongues. I did not know then for whom or for what I was praying. And honestly, I still don't know now. What I do know is that God orchestrated this conversation so that you would remove that ice pick."

"You think that whatever might have happened has been prevented?"

"No, I don't think so. I know without a doubt."

Peggy then called Aunt Alice and we talked. She told me of her dream and I told her of mine. I also told her that I prayed during the night when I got the dream. She thanked me for being obedient to pray and for having the discussion with Peggy. Aunt Alice confirmed that any concerns for someone being hurt should be forgotten. She didn't have an explanation for either dream. She just knew that all was well.

****

The Sunday School lesson at Uncle Eddie's church was about repentance. It was taken from the book by the Prophet Joel who warned the children of Israel to repent.

"Put on sackcloth, O priests, and mourn; wail, you who minister before the altar. Come, spend the night in sackcloth, you who minister before my God; for the grain offerings and drink offerings are withheld from the house of your God. Declare a holy fast; call a sacred assembly. Summon the elders and all who live in the land to the house of the LORD your God, and cry out to the LORD." The Prophet Joel's message to the Israelites was a timely message to the men in this class as well. It was clear that God was not only calling members of my family to repent and be restored but also His people around the universe. The men in this class were the ones to receive God's call today. They were the priests of their homes. Many were the Elders of that church. Could they not hear?

Joel continued, "Even now," declares the LORD, "return to me with all your heart, with fasting and weeping and mourning. Rend your heart and not your garments. Return to the LORD your God, for he is gracious and compassionate, slow to anger and abounding in love, and he relents from sending calamity.'"

God was not looking for outward signs of repentance. As with the Israelites of the Old Testament, the physical signs of today were often fake. The people did not truly repent. They only wanted people to see them as repenting.

So, they tell as many people as will listen that they are fasting for repentance. They will quickly tell a coworker that they are not going to lunch only so the coworker will ask them why. Then, they can respond that they are fasting. What was the condition of their heart? That is what is important to God. God wants true, heart-felt repentance.

His word tells us that He is slow to anger and abounding in love. He is more patient with us than we deserve. He is certainly more patient with us than we are with each other. God is not a man that He would lie. He watches over His word to see that it is fulfilled. His word in Joel says that He will relent from sending calamity if we repent. I believe it. Don't you?

The last section of the lesson focused on these words from Joel in chapter 3. "In that day the mountains will drip new wine, and the hills will flow with milk; all the ravines of Judah will run with water. A fountain will flow out of the LORD'S house and will water the valley of acacias."

This tells us that God has a day of renewing all things. He has restoration and refreshing for us. These are not things that we can do for ourselves. It is only by His grace and His mercy that He can and He does renew us.

At the conclusion of the lesson, the facilitator asked me to introduce myself. As I was doing so, I was prompted by Holy Spirit to give this word.

"The Lord says, "Men of God, I have called you here to listen to My word. Hear me well. Clean your closets of the secrets that you have hidden there. You know them. Then, return to your first love. I have great faith in you. More faith than you can imagine. I know your heart. It is a heart of gold. Your heart is pliable. It is a loving heart. So, turn it to me and I will show you My abundant love. I have sanctified you by the redeeming blood of Jesus. Now, as you consecrate yourselves to Me, I will show Myself to you in ways that you cannot imagine. You Elders are ready to assume a greater responsibility in My Kingdom. Yet, first you must complete the tasks that I have laid out for you. As you do, you will see your homes, neighborhoods, and city change. A refreshing is waiting to happen. An abundant rain is waiting to happen. The floodgates are being pressed. The water is rising. The Lord says act quickly. Place your trust in Me. The things you are to do may look impossible. But, nothing is impossible for Me, says God. So, rise Men of God. Cleanse yourselves. Take your rightful places. And act," says God.'"

The facilitator then closed the class with prayer. In the fellowship moments that followed, Uncle Eddie's barber asked if I was a Minister at my home church. I understood that he was asking if I held a position on the ministry staff. My immediate response was, "No". Yet there was a very comforting "Yes" in my spirit because I knew that God has called us all to be ministers of His word.

****

  I went back to Peggy's house and changed. I had worn a suit to Sunday School. But, God had given me explicit instructions on what to wear to the Homecoming service. It was a pair of beige slacks with a long sleeved African print shirt. The shirt was also beige with red and black designs down both front panels and across the back shoulders. It was one of the shirts that I picked up on our visit to Africa. As far as I knew, the designs were simply designs with no particular meaning. It would be very different for me to attend the family service dressed like that. I would stand out like a sore thumb. I had always worn a suit to Homecoming for as far back as I could remember. What was God up to?

  I arrived early but decided to sit in the back of the church. I looked for Chrissie, DZ, James and Rev. Brooks. I did not see either one of them. I turned off my cell phone, relaxed and focused on the service.

  Jessica opened the Praise and Worship with a rendition of "Now Behold The Lamb."

  "Now behold the Lamb. The precious Lamb of God."
  "Holy is the Lamb. The precious Lamb of God."
  "Why you love me so, I shall never know."
  "Now behold the Lamb. The precious Lamb of God."
  "Born into sin that I may live again."
  "Thank you for the Lamb. The precious Lamb of God."

  Man, that girl can sing. Singing is a generational blessing in Aunt Alice's children and her children's children. All of them can sing and sing very well. Renae, Jennifer, Jessica, Stephanie, Beverly, Melissa, and many more can really sing. They brought the congregation into high praise and worship with the very first song. Many of the songs that morning included old favorites like, 'Ain't No

Rock', 'Blessed Assurance', 'Holy, Holy, Holy', 'O Worship The King', 'To God Be The Glory, and 'Amazing Grace' of course. God did not miss a moment to minister to His people through the songs.

The minister of the hour was Rev. Melvin Reynolds, one of the descendants from Raeford. Rev. Reynolds and I were related through Samuel Reynolds. His great-grandmother was Heather Reynolds. He and I had known each other and often played together as children visiting Raeford. God's message through him was based on Mark 5:19.

"...Go home to your family and tell them how much the Lord has done for you, and how He has had mercy on you."

The context of the verse is Jesus healing a demon possessed man from a legion of demons. The man had been tormented night and day for a long time. Upon seeing Jesus, the man fell at Jesus' feet and begged Him not to torture him. It was not the man but the legion of demons that asked not to be tortured nor sent away from the area. Jesus paid no attention to the demons' request. He simply cast them out of the man. Afterwards, the man begged Jesus to let him go with Him. But, Jesus spoke the words of verse 19 to the man. The man was obedient and told everyone what Jesus had done for him. The people, all the people, were amazed. Immediately, I knew that God was talking to me. I kept hearing the Holy Spirit say to me, "Open your mouth and I will speak. Open your mouth, and I will speak."

I heard God. But, I did not want to blurt out in the middle of the service. I waited. When the doors of the church were opened, Peter's grandchildren, Brian and Sarah, walked to the front and gave their lives to Christ. Hallelujah!! In their testimony, they told how God had been working on them since the previous Friday night. Today's sermon confirmed that it was time to accept Jesus Christ as their Lord and Savior.

Just before the benediction, Rev. Reynolds called me out.

"Family, I have to tell you that for most of my time it this pulpit, I could not help but notice my cousin Willie, at the back of the church. I am sure that many of you noticed him, too. Who could miss that blood stained shirt that he has on? I believe that the Holy Spirit has given him something to say. Would you come up, please?"

I silently prayed Ephesians 6:19 and 20. "God when I open my mouth, I pray that words will be given to me such that I fearlessly proclaim the mystery of the gospel." Rev. Reynolds gave me the microphone and I began my testimony.

Like the man now delivered from the legion of demons, I told everyone what God had done for me. He had brought me through my early years of rebellion, later years of pride, and now to complete surrender in Him. I told them of my brokenness in March and my current mission on this trip. My encouragement to them was to repent for the Kingdom of God was at hand. God had a mighty work for many members of this family. Each was to search their own hearts and be obedient to the commands and specific call of God on their lives. The key message was 'Jesus Christ is real and He is coming.' Just like in Mark 5:19, all the family was amazed.

****

I enjoyed fellowship with many of the family members after the service. Uncle Robert, Aunt Lois, Uncle Eddie, Aunt Betty, Linda, Eddie Jr., Crystal, Joan, Nancy, Fred, Mrs. Lewis, Peter, Robert Jr., and many others. Nancy asked me to walk through the cemetery with her. She wanted to talk about the Homecoming. She was not real happy with the way things were done, in general. One of the things she was unhappy about was the way the family had treated an unknown lady who had recently died. This lady had no obvious record of having family members buried in Oak Hill. She was not a member of a local church and she walked the streets alone. When she died, there was no pastor to officiate her funeral.

Some of her distant relatives asked Robert Jr. to officiate and he did. After her family did considerable research, it was revealed that she indeed had a family member buried at Oak Hill. The administrators of the cemetery reluctantly agreed to bury her there. Nancy was upset with the entire proceedings.

"What should I do, Willie?" she asked.

"Nancy, the situation with this lady was ultimately worked out. Wasn't it?"

"Yeah. But, it didn't have to take the course that it did."

"Let me be honest with you, Nancy. When I have found myself in similar situations, I had to admit that God was really trying to show me something within me that needed to be dealt with."

"So, you think the problem was with me?"

"I believe there is a good chance that God is talking to you. I wouldn't call it a problem. I will say that if you listen then He will get the glory and you will receive the blessing. I want you to read and meditate on Psalm 139 tonight. Don't just read it. Listen to what God has to say to you. Whatever is in your heart will be revealed. You can then be free if you are obedient to what the Holy Spirit tells you."

Nancy and I headed back toward the church. Along the way, we saw Robert Jr. standing near The Shade Tree. He had stopped for a minute on his way to his grandmother's gravesite. We stood next to him for a while and remembered her life. We spoke of the good time that she and many of our relatives must be having with God right at that moment. 1 Thessalonians 4:13 - 18 came to mind.

"Brothers, we do not want you to be ignorant about those who fall asleep, or to grieve like the rest of men, who have no hope. We believe that Jesus died and rose again and so we believe that God will bring with Jesus those who have fallen asleep in him. According to the Lord's own word, we tell you that we who are still alive, who are left till the coming of the Lord, will certainly not precede those who have fallen asleep. For the Lord himself will come down from heaven, with a loud command, with the voice of the archangel and with the trumpet call of God, and the dead in Christ will rise first. After that, we who are still alive and are left will be caught up together with them in the clouds to meet the Lord in the air. And so we will be with the Lord forever. Therefore encourage each other with these words."

Robert Jr. concluded our reflection with a prayer. Afterwards, he asked if I would give him a ride home. His wife, Judy, had gone home earlier to prepare to receive guests.

"I'm glad you could stop by, Willie," Judy said.

"I wouldn't miss it for the world. How you doing?"

"I'm well. I am especially glad that you and Robert Jr. had a chance to talk last night. He told me that you confirmed that he should get himself checked by the doctor."

"God gave me that word of knowledge. Since both you and Robert Jr. have received it, I am confident that you will follow through."

"No problem. Can I fix you something to eat?"

"I appreciate the offer, Judy. But, I only have a few minutes. I promised Peggy that I would get back as soon as I could to talk to her girls. In the mean time though, God has given me another word for the both of you."

"What is it?"

"God says to be alert. There is someone close to your ministry who does not have your best interest in mind. Their motive is personal gain. The Lord says, Judy, you have known this for some time. But, you have been reluctant to tell Robert Jr. because of the long time friendship with the person. God says that this is not about your personal friendship. It is about His Kingdom. Robert Jr., God says that you have been reluctant to listen to Judy. She has been given a greater degree of discernment so that she can be additional eyes and ears for you and your family. Listen to her. Approach the person in love. Speak the truth in love so that all in your ministry can grow up into Him who is the head. That is, Christ. Then, the whole body to which you minister will grow and build itself up in love as each part does its work."

I went back to Peggy's house where we had already planned that I would pray for her family. Before we did, Jennifer told me that one of her friends suggested that she should hook me up with some woman in the community. Jennifer promptly told her that I was married and would not be interested in such a proposition.

"Thank you, Jennifer. It was good that you rebuked that spirit. I want you to know that you need not ever worry about anything like that. God had already warned me such a situation would occur on this trip. You have allowed yourself to be His instrument to avert it. Thank you."

"God told you a woman would approach you?"

"He actually warned me to be aware of any sexual temptations. So, I am not surprised."

"God is awesome!"

Peggy gathered her three girls, Jennifer, Jessica, and Melissa. Renae who was also there called her daughter and her husband. The Holy Spirit directed me to confess the fourth, fifth, and sixth chapters of Ephesians over the family.

"… As a prisoner for the Lord, then, they live their lives worthy of the calling that each of them has received. They are completely humble and gentle; bearing with one another in love. In everything that they do, they keep the unity of the Spirit through the bond of peace. Every relationship abounds in love. Sibling to sibling. Aunts to nieces. Cousins to cousins. In-laws to in-laws. Lord, this family is one body and one Spirit. You, God, are over them all, through them all, and in all of them … This family imitates You, God. They are sexually pure, void of any kind of impurity, and without greed ... They are children of light and live a life of love in You. They are careful to live a wise life. They are spirit filled, speak compassionately to one another, praise and give thanks to You, submit to one another, and are strong in You ... Wherever they are and whenever they speak, they speak boldly of the gospel. In the name of Jesus, we declare it to be so. Amen."

Melissa and Jessica asked for individual prayer. Melissa had a desire to do very well in the coming school year while Jessica wanted pain and stiffness in her hand to be gone. I anointed both with oil and asked God to give them the desires of their hearts with full expectation that He would deliver. He did not disappoint us. Jessica's pain left immediately. Six months later, Peggy reported that Melissa was a straight A student. We spent nearly three hours in prayer and ministering God's word. Then, Aunt Alice called.

Peggy who lived across the street from Aunt Alice had a remote talking system installed. She first called "Willie." Then, she called "William." Her daughters then said, "Willie, you had better get over there before she calls your full name, "William Johnson.'" I grabbed my Bible and my anointing oil and went across the street. Aunt Alice was waiting for me in her bedroom. She was sitting in her wheelchair. She told me to sit on her bed. She wanted to talk to me. She told me that it was finished. My mission was finished. I had done all that God had asked me to do. It was time for me to stop ministering. I had poured out. Now, it was time to just rest. She prophesied to me about the pressures in my life and the amount of studying I had been doing. She spoke directly from God's Rhema word. Then she told me that God's call on my life was to the office of Prophet.

"Be alert. Don't let Satan do to you what he tried to do to both Pappa and Grampa Ellis," she told me. He tried to pervert their ministries. He tried to make them do things that were not biblical. He tried to make them do things that were not of God.

She explained that Satan tries to reel you slowly into his camp. With spiritualism, he will set the hook with you speaking to your dead mother, for example. Then, you talk to your dead grandfather. Then, your dead brother. Before you know it, your neighbor will have you talking to their dead sister. Wham! You are the next local fortune teller. She told me to review Matthew 22:32, Deuteronomy 18:9–11, Leviticus 19:31, and Isaiah 8:19.

Then, I remembered Aunt Lois's words and the look on her face. My prophesy from the apostolic and prophetic conference then took on a deeper meaning. Here is what it said,

"…Son, even as you lay the Bible out in the midst of your family know that it will be something that will shine forth. And it is something that I want you to even begin to get into every day. Because I want you to gradually grow strong in My every word. Son, it is going to be important that you stand together as a family. That you stand together under Me because the enemy so badly wants to stop you even as he has tried to stop you in the generations past. He has tried to stop your great-grandfather because of the ministry that I had over him. But know that it is his ministry that has set you free. It is his ministry that has helped you to walk where you are walking now. Because son, I have even broken off the generational curses that have tried to come against your family and is gone now in the name of Jesus, says the Lord. And I have replaced it with my blessing, blessings, and blessings. I'm going to enlarge your territory like you have never known before because My presence is upon you, says the Lord…"

One way to stop a ministry is to pervert it. Aunt Alice took time to carefully explain what God had placed in her heart to tell me. She told me that it was my motives that mattered most. My character should be shaped not by the good that I do but by the supernatural grace of God to serve Him. I must not confuse right-doing with right-being. By the grace of God, Jesus Christ made me a new creature. I now have the righteousness of Christ Jesus. My motives must be exactly the same as those of Jesus. God must only see Jesus in me. Thus, He should see nothing in my motives to rebuke.

"Willie, receive the true nature of Jesus Christ," she said. "He has placed it in you. Because of that nature, you are different. Your personality did not change. But your character did. You have the character of Christ. Live by that character and that character only. Be ever mindful of the ways that God will give you a prophetic word. You may see a vision or picture. You may hear a word. You may get an inner witness or sense of the word. And, you may actually feel someone else's pain just as Isaiah felt Israel's pain in chapter 21 of his book. Willie, God has called you to be one of his prophets. Will you accept the call?"

Then, she anointed me and prayed over me. She primarily prayed for protection. She released me and told me to go back across the street and sleep.

When I got in the house, Jessica approached me and asked if it was OK for her to take me to Washington D. C. She explained that she did not have to be back at college for a few days. What she did not know was that her mother had already claimed at breakfast that morning that she would ride with her to take me back. When Peggy later came back, she and Jessica told me that the two of them would take me to Washington D. C. the next day, in time for my six o'clock flight.

****

Monday (Day 12)

We were to leave around 10:00am for Washington D. C. I was up again reviewing Ephesians Chapters 1 through 6. Just before leaving, I went across the street to say goodbye to Aunt Alice and Uncle Karl. Aunt Alice asked me to sit in front of her and pray for her while she lay in the bed. I also prayed for Uncle Karl who was sitting in a chair nearby. Uncle Karl among other things built headstones in the community. Many of them are in the family cemetery at Oak Hill. So, one of the things that I prayed for with him was that his children would receive the same honor within the community that he had received. I prayed that his honor would be passed to his children. I said goodbye. Then, I left.

****

Something terrible happened to Willie later that same day. So terrible, in fact, that he was unable to complete this last chapter. Chrissie, after consulting with others, finished it for him.

****

Peggy, Jessica, and Willie talked about many things on the drive to D. C. At one point, Peggy said, "You know, Willie, I have been thinking lately about the return of Jesus Christ."

"What a wonderful day that will be," he responded.

"Yeah, it sure will be. Do you remember that summer many years ago? I think we were about 10 or 11 years old. Pappa gathered you, me, and a few others under The Shade Tree right after Sunday service. He told us how God lived in eternity. He created all things including angels and the entire universe."

"I sure do. Pappa was a wise man with a very strong faith in God," Willie agreed.

"When Pappa told us about God kicking Lucifer out of heaven because of his pride, I thought who could be so stupid. Well, as you know, God created man and gave him dominion over the earth, its animals, and its trees. Then man's pride incited by Lucifer caused us to be eternally separated from God. We were just as stupid. Isn't it amazing that the All-Knowing God would provide a way out of this predicament even before the sin occurred? A Savior, a Redeemer, would come?"

"But, we are so hard-headed at times. Mankind would become increasingly sinful until God decided to wipe out everyone except a few," she continued.

"That was when He destroyed the world with the flood and only saved Noah and his family. Isn't it?"

"Yeah. But God eventually chose a people to bring His message to all nations. To be faithful to God. This chosen people rebels, worships other gods, and repents repeatedly until God takes them out of the land He promised. God establishes a timetable to finish transgression, to put an end to sin, to atone for wickedness, to bring in everlasting righteousness, and to anoint the Most Holy Place.

Willie then interjected, "Just think, for 400 years after all the rebellion, God did not speak! He was silent. I can't imagine what life must have been like during those times. But, in the fullness of time, He spoke loudly with the arrival of Jesus Christ, the Savior."

"What do you think, 'In the fullness of time' means?" asked Peggy.

"It means that the world was made ready for the first coming of Christ and the swift spread of the gospel. The Greco-Roman culture had fostered one common language, Greek. There were major central cities built across the Mediterranean. Roman highways had been built for nearly three decades facilitating the easy flow of people. There were nearly 150 synagogues throughout the Roman Empire. The Jews had been expecting the Messiah. The Law did not satisfy the heart. Noted and respected Greek philosophers like Plato concluded that reality existed in the spirit world. Then, it happened."

"Zechariah hears from God. (Luke 1:5 – 25) Mary hears from God. (Luke 1:26 – 38) The Holy Spirit overcame Mary. Simeon hears from God. (Luke 2:25 – 35) Anna hears from God. (Luke 2:36 – 38) The Magi hear from God. (Matthew 2:1 – 2) Shepherds hear from God. (Luke 2:8 – 20) Herod hears from God. (Matthew 2:3 – 18) Jesus suddenly appears in the temple at twelve. (Luke 2:42 – 50) The nations hear from God through John the Baptist. John pointed out the Lamb of God. (John chapter 1)"

"Pappa not only knew the Word of God but he could also tell the story in such a way that you would never forget it," Peggy remembered.

"Yep. And remember that Jesus lived a perfect and sinless life before dying on the cross for all of us. This sacrifice is the redemptive price Jesus paid. Everyone who accepts that sacrifice by accepting Jesus Christ as Lord and Savior now has a way out of the original predicament. We have a way to live eternally with God."

"After His resurrection, Jesus told us that He would return after preparing a place for us in God's house. It is that return that we look forward to with high expectation that it is so."

"It may be that time is getting full again, huh? Think about it. Technology is such that now if Jesus were to return in the sky anywhere visible on earth, everyone would know in about 3 seconds. Camera-phones, iPads, television cameras, YouTube, and who knows what else would capture that event in no time and transmit it for all to see just as the Bible says. That same technology makes it possible to spread the gospel much faster than people of old could travel on the fastest horse on a Roman road. The opportunities for knowing Christ are nearly limitless."

"I agree Peggy, that today's environment including all of nature's calamities seem to point to an ever quickening day when Christ will return. Yet, we know God's Word says that no man knows the day or the hour. So, until then, He gave us instructions throughout the New Testament on how to live. And at the end of the gospels, He tells us to go and make disciples of all nations. We are to continue to spread the gospel. We are to tell others to repent and receive Christ."

"More than anything else, Peggy, these last twelve days have convinced me that I have no greater mission than to fulfill this command within the sphere of influence that God gives me now and at any point in the future."

****

Jessica then shared a discussion that she and Aunt Alice had while Willie visited Robert Jr. and Judy on the way back from the Homecoming services. Aunt Alice had asked if DZ, James, or I had come back. Since we had not, she wondered how Willie was going to go back to Fayetteville.

"I told her that you could not go back to Fayetteville. God told you not to go back the way you had come," Jessica said.

"Thanks, Jessica."

"She then asked me why were you planning to stop in Raleigh on your way to D. C.? I knew that you had planned to pray with your brother. So, that's what I told her."

Willie suddenly realized that he could not stop in Raleigh. Aunt Alice had asked a very insightful question. He had already prayed for DZ's family at the beginning of the trip. It was neither necessary nor God's desire that Willie stop now. He called D Z from the car. Willie was surprised to hear that DZ, Brenda, James, and I were in Winston-Salem visiting Aunt Dorothy.

Around 5:00am Sunday morning, Aunt Dorothy quietly left my house in Fayetteville because her daughter called with frightening news of an automobile accident involving Uncle Henry, Aunt Dorothy's husband. He had apparently fallen asleep at the wheel on his way to Raeford for the Homecoming. He never noticed the train tracks or heard the sound of the whistle. He was on life support when Aunt Dorothy got the call. She decided not to interrupt my plans for the Homecoming by leaving without notice. However, I received a call later from Aunt Dorothy's daughter explaining the situation. I called James, DZ, and Willie. James and I drove directly to Winston-Salem. DZ and Brenda met us there. Willie had turned off his cell phone during the Homecoming services and forgot to turn it back on until making the call to DZ

"Chrissie, I just got the word on Uncle Henry. How is he?" Willie asked.

"He is a blessed man. He is now stable. The train clipped the back of his car as he crossed the track. It spun him around several times until he crashed into a light pole. He has severe wounds to his head and chest. The doctors did a great job of getting things under control. He is now resting with a good prognosis."

"Glory to God. How is Aunt Dorothy?"

"Better. But, she still has some worry. She is sleeping now and has been for a couple of hours. We felt like she really needed family at her side. We tried to reach you but it kept going to your voice mail."

"I know, now. I wish I had remembered to turn my phone back on."

"I am sure that you would agree that God works for our good in all things. He knew the plans He had for you in Raeford. And, He knew the plans He had for us here. It really does look like Uncle Henry is going to be all right."

"We again give glory to God. Peggy and Jessica are driving me back to Washington D. C. for my flight back to New York today."

"I know. I called Aunt Alice this morning just after you left and gave her an update on Uncle Henry and Aunt Dorothy. She told me you were on your way home."

"Well, tell Aunt Dorothy that I am praying for her, Uncle Henry, and her family. Tell my brothers and Brenda that I love them. And I love you, Chrissie."

"I love you too, Willie."

****

Peggy, Jessica, and Willie arrived in D. C. in plenty of time. The flight was a little late taking off but otherwise things went well. Willie heard the hum of the L1011 engines as he sat and meditated on the events of the last several days. What a wonderful God we serve. He had seen, sensed and been directly involved in a powerful move of the Holy Spirit. He really needed the next couple of hours or so just to let it all sink in.

Willie heard God say, "Life lived apart from obedience to the call of God is a life unfulfilled. God is faithful. He continues to reach out. He will not take back the gift. He, however, may shake things up until you realize He is serious." As Willie closed his eyes, God unfolded what He had done and was doing in Willie's life. Just like Jeremiah, He had called Willie from his birth. "Before I formed you in the womb I knew you, before you were born I set you apart; I appointed you as a prophet to the nations." From the early days of meeting at The Shade Tree in Oak Hill Cemetery right up to this very day, God had patiently planted seeds in Willie and watered them. But, Willie let weed seeds grow up in his character. He had initially wandered from the truth taught by his forefathers. Even when he returned, there was much pruning to be done.

God prospered Willie in many ways but he lost temporary sight of who was doing the work. In spite of the many successes, as long as Willie thought that he was sufficient, God's power in his life would be limited. God had to completely break Willie down, in March. Willie had to realize that he was destitute in every area of his life. Over the next five-month grace period, God slowly put Willie back together again. He brought Willie to His house, the Potter's House.

When the chapter was closed on the business at the end of the seventh month, God launched a new beginning in Willie. In the eighth month, on August 1st, he was set apart, consecrated with the spiritual anointing of a Prophet. This new life had nothing but Jesus Christ and Him crucified as its focus. Willie's time with family in Fayetteville and Raeford confirmed his renewed focus in Him. Willie could now relax and enjoy the smooth ride home.

****

It was already early evening. The dusk had triggered the automatic runway lights. The sky sparkled with twinkling stars each as bright as a 1000-watt bulb in a dark room with no windows. As Willie gazed through the portals, he could both see and sense the steady movement of the plane. The runway lights flashed by so quickly that they soon became one steady stream of brightness. Then in a blink of an eye, this huge metal air ship lifted from the ground and ascended to 35,000 feet above the earth. Willie watched as the lights below got dimmer and dimmer until they finally disappeared. When the flight attendants turned off the cabin lights, it was completely dark except for the few overhead lights belonging to a couple of avid readers. The darkness was just what he needed to fall fast asleep.

Ahhhhhhhhhh!!!! Eeeeeeeeee Help!!!!!!!! A loud scream startled him out of his sleep. Then, he could feel the bottom drop out of the plane. They were headed down. The passengers were screaming. The lady behind Willie threw up her meal all over the back of his seat. Air masks had dropped. People were frantically trying to put them on. He could barely hear the flight attendants say, "Everyone be calm. It is just an air pocket. The captain has the plane under control." No one believed her as this giant airplane continued to plummet. His heart raced. Willie fought off the panic that tried to engulf him. In the midst of it all, he remembered to put his head between his knees. Above all else he prayed.

In the cockpit, the captain tried feverishly to get the plane level. While the weather was perfect at take-off, suddenly they encountered an unexpected thunderstorm. The plane had stalled and was on its way down. To make matters worse, the ground crew faked an inspection that would have revealed faulty instruments. As a result, unknowingly, the captain was making decisions based on incorrect information. He pulled the nose of the plane up when he should have done just the opposite. The plane continued to descend ever faster and faster until …

Jesus Christ is Real And He is Coming

About The Author

Cliff Kyle (aka Clifton Kyle) is a worshipper and the husband to Shirley Kyle. He is a native of Beaumont, Texas, graduate of Hebert High School ('68), graduate of Macalester College ('72 Bachelor), and graduate of the Illinois Institute of Technology ('76 Master). As the fifth child and fourth son of Willie Mae and L. C. Kyle, Cliff quickly learned to adapt to an ever changing family environment early in his life. His mother's love, dedication, integrity, humility, and never quit spirit were the foundation of his ultimate spiritual maturity.

He currently enjoys living in the Chicago area with Shirley. Both are members of Rock of Our Salvation Evangelical Free Church where Cliff serves as Chairman of the Elder Board. His previous and current ministry work includes teaching bible study, vacation bible school, and Sunday school. He has chaired a Pastor Search committee, a rewrite of the church constitution, and the Prayer Ministry. He has been actively engaged in Men's ministry, small group studies, and church leadership. Cliff and his wife direct the Dollar Bill Ministry where every Christmas season they organize then distribute coats, gloves, hats, and toiletries to the homeless in the Chicago Loop. Cliff has mentored young men and played integral roles in the development and nurturing of multiple men's groups.

Cliff and Shirley have three wonderful children, twelve beautiful grandchildren, and a handsome great-grandson.

REFERENCES

Chapter 3

1. Hebrews 10:24 – 25
2. James 5:16
3. Galatians 5:13 – 15
4. 1 Thessalonians 3:12 –13
5. Colossians 3:13 – 14
6. Proverbs 4:1 – 27
7. 2 Timothy 3:12
8. 2 Timothy 4:2
9. 2 Peter 1:3 – 11
10. 1 Peter 4:1 – 19
11. 1 John 1:7
12. John 14:15 - 18; John 16:13 - 15; and 2 Thessalonians 3:5
13. 2 Corinthians 3:6

Chapter 6

1) These references will help you. Matthew 8:5 – 10, Matthew 9:29, Matthew 14:22 – 31, Matthew 15:28b, Matthew 21:21, Acts 6:1 – 3, Romans 1:17, Romans 4:17 – 20, Romans 5:1, Romans 10:8, Romans 10:17, Romans 12:3C, 1 Corinthians 2:5, Ephesians 2:8, 2 Thessalonians 1:3, 1 Timothy 1:5, 1 Timothy 1:18 – 19, Philemon 6, Hebrews 10:38, Hebrews 11:1, Hebrews 11:6, James 1:5 – 7, James 2:5, James 2:22, 1 Peter 5;7, 1 John 5:4